DEMON CORE

3

DEMON CORE

3

D. M. RHODES

AKA RAZZMATAZZ

Podium

Cover design by Husa

ISBN: 978-1-0394-4289-4

Published in 2024 by Podium Publishing
www.podiumaudio.com

DEMON CORE

3

CHAPTER 1

THE BEGINNING OF THE END

~ [Ruhr, the River Sorceress] ~
Half Elf | ♀ | Sorceress
Rank: SSS
Location: The Demon King's Castle, Floor Thirty-One
Level: 100

The Thing That Is Bound
Bones will crack and tongues will flay,
As come to birth—these binds to stay,
The ties that will wrap flesh around raw meat,
And hold together the men of this day,
Always one man abreast, as if they were feathers on
wings, a-splay.
If they are real, or they are not, is quite impossible for
one to say,
But as for the Thing That Is Bound—it is here, for now,
today,
In the halls of the King; in the burrow of screaming, lost
harrows,
Lives now this thing that cares not for cries—chirping like
mourning sparrows,
It will take and absorb and fuse and meld,
All of those who oppose the Lord—who deep dwells,
For these men, are too, snared, just as the creature is
itself,
A terror, prolific, amongst those who dared to delve,
Into the dark.
For they themselves are not but it, and it is not but them,

Together, aloft, a meld of flesh, of biting rats and drown-
ing men,
Horrors untold and terrors beyond the pale of children's
wild imaginations,
Have come now once again to roam the world, present as
cruel manifestation,
It is bound, and so are you—We're both down here
together,
In the core of the Beast and the halls of the damned,
In the depths of black revelation.

~ A Thing That is Bound ~
- Summoned Entity -
Cost: 50% SOUL POINTS

Trapped down in the deepest pits of the Demon King's castle, the Thing That Is Bound is a horrific, crazed entity made up out of thousands of living bodies fused together. The broken arms and legs of the thousands of men and women it has taken are fused together, like the interweaving roots of a tree. The Thing That Is Bound makes use of their connected mass as a long, chain-like extension of its own body—as it itself is, too, trapped, bound, and locked to unbreakable ties.

Its deepest desire is to catch more people, more bodies to add to itself, so that it might extend its elongated "body" further outward toward the surface that it yearns to feel.

As for the bodies it takes, death is not promised, and many remain screaming, their broken arms and legs fused to their corpse neighbors.

Class: MONSTER	Element: DARK
Type: Nightmare	Category: TERROR*
Rank: SSS	
Level: ???	

TERROR is a classification term used for all monster types that do not fall into traditional monster categories such as UNDEAD, GOLEM, GHOST, etc. Terrors tend to have unique makeups and behavior patterns, and lean toward hyperviolent tendencies.

Ruhr sinks, loosely suspended in a fully encompassing body of water that cradles her descending form. The half elf drifts, falling slowly deeper and deeper into the deep dark blue water.

Dead bodies sink all around her, together with herself.

If there is any movement in the distance, it is impossible to see, given the fading of the light from above. Also because of the simple fact that her eyes are closed.

Long strands of hair drift slowly behind her in the hot water as she drops further, bubbles slowly leaving from the inside of her soaked, heavy rucksack and from her pursed lips.

Down here, it's quiet.

Muted explosions come from the surface, only barely audible. Sharper tones, such as screams, fail to reach her down in the bleak abyss.

Flashes of lights of many colors come from above the surface of the body of water she's inside of. The ripples and waves caused by the heavy explosions do little to reach her down here, the energy of the blasts quickly muffled and absorbed by the deep.

After a moment of silence, Ruhr opens her eyes and stares off into the void.

There's something else in the water.

Swim.

She has to swim, or she's going to drown, says the lizard voice in the back of her head, but she ignores it.

Something stirs in the distance, a movement breaking the murky waters. Her presence has been noticed.

Instead of swimming, though, Ruhr closes her eyes again and sinks further still as something shoots her way from the other end of the arena. The half elf locks her hands in a pose that might be viewed as a praying position by an outside observer, her shut eyes and lowered head giving credence to the appearance of a drowning woman of pious faith.

Pressure builds between her fingers, the water around her moving, her hair and the fabric of her clothes flowing in entirely different currents than that of the water's own.

And then it arrives.

The thing beneath the water has reached her; she can feel it all around her, the water shifting in different directions as if something were pushing it to the side.

Ruhr opens her eyes, looking at the open, waterlogged face only inches from her own. It twitches, spasming, as the muscles fight to move but have nowhere to go. A man, drowned but never dying, his eyes and tongue long since rotted out despite his body remaining sustained. His broken arms and legs link him to a chain of flesh, whipping around like a tendril—one of many. Hundreds of claimed bodies are bound together like this into living appendages of the monster.

Dozens of faces press in toward her from all sides as the entity closes the tentacle of grim visages around her, the ever-screaming, spasming face of the man moving closer to hers with an open, toothless mouth that snaps rabidly.

Ruhr lifts her hand, muffling its mouth as the other dozen move in from all sides to take her.

A single word leaves her lips, muted by the water and the gnashing of boneless flesh, the glow beneath her fingers pressing so vividly out of her that the skull of the dead man, which her fingers cover, begins to glow from the inside out.

Corpses rain down from the platforms above like flocks of snow, sinking into the murk.

Pressure grabs her from all sides as the mass of bodies crushes her within them just as the spell begins to work, wrapping themselves around her—trapping her under their undulating weight which writhes against her. Broken fingers and rotting faces touch her, grab her, gnaw on her—bind her. Waterlogged hands that jut out from between layers of old bodies yank on her hair, the already dead trying to grab hold of something in an animal attempt to pull themselves free from their own trappings, rather than in an effort to drown her.

(Ruhr) has used: [{Purity} Sacred Dragon]

The ocean flashes with white, as if the sun itself were rising beneath the brink. The black, murky ink turns into a glowing, raging vividness for a brief second as, in the eyes of the holy crusade above, the presence of God is evidenced in the bleakest recesses of the world.

The skull that her hand is over explodes, a ripple of pure light and energy running down the chain of bodies in both directions, as if an arc of lightning were moving through them. A great surge of moving holy water in the shape of a roaring dragon weaves its ways through the corruption. Its open maw tears through thousands of bodies at once, filling them with a radiating energy of cleansing purity. All of the oozing, waterlogged, pus-and-fungus-filled flesh takes on an impossible tone—the color of heaven itself—as she lurches, her body being flung to the side as the wounded monster lashes out in incredible pain.

Holy water fills the ocean, the tinge of its entirety changing by the second to a lighter tone, like that of a creek in the springtime. The brackish, oily blackwater fades as her purifying power moves through it.

Soggy fingers, knotted in her hair, painfully yank her upward as the entity writhes in anguish, a thousand screams filling the underworld she's suspended in.

Ruhr flies up into the air, grabbing hold of a fresh corpse's belt, and pulls a knife out of it. Her body whips around beneath the water, the maddened monstrosity dying in its own—now purified—terrain, writhing in anger. She holds the knife back behind herself, grabbing her own hair and the wet hands holding it before sawing with the blade, cutting through gnarled fingers and blue strands as she releases herself from their grasp.

Movement comes from the water, angered at her escape and the hurt she caused.

Ruhr holds her hands together and aims down below herself, swimming up at the same time a violent burst of water from her palms shoots her upward and out of the depths. The energy of her spell propels her upward and repels the thousand screaming faces at the same time.

(Ruhr) has used: [Aquatic Dynamics]

The river sorceress breaks the surface of the fake lake, shooting far above its churning waters into the air above from the overly powerful force of the spell. For a brief second, she hangs there, aloft, looking down over the world below herself at the many platforms covered in battle groups from the crusade, which has employed many new tactics in the face of this growing adversity. Hundreds of priests and priestesses hold their hands together, aiming her way.

As she comes to a halt, her momentum lessening and her fall just beginning now, a sharp whistle cuts the air from below as someone gives a signal.

In that single, time-stopped second, her gaze turns to the spire of water she's rising up on, and then toward the ocean filled with corpses. Just below the top of the water sit thousands of faces, thousands of fingers and mouths, all turned her way, just barely breaking the surface.

The doctrine whistle comes to an end, and hundreds of people mobilize at once.

The air around her crystallizes, crackling noisily as if winter had come early and everything were freezing over in a fresh frost.

A tower of corpses lunges out of the water straight toward her, hoping to catch her as she falls back down into it.

Suddenly, dozens of prismatic, magical glass platforms appear just below Ruhr in a circle, leaving a hole free in the middle. The magical platforms created by the priests of the crusade act as a catcher, and her boots land on either side of the rim of glass. The river sorceress stands there with spread legs as her hands aim down at the hole—a tunnel that is solidifying as more and more magical barriers come into place, creating a hollow cylinder, a tube, that she's standing atop of.

Trapped and already in movement, the thousand faces of the monster's waterlogged tendrils compress, sliding over the sleek glass from the inside of the pipe they've been forced into, pressing together in graceless constriction as their total, squelching mass is much too large to fit through the tight passage. Meat and glass squeak as they rub against one another, the edges of the magical tunnel cracking and ripping from the much too large fit forcing its way through to reach her at the other end.

Ruhr's hands glow as the few faces who can manage to do so turn upward to look at her, standing there above them, her short hair matted over her wet face.

(Ruhr) has used: [{Purity} Sacred Dragon]

Again, the dragon made entirely out of holy water erupts from her fingers, the counterforce of the spell pressing itself straight down through the tube from above, the pure water raging against the wriggling flesh in the soaked passage. Steam and crackling flakes of floating magical glass fill the air, together with loud, vivid screams, as the monster—unable to pull itself back out into the blackwater—drowns above the ocean in holy water, in the small prison it had forced itself into in its greedy desire to have her.

Holy water burns away meat and sinew. It burns away through hollow sockets and gaping maws, the pressure of the spell that still continues to rage pushing down further and further, Ruhr's scream overpowering those of the thousands—of the legion—until a moment later, it is done.

The cylinder bursts, water spraying everywhere.

The magical barriers, unable to hold up against the pressure any longer, explode in all directions. Pure, holy water and pieces of meat rain down over the smoldering ocean, sinking.

This time, they remain unmoving.

Ruhr stands there, panting for breath, watching it all fade away down beneath herself, watching it all vanish into the brink.

It's done.

Another magical platform comes into existence, sealing the ripped and broken hole she's standing over with her waterlogged boots. The river sorceress stands back upright on firm footing, looking down over the edge and nodding to the priests before she then steps off into the air herself.

Before she can fall, more platforms are made beneath her feet, a staircase coming into existence as she descends back down toward the rest of the arena.

Members of the crusade clap and cheer, letting themselves be put at ease by her idle hand, which waves them off as she walks past them, swiping a strand of long hair out of the side of her face to sell the image a bit more.

Since then, since what happened before, she's taken a somewhat more active role in the leadership of the crusade, which they all seem more than happy with, considering the grim losses they've sustained just getting this far into the Demon King's castle. This is a problem they're actively working on fixing now.

This quiet change of behavior has elevated her in status in the eyes of the crusade, who, until now, had viewed her as sort of a lofty, flippant cosmic oddity rather than the tip of the spear that she was hoped to represent. Yes, she was given a holy blessing, but she hadn't really acted the part until now.

Ruhr looks at the chief officer, Mistley, who comes in rank after her. "Set it up," she orders, walking past him before he can try to catch up to her and stop her. Thankfully, he's a bit run-down after all of these days.

This should have been enough time for the others who had gone back upstairs to get ready—assuming they didn't desert or die on the way.

Mistley nods, waving over a series of casters from nearby. "Yes, ma'am," he replies without any questions or objections.

Ruhr sits down on a rock and starts unlacing her boots.

"Miss . . . Miss Ruhr?" asks a voice from the side.

Ruhr looks at the limping priestess, a young woman with black hair wrapped into a tight braid that drapes over her shoulder. She doesn't look like an actual crusader. Likely, she's just an attendant priestess to some crusader of social renown who died on the way, and now she's kind of straggling with the group she got dragged into. Given that hygiene is somewhat difficult down here, braids and buns are the best way to keep long hair out of the way, short of cutting it off entirely, so just about everyone has employed some manner of low-maintenance hairstyle. These little creature comforts add a surprising amount in the face of the true horror they're immersed in.

"Thanks for the platform," says Ruhr, taking off her boot and turning it upside down, a pool of water leaking out of the soaked leather.

"Of course," replies the priestess, lifting a hand with a weak finger to point. "You, uh . . . May I?" she asks, carefully reaching over toward Ruhr as she shambles closer to her. "You have fingers in your hair."

"It's almost like I'm a teenager again," replies Ruhr dryly, shaking her head and taking off her other boot instead of worrying about the few pieces of corpses stuck in her tresses. Wet feet are a serious problem, especially in wet boots. Foot rot is a real issue for adventurers in dungeons who don't take proper care of themselves. It's a very debilitating illness if not carefully handled.

"Huh?" asks the priestess. "Oh. Uh . . . Pardon me," she says, holding out a piece of white cloth and disgustedly picking out the dead, rotting fingers from Ruhr's hair.

"Don't worry about it," replies Ruhr, loosening the laces more on her boots to open them both as wide as she can, eyeing the woman out of the side of her vision. After a second, the sorceress looks around for a fire caster. Seeing one, she whistles sharply, getting his attention. "Would you?" she asks, carelessly throwing her soaked boots to him.

The man fumbles, barely catching them both.

Ruhr sighs, looking ahead of herself as the few powerful casters of the crusade form a circle now that the battle is over.

Of the thousand-some who had entered the Demon King's castle, only a good hundred, less than a handful, remain. And those aren't necessarily the strongest and the best. A lot of people just made it this far through sheer luck and happenstance. The Demon King's castle churns down the bones of everyone it can take equally, indifferent to the volume of their screams.

Ruhr holds up the knife she took from the corpse to the priestess. "Cut the rest."

"What?" she asks, not understanding.

"My hair," clarifies Ruhr, reaching behind herself and ringing out her soaked hair, which is half chopped already past her shoulders from her escape. She pinches off a section where she cut it below the water. "Cut the rest off here."

The priestess takes the knife. "R-Really?"

Ruhr glares her way. "If you came here to be useful, then be useful," snaps the river sorceress at her, folding her hands together, her elbows on her knees as she looks back at the ritual that is being performed. "Just do it."

"Y-Yes, Miss Ruhr."

The first assault that she led against the Demon King's castle was a failure. She led everyone into a trap below that graveyard back when this all started, and they all died. Everyone except her and Zacarias.

The second assault that she led against the Demon King's castle with the troop of nobles failed, leaving only her and Zacarias alive, until the crusade arrived.

Now, she's lost Zac too, and most of the crusade. Plus, her hair looks like shit. This is going to be disastrous for her image.

They say the third time is the charm, but as far as she can tell, that isn't the case. She'll have to bet on number four.

Nervous hands hold her hair from the side, the frightened priestess taking a moment to make sure she's cutting at the right spot, lest Ruhr snap at her again.

She has moved away from all of that in these last few weeks—her obsession with her status, with how she's perceived in the public eye during her ascent to power and fame. For a while, she was so wrapped up in this new game of life that she was playing together with Zacarias that she actually thought it was real. She deluded herself into thinking that a life like that was real.

But it isn't. It never was. Not for her.

It wasn't possible back when she was a girl, and it isn't possible now that she's a woman.

That pretend world in which people are happy, in which . . . feelings like those ones, like the ones she was feeling for Zacarias—It's not real. It's pretend. It's fake. It's a game.

The real world is this. It's ugly. It's as far from the beauty of cherished hopes, kindness, and grace as can be. Those things are just temporary illusions. They're smears of paint over a fundamentally cracked and broken facade.

Whatever.

It was fun. She had some odd hopes for a while there, some odd thoughts. But now, those are gone. Zacarias is gone. All that's left is Ruhr, the river sorceress. She's back where she started.

Ruhr watches as the circle of crusaders begins to channel the spell.

The Demon King has been playing his game now, too, but she's about done with it as well. He thinks he's trapped them here in the belly of his castle, and that might be true. But what he hasn't considered is that there is a risk to eating things alive.

Sometimes, those things might gnaw from the inside out.

A pulse of energy generates between the circle of crusaders holding together. A ripple forms in the air in their midst, the air waving in the presence of the incredible heat collecting in the circle of magical energy.

A moment later, a tear appears—a rip. A portal.

The unstable line of energy hovering in the air waves back and forth like a wriggling worm, unable to find cohesion in a straight, rigid form.

Behind her, the priestess with the hurt leg lops off the long hair, wrapping it into a little ball.

The portal comes into shape.

It's a connection to another one of the same make and energy, one which the other teams they had sent back above to the prior floors have set up, creating a chain from one portal to the next, from one floor to the next. It is a link of shortcuts that run through the Demon King's castle.

For a moment, everything looks good.

However, then the portal essentially explodes.

The ring of casters is sent flying, a few of them landing in the water. One of them screams as the wave of wild, dangerously volatile magic erupts his way, a wave of burning ash searing his hands and face. He falls to the ground, crying in horror as priests run around to help him.

Ruhr puts her hand by her mouth, calling out to them. "Do it again," she orders.

The sorceress rises up to her feet. They're going to get this damn thing set up and create a new staging area here. Without reinforcements, they're not going to make it.

She might. She's going to kill the Demon King no matter what.

But the others are not going to make it without more numbers, and more importantly, she needs witnesses to watch her kill the Demon King if she's going to become famous for this mess.

Ruhr looks back at the priestess, who is still holding the bundle of hair and knife, not really sure what to do with either of them. "Hey. You a virgin?"

"Pardon?" asks the priestess, looking up at her very quickly. "Y-Yes?" she replies, unsure. "As a priestess, I am honor bound to—"

"Yeah, yeah," interrupts Ruhr dryly, cutting the priestess off and taking the ball of blue, matted hair from her. "Come to my spot later. We'll fix that for you."

"Oh!" The priestess waves her hands nervously in response. "I, uh, I'm flattered," she starts. "But I'm not—"

The river sorceress throws the bundle of hair carelessly into the water of the arena, letting it sink away. Grabbing the knife by the blade, Ruhr pulls it from the woman's hand and then tucks it down in between the priestess' belt and robe, on the side of her bad leg. "You're going to die kicking and screaming down here anyway," says Ruhr to the gulping stranger, turning to leave, "might as well get some practice in beforehand."

The half elf walks away, grabbing her boots from the fire caster who was heating them up. She holds them under her arm as she moves toward the ritual circle. "Hey! You slime slurpers!" barks Ruhr, clapping her hands together as the singed casters get back into loose formation. "I said, do it again!" she orders, and the magic circle begins to power up a second time.

Gods know what sort of mess has been happening up on the surface all of this time they've been down here.

~ [Outside of the Demon Carnival] ~

Screams and metal clash all around them.

The man's face contorts in fear as he falls back, crawling through the dirt, his horrified and blood-caked visage staring up toward the night sky. There, on the horizon, stemming out of the darkest shadows of the world beyond his vision, protrudes a long, witchy arm that reaches toward the lofty heights. Its width is the size of castles; its length is impossible on a human scale. The entity of pure shadow rises up higher, higher, and higher still as it reaches up toward the night sky above. The hand, with fingers so long and impossibly sharp, delicately pinches a pinprick of light that dares to shine in the Demon King's sky—a star—and pulls it back down toward the world below, its delicate grip receding, as if it were holding a small, squirming firefly.

As the black hand lowers itself back down toward the ground, the star never grows in size. Instead, it simply stays a single pinprick of light that then just vanishes over into the distant horizon, leaving the sky just a little bit darker than it was a moment ago.

"GET UP, YOU DAFT FOOL!" yells a voice, another soldier tearing him to his feet.

His chest heaves in terror, his panicked breathing not keeping pace with the racing of his heart. "What? What?!"

The world explodes in a violent eruption, sending him flying, tumbling over the mud and the stones a distance away. His armor, superheated from the blast, hisses as he rolls through the wet mud, barely scrambling back upright. The lost man looks around himself, screaming in horror as he looks at the now disembodied arm still gripping his breastplate, broken bone and sinew hanging from the far end of it.

He tears the lost arm off of himself, throwing it to the ground and looking around at the chaos happening in all directions.

Legions of undead, beasts with gnarled and twisted faces, churn through swarms of men—soldiers from the distant regions and allied nations who have come together in an ambush on the demon carnival. It sits, stopped in its route in the middle of the way.

Hordes of demons pour from every shadow in and around the caravan.

He runs, not even sure to where, just in the first direction he picks in his mindless terror. The sky is filled with claws and teeth and screaming bodies, torn from the soil by things that reach and take.

The shadowy arm, the Thing That Gathers Stars, reaches up again to take another pinprick of light from the night. Every star it takes makes the world a little darker, makes the battle a little harder to fight. Soon, they'll be fully immersed in nothingness—in total entropy.

He slips again in the mud mixed with blood and rainwater, tumbling forward. Crawling for a second, he then continues running through groups of soldiers holding formation and fighting the armies of the damned. Fairy lights and hellfire overstimulate his thoughts and vision as he, frantic and lost like an animal, finds no footing anywhere in body or in spirit.

His eyes are torn between the sight of a screaming priest holding on to his own entrails that are being yanked up into the air out from his guts by a sharply taloned harpy, like a marionette's string, and the sight of the shadow behind it, stealing another star from the night sky.

~ The Thing That Gathers Stars ~
- Summoned Entity -
Cost: 100% SOUL POINTS
Sitting on the edge of the realms of physicality and the collective dream state of the world, the Thing That Gathers Stars is an egregore, made manifest by the shared nightmares of the world. The total despair of humanity has been made manifest through the powers of the Demon King, the threat of the total extinction of the flame of their world given shape and form as something that quite literally steals the little light that remains.
The Thing That Gathers Stars will do nothing else except tenderly and gently reach up toward the sky for all to see, plucking the stars from the night one by one. It will work its way through the countless thousands of them until there is nothing left but total blackness.
The dimmer the world becomes, the more the creatures of tooth and claw thrive in the darkness.

Class: MONSTER	Element: DARK
Type: Nightmare	Category: TRUE TERROR*
Rank: TRUE SSS	
Level: ???	
*TERROR** is a classification term used for all monster types that do not fall into traditional monster categories such as UNDEAD, GOLEM, GHOST, etc. Terrors tend to have unique makeups and behavior patterns, and lean toward hyperviolent tendencies.	

The storm that never stops howls all around the world, the raging heat that stems from the Demon King's caravan causing the mud to bubble and boil in several places, creating a screaming quagmire that others sink into, desperately trying to pull themselves free as they're boiled alive while they slowly sink into the muck. Some of the unfortunate have their faces gnawed on by long-necked monstrosities—vampires—whose pale, sickly, and wet protruding necks they fail to hold back.

He tumbles, falling again as a fresh shock wave blasts through the air.

Crawling once more, he lifts his gaze, looking at the source of the blast.

A man wielding a thin, elongated rapier holds firm, the blade resting in the claws of a demon the likes of which he has never seen before in any text or story. Clad in scales that have grown onto its exterior like a knight's armor, the tall, lean monstrosity radiates raw power from itself. It has spindly, sharp legs that rest at a needle point which glide over the soil. Its befoulment is so much that the very air here makes him nauseous to even be in, the sensation of its raw presence too vivid to ignore—like a corpse, rotting in a room one is trapped in.

A shadow moves behind the locked combatants.

"LOOK OUT!" yells the man down in the mud as a second demon knight moves out of the mass of bodies and warfare, its towering form having been hidden in shadows and wildfire as it lunges out toward the fencer from behind with long, sharp claws of metal of an unspeakable origin.

The fencer's thumb clicks down onto a mechanism on the hilt of his rapier as he ducks, pulling on the hilt at the same time, which comes free from the elongated blade of the weapon, inside of which was socketed a smaller knife. The knight he was fighting falls forward as his counterbalancing weight leaves the spot, holding on to the unmounted long blade. A second later, the other knight collides with the first, its claws cutting into his demonic armor.

The fencer kicks his leg off, sliding back and away through the mud, out of harm's way. Without a second of peace, he ducks down over a swiping arm from behind and plunges the knife into the throat of a reaching ghoul, severing its spinal cord.

The wounded demon knight opens its mouth, snarling at the other with a meat-and-gore-filled maw. The other one, perhaps at fault or perhaps not, roars back as she pulls her claws out of his bleeding chest, and the two of them begin to fight one another in something akin to a lover's quarrel, tearing into one another's bodies in a carnal ritual now that they are distracted from their prey.

The man in the mud gets up and runs again, froth and tears running down his face.

~ [The Demon King] ~

"Look! I drew a goat!" says Kirsch the ghost.

Swain, the monstrous beast that is the Demon King, lifts his head and holds out his hand, taking the paper made from a flayed, screaming soul, and looks at the drawing on it.

Depicted on its surface is a goat, crude and clearly drawn by a child's unskilled hands.

"Excellent," growls the Demon King's harrowing voice, his foul candor being the scourge of all that lives and is good. His massive, wretched, clawed hand—the size of many men's crushed bodies—moves over to the side and presses the sheet against the wall. It sticks there, next to several other drawings of such a nature, as the flayed soul, screaming, burns into the scorching-hot brickwork of the throne room, fusing with the rock because of the heat. "You have served me well, Kirsch," he praises as the screams of the tortured damned fill the air.

Kirsch the ghost beams as best as she can. The sheet that covers her body, ever dripping with blood, leaks down onto the hissing floors, steam rising into the air between the feet of the hundreds of statues that fill the throne room. The ground between them has begun to crack and break from the intensity of the inferno, giving the appearance that they were all about to fall into the deepest recesses of the underworld itself—even deeper than they are now.

"You like it?!" she asks excitedly.

"I am pleased," replies Swain, leaning back on his throne, his massive arms lumbering down onto its rests.

The ghost spins in a little circle, clutching her gore-soaked doll as she looks around for a new sheet of paper to catch. The souls flying around the throne room, sensing her intent, swim away like a trapped school of fish trying to escape a shark in their midst.

"My lord," comes a voice from below him. Swain lowers his gaze, looking at his servant, Cartouche. "We are getting closer to the human capital," says the gallu, lifting her gaze to look at him.

Swain nods. "We are, Cartouche," replies the Demon King.

"But we're stuck," she adds.

"We are," repeats Swain again, resting his head on one of his massive fists.

The dancer looks his way. "What would you have us do?" she asks. "Should we go and remove the problem?" inquires Cartouche, referring to herself and the other gallu—the Demon King's most powerful servants.

Swain shakes his head. "There is no need," he replies, lifting his hand. "It will solve itself soon," he explains, his many eyes watching the crusade work. "Spend your hours on perfecting your craft, Cartouche," instructs the Demon King. "The final stage is almost set," states the beast. "And the world will be there to watch the beauty of your creation unfold," he promises. "I look forward to it."

"Yes, my lord," replies Cartouche, smiling. ". . . There is something else. A human is in the depths. Abydos—"

"I know," replies Swain, lifting his other hand to stop her. "It is also no bother."

"My lord?"

He shakes his head. "We all have our playthings," says the Demon King. "If the painter needs her for his musings as an artist, then it is not my place to stop him."

Cartouche tilts her head, looking at him. "This is a threat to you, my lord," she explains. "A human this close to the throne, even if she's weak—"

"No . . ." replies Swain, staring off into the distance as he thinks. "I tolerate her presence," growls the Demon King, but not able to really tell her why. There's something there in the priestess's mind . . . something familiar. A sense of rejection from her own and also acceptance from another that is vague and oddly . . . homelike. There's something he knows deep in the thoughts she radiates, in the feelings she emanates. It's something that reminds him of . . .

The Demon King shakes his head, not quite sure of what exactly he is reminded of, actually.

"The pursuit of beauty comes in many shapes, Cartouche," explains the Demon King, his voice hissing together with the baking rock of the darkness below the world. "And some of those shapes are unconventional."

"Yes, my lord," she replies, nodding. After a moment, she vanishes, teleporting away.

Somewhere above him, a soul lets out a horrific scream, having been caught.

~ [Ruhr, the River Sorceress] ~
Half Elf | ♀ | Sorceress
Rank: SSS
Location: The Demon King's Castle, Floor Thirty-One
Level: 100

It is later on that night, and the chamber is filled with thousands of voices, being unusually loud.

The portals were a success, only for the modicum price of a few fingers and a bit of skin, but they've connected the floor they're on now to the entrance, and have made a sweep back to the exit of the castle, funneling in several thousands of warm bodies from the armies that had surrounded the demon carnival outside. It took some doing and blood, but with the counterassault that came from inside the castle itself, the combined forces managed to repel the exterior demon onslaught, at least long enough to get everyone inside.

The demonic caravan is moving again, but they couldn't have stopped it for much longer anyway. The other army is better off acting as a force multiplier inside, rather than outside of the castle anyway. The crusade and the officers are organizing themselves now, reestablishing a chain of command.

The plan now is to use the portal mechanism as they push deeper, always returning to a fortified position where they can heal the wounded and rest.

As for food, many gave up after days of hunger and just started eating whatever they could find. The concept of being damned to the underworld if one eats in it means nothing to many of them now, as they assume they will die here soon anyway, given what they've experienced. And, given what has happened so far, they might really not be wrong to do so.

Ruhr lets out a long, deep exhalation, rolling back over on the bedding onto her back, a slender arm draping over her front as two sweaty bodies lie next to one another.

The black-haired priestess lies there, her fingers tracing patterns on the half elf's skin as Ruhr stares at the ceiling, thinking.

"Hey, you still got that knife?" she asks, turning her head to the woman.

The priestess opens her eyes. "Huh?" After a confused moment, she sits upright, holding the blanket against her chest to look around for the pile of clothes just next to them. She pulls out the knife, handing it to Ruhr. "That's kind of a scary question . . ."

Ruhr takes the knife and stands up next to her, the blanket falling off as she walks past the somewhat overwhelmed stranger, who isn't sure if she should look this way or that. "I gotta go do something real quick," says the river sorceress, bending over and grabbing her clothes to get dressed.

"That's also kind of a scary thing to say," remarks the priestess. "Should I, uh . . ." She stops for a second. "My name is—"

"Ah-ah!" Ruhr stops her, adjusting her belt. She kneels down and looks at the priestess from up close. "Don't," she says, a hand below the woman's chin, holding it up as they look at one another.

". . . Oh." She looks at her, rubbing her arm nervously as Ruhr stands back up and lets her go. "Well, this was . . ." She looks away. "I—I should. Uh, I think I'll—"

"Stay here," says Ruhr, walking to the flap of the tent and looking back at her. "I'll be right back." She looks down at the knife and then back at her. "Don't get dressed."

Ruhr closes the tent behind herself, looking around the crowd. Everywhere, soldiers and crusaders are celebrating. Dehydrated crusaders are drinking water as if it were pure Amrita from the heavens, and they're eating military rations as if they were the first food they'd ever received.

She doesn't blame them. They've all reached a point where faith and piety have collided with human needs and desperation.

Walking through the crowds of celebrating revelry, she moves toward the officer's circle, walking past the row of guardsmen who keep it separate from the rest.

"Ah, look who's decided to join us!" says a voice from the circle. An officer from the military claps his hands together at the sight of her as she walks toward them. "The famous Ruhr, the river sorceress!"

Ruhr instinctively reaches up to flick her hair away, but it's shorter now, and her fingers find no grip at first until she reaches higher upward. "The one and only," she replies, looking around the circle. "Glad you made it to my party. Ah—Officer Mistley?" she asks, gesturing for a man to come over to her—the chief officer of the crusade.

"Yes, ma'am?" he asks, stepping away from the improvised planning table toward her.

Ruhr nods to him. "I just wanted to say thank you," she says. "For your excellent work today with the portals." The sorceress holds out a hand in an unusual gesture for the hard social image she has made for herself this last week. "And I wanted to apologize for stressing you this afternoon about it."

The man blinks, looking around the table for a second before turning back to her and taking her hand. "Of course. I understand; we're all just doing our jobs," he says, clasping his second hand over her outstretched one in a firm gesture as he smiles warmly her way. "Thank yo—"

Officer Mistley gurgles, black blood oozing out of his neck as she stabs the knife into it from the side with her free hand.

People scream around the table in confusion, the camp rising to alert as he stumbles back, grasping at his oozing throat, blood leaking everywhere as long, sharp, spindly legs like those of a spider flail out in all directions from the cut. Kicking and screaming, people back away from him while his body violently spasms as if a terrified spider were trying to work its way out of his flesh, where it had nested itself, but finding nowhere to go.

Ruhr stands there, staring at him intently as she lifts her hands.

"I figured you out," speaks the river sorceress, looking at the possessed corpse. The officer is long since dead, his body taken over by a thing, a monster of the Demon King's employ. "Don't think I didn't recognize you from last time," continues Ruhr, never blinking as she lifts her hands toward it.

As long as somebody is watching it, it can't leave. It can only ever be places where nobody is looking.

For days, weeks, people have been going missing here and there. Not even because they died in the fights; they've just been . . . vanishing. It took a while, but she pieced it together. They've met before, she and this thing, when she and Zac made it to the safe room on floor eleven.

She thought it died when it fell down the pit, but clearly, she was wrong.

Ruhr narrows her eyes.

"Get the fuck out of my castle," says the river sorceress, aiming her hands at the Shambler, glowing water condensing around her fingers.

(Ruhr) has used: [{Purity} Sacred Dragon]

CHAPTER 2

BRACK

~ [Ruhr, the River Sorceress] ~
Half Elf | ♀ | Sorceress
Rank: SSS
Location: The Demon King's Castle, Floor Thirty-Two
Level: 100

Mud.

Arcing spires of fresh mud fly through the air as massive stones crash downward from above, splashing through the ankle-deep, foggy water that rises up the boots of the crusade's forward legion. The arcs of disturbed water cascade through the air in sharp waves and crescents as the raging battle disturbs the rest of the pool.

A row of tower shields lined up in a single formation rushes forward toward the enemy, creating a wave in their wake as the shields, scraping against the stone floors, push forward against the water and into the mass of claws, teeth, and screams that is the horde of the Demon King, the demons mounting an interior defense of this floor of the castle.

One of the crusaders holding the shield wall together falls forward a bit as someone kicks off his back from behind the lines. Ruhr leaps over the barrier, flying forward together with the wave of unclear water and the roaring dragon of water trailing in the arc of her descent toward the enemy.

A giant frog's tongue slaps right against her, the sticky mass gluing itself to her arm and face as her zealous attack is cut short before it ever has a chance to begin. Before she falls out of the air with her lost momentum, it begins to pull her back in immediately toward the mass of demons.

Something cuts through the tongue at the base. Ruhr flops into the muddy waters, tumbling and rolling for a second. The half-glued segment of frog tongue still sticks to her as she rises to her feet, blasting a wave of holy water out of her hands just in time, as a member of the swarm that she's been pulled down into runs toward her with its massive claws bared.

(Ruhr) has used: [Aquatic Dragon]

The aquatic dragon blasts free from her palm, crushing the demon it hits instantly, the force of the waters held behind a now broken dam crashing against the demon and the hundred behind it, cutting a line through the horde.

The half elf turns her hands, the dragon arcing downward below herself against the stones. The pressure of the spout pushes Ruhr back up into the air and away from the circle closing around her, dozens of claws and teeth landing where she was just standing a second ago.

The piece of frog tongue falls off her side, and she looks toward the body of the monster who had stolen her from the air a moment ago. A prismatic barrier, a glassy magical wall, had been created in the middle of its tongue, severing it and freeing her.

A sharp whistle comes from behind her as she flies. A second later, several dozen tower shields slam against the stones through the water as a new row of magical barriers is created at once—all together in a perfect line—across the room by the shield bearers and priests. The prismatic wall divides the full room in half. The room begins to shift in its composition as the shield-wall marches forward.

As she falls, another barrier is created below her feet, attached to the outer wall of the room. Ruhr lands on the elevated platform, watching the room from above. The demon swarm—full of strange, swampy monsters—begins to fight and push against the wall. Hundreds of claws and thousands of teeth gnash, bite, and cut against the glassy barrier, cracking it here and shattering it there, only for the damaged sections to be renewed with fresh magic while the soldiers with tower shields continue to advance. They cross half of the room's distance, then another quarter, slowly pushing against the demons who are running out of space to move, to run, crushed against the back wall of the chamber. Muddy waters rise up higher and higher around them, toward their waists and then their chests, while the space they have is reduced further.

The wicked stampede begins to crush itself in its lack of space, the demons clawing and descending on one another in an attempt to move as they're suffocated amongst their own bodies and mass. The shield wall presses further. Demons are stuck shoulder to shoulder, then elbow to elbow, as their space continues to be stolen. Wet, wretched screams come up to her in the air as the muddy water rises to the demons' necks and then, soon, over their heads while the wall advances further, indifferent to the noises of crushing bones and ripping flesh.

Ruhr stands there, watching from above, as the legion of cruel, terrible things is compressed and crushed—compacted further as the wall moves forward again.

The muddy waters turn into an indiscernible brack as gore and viscera leak out of ruptured bodies, filling the constrained pool with more bile, urine, and blood than water by the time everything is done. The water begins to bubble from the heat of the Demon Core, causing an indescribable stink to start wafting upward toward her in clouds of thick steam.

The river sorceress turns away and descends down the staircase that is made for her out of magical barriers. The shield wall is slowly released, and the water level floods back slowly all around the room. The gore of the scene is floating around the boots of the crusade as the dam of shields and barriers is lifted.

Ruhr stands on the last step, looking down at the mess before she steps down into it. For a moment, she considers, oddly enough, if this is supposed to bother her, a glimpse of a long since dead version of herself coming to the surface for a brief moment. The half elf shakes her head, her gunked-up hair sticking to her face as water splashes around her ankles. The old, pre-Demon King Ruhr was a bit of a delicate, snobby creature with highly refined tastes and desires. The new Ruhr is less so, that polish she once had ground down into something more base and pragmatic.

She's still going to get famous, even more so than she already is, by killing the Demon King. But it's going to be for different reasons now than they were when all of this started.

The half elf looks toward the end of the chamber, toward the gaping maw where bloodied fluids now flood down into, draining into the deeper section now that the exit to the next floor has opened up.

The Demon King is running out of space to hide, just the same as they're running out of time to stop his collection of innocent souls.

Pressure is mounting, and the crusade as a whole is in a race against the clock to stop him before it's too late for them all—for the world.

Ruhr waves a hand listlessly into the air. "Send the wounded back up," she orders. "Get me replacements. We're moving to the next floor," orders the river sorceress as crusaders begin to carry and drag the wounded out through a violently unstable portal behind them which leads back up the staging area they've set up. As she walks to the next floor, fresh bodies come out of the portal from above, ready to fill the gaps in the offensive force.

A priestess runs after her, holding the bottom of her robe up with her hands as she wades through the surging water that is flowing downstairs. "You're still alive?" asks Ruhr, looking at the black-haired priestess from the other day.

"I, uh, I just wanted to see if you were okay," replies the woman. "That frog demon looked like it hit you pretty hard."

Ruhr looks at her. "We're not making this a thing," says the half elf.

"Huh? I'm—No . . . I—"

Ruhr lifts a hand as she walks. "Not a thing," she repeats, pointing at herself and then at her without stopping. "Thanks for the wall," says the river sorceress, her hand shifting to a listless thumbs-up.

"You still have some tongue on you . . ."

Ruhr lifts her arm and peels off a strip of slimy frog tongue that is still stuck to it. She flicks it away. "Lots of repeating patterns in my life these days," remarks Ruhr, shaking her head as she walks on.

"See you later?" asks the priestess, falling behind.

"We're not making it a thing," replies Ruhr, waving the woman off as she goes.

The crusade marches after her as they descend deeper into the darkness of the Demon King's castle.

~ [High King Mercator] ~
Half Elf | ♂ | King
Location: The Capital City in the Nearby North
Level: 100

The man's sleep is filled with screams; his moments of brief wakefulness are indistinguishable from the questionable ambiguity of his sleep as he fades between a state of fugue rest and uncertain awareness. Every time he tosses in patterns of a few minutes, it feels like hours have passed, and every time he opens his eyes, new shadows stand all around his bed, hovering over him in such abundance as if it were night—as if it were totally dark in his chambers.

But he can see the lights glowing behind them, through them. The lanterns that adorn the walls of his room continue to shine, their meager flames pressing through the curtain of shadows that hovers around him.

The king screams, shooting upright again another time, just as he had done a dozen times before. Is he awake? Or is he still asleep, and this latest waking is just another layer of the dream he cannot escape from?

His body feels heavy. His eyes look around the room, and the bed vibrates beneath him for some reason. His mass sinks lower and deeper into the mattress, as if it were swallowing him whole. The shadows surround his bed.

The king screams, sitting upright again and clutching his face as he "wakes up" again, presumably. Sweaty and panting, he looks around the room. He can't get up. He can't get out of bed.

Did he make it out this time? Did the sleep paralysis break?

Shadows creep toward the edge of the mattress. A voice rings through his head. *We have to get out of here.*

He sinks into the mattress that his back feels glued to.

His eyes open again.

He sits upright, lost in an animal fear, as the cycle of the dream he cannot leave continues on over and over and over. He's locked in this state, this pattern. He's repeated it hundreds of times, and each time, he thinks that he's about to wake up for real, but then he never does. How long has it been? A night? Days? He isn't sure. His exterior and interior senses are totally lost, numbed by the fake sensory input of the dream.

Shadows surround his bed, staring down at him. One of them is sitting on his chest. The bed vibrates, and despite being in his own chambers, he can feel roaring winds rushing over his skin, as if he were falling, as if everything were falling.

He sits upright, covered in sweat again.

~ [Military Advisor Blumen] ~
Human | ♂ | Royal Knight
Location: The Capital City in the Nearby North
Level: 100

Blumen sits at the table.

His heavy head rests there in his folded palms, and his eyes are closed. People run around the room all around him, organizing all manner of defensive and offensive operations. Special military advisors and diplomats hurry in frenzies as they try to enact last-minute measures.

There is a soft shuffling sound as something moves over paper. The noise, clearly discernible from all of the rest of the chaos, causes his body to twitch together in response.

Weakly, Military Advisor Blumen, who has taken over the central defense in the king's place, lifts his exhausted gaze to look at the most hated man in the room. The court artist, well aware of his own poor fortune, makes eye contact with nobody else as he quietly slides the miniature caravan figurine across the map, ever closer to the capital. It's not his fault. He's just doing his job. But everyone hates the artist nonetheless because he's associated with their troubles by being the one who has to represent their ever-worsening situation.

Nobody likes the bearer of bad news.

The Demon King is almost at the gates of the nation's capital. The final siege is going to begin soon. There are a few tricks and games left to stop him, some final desperate acts to be given a chance, though everything they've thrown at the Demon King so far has been intercepted, has failed, or has been subverted.

Not a single one of their most creative strategies or spontaneous plans bought them more than a day at best. Hundreds of thousands of people are dead or worse. The country is in disarray. The nation's greatest fortifications have all but fallen. Their experimental weapons and technology have failed and lost, setting them decades back in the fields of magical research alone, which will cost them more than dearly should they even survive this mess—and that's not including the damage to infrastructure and the spirit of the country. The king is lost to madness. The world is soon to end.

All in all, it's really not going that well.

"Sir," says a voice from the side. Military Advisor Blumen turns his gaze, looking at the knight who has lifted a hand. "A suggestion."

"What is it?" asks Blumen.

The knight shrugs. "Why don't we just ask the Demon King if he'll give us a day?"

The room is quiet as everyone immediately stops their work and looks at him.

"Soldier," starts the tired officer, looking at him. He lifts an arm, pointing to the window.

Everyone turns to look at the darkness beyond the shattered windows of the castle that haven't held against the ever-increasing intensity of the storm. There, on the far horizon, the arm of a demon of impossible scale and size reaches up toward the sky to steal another star of its many thousands.

The knight looks around the room and shrugs. ". . . It's just an idea . . ." he mutters silently, his gaze lowering to the floor.

Someone clears their throat from across the room as people slowly look at one another.

The exhausted head of defensive operations, Blumen, sighs and holds his face in his hands. ". . . Get me a scryer," he instructs after a minute of silence.

Their only hope is that the capital can hold on long enough for the crusade and its reinforcements to break through to the Demon King.

~ [The Demon King] ~

"I don't understand," says the reengineer, Peribsen. The young gallu looks at his plans, ripping through sheets of flayed souls as he tries to spot something that he's missed. "How are they getting through my designs so quickly?" asks the demon, referring to the crusade. He scrunches his face in frustration, throwing everything away to his side.

"They're slippery creatures," growls a heavy voice from up above. The gallu looks up at the Demon King. "Humans," explains the lord of monsters, staring at his hand as he curls his fingers as if he were trying to grasp hold of something he once held on to but that would no longer fit in the grisly, monstrous appendages he has now. "They are unpredictable and strange." He shakes his head. "Even worms have a beauty to them," explains the Demon King. "They have a pattern of motion, a rhythm of nature that guides them through the simplicity of their days." The beast looks toward the architect. "Ugliness, however, is the only repeating dance that humanity as a whole carries with itself."

The gallu thinks for a time, souls swirling around the throne room of the Demon King's castle in a raging torment as the intensity of the

Demon Core grows with every minute. After a minute, he lifts his gaze, looking back toward Swain. "I've learned, as an engineer, that all materials can be useful in their own way. Some woods fracture easier than others but have incredible properties against moisture," says the demon engineer. "Some stones weather terribly, yet make for the sturdiest foundations." He shakes his head. "Surely, there is a flaw in judging the collective whole of a species?" asks the gallu, questioning the logic of his king, who doesn't reply, his head simply resting on his massive fist.

Something disturbs the swirling anarchy that is the throne room. A light, an orb, forms together in the air between them.

"Let me prove you wrong, Peribsen," says the Demon King. "Watch as I demonstrate to you that there is not a single light within the skyward span of the collective totality of humans. They are depraved, lost things far more wretched and cruel than anything that I could ever hope to imagine." He lifts his hundreds of eyes, staring at the mass of flying souls. "They will do whatever they have to if it means they get what they want." His fingers close again, trying to grab something that isn't there, trying to grab hold of a hand that had once held his own. It is not something he remembers with anything more than base instinct from the moments that led up to his transformation into what he is now. "Any flower, no matter its beauty, will be trampled," he says. "Any song will be crushed within its windpipes, any bridge burned, Peribsen, if it means they can have just a little more of what they want."

A message comes through the scrying orb, a human communication and observation spell that has been cast into his castle—allowed through his permission. The humans' predictable groveling comes at an opportune moment for him to demonstrate the clarity of his mission to a kindred soul.

They have come to ask for mercy, pleading like sniveling children, now that it looks like they won't get what they want.

The Demon King looks, listening as a human voice speaks from the other end of the spell, asking for exactly that—a stay on his offensive for a single day.

A single day longer than they deserve to live in his eyes, and they will prove it themselves.

~ [Military Advisor Blumen] ~
Human | ♂ | Royal Knight
Location: The Capital City in the Nearby North
Level: 100

This is stupid.

Military Advisor Blumen stands there, his hands gripping the edge of the table as the winds of the spirit world coming to claim their lives howl outside of the castle, carrying over the city's walls. The gale's whistle sings the tune of the end of days, upon the precipice in which they find themselves as a collective.

His eyes lower away from the scrying orb, looking around the room, tense.

Of course it's stupid.

The last scryer who tried to send a message to the Demon King spontaneously combusted, yet this one persists—sweating very profusely. A final act of desperation. The city's defenses might hold when the Demon King arrives, but they also might not. There are still a few regions left before the demon carnival arrives at their gates, but . . .

He looks back at the orb, toward which every face in the room is turned.

The orb floats there, crackling with wild energies as it begins to fail to sustain the power of the spells moving through it in both directions, like a glass tunnel trying to funnel the ocean.

Priests surround the scryer, readying themselves for him to start melting on the spot.

The lantern lights around them waver, a wind creeping in through the broken windows like a witch's fingers crawling through the slats of a crib, creeping forward toward them all. The lights dim in and out, the magics of the spell fading at first and then brightening in an overpowering up and down. The room is filled with wavering light, the features of their tired, horrified faces dancing first to hide in the shadows and then to be over-exposed. Papers fly around the room, the corners of the pinned-down map rising up and ripping free from its constraints as a heavy heat billows around them, hammering the exhaustion deeper into their frames. The moving air does not have the grace to wick the sweat from their brows, and the moisture of the storm that never stops only worsens their breathing difficulties.

The orb in the center of the room crackles.

The lights all fade, the candles die out, the lanterns suffocate, and the magic of every spell present within the chamber dissipates into nothingness. Only the scrying orb remains, but it is no longer under the control of the human scryer who cast it. He lies unconscious on the stones, blood leaking from his eyes and nose. Strands of white come from the orb, peeling off as if it were an unraveling cocoon. Some threads fall down to the table, while others rise up to the rafters above, wrapping themselves around the beams. All of them expand outwardly like the arcs of multipronged lightning bolts.

A web is created; a spider's silk is spun across the room of the castle, above their table. And the orb from which it all stems, the egg that the Demon King has now made it into, breaks. Two sharp, long, black chitinous legs appear from within, resulting in the horrified screams of everyone in the room. People start to run, trying to get to doors that have locked themselves.

Two more legs appear, then two more. Sharp, needlelike protrusions, each joint alone the length of a healthy oak, come to span. They are covered in fine, thin hair—soft and white. The legs arc themselves, trying to fit inside the ceiling of the castle room, which they are much too long and spindly for.

Two more legs appear, bringing the total to eight, and then follow eight glossy ruby eyes that catch sight of every person in the room. The chittering mass clicks with its mandibles. The giant spider, the size of a dragon, clicks and snaps as it spreads its legs around the magically spun web.

Crying and screaming, people hammer against the doors and try to climb up to the windows, but none find success.

A voice fills the air around them; the screaming harrow, the growl of the true beast, the Demon King speaks. "Sacrifice yourselves," it instructs, the stones all around them rumbling. "If you really love your people, your world, then step into the web," it says as dozens of eyes look up toward the spindly monstrosity that stares back at them, hungry. Foamy venom leaks from its jagged, meat-sheathed fangs, which are the size of crooked swords. "For every willing volunteer, I will stop for one precious, beautiful hour."

The wind lessens. The howl quiets. The spell fades, leaving only a dark room filled with dozens of people and the docile spider, clinging to its web above them.

"Or was that not why you were interested?" he asks in a mocking tone as his voice fades away, leaving them to their choice.

~ [Ruhr, the River Sorceress] ~
Half Elf | ♀ | Sorceress
Rank: SSS
Location: The Demon King's Castle, Floor Thirty-Three
Level: 100

Bones crunch beneath her boot.

Ruhr screams, violently stomping down again on the skull. It cracks, pieces of fractured bone pressing out through the soft meat on the sides of the compressing head. The demon's arms flail, its broken body either trying to mount a defense or simply reacting to the senseless signals its own brain is sending in its death rattle. Her boot cracks down again, mush oozing out beneath her foot.

The battle has long since ended.

"Are you . . . are you okay?" asks a voice from the side.

Ruhr's boot breaks through the top of the skull as it fully caves in, her foot sinking into the broken bowl of the cranium. Panting, she turns her head, looking at the priestess who is still tailing her. "I'm working through some stuff," replies Ruhr dryly before turning to the crusaders with whom she had been fighting against the enemies of this next floor. "Bring me another one."

The crusaders look at each other before turning to her. "Ma'am . . ." starts the first one.

"Bring. Me. Another," repeats Ruhr, tapping her finger into her open palm.

"Ma'am," speaks up the other crusader. "There aren't any left," he says, gesturing around the room.

Ruhr looks.

The battle has long since ended. After the flooded room, they moved on to the next floor and cleared that one just as violently. Although, she might have gotten a little too into it. The fight has been over for a good ten minutes now, but she's just been here letting out some rage.

The half elf's eyes wander down around her, at the other dead demons who lie strewn at her feet, all of them with caved-in heads and broken necks that have been stomped down on. Her boot is perforated with shards of sharp bone fragments. There aren't any living ones left to kill.

"Next floor. Let's go," says Ruhr, shaking her leg off before she starts walking to the next staircase.

"Ma'am —" speaks the crusader officer again. Ruhr turns her head his way. He lifts his hands. "The soldiers need a few minutes at least. Let them heal their wounds," he explains. "This pace is too much."

"The world is going to end," replies Ruhr, narrowing her eyes. She stops and then steps toward him. "Everyone you know is going to die," continues the half elf, grabbing him by his breastplate and looking him in the eyes. "Everything, everywhere, is going to die," she says. "Because you slackers need to take a pee break?"

To her surprise, the soldier, very bravely, grabs her wrist and pulls her hand free from his armor. He looks her in the eyes. "Ma'am, respectfully," he starts. "Families died today. Rein it in."

Her eyes go wide as those words ring through her head. Those familiar words, which are one and the same as Zacarias once told her back in the castle before they left on this mission. She should have told him back then to fuck off, and that she'd go without him.

If she had . . .

He lets go of her arm and turns around, walking back to the piles of the dead. To the heaps, where not just dead demons but also dead people lie. Soldiers tend to their own wounds and the wounds of their brothers and sisters. However, they also sit and kneel together with the dead. They weep over them, mourn them, dress their faces with clothes, and hold their hands tightly, as if they were guiding them over the precipice.

Ruhr hisses, turning away and gritting her teeth.

They have to get to the bottom of the castle before that bastard expands it again. They're already at the razor's edge of their timetable, even now. If the Demon King adds another ten floors like he's done twice to them now . . .

It'll be over.

This is their last, final shot. This push, this continued assault, is all that's left for humanity.

"Hey, do you wish to speak about it?" asks a voice from behind her.

Ruhr's fingers clench together as she turns around, glaring at the black-haired priestess who is still here for some reason. "This. This here," says Ruhr, her finger motioning between the two of them. "This isn't a thing. It needs to stop." The half elf looks at her. "I was just using you as a quick rebound to get over someone who actually mattere—"

A slap cracks through the room.

Ruhr holds her red cheek, looking at the priestess, who lifts her nose and nods as she speaks. "While we're opening up, don't forget to mention you're a loveless bitch with daddy issues and a broken ability to bond to anyone and anything."

". . . What?" asks Ruhr, taken aback by the quick rebuttal. She has the feeling this might not be a spontaneously generated thought from the woman.

The priestess turns around, looking at her scornfully over her shoulder. "I'm sure your dead friend would be proud to see you acting like a shithead. It's very kind of you to be so respectful of his memory." She looks away. "You should be glad he's dead so he can't be let down by you."

Ruhr stands there, holding her face, watching the woman walk away. The skin on her face stings, and those fresh words ring around her skull. Confused, she looks away for a moment through blurry eyes as she tries to understand something.

Why did it feel good that somebody had finally yelled at her?

The river sorceress stares into the distance.

"Hey," says Ruhr, turning around after a moment.

"What?" asks the venomous priestess, stopping but not turning around.

"What's your name?"

The priestess walks off, shaking her head. "What is wrong with you?" she asks as she leaves.

Ruhr shrugs, staring off into the distance for a moment. The half elf mutters to herself, "Apparently, I have daddy issues," adding the pieces together in her head. It checks out. It's not like she didn't know that already. Her childhood was . . . Well, it was. That's about it. It just was.

Having someone acknowledge it for her externally, along with the rest of her characteristics is nice, though.

"Fuck," mutters Ruhr in a revelatory tone, turning back and then running after the priestess, shards of broken bones crunching beneath her boot as she goes.

~ [Military Advisor Blumen] ~
Human | ♂ | Royal Knight
Location: The Capital City in the Nearby North
Level: 100

There are no volunteers.

Everyone stands with their backs against the walls, not daring to get too close to the spider, which is content on its web. All attempts to batter the door down from either the inside or the outside have failed.

Would he give his life for his country on the field of battle? Sure. Of course he would!

But this is different, isn't it?

This is . . . It's not the same.

Blumen turns his head, looking at the many knights of the castle's legions and at the higher officers and noble born of the high estates who were in here when everything happened. From them, too, nobody steps forward.

Besides, if he dies, who's going to run this operation? They need him. He's important. With the king absent, nobody else could do this work like he does this work. He's important. He's vital.

His presence alone is worth more in value toward the defense than the single hour his life would buy. It would be a waste for him to sacrifice himself for a vague promise made by the Demon King of all things. Who says that he'd even keep it? You can't trust the Demon King.

Blumen shakes his head, having fully finished his argumentations to himself for the third time now, just in case anybody happens to ask him to step forward. However, nobody has yet done so, because nobody wants to be asked themselves to step into the web.

And so, they all stand there quietly, waiting for something to happen, but nothing ever does. Only the darkness outside grows ever bleaker as more and more lights vanish from the sky above.

~ [The Demon King] ~

He sits there with his head on his palm, his point having been made clear to the gallu, Peribsen.

"You see, Peribsen?" he asks, his voice shaking the walls of the castle. "Not a one," says the Demon King. "Not a single one of them has within them the capacity of love for a thing greater than themselves. Those who truly do are rare and few." The Demon King leans back on his throne. "And they are destined for better graces than what this world is now, after our work is done. After we reach the apex, the pinnacle of beauty."

". . . I see . . ." says the gallu, watching. "I admit, I am . . . disappointed."

"We all were, Peribsen," replies Swain, looking at him. "People who are truly satisfied with the world do not make art, for they would perceive it to be such already," explains the Demon King. "Art is the manifestation of that which does not exist; it is the collective wishes and memories of a person, both brought to life as an avatar, an imprinting of the soul." He shakes his head, looking at the humans cowering against the wall. "What their problem is, is that they have nothing to wish for. Nothing except for life itself, which is an empty, token prize."

The Demon King slowly rises to his feet, the stones of his grim seat crumbling. "Living is only sustenance, Peribsen." He steps down from his throne, looking at the gallu. "Beauty is what nourishes." He looks up toward the wall, toward a picture of a goose, and then at his own long claws. "It's what lets us . . . grow," says the demon curiously as his senses reach through the castle, reaching toward something that was festering and now begins to break through the rot.

~ [Ruhr, the River Sorceress] ~
Half Elf | ♀ | Sorceress
Rank: SSS
Location: The Demon King's Castle, Floor Thirty-Three
Level: 100

"So I used to have this really neat owl doll," answers Ruhr, staring upward at the top of the tent and responding to the question about her favorite childhood toy. "When I was a girl."

". . . An owl?" asks the voice next to her. "I somehow figured you were a frog person."

"Yuck!" Ruhr sits upright, looking at the priestess who is lying next to her. "As if," she says, lifting an eyebrow. "Frog people are weirdos. Total creeps."

"Hmm," replies the priestess, staring at her blankly.

"For real. Have you ever seen somebody who is super into frogs?" asks Ruhr, leaning down with wide eyes and shaking her head. "Wackos."

The priestess leans sideways with her head resting on her palm. "Springer."

"Huh?"

"My name is Springer," says the priestess. "And I like frogs. A lot."

Ruhr purses her lips, the two of them looking at one another.

Quietly, Ruhr leans over to the side, grabbing her clothes. "Okay. Maybe this was a mistake after all," she starts before they're yanked out of her hands, and the two of them get into a play fight over them.

Perplexingly enough, laughter finds itself present inside the Demon King's horrific castle.

In honor of this rare blossom, the demon carnival stands still for one hour—but not a second more.

As for the castle in the human capital, the spider gruesomely and hor-rifically eats someone randomly in exchange and then vanishes. If only because the Demon King cannot let it be known that he is a softie.

A DARK AND GLOOPY NIGHT

~ [A Strange Village Down in the Dark Forests] ~

Y ou must not go that way, girl," explains the old woman, clutching the arm of the sorceress as she steps into the carriage, stopping her. She turns her head, letting out a hacking cough. Splatters of blood coat the elbow of the sleeve she coughs into, adding to the already dried stains there, present from past episodes of the symptom.

The caster, with a very monotone expression, looks at the elderly stranger clutching on to her bony arm. "That place is not natural, child," the old woman explains, her eyes going wide. "It is where . . . where it lives . . ."

Her voice falls silent.

"Die Kreatur . . ." whispers a man on the side of the crowd ominously, the others nearby shying away from him as he speaks the odd phrase. A small child cries in the crowd surrounding the carriage, its hooded mother tucking the baby in below her large, bobbled shawl as if to stifle its cries with the fabric.

"I must go," replies the sorceress without any emotion in her voice, pulling her arm free and stepping into the carriage. The gray-feathered anqas tied to the front of it scratch their taloned feet into the damp dirt in an uneasy gesture as they stare around the full crowd. The birds aren't used to such large gatherings and are uneasy with the unusual behavior of the people in this village, where they've stopped for directions.

Before she steps inside, she looks out over the carriage toward the castle high atop the nearby mountain. Its black silhouette contrasts with the hauntingly blue night. Crows caw in the trees all around the little shanty village.

The carriage creaks as she steps inside and pulls the door closed, sitting down next to her compatriots. The wood groans as it begins to move, rattling onward and upward down the mountain road, which is entirely overgrown on the sides yet kept meticulously open in the middle, as if they were all but too welcome to head that way, despite the villagers' many warnings.

She looks down at her hands, at the slip of paper she received, and reads it again as the shadows begin to consume the carriage that rides into the night that never ends.

A Thing That Harbors
Whispering winds entice weary feet within,
Of men who wander, leaving prints of crimson sin,
Into the den of the cruel thing that lies therein,
The prince of all beyond the world's virtuous kin.
For days and weeks and hours uncounted,
And every speck of time, somehow lost, surrounded,
The spirits wander into the harbor's bleak embrace,
Of the thing that dwells within this darkened space.
Like moths drawn to the brilliance of the flame,
They're pulled towards this heartless being's claim,
And bring unto it the bounty that their lives bestow,
In quest to find shelter from heartbeats' echo.
For they're reminded of their pasts, now long passed,
And screams dried out but persistent in memory's grasp.
The thing that harbors has beckoned them inside,
And they, the guilty, couldn't resist its siren cry.
For no man is without sin, when closely viewed,
As ships come to harbor with their journeys subdued,
So too must souls eventually come to rest,
In the shadowed refuge of a darkened, damp nest.
Return.

~ [Inside of the Carriage] ~

A great evil has nested itself in the peaks of the mountain.

In the midst of a seemingly endless black forest, a rickety old carriage meanders its way up a winding mountain road, its loose wheels creaking

in protest with every rotation. The gnarled branches of the surrounding trees reach out as if to claw at the intruding carriage, casting elongated, sinister shadows on the darkened path. The atmosphere is suffocatingly haunting and silent, devoid of the melodious songs of the forest-dwelling creatures; even the whispering wind dares not disturb this eerie void of noise. They are far away from the Demon King's immediate influence, yet even here the world has become bleaker and darker.

The desolate tableau is punctuated by the disquieting sight of countless crows perched upon the skeletal limbs of the lifeless trees, their beady eyes fixated upon the unwelcome interloper with an unnerving intensity. The once vibrant foliage that decorated these arboreal giants has long since withered and crumbled to dust, leaving naught but a monochromatic landscape draped in varying shades of darkness.

The beleaguered anqas pulling the carriage snort uneasily, their breaths forming ghostly wisps in the unusually damp air as they struggle to ascend the steep incline. The strain of their efforts is palpable; their muscles tremble beneath their slick feathers, and their talons slip on the slick cobblestones as they fight to maintain their footing. The passengers within the carriage are shrouded in shadows, their identities and intentions obscured.

As the carriage continues its arduous journey into the heart of this forsaken forest, an almost imperceptible sense of foreboding seems to seep from every nook and cranny of this haunted landscape. The omnipresent crows appear to multiply in number with each passing moment, their obsidian feathers melding into one indistinguishable mass as they maintain their unwavering vigilance over their silent kingdom. In this almost otherworldly realm where darkness reigns supreme, hope and optimism are but distant memories, swallowed whole by the ever-present maw of despair that has clamped down on the world ever since the birth of the Demon King. The carriage, a mere speck of glowing light in the vast abyss of shadows, perseveres in its ascent.

Within the confines of the creaking carriage, a cadre of grim adventurers sit in oppressive silence, their eyes downcast and their thoughts buried within the depths of their own minds. These hardened souls have each faced countless perils, and yet, in this darkened space, an undeniable tension weighs heavily upon them, causing even the most stalwart among them to shift uncomfortably. They are bound for a forgotten castle

nestled precariously atop the mountain summit, where evil has woven its insidious tendrils into the very stones forming the once glorious ancient fortress. The walls, which once stood as a symbol of strength and defiance against the encroaching darkness in long gone days lost to history, now serve as a breeding ground for malevolence and corruption.

The local villagers, desperate to be free from the plight of evil over their heads, had hired them to go there.

The adventurers are an eclectic assortment of individuals, each bearing the scars and tokens of their harrowing pasts. The leader of this somber ensemble is an enigmatic figure clad in worn leather armor; his battle-hardened hands grip the hilt of a sword that has as many knicks and notches as he himself does.

"It's not the Demon King," says the man, looking out the side of his eyes.

Beside him sits a lithe sorceress cloaked in shadows, her eyes smoldering with an inner fire; her fingers idly trace intricate patterns in the air as she mutters incantations as practice.

"It is unlikely," she remarks in a dry, monotone voice.

Across from this duo sits a stoic cleric bearing the symbols of a long-forgotten deity, his faith unwavering even in these dire times; his calloused hands clutch a sacred amulet as he whispers prayers for protection and guidance. He doesn't interrupt his prayers to argue with the others anymore, although he is fairly convinced that whatever is happening here is the work of the Demon King. What else could it be?

Beside him is a silent crossbowman, his presence nearly imperceptible in the gloom; his keen eyes, peering from beneath a face-obscuring wooden mask and a hood, scrutinize every detail of their surroundings rather than looking at any of them. His hand rests on the handle of the door as if he were ready to escape at any moment, even if they're moving far too fast for anyone to be able to exit safely.

Regarding his personal opinion on the Demon King matter, it's difficult to say for sure. He simply doesn't talk all that much.

As the carriage continues its ascent toward the summit, an oppressive aura of dread permeates the air, causing the adventurers to cling ever more tightly to their weapons and talismans.

From the walls of the castle, a figure stares down over the horizon, watching from the shadows.

Deep within the bowels of the forgotten castle, a malevolent entity broods in the darkness, its sinister gaze fixed on the distant carriage as it laboriously ascends the treacherous mountain path. The air within this forsaken fortress is heavy with a sour, acrid stench that seems to permeate every nook and cranny, clawing at the senses with its rancid tendrils.

From its shadowy perch, the vile presence observes the slow-motion procession of the carriage, its formless visage twisted into a grotesque facsimile of a smile as it revels in anticipation of what is to come: a feast. The decaying walls surrounding this abhorrent being seem to absorb the very darkness that cloaks it, their crumbling surfaces tainted by the indelible mark of malevolence. The moonlight filters through broken windows and cracks in the castle's facade, casting eerie patterns upon the rotting tapestries that adorn the desolate chambers. The once resplendent halls now lie in ruin, haunted by the whispers of long-dead inhabitants and consumed by an insidious corruption that gnaws at their deep-set foundations.

There is a rot, an eating, that happens deep down below the stonework.

As the carriage draws ever nearer to its harrowing destination, the air within the castle seems to thicken with an oppressive tension that chokes every breath. The entity's dark essence reverberates through the ancient stones with excitement. The brick seems to ripple unnaturally, moving as if it were an organic fluid, rather than being a strong, sturdy construction.

As they approach their final destination, unaware of the watchful eyes that observe their progress from within the castle's depths, they remain blissfully ignorant of the true nature of their journey's end, for amidst this miasma of decay and malevolence lies an evil far beyond their comprehension—a darkness that hungers for their very souls. And as the carriage approaches the castle's foreboding gates, the being there within stirs with anticipation, eager to welcome its unwary guests into the cold embrace of eternal night.

The castle squelches, which is quite the odd thing for a castle to be doing. But it is best not to question that.

~ [Inside the Castle] ~

Bats screech in the air above their heads, fighting to fly away now that their nests have been disturbed by the glow of raging cinders.

Falsch, the sorceress, holds her hands out before herself, letting out a torrent of flames that swallows a shambling mass that had come to greet them the moment they arrived. Undead, a swarm of them, had crept and crawled out of the shadows the instant they opened the massive oakwood doors into the old castle.

Dust and cobwebs, strangely, fail to catch fire or burn. Rather, it all just fades away, as if they were being retracted by an unseen force.

As the world before her glows with fire, the world behind her glows with holy light. The monotone sorceress looks back over her shoulder at the priest, who has created a magical barrier to block the open door they had just entered through. A legion of drooling, sloshing undead hammers at it from the outside, trying to reach them.

"Now!" yells the party fighter, the man in the leather armor, Erfunden. He presses against one of the massive doors, and the obscured crossbow-man, Unecht, presses against the other one. The two of them move the swinging doors, slamming them shut against the magical barrier. The priest, Gelogen, dives out of the way just in time to avoid being crushed as the heavy barriers crash closed with a resounding clap akin to thunder.

A pillar of broken wood is shoved in between the grips, barring the door from the inside.

Erfunden, the human fighter, looks down at his hands and then wipes them off on his clothes as he looks around at the grand entrance hall of the castle—if it can be called that still in its current state. The structure is dilapidated beyond repair. There is a hole in the floor above that lets the moonlight creep in through the upstairs windows and illuminate the entrance below in a circle, as if it were marking a ritual space.

The flames have died, the sorceress's spell having come to an end.

With his hand on the hilt of his sword, he looks around the area, stepping over the crumbling debris on the floor.

Their carriage had arrived at the castle; however, the anqas had been greatly disquieted, and as soon as they'd stepped out, the animals had bolted in terror with the carriage in tow. It hadn't taken a minute more for the undead ambush to roll over them. There were too many, so they had to run into the castle. Also, there was something else—something big.

"This was a mistake," says the priest, slowly rising up to his legs and looking around himself as he clutches his talisman. "We shouldn't have come here!"

"Shh," hisses the crossbowman, his blackened leather glove creaking as he lifts it to shush him. Warily, he stares around the hall. The entrance to the castle's first area is a grand, open room with an inner balcony that has long since crumbled down onto the ground floor. There is a winding staircase that might have served for grand entrances back in the day, long, long ago. However, now it only acts as a rest for the beams that have fallen from the upper floors.

No noises fill the air other than the haunting whisper of the winds outside the castle.

The two men turn their heads, looking back at the entrance door behind them, which has fallen silent. There is no hammering on it any-more. The undead have stopped.

". . . Where did they go?" asks the priest, nervously.

The hooded man lowers his hand and walks onward without replying, causing the priest to look toward the sorceress instead for answers. She looks at him and then keeps walking too. "They're taking another door," she replies quietly.

". . . Other door?" He receives no other answer. "What other door?! Hey!"

The man runs after his party, which begins moving through the castle in search of what they came here for.

Through the nebulous gloom of the forsaken castle, the band of grim adventurers cautiously advances, their hearts pounding in perfect har-mony with the ominous rhythm of their own footsteps. The haunting atmosphere of the forgotten castle clings to them like a shroud, and each oddly wet creak of the ancient floorboards beneath them sends a shiver down the spine of the nervous priest as they all traverse the labyrinthine network of shattered chambers and desolate halls that never quite seem to come to a sensible end.

It's as if the castle kept making more of itself every time they opened a new door, as if it were intent on keeping them inside for as long as it could.

All the while, something large moves elsewhere. It's not clear where, but its presence can be heard—ambling, shuffling, lumbering.

The walls of these once stately rooms now stand ravaged by the relentless passage of time, their moldering surfaces having borne witness to untold tales of terror and suffering that have now long since passed. Tattered banners with the iconography of a forgotten house of nobles hang limply from cracked rafters, their once colorful sigils long since bleached by darkness and decay. Shattered remnants of gilded mirrors reflect twisted fragments of reality, casting eerie illusions that dance along the periphery of the adventurers' vision, as if they were looking into a disturbed body of water rather than at the shards of looking glasses.

As they delve deeper into this oppressive realm, the sounds and sensations of creeping horror serve as constant reminders that they are not alone. The faintest whispers echo through abandoned corridors, voices that seem to have clawed their way out from beyond the veil of death to torment those who dare trespass upon this cursed domain. The undead shamble and groan, always nearby but never quite on their heels—as if the horde were a minotaur, chasing them through a labyrinth.

In one forsaken chamber, the impossible remnants of an opulent feast lie strewn across a vast dining table, as if frozen in time at the very moment when darkness descended upon this doomed gathering. A once resplendent chandelier hangs precariously above them, its crystal pendeloques no longer reflecting light but instead absorbing it like the endless void between the many stars in the night sky.

In another room, they chance upon a macabre gallery lined with portraits whose subjects' eyes seem to follow them with an unnerving intensity. The faces on the paintings never move, but they do not need to. Their screaming visages speak for themselves. One of their many eyes is yellow, which is inexplicably out of place.

As they delve farther into this unhallowed fortress, navigating through the suffocating darkness that threatens to envelop them whole, the adventurers are plagued by a mounting sense of dread. They can feel the oppressive weight of the malevolent presence that resides here, its very essence seeping into the very air they breathe. It smells . . . acrid and acidic. There is a dankness to the damp air that is akin to the deepest, oldest, and mustiest dungeons in the world.

"Hey," says a voice from the front of the group. The fighter, Erfunden, turns around to look at them for a moment. ". . . Where's Gelogen?"

The sorceress and the crossbowman look at one another and then around the hallway they're walking down for any signs of the missing priest. No doors are open anywhere that they themselves haven't opened.

He's nowhere to be seen.

"Ge—!" starts the fighter, calling out. Before he can finish, a leather-gloved hand is over his mouth. In indignant anger, he swipes it away, scowling at the crossbowman, who shushes him just the same as he had shushed the missing priest before. His lifted, gloved finger moves through the air as his outstretched hand switches from gesturing *Silence* to gesturing *Wait* without ever changing anything except its position in the air between them.

The three of them stand there, listening.

But it isn't so much what they hear that they notice. It is what they sense.

Something very large is moving nearby; its presence is made clear by the vibrations in the stonework beneath their boots—vibrations that travel deeply, unnaturally for this sort of material. They look down at the ground below their feet, watching it tremor strangely. The little pebbles on its surface, the puffs of dust, the fractured wood—none of it ever shakes or vibrates as something heavy thuds along. Instead . . . the fragments are perfectly, unnaturally still.

Only the brickwork floor itself somehow carries the sensation of the other toward them, not as a shaking vibration but as a soft ripple.

"This place is fucked . . ." whispers the fighter. "What do we do?" he asks, receiving no answer from either the crossbowman or the sorceress other than their continued walking onward.

It's in the room with them.

With her back pressed against the bookshelf, Falsch the sorceress quietly shuffles down the row in the old library until she reaches the end. Her fingers grip the edge of the shelving behind her as she cautiously leans out a few inches, staring into the darkness of the central library.

A smell is in the air—the smell of foul, rotting meat. It reeks of something that had been digested and then never fully completed.

Moonlight ekes in between the shelves of the upstairs library, entering through the half-atrium glass windows on the ceiling above. Many of the panes are broken, allowing previous rain to enter and flood the library. Crow droppings from nests above mark the shelves. The books are soaked and molded, many of them rotting and fallow. The acrid smell of their presence comes together as if they were themselves their own horde of undead.

But they are nothing compared to it—to the creature, the large thing.

She can't make it out clearly, but it is a hulking entity, the size of several men. Its torso is stiff and elongated, almost dragging down to the floor itself as if it had no legs. Its arms are what look like two long clubs that it uses to drag itself around, each of them easily enough to crush a knight in his armor with a single swing.

They say that a vampire used to live in this castle a long, long time ago, but that was ancient history. It was killed generations ago. At least, so everyone thought. However, now the castle, which was reduced to nothing but a heap of bricks, has reconstituted itself in an odd manner. It has come back—broken and destroyed, but returned nonetheless. It is as if the castle itself were an undead entity, just like the things that fill it.

The lurching thing slowly turns.

She hides back behind the shelf, quickly and quietly shuffling back down the other way toward the end of the row as its heavy steps come closer and closer. Each lumbering movement of its thick, clublike appendages against the floor ripples out unnaturally and lets her feel its presence.

Aiming a finger across the room, she points it at a book on the other side of the library and casts a spell to let it start smoldering.

The wet paper doesn't catch.

However, the magical glow persists nonetheless as the flame tries at least to eat away at it for as long as the effects of the spell remain. The lumbering stops for a moment, and she uses the time to sneak further toward the end.

There's no way out of this row. The open gap between this row and the next one is full of debris. She's trapped at a dead end.

Quietly swearing, the woman grabs an armful of soggy, mold-eaten books and quietly sets them down on the floor before repeating the pattern a few more times while the lumbering sensation returns.

She crawls sideways into the open shelf, squeezing her body against the little hollow space, flat and long, with her back out in the open and her face toward the wood. Quietly whispering, her palms pressing against the inside of the shelf, she works. Flames crackle and pop as they come into contact with the wet, soaked wood of the shelves that have collapsed in many places. The wood doesn't burn; rather, it just . . . sort of melts away in a deeply unnatural manner.

The ground ripples, quivering as the heavy thing moves. Its unnaturally large body forces itself into the tight gap between the shelves as it tries to enter the row she's in. Its long, stumpy growths churn in through the pulp and indiscriminate black slush that covers the floors as it forces its way inside, violently pressing its hulking gestalt in where it does not fit.

The ground shakes—together with her body—as it approaches, coming further and further inside, tearing and breaking everything delicate and soft on the way to her. It's closer now. Steps away. She works, feverishly whispering, as a heavy thud lands just behind her body.

The inner wall of the long shelf she had been burning gives way, and she rolls through the hole into the adjacent row before quickly crawling away on her stomach as something big looks down where she just was but sees nothing there.

Quietly, she sneaks out and down the row as fast as she can, heading back into the central library before it can, too.

Looking up, she sees the human fighter, Erfunden, quietly waving to her from the upper balcony of the library.

In a hurry, she runs through the library toward him, her steps coming to a stop as his full silhouette comes into light. He's just hanging there over the edge of the balcony, his entrails tangled and torn out of his sides. The many undead swarming behind him eat his insides as he drools and fails to scream—still alive.

He reaches out for her.

The shelves behind her shatter apart as this thing, the creature, breaks free.

She runs, sprinting down through the library on her way to the door and over a heap of broken glass that does not crunch as her boots press down on it.

The crushing monster slams into the open door behind her, the walls around the frame cracking at its forceful impact, too substantial to fit through immediately. By the time it is done rupturing the entrance open wide enough, she has already vanished.

The sorceress now finds herself alone in this wretched castle, her heart pounding with an echo of her companions' absence. The atmosphere is oppressively bleak, and the air hangs heavy with a palpable sense of malevolence.

As she traverses the desolate corridors, her footsteps muffled by the oppressive silence that envelops this forsaken place, she becomes acutely aware of a series of chillingly wet slurping and sloshing noises that appear to emanate from all around her. These grotesque sounds seem to taunt her with their dissonant cacophony, sending icy tendrils of dread snaking down her spine and causing the hairs on the back of her neck to stand on end.

Each step she takes is tainted by a creeping sense of despair, and as she passes through the gloomy chambers that lie strewn with the detritus of unspeakable horrors, she cannot shake the feeling that she is being watched by unseen eyes—predatory gazes that linger on her every movement from within the depths of the surrounding darkness.

The walls themselves seem to close in on her, their cracked surfaces whispering unspeakable secrets into her ears as they ooze some foul ichor that drips onto the cold stone floor beneath her feet. The very air is thick with tension, and it feels as though even time itself has become distorted within this hellish domain.

With each passing moment, it seems as though the darkness grows even more oppressive, and the grotesque slurping and sloshing noises that surround her take on a life of their own.

Falsch, the sorceress, keeps walking. She's almost there. She's certain.

Opening the next door, she walks through a room resembling a grand bedroom and looks to the side at the wall. There, the missing priest, Gelogen, is present.

In the context that his physical form is so.

The man is dead. He's merged into the wall. His body is plastered against it, his arms splayed out wide to his sides, as are his legs. His skull and chest sit half within the brickwork, as if it had been sucking him inside of itself. Ooze dribbles down out through his sockets and nostrils, the fluid that has already long since eaten his back and insides leaking down through his front.

That acrid smell is in the air again. The smell of something sour and foul.

Falsch looks away from the dead man and keeps walking, turning to go down the staircase he is plastered next to. His outstretched fingers were reaching for the corner of the wall but never quite managed to touch it.

They say that the vampire returned after all these years. That is why they are here.

The sorceress keeps a cinder aglow in her clasped fingers as she descends now deeper into the castle, if only to be ready for anything as she approaches the final chamber.

Something moves behind her.

Quickly, she turns her head and looks back up the staircase, but sees nothing.

Then, quietly, she descends.

The vampire's chamber.

Falsch looks at the hidden room she's found.

It's a dark, underground chamber akin to a castle dungeon. Chains and brickwork lie scattered all around the area, as if it had been under construction and then simply never finished.

Here, in the center of it all, sits a sarcophagus.

Vampires can only ever move about during the night, for they must rest during the day. However, in the era of the Demon King, in the era of the night that never stops, there is nothing around to stop such a creature from ever roaming the world again.

Hand lifted with a glowing spell, she creeps toward the coffin and gets ready to open it.

The castle above her shakes as something heavy moves nearby.

Her fingers grasp the edge of the coffin, and she yanks it open, the cinders glowing around her fingers aimed at the inside.

A gloved hand covers her mouth from behind as her body lurches, a painful heat shooting through her core as something presses into her flesh. She looks down at the old knife sticking through her, then back at the crossbowman behind. The man with the obscured face is holding her.

"Shh . . ." he says, pressing the knife through her. "You did well," he adds, restraining her as the last of the fight fades from her body. He pushes her face down into the open coffin and then looks around the room, listening to the noise of the heavy thing moving and lumbering above and around him.

It had tried to stop him from returning.

The crossbowman drops the knife, lowers his hood, and takes off his mask.

"It's over," he speaks out loud to the chamber. "I've won," says the man as his pale face is revealed to the world. His sunken features, cold, off-blue skin, and sharpened teeth reveal his nature as an elder vampire. He looks around himself. "Leave this place and never return."

There is no response.

But that is because it does not fear him, for it does not know who and what he is.

Sanctioned by the Demon King.

It has been generations since he last walked the world's surface, generations since he tasted the blood of the living, and generations since his castle stood whole and true. All of those many, many years ago, he had been slain by a man, a hero, an avatar of the sun and the day.

However, now they find themselves in the truest of nights, and he, by the graces of the Demon King, has been resurrected to fulfill his purpose. Even here, on the other end of the world, far, far away from the demon carnival and its grim parade toward humanity's last bastions.

The roof above him gives way.

But it does not break.

Rather, it simply forms a hole in itself, as if it were a liquid, as if the bricks and the wood and everything there were something else. Almost like they just looked like it—like they were made from a fluid substance pretending to be solid, pretending to be a destroyed castle.

Because that is what it is.

A heavy, lumbering thing falls down from above, the fake stones below his boots quaking and rippling as its heavy weight comes to a crash before him. The vampire's excellent vision in the dark lets him see what the lumbering monster truly is.

A slime.

To be exact, it is slime that has bitten off far more than it could chew, as one might say.

"Hmph," he says, flicking his wrist as if overcome by amused boredom. A sharp line of energy cuts through the hulking thing.

Its long, elongated torso with no legs is a slime-covered sarcophagus.

The little beast somehow wandered to the ruins of his castle and ate his old gravesite, his staked coffin with his old bones in it and all.

However, it was far too much power for a thing like it to handle. It couldn't digest it or absorb it, and so his magic has been restoring his castle in his absence, but with the slime's properties. The fake vampire has made a fake castle.

After his return, he needed a little help to make his way through. The slime had altered the layout of his castle so that its core, this chamber, could not be reached.

It is cut in half, with acidic goo splashing everywhere. His old coffin crumbles into two pieces, as one of the only really solid things in this entire structure.

The false vampire splashes, falling apart in an instant as its stabilizing core is destroyed. His old bones scatter, rolling around the floor in a mess of ooze. The castle rumbles and quivers, the walls and stones shaking like a gelatinous mass. "I shall not tell you a second time," he says, lifting his hand and a long, clawed finger that pierces through the black leather glove from the inside out.

Droplets of slime pull themselves together, a single, yellow eye forming in the oozing mass and looking up his way.

A slime that is deeply out of its league now that it has been robbed of its nigh-infinite power flattens itself down into a meek puddle and quietly begins to ooze away. The castle's walls melt, and the entire structure starts to break apart into a leaking mass, as if it were entirely made out of ice on a summer's day.

The elder vampire breathes a sigh of relief as the sour smell of the slime begins to fade, and the cold night air finally reaches him again. The fake castle, the fake undead, the fake *everything* fades, melts, and vanishes. An entire castle simply disappears.

And if anyone was watching from a village below the mountain, watching the silhouette break, crumble, and fade, then they might perhaps think that the castle and the creature inside had been destroyed.

As if such things were possible in the year of the Demon King.

He looks out over the landscape that reveals itself to him—a world that he once failed to best. But now, the era of heroes is over. Now, he has risen once more from the grave, this time in the service of a king.

~ [A Strange Village Down in the Dark Forests] ~

The villagers cheer, adorning her with beads and trinkets as she quietly walks down the road away from the castle, the forest, and the village.

"Thank you!" says the old woman, grabbing her hand and squeezing it. "I am sorry for your friends," she adds.

The quiet sorceress looks her way with a monotone expression and shakes her head. The fact that she has one yellow eye is not noticed.

Without much more than that, she simply walks off in the direction the carriage had come from earlier that day. Lowering her gaze as she wanders the dark road at night toward the thing that calls her, she looks down at her hand.

Her skin is compressed. Her hand, boneless, is squished into a flattened oddity.

After a second, it begins to reshape itself. The beads and trinkets adorning her body are absorbed and taken in. They begin to fade, sinking into her body and through her clothes that are as fake as her hair, eyes, nails, or anything else.

She clenches her fingers, a jiggle running down along her arm and to her shoulder.

The slime, pretending to be a person, quietly marches on toward the horizon, toward something even bigger that it wants to eat now that it is free from the spell it was trapped within. It doesn't know what it is yet. But it is getting closer and closer.

The body melts down into a featureless puddle of green goo with one yellow eye, and it begins hopping through the endless night.

LUCKY RABBIT'S FOOT

**~ [Akrasia] ~
Human | ♂ | Classless Child
Location: The Human Capital**

"What is this place?" mutters the boy to himself, peeking through the hedge in confusion. He pulls his head back out, looking around himself at the busy street in the middle of the human capital. He's out here on errands. His shoulders are ladened with a heavy, wax-coated sack of flour. All around him, people are running around in their usual panics. They say that the Demon King is coming, that he's almost here. A lot of people have left the city, but just as many have come, thinking that this is the safest place to be.

He doesn't know anything about all of that. He's a young man, not yet at the cusp of adulthood but past his formative years.

A large patrol of soldiers in uniform, water running down their armor, marches through the city in order to keep an established presence within the minds of the people, who are likely to fall into anarchy. There are rumors that monsters, shadows, and creatures of the like have managed to sneak into the capital city despite its formidable defenses, both physical and magical, but he doesn't know if he believes that.

Still, the stories persist, particularly in the nightmare-riddled dreams of the citizenry.

Akrasia turns his head back around, looking where the flush, green hedge was just a moment ago on the side of the street. He's walked this road a thousand times; there was never such a thing here. However, now that he looks back, there is nothing there except for a stone wall.

Confused, the boy blinks, looking around himself. But he sees nothing out of the ordinary anymore.

Water runs down the wax-coated sack of flour, stamped with the logo of a rabbit. Akrasia fusses in a panic and runs off. He needs to hurry back home before the coating breaks through from the rain and makes the flour wet, or he's going to get in trouble.

Hurrying, he runs down the road to make up for lost time.

A small, green leaf falls out of his hair as he goes.

Would he stay or would he leave the city, if given the choice?

Akrasia winces, sitting down on a wet, broken crate as he looks around the street. It is the next day. The boy stretches out his throbbing leg, covered in sharp red welts.

The flour got wet yesterday before he made it home.

If he could, he'd leave the city. But not because of the Demon King. He'd just always leave, no matter what. Some of his very first memories are scenes of his own mind telling him he has to go. His very first sentence to himself was something along the lines of *Run*. However, he didn't, and he's still here.

Where would he even go?

Besides . . .

Akrasia leans with his back against the stone wall behind himself, just outside of an alley, as he looks up toward the blackened sky.

A barrier covers the city. Magical sigils the size of houses float overhead, projected into the sky by the shield around the human capital that is held up by thousands of priests and casters from all around the nation who have come here. It still lets the rain through, but everything else is blocked from leaving or entering. The entire human capital looks as if it were trapped in an ornamental globe.

He sighs, relaxing his shoulders.

Then, a second later, he lets out a terrified yelp as his balance shifts. The solid wall he's sitting against gives way, and he pushes through it as it becomes oddly soft all of a sudden. Sharp twigs and branches scratch at him as the weight of his body drags him through the changed barrier, and a moment later, he finds himself lying on his back and looking around in confusion.

A hedge?

Lifting his gaze, his legs still sticking through to the other side where he just was, Akrasia stares at the verdantly green hedge he has fallen through.

"Huh?" he blinks, staring at it, then around himself. The boy pulls his legs in, wincing again as he gets up before brushing himself off. Confused, he looks around.

It's the place he saw yesterday. The garden.

His wide, confused eyes examine the space, which is entirely the opposite of the city he was just in. It stands in full contrast. The air is . . . fresh and dry. There is a crispness and a cleanliness to it that the grimy city couldn't ever contain within itself. The grass below him, blowing in an impossibly soft, spring wind, is so vividly green that it almost hurts to look at. It looks fake, like oil paint. However, as he bends down and plucks a blade free to examine, he finds that it is very real.

The garden looks not like a tended, well-kept park—like a garden one could see through the fences of the estates of the wealthy. Rather, it looks more organic and wild. There are flowers in bloom, but they don't look as if they have been planted; rather, they look as if they simply grew. There are trees, but they are not in clusters or in singular rows; they are in misshapen bunches here and there, as one would expect to find in the wild.

However, what has stolen his eyes and his breath the most is the sight of the unfettered, bright sapphire sky above his head.

There is no barrier blocking his sight. It's not dark, like it has been for weeks and weeks now. It's . . . the sky. It's like he remembers it being before this all began. It's not raining. The ground is as wet as one would expect a healthy meadow to be in springtime.

Akrasia turns around, looking at the hedge behind himself that is still there, and then back toward the garden. Deeply curious, he wanders, looking around, trying to understand how exactly this could exist?

He doesn't see the city at all. He doesn't see any houses, any masonry, or any sign of a street or a road other than a meek desire path that goes up a slight incline and around a little bend hidden by large stones covered in moss, wood, soil, and mushrooms.

Lost to his curiosity, Akrasia wanders through the garden, which seems to be confined in a strange space. He can't see the horizon; rather, it's like there's a fog on the distant edge of the area that, while being transparent in a way, is not transparent enough to allow him to see through. At least no more than to see a few, misty details. It's like being inside of an overturned, scratched glass bauble.

There is a chattering of glassware.

Holding the large rock, he curiously peeks around the side.

A face is looking straight at him; however, something is clearly wrong with its features. Its eyes are where its mouth should be. Its mouth is where its eyes should be. Its . . .

Oh.

It's actually just upside down.

Akrasia screams, stumbling backward and swiping with his arms instinctively as if he had seen a spider inches from his face.

"Lucky, lucky," says a girl's voice from behind the large stone as something drops down and rustles in the underbrush. A black shadow, something that stands in contrast with the rest of the garden, hides in the overgrowth before him, pieces of it sticking out in many places.

He runs away, scrambling back through the hedge. He lands on the other side, covered in scratches from the bramble. By the time he looks back from the wet stone paving he's sitting on, the greenery is all gone.

There is only a brick wall there.

He told the city guards about what happened.

They inspected the area and found nothing, and then escorted him back to his home, warning his parents for him having wasted their time.

He got the belt again, more severely today than the day before when he let the flour get wet. Sometimes, they'll use different spots—his back, his arms, his legs—to spread it out. But other times, they'll focus on one area for a week or two to make him feel it more. They don't really seem to be able to decide which strategy of punishment they prefer, so they switch it up every now and then. Currently, they're fixated on his left leg.

It is the next day.

Akrasia hobbles down the road on his errands again, looking around at the many windows of the many shops all around him. The influx of goods into the city has come to a total standstill, and as such, so has most of the commerce. There is a dungeon at the core of the city, so the adventurers and the city guard supply most of the food and necessities from hunting in there. However, it is a significant downgrade in luxury and abundance compared to a few months ago.

Still, it's enough for the city to survive on heavy rations for now, though they've had to adapt to things like eating monster meat instead of just animals. Before all of this, that was extremely taboo and seen as very uncouth.

His left leg isn't broken, but an outside observer would assume that someone had done their best to try and make it that way. The welts and marks are layered over one another, raw skin blistered and open where old marks had been lashed to create new ones. The area is red and bleeding.

The boy walks, needing to go to the market.

Whatever that place was—*that thing he saw was*—nobody believed him about it. The city had explicitly asked everyone to mention any oddity, any strange thing to the guards immediately. But he did, and this is what he got for it.

Sighing, he looks away from the shops he can't afford anything in anyway and keeps going toward the market until he sees a flash of green out of the side of his eye where one of the windows for a store should be.

Akrasia looks at the hedge that is quite literally growing in the place of a pane of glass, but nobody seems to care. Everyone is just walking by the shop as if it had always been that way, as if it weren't interesting.

Metal rattles as three soldiers in armor walk by on their patrol. He almost reaches out to grab one of them to point out the strange store, but his fingers stop in midair, and he quietly drops his palm, turning his gaze back toward the hedge.

. . . What should he do?

Is this . . . Is this something he should be worried about? Some magic of the Demon King?

The glass around him glows, reflecting the aura of the bubble over the city.

No, how could it be? They're safe in here. But what is it, then? Is it dangerous? Should he keep trying to warn someone, anyone?

His mind goes to the garden, which, compared to this place, was beautiful beyond comparison. However, what about that thing? There was something in there with him; someone, maybe.

Quietly, he stands there for a time before looking around himself and then back toward the window.

The hedge is gone.

Akrasia lies in his bed. It is night, and he closes his eyes, ready to sleep. He didn't mess up his errands today, and so, he wasn't physically punished.

However, his growling stomach and aching leg are enough to make him continue to feel it. He won't be allowed to eat for another day.

His eyes fall shut despite all of that, his weak and hurting body thankful for the feast of sleep, if nothing more than that.

His body spasms, immediately having the sensation of falling inside his bed. His eyes shoot open, his fingers grabbing the blanket as he falls through the hedge that has replaced his mattress.

He lands on soft grass with a light thud, his eyes staring up toward the ceiling of his room, only to find it missing. Instead, he's staring at a bright, vivid canopy of stars. They shine with an intensity that he has never quite seen before. They're so impossibly bright. The lights of the city usually dim them from the human eye.

In a panic, he sits upright and looks around himself at the garden.

"So lucky. Wow . . ." says a voice from the darkness.

Akrasia jumps to his feet in surprise but puts too much weight at once on his hurt leg and falls down again. Instinctively, he instead grabs his blanket, which had come with him, and pulls it over himself, like a child hiding under their covers at night from a monster—which he essentially is at this moment.

He huddles himself together, the fabric draping over him as he lies in the grass, listening to the sounds from outside the blanket. The blades crunch lightly as something walks over their rustling bodies. Soft, wet snaps give credence to the presence of some other thing here with him. There is a smell in the air that is lightly floral and pleasant, a soft perfume that reminds him of gentle teas.

Whatever it is, it walks around him. He can hear it within touching distance as it makes the small circle around him with a very odd gait. "So lucky. This is your fourth time now," says the woman's voice.

"LEAVE ME ALONE!" yells Akrasia, not really having anything better to shout than that as he clutches the blanket in fear.

He feels something press against his back on the other side of the blanket. A presence. A weight crawls over his side, pressing down on him from above as it crawls over and reaches toward the direction he's facing, grabbing the blanket.

"But you're so lucky!" she argues. A second later, pale fingers yank on the edge of the fabric, pulling it up and away from his grip to expose him to the night. Vivid, yellow eyes look at him up close from a human face that twitches its nose. The smell of perfume comes his way. Large, black-furred rabbit ears are pressed against the grass, flattened as her head rests upside down to look at him. "Such a lucky boy," says the black rabbit, flopping off the top of the blanket and then crawling inside.

Akrasia screams.

Akrasia wakes up.

He sits upright in his bed, looking around the area. His body is covered in sweat, his blanket sticking to him because of it. The boy peels it off, looking around his bedroom. It's exactly as it should be.

He's exactly as he should be.

It was just a bad dream.

His heart begins to slow down as his breathing calms.

After a minute, he rustles his hair because it feels off and pulls out a twig.

He's carrying a knife with himself.

He's not allowed to have it, but he has it tucked away in his trousers. He doesn't know what that thing is or why it's haunting him—the black rabbit. But he's going to defend himself if it tries to get him again.

Not that he's really even sure what happened.

He was there under his blanket in the garden, then it—*she*—crawled in toward him, and that's the last thing he remembers.

Is she some kind of monster? Some spirit or something? Maybe it's some kind of creature who escaped from the dungeon? That happens from time to time. Usually, it's just some odd goblin or something who slips past the guards, but it could be that something more unusual broke free from its underground confines. It's possible, right?

It can't be because of the Demon King. The shield keeps the city safe from him.

Akrasia stops in the middle of the busy street as he looks around himself. The smell hits him. The perfume.

In between the smells of mud and filth, past the smoke and the smell of alchemists at work, past the odors of leatherworkers and smiths and bakers and everything else within the city comes a single note, creeping its way through all of that toward him.

He looks around himself but sees nothing.

Quietly, Akrasia keeps walking, his hand hovering over his belt so that he's ready.

It is an hour later.

The city guards thought the way he was walking was suspicious, so they stopped him and found the knife he's not allowed to have and certainly not allowed to have in public.

They're taking him home to his family now.

Out of the corner of his eyes, the boy sees the familiar hedge growing in the wrought iron fence of a local graveyard this time. A part of him wants to run and jump into either one of them, honestly, but the strong hands holding his shoulders firmly won't allow any escape.

The door slams and locks behind him seconds after he roughly tumbles over the wooden floors in a heap, having quite literally been thrown into his room.

It takes a moment for him to recover and orient himself, throbbing pain shooting through him from the beating. His leg moves between a state of numbness and pain.

His trembling hand reaches down for the fabric of his trousers, causing him to scream and hold it down at the same time. Tenderly, he pulls the fabric around his leg up. The crusted blood that had fused the fabric together with the mangled wound covering his shin and calf cracks as he peels it away. Red ooze, a mixture of blood and thick wound fluid, runs down his leg as he cries, exposing it to the night air.

The limb is raw and essentially flayed. There isn't a single free spot left anywhere that hasn't been marked, scarred, or whipped with the belt. There are deep imprints and tears where the metal buckle had struck. Tenderly, he tries to touch his shin bone, not able to do so for more than a second as he pushes around a small fragment of bone shard.

It hurts so much. He hates this place. He hates them. He hates this stupid city and his stupid home, and he hates his stupid family.

Akrasia pulls the fabric up to around his knee, exposing the leg fully. Any adventurer with wounds like this would be taken to a fainting priest. But as a child, he is essentially just the property of his family and can be treated as such. Nobody cares, and anyone who might is too busy with their own problems, brought on by the incursion of the Demon King.

Quietly sniffling, he breathes in deeply, trying to calm himself.

This is all the fault of that stupid rabbit. If she hadn't . . .

He turns his head, looking at the hedge that, of course, has taken over the side wall of his room. Full, flush, verdant growths spread from wall to wall, the thick, full leaves billowing and moving as if there were a breeze in his tiny bedroom. The smell comes his way. The smell of that sweet perfume.

His trembling lips break his words as he cries out.

"What do you want?" asks Akrasia, not able to stand up anymore. Hands reach through the hedge from the other side. "What do you want?!" he yells.

A loud thud comes from the other side of the house as someone kicks against a wall. The signal for him to shut up.

A hole opens up in the hedge as she pries it apart, a bright, vivid light shining into his room from her side of the partition. He looks at her. She's a woman, like a human, but with the features of an animal. A black rabbit. Is she a Vildt?

Black, messy hair and yellow eyes contrast against the bright greens and blues around her as she looks at him.

"Hello, lucky boy," says the creature as she works away the hedge enough for someone to walk through. He looks at her in terror, not able to run or fight, or even scream. He knows that if he tries to get anyone here, she and the hedge won't be seen by them, and he'll get hurt again for making noise.

He grabs hold of his bed frame, trying to pull himself up off the ground. "Why do you keep calling me that?" he asks, looking at her as she works, opening up the hedge some more. The smell of the garden enters his home.

"Because," replies the black rabbit, looking his way. She clears the rest of the hedge away, letting him see her full body for the first time. She's missing a foot; it's gone at the ankle. "Humans like to take off the feet of lucky rabbits," she explains, lifting the sock-covered stump to show him. She lifts a finger, tapping her sharp nose. "So you must be a really lucky boy," finishes the creature.

". . . Huh?" he asks, looking at her in disbelief. "Are you kidding me?"

She shakes her head, thinking. "No, really. They think they can steal our luck that way." Her finger taps her chin as she stares toward the ceiling.

"You're super lucky, actually. I lost my foot the first time I got caught," she explains, waving her fingers at him a moment later. "But look at you. Number five now, right?"

"I'm not . . ." Akrasia looks at her. "This only happened because of you!" he hisses, instinctively lowering his voice.

". . . Huh?" she asks in a somewhat droopy tone, looking his way. Her nose twitches from side to side, her ears changing posture. She lifts a hand, waving him over. "Hey, come over here! Come on," she urges, entirely ignoring his accusation of guilt. The black rabbit nods her head, gesturing for him to follow her into the hedge.

"Leave me alone!" he snaps at her.

She frowns, tilting her head, and then shrugs. "Okay. It's your loss," she remarks, closing her eyes and shaking her head as she grabs a stick to balance herself and then hobbles back and away. "Just remember that after they take your foot; they'll eat you too if they can," she explains. "Good luck"—the black rabbit taps her nose as the hedge begins to close again, the leaves slowly obscuring her features as the hole closes, the vines that are spread from wall to wall beginning to retract as everything pulls back and away from this place—"lucky boy."

Thundering footsteps make themselves heard as someone moves through the house, very likely provoked by the noise of this conversation. His eyes go wide as the steps come closer and closer, the vibrations moving through the floorboards beneath himself as he hangs on to the side of the bed. He can't . . . He can't survive another punishment.

The sound grows louder and louder.

In terror, he lets go of the bed, hopping on one leg before falling down, leaving him nothing but the act of crawling forward desperately as the rumbling grows louder and louder. There's a clinking of metal on the outside of his door as a belt is undone from a waist and a hand begins to fumble with a locked door handle.

Akrasia reaches out for the hedge closing before his eyes. He's not going to make it.

A pale hand reaches out, grabbing his. It's warm; hot, even. A face down on ground level with him looks his way, smiling a strange smile.

"Such a lucky boy," says the creature again, and he is yanked into the hole just in time as the door opens behind him.

* * *

The two of them fall through the hedge, tumbling through the air together in free fall for a moment, having entered the garden from an unusual angle this time—that is, from the sky above. The black rabbit grabs hold of him in the air as they fall, Akrasia yelling in shock.

She lands on her one leg and then bounces off immediately, jumping a few steps to break off the momentum of the movement before letting him go. He falls down immediately and rolls onto his back, watching as the hole in the sky grows closed—a looming shadow standing beyond the closing dot.

Akrasia turns his head, looking at the one-footed rabbit who has, after letting him go, hopped one more time and is now just floating in the air, her long, frazzled black ears dangling and twitching at the same time.

"What are you?" he asks. "What is this place?"

The creature holds on to her walking stick, placing it on the ground but continuing to float as she holds on to it. "I'm a rabbit," she answers.

"Huh?" He looks at her, not able to get up onto his legs. "You're not!"

She blinks. "I am." The girl holds her arms out to her sides. "And this, you lucky, lucky boy, is a secret place." She floats upside down now as she climbs down the stick, which is stuck in the soil, her legs dangling up into the air as if she were fighting to not float away. The rabbit holds her finger over her lips. "You can't tell anyone about it. Ever." She shrugs. "That is, if you decide to leave."

"Look, I'm not lucky," he argues, grabbing hold of her walking stick and pulling himself up onto his feet. He lifts his gaze, looking at the face hovering over his smiling a knowing smile. A hand reaches down, touching his nose.

"But you are," she replies. "Because you," she starts, her ears flopping down against his head, "you lucky boy, are very special," says the rabbit. "Because you can leave if you want to."

"What?" asks Akrasia.

She nods, letting go of the stick before slowly drifting away into the air. "That is, if you want to."

"Leave?" replies the boy. "What, the city?" He pulls the walking stick free from the grass and hobbles after her, his mangled leg throbbing. She nods. "How? I don't have any money or anything," he explains.

The black rabbit nods. "I have a friend," she says, twirling a strand of hair as she watches him from above. "He made me into this. From a rabbit. He's very powerful." The black rabbit leans her head onto her fist, her elbow outstretched as if she were lazing on a bed. "He can help you. In fact, he wants to help you," says the entity.

"Why?"

"Because you're—"

"I'm not!" interrupts Akrasia before she can say it again. "If your friend is so powerful, then why don't you have your foot back?!" he argues, perhaps somewhat offensively.

She shrugs but doesn't seem too offended. "Because if I did, we wouldn't be similar," she says, tapping the side of her head. "I was chosen because you were chosen." The black rabbit nods. "It's very simple."

Akrasia looks around the garden, which is as serene and peaceful as ever—so perfect it may as well be paradise.

His gaze turns back to the sky, but she's gone now. The rabbit has vanished.

"What do I have to do?" he asks. "And what do I get for it?"

A pair of hands rest on his shoulders from behind, a head resting next to his, smelling of floral perfume. "You just have to do a little, tiny favor for him," she explains. "A little help that only you can provide, and then he can give you anything you want," promises the black rabbit. She grabs the tops of his ears, gently pulling on them as if she were stretching them out. "Any little thing at all."

It's quiet for a time as he thinks, trying to piece together these nonsensical circumstances. The wind blows, the grasses rustling, the smell of flowers around him.

"Unless you want to go back," she continues, letting go of him and gesturing to the edge of the garden where the hedge, the exit back to the city—to his home—sits. "There are many other lucky boys out there." She sighs. "But it's a shame." The black rabbit shakes her head. "I thought you were really the lucky-lucky one," says the entity, holding out her nub leg next to his mangled one. "Oh well. I guess we'll find someone el—"

"Okay!" says Akrasia, turning to look at her, fists clenched. "Okay!" he repeats, lifting his gaze to look at the black rabbit. "I'll do it. I'll help."

The black rabbit beams, grabbing hold of the walking stick that he's still bracing himself with, her shadowed face contrasting the reflection in her off-yellow eyes and smile that seems almost haunting.

She thumps her good foot against the ground a few times in quick succession, a vibration moving through the soil.

The grass pulls away, peeling back as if it were a layer of skin being removed. It rolls together like a closing scroll in either direction as the ground beneath them, bare, begins to shake and rumble. Dirt and rock shift to the sides, a hole opening up next to them in what looks like a burrow of sorts. A tunnel.

"Hold on," she says, taking the stick from him and using it herself to walk. Instead, she holds her other arm out his way and lets him brace himself against her body as they walk down an incline into the deep hole from which a sweltering heat comes out, blasting like from an open stove door.

"Where are we going?" he asks. "What is this?"

The black rabbit smiles, her yellow gallu eyes glowing in the subterranean darkness. "We're going to meet my friend," she explains as glowing fires line the edge of the distant darkness below the core of the world. "And he's going to be your friend, too, very, very soon." She shakes her head, sighing. "Such a lucky, lucky boy."

He can't help but look out of the corner of his eyes at the mangled corpses and skeletons that sit in a heap at the side of the tunnel.

C H A P T E R 5

A CHOICE OF MONSTERS

~ [A Cathedral in an Irrelevant City] ~

They're almost there.

The organ screams as fingers furiously pound down on its stained ivory keys, the blinded woman next to it singing her song on the precipice of the altar. Her black-gloved hand rests over her chest as the notes of her wordless aria resound around the crumbling cathedral, together with the metal cry of the instrument. Both sounds of music overpower the clashing of steel, iron, and teeth as boots press their way, cutting through swarms of monsters in a determined effort to reach the end of the cathedral gauntlet. The ceiling of the structure has long since collapsed from the heat and the rain, the wood and stone giving way.

Through the broken rafters and crumbling upper floors, the true night is visible. Thousands of stars shine above the battlefield, watching them like the curious eyes of a grand spider—only for its pupils to be plucked away, one after the other, by the great arm the rises up toward the night sky and steals them from it. The Thing That Gathers Stars plucks them down over the edge of the horizon, leaving the night a little darker than it was before.

That's how it always is; always just a little bit darker.

The adventurers pull back together in a tight formation, looking at one another as the dead bodies of hundreds of monsters lie strewn around the cathedral that has been acting as a monster-spawning location—a nest—created by the Demon King. Usually, wild monsters outside of dungeons simply breed to multiply, like any other animals. However, in high-magic zones, there are instances of monsters just spawning like they do inside of dungeons—just materializing out of thin air, essentially, as an area's natural ambient magic is condensed into monster shape.

The Demon King's corruption has left many places across the world in such a state, or is actively transforming them into one.

This cathedral they're fighting to destroy is one such place. After the Demon King's hordes razed the city, thousands of undead, demons, and monsters of intangible shapes swarmed the walls. Then the corruption took root.

The voice fills the air, singing in the presence of the organ.

All around, glowing lights begin to take form, manifesting as bodies. Fresh monsters begin to rise as the energy of the corrupted cathedral, an incredibly powerful holy place, is twisted and channeled into this dark task by the manifestation that guards it: the boss monster, the spawn guard—the once virtuous high priestess of the cathedral, who has succumbed to demonic influence.

Her arms rest together over her chest, two hands folded there as she sings. Another two arms spread out to the sides, gesturing around the area. Another two arms reach around behind her back, hammering against the organ as she plays it, the original organist lying as a charred skeleton down below it. Two more hands clutch her face, pulling on the sides of her own mouth as she practically screams her song, her lips never closing.

The relentless cacophony of battle and the discordant symphony of suffering intertwine, creating an unholy dirge that resonates throughout the desecrated cathedral. The adventurers, their faces etched with terror and determination alike, forge onward through the gauntlet of monstrous abominations. With every swing of their blades and flash of steel in the ever-darkening twilight, they cleave through grotesque flesh as if seeking to carve out a path toward salvation.

Their gazes are drawn inexorably to the source of that eerie lamentation, their breath catching in their throats as they behold her: the boss monster, spawn guard—once a virtuous high priestess, now twisted into an agent of demonic influence. Her multiple arms move with unsettling grace as she hammers against the organ's aging keys while her other hands continue to act as she sings her dark song.

As her soul-chilling aria reverberates throughout the cathedral's shattered remains, fresh monstrosities materialize from nowhere—tangible manifestations of the ambient magic that suffuse this accursed place. They rise up like an unyielding tide driven by forces beyond mortal ken, threatening to engulf all who dare to defy their dark master's will. With grim resolve etched upon their faces, the adventurers ready themselves for yet another onslaught, steeling themselves against insurmountable odds as their hearts pound within their chests like funeral drums heralding a dirge for those brave enough to stand against darkness's relentless advance. Yet, in the face of such horror, one truth remains unbroken: they cannot—*will not*—falter, for failure would mean plunging not just themselves but the entire world into eternal shadow.

A new wave of monsters spawns, hundreds of corpses glowing all around them.

They're almost there.

The music of the organ intensifies, the high priestess screaming as if begging to be put to mercy.

~ [A Tower, Somewhere on the Edge of the Nation] ~

The deaf girl yells in fright, falling forward as her foot catches on the edge of a step in the spiral staircase. She roughly falls down, barely catching herself on all fours on the incline, and then scrambles, not stopping to nurse her palms and shins. She only spares a moment to look back down behind herself at the section of the stairwell she has just traversed.

It's there. The thing. It's right behind her.

Screaming, she runs as fast as she can up the tower, trying to escape the monster that's in here with her, her legs burning like wildfire.

There's a problem, however.

Crying and gritting her teeth, she does her best to manage her breathing as she ascends.

The problem is that the tower never ends. She's walked up so many flights of stairs that she feels like she should have reached the moon by now. However, every time she passes by the little exterior window of the tower, all she ever sees is the exact same view, as if she hasn't gained any height at all.

Sweat runs down her face, mixing in with her tears and snot. Her clothes are drenched, clinging to her and chafing, the skin rubbing raw where the fabric meets her body, including her feet in her soaked boots. She's been going for what feels like hours now, but she can't stop.

If she stops, it will get her.

It's right behind her, it's so close. She can feel its breath on her neck; she can feel it looking at her from right there—the monster. It doesn't make any vibrations. It doesn't have a smell. It doesn't have any tangible presence other than her sight of it, and so she runs and runs and runs, knowing that if she ever stops, it's right there behind her.

But she can't keep this up—running is one thing, but running up the stairs is another. Her body is just about to give up. It can only do so much. Ignoring her raw soles, which are swimming in her own blood, she looks to the small window that she passes as she runs by it again.

The monster is outside, looking in at her. She yells in horror, tripping and scrambling to her feet again.

~ [A Shaft, Somewhere Down in a Collapsed Mine] ~

It's so quiet, apart from a single, repeating noise.
Drip . . .
Drip . . .
Drip . . .
That's what he feels and hears.

The portly man with a strong build leans with his back against the wall. His thickly mustached face, invisible in the darkness, is covered in soot and dirt. It's surprisingly warm here, but that's how mines operate. When people think of the underground, they think of cold, dark places. The dark part is true for sure. However, the coldness is debatable. Actually, it's very warm down here. It turns out that the world, like a body, makes heat. The deeper you go, the warmer it gets.

He smirks, holding down a laugh as his mind makes a crude joke at that thought.

It drips again.

He can't see it, but he can hear it. The dripping. More importantly, he can sense it. Every droplet lets loose a soft vibration that runs through the stones toward him.

It's only a matter of time now. He can't see shit, but the others have stopped talking, stopped making noises, stopped making vibrations. As far as he can tell, he's the last one left.

His head rests against the wall as he stares up toward nothing. Given that it is dark as all fuck down here, there is nothing to see. He's a good half hour—at least—beneath the dirt. This mine was originally started because they found a strong vein of silver; however, as they dug it out, they began finding . . . other things; things of a curious nature that he can't rightly explain—not that it was his job. He just dug, like all of them.

A droplet runs down his mustache and lands on the floor.

Drip.

It's right above him.

If he reached out, he could touch it.

Drip.

The thing that was down here with them when the mine collapsed, the monster—he can't see it. He's not sure if any of them ever did. But it's real.

Drip.

And its saliva is dripping down onto him from above.

He just sits there quietly, his legs outstretched with his hands resting on his lap, and the monster, the thing that lives in the underground, remains just as still.

There's no way out. The core shaft collapsed. He's trapped down here. Honestly, this is probably it. It already ate the others. He's not sure what triggers the monster to strike, but given that nobody else is making any noises, he's confident that it has taken all of them into its belly already.

The man idly claps his hand out, drumming against his own substantial belly in the dark with his fingers as if he were bored and waiting for something to happen. The vibration runs through his body and into the stone.

"Hope you choke on me, asshole."

Something claps back from up above, soft appendages hitting against flesh over his head.

Drip.

CHAPTER 6

A THING THAT DRIPS

~ [Tenebrous] ~

Everybody is locked, inside cages with no keys,
Behind the bars of doubt that their uncertainties do
weave,
And in these prisons—rigid—only time passes them by,
As their glassy, dead looks, consume the white of their
eyes,
For life is but short, so very fleeting and quick,
Like a flame on a candle, it burns down the wick,
A droplet against stone will harm not, first days,
But on days therefor after, it will begin to form ways,
Droplet by droplet it will break through a rock,
And dig down a hole, to which comes the rot,
It will fester and bubble and drop down through the
stone,
Until nothing comes through more,
Not blood and not bone,
The Thing That Does Drip, does not so in hunt,
It does so instead, to soften the brunt,
A stalker that bites not, nor claws, tears, nor howls,
A monster that deeply below the dark prowls,
The death comes from within,
From inside of the man,
Who stands not against,
The droplets that land on his hands,
It fears not the blade,
And it hides not from light,

For it is always within you,
And never in sight,
A Thing That Drips

Darkness . . .

There are different kinds of darkness, different depths and levels.

There is the darkness of the nighttime, when the sun has left to rest and the heads of the many lie upon their soft pillows. Within the confines of cities and towns, this is perhaps a more limited manifestation, as many able bodies are still around and about, carrying the light of their lives within themselves. There is darkness, but there is company.

Then there is the darkness of the wild, far away from places like homes and things like hearths. It is more absolute, more concealing. The wild darkness is full of endless, skulking threats—monsters and beasts with yellow fangs. It's like an endless ocean. There is darkness, but there are other things with you in it.

Beyond that, however, is the darkness of the underground.

Even in the wilds, in the forests and plains, there are things like stars and moonlight to accompany oneself, even when said person is walking alone.

However, underground, there is nothing at all. When it is black, it is absolutely so. It is beyond compare; it is an all-consuming, all-encompassing true blackness that coats a person and obscures them, swallows them and hides them from the world's many eyes.

There is darkness and there is nothing else here with you in it.

No monsters, no men, no animals. It is total, full solitude in the coldest, most loveless place that could exist.

Being underground is not where a man wants to be in the best of times. It is limiting, imprisoning. There are few ways in, few ways out. In theory, this might sound like a walled city; however, the difference is the number of ways out that there are, and the context of the shallow tunnels, tight passages, and hard, loveless walls. Even a man locked inside of a city might find joy in the sight of the sky, the wind on his skin, the pleasant architecture, and the voices all around him. Here, man is reliant on his oldest companion: fire.

Lanterns light the underground in the absence of sunlight. Lanterns lit with glowing flames, magically wicked candles, and spells contained in glassy orbs are commonly used to show the ways.

Tenebrous sits there, the portly man fiddling with his mustache in the darkness that has taken him.

He's a miner in the silver mine off to the distant northeast. Silver is a very precious metal, not just for its value as a rare material in terms of things like jewelry and plating, but also for its specific properties. Silver, as a metal, is unusually effective as a material for weapons and armor meant to be used against dark forces. Creatures like demons and undead have a particular dislike for silver, making it an extremely popular resource for those who dedicate their lives to fighting such evils.

And, of course, in times like these, it is of incredible value. When the Demon King rose and the crisis began, every silver mine across the nation was staffed to full capacity. Other mines for less important metals were closed in the name of national security, and those workers were carted off to the many silver mines of the country to flood them with labor. For weeks, they were working brutal shifts on few hours of sleep in the name of national security. Silver was flooding out of the depths of the world to be used for swords and shields that would be held against the Demon King's forces.

However, a few days ago, something went wrong.

The mine collapsed in on itself, the main passage entirely blocked off by tons of rocks, stones, and dirt—far more than any of them could move with the tools they had here. Even the casters who were left on this side had nothing to offer, their ability to use magic waning by the day as they worked and grew hungry.

That's when it showed up.

Tenebrous lifts his gaze despite the uselessness of the gesture.

Down here, down in the deep, dark pit of the world, is a thing.

He doesn't know what it looks like; he doesn't know what it wants, what it does, or even where it is. None of them ever saw it. When the lanterns were lit, it never appeared. But then, the first lantern burned out, and the first man went missing. There was nowhere for him to have gone in the closed off mine, yet he was just . . . gone. As if the world had swallowed him down into itself.

Then the next lantern died, and another man went missing.

And so on and so forth. All the while, droplets fell from the ceiling every now and then. They had presumed the caved-in section was flooding from the rain on the surface; however, it began to become clear that was not the case. The droplets aren't rainwater—they're drool.

The damned thing is gone now. It was just over his head. But he has no idea where it went or why it hasn't eaten him yet.

Time is . . . difficult.

Has it been a day? A week? There is, quite honestly, no way to tell.

Tenebrous has risen to his feet. His hand is held against the warm stone walls of the underground, his hand outstretched as he slides along the wall. Moisture condenses on its surface, making his palms damp.

When the cave-in happened, it felt like they tracked the first days. But by the time "day three" came around, it was already a mess. One man said it had been forty-eight hours only since; another said it was seventy-two, but none of them really knew for sure. Without the sun, the moon, it's impossible to know. Being underground like this is entirely separate from what life on the world's surface is.

This is it. Hell. There doesn't need to be anything more than this. All it takes is a little darkness and a little solitude, and the human mind and heart both very quickly find their way to the edge.

His hand finds a trickle running down the stone. He pauses there, cupping his palms against the wall to let the water flow into them so he can drink. After a moment more, he takes the old flask off his hip and fills it under the drip with cold runoff.

Behind him, something drips.

"Gritty?" asks Tenebrous, his hands feeling over the walls. A noise comes from the other side. "Gritty, is that you?" His fingers move along the rough surface until they find a gap between the stone. On the other side, he can hear someone moaning or wailing. It's not really easy to say. However, the voice is familiar, belonging to one of them. The man doesn't reply. "Gritty, you fuckhead!" barks Tenebrous through the hole. "Say something instead of crying like a damn homesick zombie, boy!" The noise continues.

"T—Teb?" asks a voice from the other side of the rock, replying. "Teb, is that you?"

"I'm here, boy," says the man, feeling around the wall. Where in the gods' name is he? He's been working down in the mine for so long that he knows its many passages like the veins on the backs of his own hands. But . . . this feels different. Or is it just the darkness disorienting him? "What tunnel is this?" he asks. "Is this Queen Bee?"

An incoherent muttering comes from the other side of the hole that he's not sure has ever existed before. "GRITTY!" barks the man, the young adult trapped on the other side coming to his senses with a ferritic yelp at the loud noise that echoes down the many passages, the word being swallowed by the darkness.

"S-Sorry," replies the boy. "I think . . . I think it isn't," he continues, sniffling. There is a sound of scuffling rocks and some other noise. "I'm stuck here in this fucking hole, Teb. It's over for me."

"How the hell did you get in there, boy?" replies Tenebrous, feeling over the walls for a way in. But there's nothing. There's just a small hole his hand could fit through at best to what leads to a perfectly sealed chamber inside of the solid rock. "Don't talk nonsense!" barks the old man, pulling on the rock, trying to budge it loose.

"N-No, Teb," replies Gritty. "It's here. It's in here with me."

Tenebrous stops, listening. He hears the man's breaths, the noises of his hurt body. He hears him scuffling over stones, moving against a wall. He hears his own heart and air.

And then, he hears the noise he had been hearing this entire time—droplets.

"I-It's in here with me, Teb," sobs the boy, breaking down. "I don't wanna fucking die, man."

"You're gonna be fine, boy," says Tenebrous, thinking.

"I'm not. I'm fucking *NOT*, TEB!" yells the boy. Seconds later, there's a scuffling sound. Something grabs the man, a hand shooting out of the hole in the stone, wrapping its fingers around the straps of his coveralls. "I DON'T WANT TO D—!"

"Get the fuck off me, Grits!" barks Tenebrous, his hand shooting up to grab the boy's wrist.

But his fingers never grab anything.

The man stumbles back, fumbling around in the darkness. He feels the hole, but his fingers find no arm, no hand, no boy. "Gritty?" asks Tenebrous. "Gritty, what the fuck was that?"

No response comes from the other side of the hole.

"Gritty?" His voice carries away down the many tunnels, echoing as it goes off into the distance. ". . . Boy?"

The only noise that comes from the other side is the sound of dripping.

He slowly backs away from the hole, feeling his way along the wall to try and figure out where he is.

Queen Bee is the name of tunnel section Q-B. *Q* stands for the horizontal position of the tunnel. *B* stands for the lateral position. They use these names as a way to help communication.

That's where they were when the cave-in happened. They didn't move too far away from the site after that in the hopes that the people on the other side would break through, but they never did.

He's not sure why. Maybe they're all dead too? Maybe the whole mine collapsed from top to bottom, apart from some pockets down here? Or maybe they've all been killed by something relating to the Demon King? Or maybe still, they've just been left here, abandoned because a rescue effort would be too much work.

It's impossible to say.

Queen Bee is also when things started getting . . . weird.

His foot kicks something. It loudly rattles across the stones, tumbling. It sounds like a hollow container made out of metal. Rectangular.

A lantern?!

Tenebrous curses, fussing under his breath as he slowly drops down, feeling around the area for the lantern. What he wouldn't give to be able to see a single goddamned thing. It's been days since his eyes have worked. There isn't a single source of light down here in the deep underground without the lighting system that has entirely failed.

His fingers graze something soft lying on the stones. He stops, confused, running over it again with his hand, trying to identify what it is. There's a lump on the floor. It isn't stone; it's softer, to a point, until it becomes hard inside. He presses down on what feels like a body, convincingly so. However, it doesn't move. It's not something lying on the stones, like a corpse would be. Rather, it's some sort of . . . supple protrusion growing out of the rocks. It's naturally melded to it.

But what the hell could be growing down here? Nothing lives down here. If they were higher up, he'd suspect some kind of fungus or lichen, maybe. But they're too deep, and this is far too large.

His fingers touch cold metal.

Tenebrous grabs the handle of the lantern, pulling it toward himself. "Come on, come on . . ." mutters the man, fumbling with it. His fingers run over its sharp exterior until he finds the small ratcheting knob on its base. He grabs hold of it, twisting it. A sharp clicking noise fills the air. The old miner prays silently as he fumbles with it using the only method he knows: furious swearing and threats toward intangible forces.

The little ratcheting wheel clicks as he turns it, but no sparks or light ever form. It's broken.

"FUCK!" yells the man as loud as he can, his voice carrying down countless tunnels he can't even begin to sense. He rises to his feet, screaming, his arm arching outward as the lantern flies off into the distance, crashing noisily against a wall, the metal noisily rattling as it lands somewhere.

What the hell is this supposed to be? Why is this happening to them?!

Tenebrous lets out every word he knows, indifferent to who can hear them. This deep down below the world, he's closer to hell than the heavens, anyway.

He's actually going to die down here. He's actually—

A droplet strikes his face from above.

Tenebrous stops, looking up. "What do you want?!" he screams, not even sure if *it* is there, or if he's screaming at some damp rock. He reaches around, fumbling for something else to throw. The man finds his flask, and in anger, throws it straight up toward the roof of the shaft, hoping he hits whatever is there right where it hurts most. Wet splashes against his face, running down his cheek.

"Hello?" calls a voice from the distance. "Is anyone there?" cries a woman. "I'm stuck up here!"

He turns his head immediately, the flask crashing back down against the stones and rattling as it slides.

"Hellooo?" calls her voice again from the distance, down a dark passage.

Tenebrous shuffles forward, reaching for a wall. The man holds himself against it, stumbling onward toward the voice. It sounds like its coming from this passage? It's hard to be certain, given the echoes.

"I'm here!" he calls out, making his way toward the source.

"Where are you?" he calls.

"Up here," replies the woman's voice. He doesn't recognize her, but she sounds rather distant.

In confusion, the man looks up. "Up where?" he asks. The shafts of the tunnels aren't usually tall enough to be *up* anywhere, let alone as far off as she sounds.

It's quiet for a moment.

"I don't know?" she replies in an exasperated voice.

"What does it feel like?" he continues, trying to figure out where she could be.

There's the sound of someone scuffling around for a moment. "I . . . I'm on a platform of some kind," she guesses. "It's . . . circular. Flat. I can crawl to each edge in a few seconds," she explains. "It's very small."

"How did you get up there?" asks Tenebrous.

"I don't know," she replies. "I just kind of . . . got here," says her voice, confused. "I can't climb down."

Tenebrous feels the wall, walking along it. Her description sounds right, but he can't find anything like it in his memory.

There's a stone column with a rough exterior, like the rest of the cave. It's massive in diameter. Its exterior is soaked, water trickling down on all sides. It takes him a minute to feel his way around the cylinder set in the middle of the mine.

Nothing like this was ever here before.

"Can you climb up?" she asks.

". . . What?" He thinks about it for a moment. "Even if I could, then what?" says the man. "It's a dead end up there."

Feeling around the area, he touches something soft again on the floor, like he did before outside the hole Gritty was trapped in. Confused, the man touches the odd organic growth, and then works his way forward in the dark.

Something drips onto his shoulder, cold water pressing through the fabric of his shirt. "FUCK OFF!" yells the man, swiping his hand through the air.

"What?"

"Sorry. Not you," says Tenebrous. "There's . . . Never mind."

"It's a dead end everywhere . . ." she replies quietly to his prior statement. "Maybe if you climb up, you can help me get down? Please?"

Tenebrous frowns, rubbing his greasy hair as he thinks. A fall from a place like that is dangerous. If he climbs up and slips halfway up some rocks and breaks his ankle, it's over for him. He'll never get out.

Something drips.

Shaking his head, he grabs hold of the side of the column and begins looking for a way up.

Tenebrous climbs, listening to the woman talk as he focuses on finding good footing.

"I wish I never came here," she says, her voice floating around his ears as he reaches up to find a new place to grab on to. He's already high up; high enough that a fall would be more than substantial, especially with his size and weight. "I wish I'd just stayed in the west."

He keeps climbing up the wet column, listening to her monologuing, not really having the capacity himself to participate. He has to focus.

Tenebrous climbs, reaching farther and higher. He has no idea where he could possibly be. "Do you know what section this is?" he asks, interrupting her rambling.

"And then . . . Huh? Section?" asks the woman, thinking for a moment.

"Of the mine."

"Oh . . . Uh . . ." She is silent for a moment. "I was in Jester-Jester. Before the cave-in."

He stops. "How's that possible?" asks Tenebrous. "I was in Queen Bee." Jester-Jester is a section to the back right of where he was and even deeper. How did she get here?

"Huh? Wait, but that's . . ." she replies, realizing that she somehow managed to go deeper underground instead of going toward the surface from where she started. ". . . Oh gods . . ."

His hand reaches a ledge. "Don't worry," says Tenebrous. "We'll figure it out." He slaps the stone surface of the upper platform with his hands. A puddle of stagnant water splashes beneath his fingers. "Help me up."

"How did I get here . . . ?" she mutters to herself in a tone of increasing worry. There is a noise of something shuffling, displacing a large amount of water. The entire top of the column is apparently a flooded pool of sorts. "I've been walking for so long," says the woman's voice as she splashes around. The ripples reach the tips of his fingers. "We're going to die."

"Don't say that," he replies, feeling soft hands touch his skin. The warmth of another person, the smell of another person, these come to him. But not the sight. It is as pitch black as always. "We'll get out of here."

"We won't!" she cries, her fingers tightening around his wrist as he pulls his weight up over the ledge. "We're not going to get out of here!" She starts to panic. "The last thing I'm going to feel before I die is the fucking water dropping on my GODDAMNED HEAD!" she screams at the top of her lungs as he hoists himself over.

Water splashes as he rolls over the ledge and into a very shallow pool of sorts at the top of the column. Tenebrous sighs in relief, amazed that he made it. Someone with his build isn't exactly built for climbing something like this in these conditions. A spider might have better luck.

After a moment to catch his breath, he turns his head. "Listen," starts the man, "we're going to . . ."

He stops.

". . . Hello?" asks Tenebrous.

The woman's smell is gone; her warmth is gone. He reaches out, crawling through the water to try and grab around the area. But she's just . . . gone. Vanished.

The man sits there in the pool of stagnant water, listening to the sound of a single droplet dripping down from above.

He sits there in silence for a while.

"So, are you gonna fucking eat me or not?" he asks the darkness, but it does not respond.

Tenebrous feels around the edge of the platform, reaching around for anything to touch in the hopes that he won't have to climb back down again. He's so hopelessly lost that he has no idea where to go or what to do.

His fingers find something.

Confused, the man reaches out over the edge, touching what feels like solid rock. There's an opening, a cave mouth. There's a slight gap between the cylinder and the entrance, but it's definitely there.

The man hoists himself out of the water, carefully straddling the edge as he feels the distance before scrambling over in an awkward combined jump and flop. His heart racing in his chest, lurching at the prospect of falling, he clambers forward then gets up to his feet again.

Feeling around the area, he works his way forward in the dark.

Every footprint he leaves behind as he walks acts as a container for a single drip coming from above and behind him.

* * *

He walks until he comes to a wall, feeling his way around.

It's a dead end.

Tenebrous, exhausted, falls down and slides against it with his back. His head rests against the rock. The man isn't even sure if his eyes are open or closed anymore.

He can't do it anymore.

He doesn't *want* to do it anymore. There's no point.

The man stares blankly at the darkness above his head as he thinks about his journey so far.

"I give up," he says, relenting. He tiredly bows his head, listening to the dripping droplets strike against the stones one after another in slow, tedious procession. "I don't . . ." He sighs. "I just give up."

He's going to die.

He really is going to die down here. He gave it a good try, but there's no point. After all, the main shaft collapsed. It doesn't matter if he walks all the way from Arrow-Arrow to Zircon-Zircon in the dark, feeling his way along every damned wall, if the only way in and out of the mine is sealed. That's apart from the fact that he has absolutely no idea where he's supposed to be right now anyway.

A droplet strikes against his leg.

It was a good try: the trick his brain had tried to play on him, the survival mechanism, the hallucinations it had played to get him to keep going, to get him to keep pushing forward so that it wouldn't be interested in him.

The Thing That Drips.

There is a lie at play here; a lie he told himself, really.

Gritty was never alive. He was never in that hole.

Gritty was the soft, organic thing lying on the floor. The boy drank the lantern fluid. It's highly poisonous to ingest. It must have burnt like wildfire. That's why it was empty. He took his life, to keep control of it.

Something drips on his thigh.

The woman whose name he didn't know—she was never up on the cylindrical platform. The soft thing that he felt down below the towering spire was her corpse. She must have jumped off the edge to end it before he got there, choosing to end her own life rather than letting it slip away.

Maybe it was the smell of decay that let his mind know where she was. Maybe it was the acoustics of the area that let his mind know there was a structure of this nature to begin with. It's hard to say.

He's been seeing ghosts, seeing people who chose to hold control over their destiny until the very end.

Something drips on his face.

"Come on, you fuck," says Tenebrous. "I'm ready."

Whatever it is, he's not going to fight it. He's ready to let whatever happens, happen.

The smell of sulfur and rot becomes present, moving closer and closer toward him, overpowering his senses.

A roar shoots through the world, the mine shaking, the stones rumbling. Tenebrous covers his head instinctively, yelling himself now in surprise as the ceiling above him breaks, having erupted away from an explosion that sends hurtling debris out in all directions. Somehow, they miss him, despite the impossibility of it . . .

It is as if something had been blocking the shrapnel.

"There's one here!" yells a voice from above.

He can't open his eyes. The light coming from over his head is too bright.

Rain rattles outside the structure, hammering onto the wooden roof.

Tenebrous lies in bed in the field clinic established outside of the mine. All around him are full beds. Hundreds of injured people have been recovered from the site.

He's been rescued. Despite the impossibility of it, he made it out.

"You must sleep," scolds a voice from the side. He turns his head, looking at the strict priestess who comes to give him his medicine every few hours. She's cutting some bandages with a knife.

His bloodshot eyes stare at her. Deep purple, almost black bags hang under his eyes as if he hadn't slept in a deathly long time.

"I . . . I can't . . ." replies Tenebrous, rolling his head back to look at the ceiling above his head.

She sighs. "I will get you your medicine," she says, walking off and setting her tools down.

But he knows it won't help.

His body flinches together again as the next droplet hits him right in the middle of his forehead.

Tenebrous stares up toward the ceiling, toward the drip from the roof that centers itself straight above his bed.

A droplet strikes his face, as they always do, no matter where he sits, where he lies, where he tries to rest. It always drips. It always *drip-drip-drip*-drops right onto his head, into his eyes, into his mouth.

His shaking hand reaches toward the table at the side of the bed, toward the knife the priestess left there.

And all the while, the dripping becomes faster and faster, the storm outside that never stops howling with intensity.

CHAPTER 7

PRIMAVERA

~ [The Demon King] ~

Translucent, ghostly silhouettes dance through the rain.

The rain splashes down from the dark sky above, the droplets hissing as they strike against the superheated stones all around the area. The sky is dark, as it always is, and the stars nested inside of it hide behind heavy, thick clouds, as if they were children hiding under their covers from the monsters below.

The sound of water fills the air—not just from the rain but that of runoff, that of the creek, the pond, and the puddles, all of which give off steam as the water evaporates from the power of the Demon Core, only to then be replenished immediately by the storm that never stops.

Dead water rises into the air, vanishing, only to be replaced with fresh, new abundance. The hot steam carries off and upward, drifting between the interlocked hands of a hundred ghosts who spin in a waltz through the air. The souls of the dead who he has claimed have come here, together in their abundance, to put on an unnatural display.

Standing there, having risen from the depths of his castle, is the Demon King. He has, for the first time in a while, returned to the outside world.

The giant beast stands there, not sure what it is that has called him here, what has called off his hounding of humanity—if just for a breath.

All around him crumble the ruins of old houses and walls, destroyed by the power of his presence, their owners having long since abandoned them to the elements. The demon carnival has stopped here, at his wish, on its way toward the human capital. He has left his throne room, ascended the castle past the intruders, and climbed out of the carriage into the light of the world once again now that his season of burrowing is over.

Rain strikes against him, the droplets screaming as they hit his glowing mass.

Swain holds his hand out, water pooling in his palm and bubbling. Ghosts drift past the monstrosity, the trailing whispers of their presence hissing past his ears.

"What is the meaning of this?" asks the Demon King, his claw grabbing a dancing ghost from the air, the spirit having been spinning through the rain. The fabric of its whole pulls apart and stretches as it attempts to continue its dance, despite the beast that devours all clutching it. The fear of its core is not extinguished—it is still there, still terrified—but rather, it's being buried beneath something even greater than that.

What is the meaning of this? Not only for souls to leave their imprisonment, but for them to take part in such a spectacle, in such unearned, nonsensical acts of happiness? What propels the dead and sorrowful to dance beneath the night sky?

The ghost answers not, simply drifting away as its dance continues once his claw loosens.

Swain turns his head, watching the spectacle unfold—the celebration of the dead, dancing amid the ruins, dancing among the graves, dancing within the heart of the deadlands to nothing but the song of the rain splashing against the water. He looks down, staring into it, seeing even more ghosts than those on the surface.

Floating among them is the ghost of a bird, a goose, simply drifting over the waters. It never looks their way, nor does it look his. It simply is.

Countless eyes on his body turn to look at the spirit beneath the water. The Demon King, most terrible and foul, kneels down to observe the specter. It haunts him the most of the ten thousand ghosts. It is . . .

His hand reaches out to touch the water.

However, the superheated exterior of his body disturbs the surface, causing it to bubble and boil over immediately with a violent reaction. The shimmering, rain-broken reflection of some other world is destroyed.

His hand reaches out farther in surprise, trying to reach after the illusion in vain. By the time his fingers manage to touch the water, to try and grab hold of the strange thing he had witnessed, the simple truth of his being near it at all has already destroyed his opportunity to touch the gentle thing he saw.

Swain kneels there for a time, not understanding.

A moment later, overtaken by his burning, he rages. Great, thunderous fists smash into the water, sending a quake out in all directions. The ruins crumble, what is left of them falling together into a heap of fire and cinders. The ghosts all around him scream for a final second as they are turned into something less than ash. The chasm that forms cuts the valley, ripping it deeply asunder as the howl that never stops carries across the world.

In rage, he lifts his gaze, following it toward the distant horizon, where the next location is.

The next stop of the demon carnival on its way to the human capital.

"My lord," says Cartouche, teleporting next to him. "The caravan."

Swain stops, looking back at her. "Stay where you are," he orders.

The gallu lifts her head, looking at him as he walks toward the human fortress in the distance, which is buzzing like a hive in alarm. "Do you have anything to do with this?" he asks, nodding his head toward the ghosts. Cartouche shakes her head.

The Demon King grunts, turning away and walking through the rain toward the thing in the distance, chasing after a white shadow he sees drifting from puddle to puddle, yet cannot explain.

~ [Cadet Advanced Botticelli] ~
Location: Primavera Bastille
Human | ♂ | Soldier
Level: 50

"What is it, Captain?" asks the young man, standing on the edge of the walls and staring up into the sky, his hands resting on the palisades of the walls of the fortress which lies on the outskirts of the capital's territory.

The hundreds of soldiers there, either in training or on duty, have stopped their activities as something unusual happens in the world.

The Primavera Bastille is at a standstill as hundreds of eyes stare up toward the sky. There, through the rain, through the roaring winds that never stop, drift and dance a thousand ghosts. Shadows and lights move through the night with no end, like rolling lightning that never cries out as booming thunder.

"The dead," replies the captain of the guard, water running through the thick grooves of his wrinkled, timeworn face. "They're ghosts, Cadet," he says as a pair of silhouettes drift past them, forceless hands grazing past their faces but never touching.

"Why are they here?" asks Botticelli, his voice carrying over the muttering of the many soldiers of the fortress. "They're jus—"

A shock wave crests over the horizon, a blast of inferno heat crashing against the fortress. Several people fall off the wall from the pressure. Botticelli loses his footing, too busy covering his face in shock, but a pair of hands grab him midfall and throw him back against the wall.

A moment later, the blast wave fades. Stones all around them hiss with heat as the rain strikes against the castle fortress.

"If I had to guess," starts the captain of the guard as Botticelli rises up to his feet in a daze. He turns his head, looking over the wall. "It's because of that," replies the captain, pointing out toward a distant horizon glowing as red as a violent eruption. Trails of fire rise over the distant hills and mounds like cresting serpents rising from the waves of the ocean. The air shakes and wobbles, a hiss screaming like the voice of a banshee. There, in the center of it, is a mass, a shape, a thing. It is a thing that moves toward them, closer, nearer, step by step, bringing with it the hellfire on its trail.

The ghosts continue their waltz, entirely undisturbed by any of this.

"Get in formation, Cadet," orders the captain, walking down the wall.

Cadet Advanced Botticelli looks after the captain and then back toward the distance, toward the thing that approaches. Each step it takes, even at this distance, he can feel reverberating beneath his feet as it crawls over the landscape and up the walls. Each movement it makes displaces more and more hot air, which blasts out toward him with powerful gusts—like he was an insect someone was trying to blow off their arm. The heat intensifies by the second. The crushing weight in the air all around him is a tangible force that feels like it is hammering down on him from above, making it impossible to move at all.

Burning, screaming cries from demons and monsters fill the world as the true beast moves toward them, toward him.

The Demon King.

Botticelli stumbles over himself, turning to run as fast as he can down the wall while alarm bells begin to ring all around the bastille, thousands of soldiers moving into their many positions and formations to await the arrival of the monster on the doorstep of their home.

He's finally here.

* * *

The fortress of Primavera stands tall as the stormy night sky brightens with the impending presence of the Demon King. Despite the heavy rainfall, an unusual heat fills the air, its stifling nature causing beads of sweat to form on the brows of even the most stoic soldiers. All around, panic takes hold as they hurry to prepare for a battle unlike any they have faced before. The alarm bells sound urgently, breaking through the noise of rain and thunder, their desperate cries alerting every man and woman within earshot to brace themselves for what is to come.

Soldiers run across damp cobblestones, their boots slipping and splashing through puddles that form between uneven stones. Orders are barked loudly over the deafening clangor, commanders struggling to maintain order amid a sea of chaos. Knights clad in armor that seems far too cumbersome and restrictive under such oppressive conditions hoist themselves onto their equally burdened mounts. The anqas snort nervously, sensing both their riders' trepidation and the unnatural heat lingering in the air.

"FORMATION!" cries the commander of the legion from an upper platform, repeating himself for those who hadn't gotten the signal yet.

Formations begin to take shape in an attempt at organized defense, archers hastily stringing arrows while shield bearers shuffle into position just behind them. Swordsmen sharpen their blades one last time before aligning themselves in rows designed for maximum impact against whatever towering evil emerges from this approaching darkness.

All around them is a cacophony of frenzied activity: blacksmiths hammer away at makeshift repairs, mending dents or sharpening weapons; cooks rush about with provisions for those who may not see another sunrise; healers prepare bandages and salves, all too aware that they will be needed before long—if at all, as this may very likely escalate beyond treatable wounds.

As the last faint echoes of alarm bells fade into the stormy night, a troop of riders clad in armor gleaming with rain and anticipation emerges from behind the fortress gates. Their war anqas snort and claw at the ground before breaking into a thunderous stride outward, muscles rippling beneath wet feathers. The riders grip their reins tightly and lean forward as they disappear into the black abyss outside Primavera's walls.

Botticelli watches them vanish into the darkness.

"We're fucked. We're fucked. We're so fucked." He turns to look at the man standing next to him, muttering to himself, much to the annoyance of his other neighbors.

Nearby, siege engineers scramble to man ballistae, hauling back immense bowstrings with all their strength, gritting their teeth against the strain. The colossal bolts they load are tipped with iron heads designed to puncture even the most impenetrable armor, each projectile a testament to human ingenuity borne out of necessity in such desperate times.

As for the least fortunate of all, the humble footmen to which Botticelli belongs, gather in large formations in the mud. Their faces betray myriad emotions, fear and determination mingling freely beneath helmets that seem both protective and suffocating in this sweltering heat.

A horn blows from up above.

As one whole, they collectively turn and march toward the gate.

Botticelli, the cadet footman, still unaccustomed to the weight of his armor, marches in unsteady rhythm with the rest of his troop. The air around him is dense.

His gaze flits about their surroundings; he takes in the familiar stone walls that had once felt so encompassing but now felt like a fragile barrier, like thin glass walls beneath the black ocean, about to burst at any moment. The lanterns flicker with an eerie glow, casting dancing shadows across wet cobblestones and causing beads of rainwater to sparkle like shattered glass before dissipating into steam from the unnatural heat suffusing every breath they take.

". . . fucked. So fucked. Everything is—"

"Will you shut your trap?!" snaps the man marching behind the nervous man, hitting him on the shoulder with a fist.

As Botticelli and his fellow footmen approach the massive gate leading outside Primavera's protective embrace, he glimpses beyond it a landscape barely recognizable as that which he had called home before this whole mess with the Demon King began. The fields that once flourished under the nurturing touch of sunlight now lay shrouded in an oppressive veil of shadows cast by clouds pregnant with malevolence. Untamed winds whip at tall grasses, bending them into twisted shapes as if bowing down before the unseen Demon King. The once lush landscape surrounding them is now a hellish tableau; grasses scorched black by unnatural forces crumble underfoot, while skeletal remains of trees loom overhead like gnarled fingers reaching for some semblance of salvation that has long since been snatched away.

From the distance, an ominous wave of heat surges forward like the prelude to a cataclysm, signaling the relentless approach of the Demon King. The sheer force of the shock wave is enough to cause some soldiers to stagger, their faces contorted with pain as the sweltering air threatens to choke them. Amid this palpable tension, a trumpet sounds, its clear notes slicing through the cacophony of wind and rain like a beacon beckoning them forward into battle. As one unified mass, thousands of voices rise in unison. Screams filled with equal parts fear and defiance echo across the ravaged landscape as Primavera's last line of defense charges forth.

Botticelli feels an unfamiliar surge of adrenaline course through his veins as he joins this tide of humanity advancing toward its darkest hour. Boots trample over mud-caked ground which seems almost eager to swallow them whole; weapons held aloft glint menacingly beneath the lightning-streaked sky as they race toward an enemy whose mere presence has suffocated all hope from within these desperate souls. Their hearts pounding fiercely against rib cages clenched tight with dread, Botticelli and his fellow soldiers press onward, each fully aware that their charge into battle may well be remembered as both a testament to human courage and a final act before succumbing to darkness eternal.

As the soldiers of Primavera draw closer to the Demon King, they first glimpse the full extent of the monstrous entity that looms before them—a hulking, red-skinned behemoth who exudes an aura of twisted, horrifying malevolence potent enough to make even the bravest warrior falter, causing the march to slow to a halt.

Ten thousand and then some men stand out in the mud and the rain, watching the bleak silhouette draw closer and closer, its steps pounding in their heads like the striking of their own heartbeats.

It stops not far from them, a thousand horrific eyes turning their way.

The air crackles with tension, and then, in an instant, chaos erupts.

CHAPTER 8

THE ELONGATION

Fire flies through the night, streaks of crimson tearing through the darkness, like the color visible behind a rippling curtain which had been obscuring the day beyond. Screams fill the air as men fly across the landscape, charred armor and bones rattling as they strike against tower shields, rolling and sinking into the mud. Half-dead men scream, clawing at the surface as they try to fight their way above the muck, to stop themselves from sinking, their scorched and battered bodies unable to resist the pull of the ooze. Hundreds drown in ankle-high sludge, their screams vanishing below the brack before the splashing of their comrades' boots even finishes, trampling over the wounded masses as they storm toward the Demon King.

He stands there in the middle of the onslaught, surrounded by a swarm of thousands of blades, his silhouette entirely invisible beyond the great mass of explosions, blasts, and arrows that never stops, targeting him as he stands there in their midst. His form is entirely indistinguishable amid the chaos. The mud all around them bubbles and boils, vapors of steam rising into the air like the souls of the departed. Ghosts howl, spin, and dance all around the battlefield, their voices and lights joining those of the spirits of the thousands of soldiers of the garrison.

Cadet Advanced Botticelli slips, falling down into the mud as the world explodes next to him, pieces of meat and metal flying in all directions past his blurred vision.

The spinning world is filled with a loud, high-pitched whining. In a daze, he sits there, turning his head to look toward the blackened smoke. The area where the Demon King had been is entirely charred, crusted over and covered in soot from the countless explosions that had taken place there.

Someone yanks Botticelli below his arms, pulling him up to his feet from behind. Mud sloshes around his legs, as if desperate to swallow him down.

"Get the hell up to your feet, Cadet!" yells a voice in his ears, finally breaking through past the whining that had been ringing in his head. Botticelli turns his gaze, looking at the captain.

He closes his eyes for a second, trying to stop the spinning of his vision. Everything is quiet. "Did we . . ." Botticelli stops, holding his head as the captain lets go of him. "Did we get him, sir?" he asks, looking back toward the clearing smoke that endless ghosts drift through, flying over the landscape.

Everything is quiet, apart from the sloshing of wet, thick mud.

"Sir?" asks Botticelli, looking around himself in confusion. The battlefield has fallen silent. Too much so. The men of the forward assault group have stopped screaming, stopped talking, stopped crying. The sounds of metal have come to an end. The sounds of screeching anqas have fallen still. All he can hear is the sloshing, the damp, pressing sounds of something moving, something writhing. Something . . . Something is present all around the scene that he can't quite make out. A squiggle; a line. There's something . . .

. . . There's something wrong.

Everything is too . . . still.

Botticelli's eyes scan the smoke-covered battlefield as his head slowly turns back toward his captain, standing behind him. The old man's hands are still below his shoulders, as they were when he helped him to his feet.

He screams, pulling away and trudging back, stepping through the mud in horror as he looks at the captain's eyes, which are full of life but without the spark of possession. His gaze lifts only an inch further to the long, tubular protrusion that presses in through his captain's left temple and exits out of the opposite side of his head, piercing it from side to side.

It's a long, fleshy, tubular thing, like a rope or a . . . a string. A cord, perhaps. It has a softness to it, like such an object if let slack. Yet it now holds a tightness to it, as if something were pulling on the opposite end.

"Ca . . . Captain . . ." mutters Botticelli, taking another step back as he looks around himself, his eyes following the elongation.

It presses in through the next man's skull, always through the temples, and then moves on to the next and the next, creating a daisy chain that is as long as every face his eyes manage to move toward. Some of them try to move their mouths, but no words come out. It's more of a spasming of their lips than a coherent movement which would indicate intent, really. Yet the spasming indicates a signal being sent, a command that never arrives.

All around him, a great movement begins, and a thousand not-quite-dead men and women slowly rise from the deep mud. Those who were trampled and drowned beneath it are spared not, arising just the same as their compatriots with fewer shards of loose bones in their shins, jaws, and fingers.

"Give me a word," says a voice from the distance behind him—a commanding voice, heavy in tone and so thick and coarse that feels like someone was pushing sharpened rocks against his ears.

Botticelli looks toward the smoke as the elongation rises. A cord of a thousand strung bodies—all pierced through their temples and freely dangling—silhouettes the night. Their blank faces and expressions are only barely visible in the tense firelight that now begins to drown within the rain and steam.

The smoke begins to dissipate, overpowered by the heavy rain. The ground quakes, the thick, gore-stirred mud rippling toward him, splashing up toward his waist and stomach, sloshing around inside of his boots and trousers.

Within the gray cloud hovering over the bog towers an indistinct mass, and all along behind it slides a chain of bodies strung up in the air, suspended from one point to another—both of which he cannot see.

Botticelli screams as loud as he can and runs.

Bodies slide past him on all sides, stuck to the elongation. Their limp limbs, torsos, and legs dangle freely on necks that crack from the sharp, quick movements. Blank faces rush past him, together with hundreds of suits of armor, like clothes on a drying line being stretched out from tree to tree.

The man flails, swiping his arms around himself in terror as he goes, running toward the next regiment as the sole survivor.

"RUN!" screams Botticelli as loud as he can as the second wave readies their bows, aiming hundreds of them up into the air, toward the towering colossus that approaches, the scorching heat reaching them, reaching him. "RUN!" repeats the man, his voice carrying through the air as new screams arise, overpowering his tone.

Arrows hiss, the whistle of a swarm filling his ears as countless feathers shoot through the night that never ends, a flock of needles flying toward the enemy. Half of them ignite in the air before even reaching their arc, their feathers burning and causing them to fly wildly off course.

"FORWARD!" screams a commander.

Botticelli runs in horror toward the wave as thousands of armored soldiers press forward. Support crews solidify their footing, casting magical barriers over the mud to make platforms for them to run over as they charge in the exact opposite direction of him. He covers his face as he runs, the wave of bodies running straight toward him, weapons drawn, heavy armor stampeding forward.

Metal grazes his elbows. Screams fill his ears. The thudding of boots next to his own vibrates up his spine as he sprints.

By the time he opens his eyes in confusion, he realizes he's somehow run straight through the assault group, as if they had opened a channel of bodies for him to move through, as if not a single man in heavy armor had collided with him.

He watches in silent horror as they vanish into the night.

A hand yanks him to the side.

"CADET!" screams a voice next to him. He turns to look, his wide eyes carrying the same terror as before as he looks at the commander.

"Sir!" says Botticelli. "We have to pull back!" he yells. "We have to retreat back to the Primavera!"

The commander of the legion narrows his eyes, pulling him in. "Do you know what the punishment for desertion is, Cadet?" asks the man. "I'll put you in irons!"

"S-Sir!" starts Botticelli. "We're dead! Everyone's dead!" he argues, pointing back toward the darkness from which he had come. Fires glow in it at a hauntingly far distance, off on the horizon. Yet none glow in the span between here and there. It is as if the middle of the world had been consumed whole. "The Demon King is too much!"

"Cadet!" barks the commander. Botticelli's terrified gaze looks back his way, staring at the fiery eyes of a battle-hardened, world-weary man who has seen everything there is to see. Although, one wouldn't guess this, given the blankness on his pupils. A tendril presses in through the side of his skull, worming out through the other end. His feet slowly start to lift off the ground. "Do you have a word?" asks the commander in a voice that isn't his. "I'm a little stuck, you see," explains the corpse as his neck cracks, as his hands—spasming—hold on to Botticelli and lift him into the air. The cadet advanced kicks and screams for his life, his sense and logic leaving him entirely as his animal drive to survive overtakes him.

He's not sure how, but a second later, he's reached for the commander's belt, taking off a knife. The next moment, he's hacking at the other man's wrists as they rise higher and higher into the fog, into the storm. Blood sprays everywhere as he severs the tendons, the sinew, the bone, before he's plummeting down again to the world.

Everything goes black. He can't breathe. His body feels like it's being crushed from all sides.

Botticelli sinks deeply into the mud before he realizes and fights against it, kicking his way up and scrambling toward more solid ground.

A second later, a magical barrier is created over his head, just as his face presses out from below the surface. His face pushes against the glassy wall from below, smearing mud and grime all over it.

He has no room to hack out the wet soil from inside of his lungs, and he has no room to breathe with it inside of him. Hundreds of boots, of bodies, trample over the thin, magical floor above his face as if they were running over his grave. His chest burns, his lungs burn, his body burns.

Between the boots, the legs, the running soldiers, a face presses down onto the glass just above his own, the thin barrier separating them by a hair's breadth. It floats impossibly out of place within the charging army, none of whom trample its owner, a priestess of the Holy Church.

"Just one," explains the voice that doesn't belong to her. Her face, skewered by the tendril through her temples, presses itself against the glass, her nose breaking flat from the pressure, squirting blood out between them like a mask. "Just a single word to help me figure it out."

Botticelli kicks, trying to scramble away as he half drowns, coughing out the mud from his chest but also not having enough room to breathe in fresh air as he slides between the overflowing ground and the glass floor crushing down on him from above. His fingers slide against the glass as he worms his way forward like an animal frantically trying to leave a burrow. All the while, the face of the priestess smudges over above him, her body limply sliding along behind her as countless soldiers run straight past her and over him, as if neither of them were relevant.

Wildly, he claws and digs until he reaches the end, and by the time he does, by the time he climbs out of the slime and looks up over the edge of the platform, the priestess, as well as the thousands of soldiers, are all gone.

And there, in the distance, continue the loud, heavy, thunderous steps of a creature he is spared the sight of.

Not sure how he's still alive, Botticelli pulls himself out and runs, covered from head to toe in gore and grime, sprinting back toward Primavera as the only man remaining of the thousands who had just left.

He turns back to look over his shoulder as he reaches the gate, staring at the silhouettes suspended in the air, at the rope of decorations. Thousands of corpses hang there limply, loosely, with only a single thread running through each and every one of their heads connecting them.

All of them turn his way at once, each lifting—despite the mangling and brokenness of many of their limbs—one finger toward him while he scrambles into the fortress.

"Damn, what the hell happened to you?" asks a man next to him.

"CLOSE IT!" screams Botticelli, grabbing him. "CLOSE THE DAMN GATE!" shouts the cadet, the look on his face enough to convince the guard to do so but also to throw him off himself—to win safe distance from the man who looks to be on the very edge of sanity.

Metal slams against stone as the portcullis closes, Botticelli already having risen up to his feet by then, already on his way again.

Forget this. Forget all of this. Forget being a soldier; forget being anything. He wants to get the hell out of here—that's it.

He runs toward the first place of safety his mind can think of, barreling past the open doors and into the keep of the fortress. The doors are unguarded, as all of the soldiers are in the fray now. The man sprints, turning to put as much distance as he can between him and the outside, barreling down a corridor into the chapel. His hands push the door open, looking inside. He's not even sure why he's here. It just felt like the place to go.

Red drips over the stones, the two attending priestesses in charge of the chapel sitting on a church pew together. They've both slit each other's wrists and are slumped over, dead. Their pale faces are devoid of blood.

But that doesn't stop one of them from turning his way, a hint of black near her temple.

He runs the other way, scrambling up the stairs toward the upper floors of the tower, running past the windows that look out over the walls, over into the battlefield. Arrows fly like raging swarms of fireflies from the archers on the walls, the projectiles lighting up in the night from the intense heat of the Demon Core. The ballistae hammer away, the engineers manning them feverishly running back and forth, loading in great projectiles each the size of a beast of burden.

The night is filled with movement and motion. It's filled with dancing lights and shadows, both of fire and spectral glow, as countless ghosts spin through the air.

And there, in the midst of it all, is the silhouette of the creature. There, breaking the sight line of the colorless horizon, which is made clear only by the endless fires raging on it, is the tyrant of the underworld—the beast of black jubilee.

Great knights charge toward it—men who have spent their whole lives being hardened by blood and steel—only to be tempered immediately by massive fists that barely swing; by its crushing indifference, simply stepping into and over them; by its raw presence, which is enough to drive hundreds to madness and fear.

He watches as the engineers load a projectile and fire a ballista from the western tower. The great arrow flies with incredible speed straight toward the heart of the monster. However, any hope they might have had for their launch is lost immediately as it lifts a hand, catching the massive arrow the size of a fallen log and violently skewering a half dozen men with it at once, lifting them up into the air like a grim banner, the arrow catching fire, the flames trailing up toward the impaled, screaming mess of bodies.

Botticelli runs up the stairs, pulling himself away from the window. He runs up the keep, past the many rooms and quarters, all the way toward the very top—if only because this is the farthest point he could run to from where he was.

The man presses open the door to the roof, the superheated air hitting his filth-covered face as he reenters the night.

But now, there's nowhere left to run except to the edge of the upper walls, which he grabs as he looks down toward the gate, where the fight should have moved to, where the remaining of the ten thousand knights should be locked in mortal combat.

And he stares.

And he sees nothing there at all.

Everything below the keep is gone; the walls, the gate, the men, the Demon King. There's only full, total blackness and the rain that falls from above, creating even more mud than there already was. Botticelli pants, his soaked hair stuck to his face, his ragged breath causing his chest to heave as he looks around in confusion.

Then he sees them.

The faces.

From below, ten thousand faces have turned to look up his way, all of them lining the keep, lining the walls, lining the night, strung from one to the next all through their temples by a single, black elongation that has no end and no beginning.

"Give me a hand here," asks a voice from behind.

Botticelli spins around, his back pressing against the edge. "I . . . I . . ." stammers the man, looking at the drowned, soggy faces that have come to surround him. "I . . ."

A second later, a scream fills the night as the man throws himself over the edge.

Swain looks down at the paper in his hands as he sits there in the ruins of the fortress, the sounds of jangling metal and grim laughter filling the air as the demon carnival, which has always been closed, moves in toward the bastille.

He rests on the rubble of the thing, staring up toward the skies, toward the ghosts who continue to dance as contentedly now as they had been doing before the destruction. The white shadow, the shape, the . . . feeling that he had been chasing is gone. The goose and whatever it represented has fled from his heart and senses, leaving his mind to teeter on the edge of knowing a word but never quite finding it to deliver to the tip of his tongue.

Oh well.

It is no matter.

The Demon King looks down at the poem he had written and drops it down onto the rock as he steps toward the caravan. The carriage that is his own opens its side, the stage unfolding as his gallu and servants stand there to greet him, to welcome him back to his castle.

"Did you find what you were looking for?" asks Cartouche as he walks past them all.

"No . . ." replies Swain. "But I'm not sure what I was looking for anyway," explains the Demon King as he enters back into his domain.

The demons look at one another, confused, but shrug. The carriage closes itself, and the demon carnival continues on toward the human capital, leaving behind a scene of destruction and grim horror—all painted under the glow of inexplainable pageantry as ghosts waltz overheard and over the string of ten thousand bodies that hangs in the air.

That single piece of paper he had dropped—a poem that was missing a word—lands on a burning stone and begins disintegrating into ash.

The Elongation
For I am there where you are not,
And here within this tie of heart,
Is tied a knot, so tight and wound,
So that I may not see what I have had once found,
I think you are here, so close and abreast,
Yet when I try to understand the nature of this grace,
I find not, within my mind, the smell of your hair,
Or the touch of the sight of your face,
My memory stretches on to reach far and oh so wide,
So that I might find you,
The one who there hides,
In a place that is dark.
I'll stretch and I'll reach, I'll crawl and I'll press,
Until I find where you went,
Until I find where you rest,
My days are now short,
The nights are now long,
And longer, longer, still longer I long,
For you, the one I once knew,
Whose voice in siren song did once so strongly sing,
But a simple trick, to lure me in,
But a simple thing, a word, a sound,
A sound that went wrong

The poem ends there. The final word, *wrong*, is scribbled through.

CHAPTER 9

THE MAN WHO IS

Hands run over his body, passing as the people of the city, of the region, run across the bridge. As they go, one after the other, their palms swipe over the body of the old bridge guard, the knight errant, Orson. He serves no master, no lord, having found a quiet contentment in this strange position he had stumbled into decades ago as the sole guard for a lonely bridge, road, and region that had been plagued by banditry and monsters, neglected by the capital city.

He'd wandered in by sheer happenstance, or maybe fate, and taken care of the problem. For all of those years since, he has remained here, guarding the roads, guarding the bridge, guarding the people who live not in the heart of the world but just a little off-center and to the left of it.

It makes little sense from an outside perspective; however, his life led him here, and he has been here since, finding contentment and purpose in the simplicity of his task in a way he had never manage to find in any court of king or queen.

"Orson!" yells a girl, pulling on his other arm as best as she can while her own mother yanks her away as they flee.

A hand runs over his back.

"Go!" screams the man as loud as he can, his voice carrying through the night as the carts and carriages roll, their axles screaming as they veer, almost falling off the bridge in their uncontrolled escape. The girl's hand slips free from the sternness of his voice and face. Soldiers and people of the villages run, scrambling. Thousands of people, survivors of the region, are evacuating after the unexpected and sudden destruction of the bastille to the south. Even if it was the Demon King . . . the fortress has been there for so long, has always been seen as the steel shield that guards the beating heart of the nation, that its loss is surreal in a manner they can't quite grasp, even after everything that has happened to the world.

Two women, the seamstresses from a village nearby, graze his shoulder as they run with the crowd.

"Orson, you idiot!" barks a man's voice from up close to his face, which is reasonable, given that he's yanked the man toward him by his tunic.

It's all come close to home now.

Knight Errant Orson lets go of the fabric of the other man's top. "Get out of here!" he barks at him. "Fool." He looks past the man as people stream down the bridge in a caravan, a deep ravine below.

Power . . .

The ground resonates with it, rumbling and shaking. The air is thick and heavy with a miasma that could choke a beast, crushing its lungs from the weight of it. The raindrops seem to shudder, vibrating as they fall down toward the ground in a rhythmic cascade, sounding to his ears like the endless steps of a skittering thing with more legs than there are stars in the night—so many of which gleam and shine, watching the world down below despite the danger to them being present and unhidden by the thick clouds.

"Why are you still here?!" barks Orson, looking back at the man standing in front of him. He shoves him back with both hands, but the other man grabs Orson's wrists and presses his palms against his own chest, rather than being offended.

"Just giving you something back," he says.

An old woman hurries past as best as she can, carrying an infant that can't be her own. She stops, grabbing its small hand and pressing it against Orson's shoulder.

Everyone runs, everyone leaves, but everyone touches Orson as they go, apart from the man who stands apart from him. The man nods and lets go. Orson nods back, watching as the familiar stranger runs off with the crowd.

The laying of hands.

It is a ritual of the Holy Church, the laying of hands. A person who is meant to be blessed is touched, embraced, felt, by the hands of those there. It is meant to signify the fact that a person is not alone, meant to reinforce this feeling of community, of togetherness, by the act of touch rather than by pure words. It is meant to signify to a person that they belong to a collective in a deeper, truer way than just words and promises could hold. In theory, it imbues the blessed individual with the magical residue of everyone involved.

And while this region here is not too deeply religious in the traditional sense, they are, indeed, superstitious, and old Orson has become sort of a local legend—a good luck charm, almost—that people always touched as they passed. When they went to the city and crossed the bridge while he was there, they would stop for him. When they went down the roads that had once been eyed by bandits and found him clearing the way from fallen branches, they would stop for him. When they went through the forests, once plagued by goblins and monsters while foraging and hunting, they would stop for him.

It's one of those obscure traditions that only really make sense when you grow up and develop in them. A man from the high court would hardly understand.

In fact, old Orson hardly understands it himself. But he doesn't mind, as odd as it might be to have others touch you all day, because these people are his.

He turns to look back toward the distance, toward the looming danger coming closer and closer: the Demon King, its presence undeniable beneath the deeply crimson, ruby sky in which the clouds burn and the stars shine with a screaming intensity, as if in anguish themselves.

A knight errant is a wandering knight, a knight who serves no master, no lord. A knight who is looking for quest and purpose. It would perhaps not be correct to call him such anymore, as he has long since found his place in the world here, between the forest and the trees.

Hands run over his body as he stands in the crest of the tide, breaking the flow of people who are running to his left and to his right, and soon, the tide ebbs. Fewer and fewer people come, the flow trickling, as the majority of them have already crossed.

The demon tide draws closer as well, the horizon itself seeming to move closer and closer toward him, as if a rushing surge—a tidal wave of flames—were cresting and devouring all there is to see, all of the world in its entirety.

Old Knight Errant Orson stands there, his hands resting on the hilt of a sword that shares his years, his feet planted firmly in the muddy ground that he has tended to himself for years now.

Everything around him withers. The leaves have already fallen from the long since drowned trees. The grass is withered where it remains in the few high places, and the low places are brackish and swampy. The river down below the bridge has grown to an uncontrollable size and is full of dead wood and debris. The villages visible from the top of the slope all burn. Shadows walk the landscape as reavers, their silhouettes visible only against the fire that takes everything that remains.

This place that he has tended to, this beautiful garden that he has loved, dies before his eyes as horror approaches.

However, he is well at heart and at soul because the fruits, the joys, the precious things he has let flower in this garden have already been picked, plucked, and experienced.

A remaining villager runs out of the underbrush, tripping over herself and scrambling in fear, looking over her shoulder in terror as she runs past him, not stopping but her fingers gracing his side as she hurries down and across the bridge.

Old Orson stands there now. It's become quiet.

The rain patters on. The river roars in its constant drone. The heat crackles and pops, steam hissing wherever it begins to form from the boiling pools.

And then, the horizon becomes black as things emerge out of the fir-escape—demons, ghosts, hounds, and beasts. Great monsters the size of towers walk among shrieking armies of ghouls and legions of howling spirits. Fire trails alongside them like a scavenger following in the steps of a great predator. The countless hordes of the Demon King shriek and cry as they maraud, ravaging the lands that remain, and within their midst, within the great formation of the screaming damned, rattles a procession of carriages and carts covered in almost mockingly bright colors, banners, and displays—like those of a carnival.

Things that crawl and things that bite, things that lash and things that swipe—all of them rush in their bloodlust toward the destruction of humanity, toward the heart of the nation and the world, toward the final collection of souls that the Demon Core needs to finally erupt, to finally break the barrier between the physical and the spiritual worlds once and for all.

Something he can't identify lunges out of the shadows toward him.

Old Orson twists the handle of his sword, pulling it free.

Thousands of indescribable creatures lunge, each vying to find a rare bite of fresh flesh. The carriages of the demon carnival, however, sharply careen over their sides, making emergency breaks and sharp turns, many of them tumbling over sideways and skidding through masses of the bodies of their own legions after having noticed something that the drooling, screaming masses did not.

Metal clicks, and then the world becomes something else.

A blinding flash erupts through the sky, a vivid light arcing all around them at once in the shape of a grand cross that stretches from one end of the horizon to the other, from the ground up to the sky, as if the sun had broken into four and was trying to reconnect exactly where he stood.

Power radiates through the air, radiates through countless heaps of bones and flesh, through gnawing teeth and snatching jaws. Power leaks through greedy eyes and selfish, sharp fingers.

Ten thousand demons die at once. Ten thousand ghosts and spirits, ten thousand goblins and ghouls, shrieking undead, banshees, and obscure beasts from forgotten regions and lands. Ten thousand things that crawl and snatch, as well as ten thousand things that stalk and grab—so many different things were, and then were not.

The flashing light pulsates in and out, the reclamation of fire coming back over the landscape as the scene returns to what it was, with old Orson standing there in the darkness by a bridge that none are allowed to cross anymore.

Smoke fades. The light fades. He stands there, his sword drawn, as ash rains down around him, together with so many bones.

The demon carnival has halted, several carriages having crashed over sideways in their emergency stops, the undead birds pulling them squawking and shrieking in their usual way—unbothered entirely by their crushed torsos and necks—as they keep trying to kick off the ground that their feet no longer touch.

And then come the voices from around him, whispering things, curious things. The voices of witches in the night, skulking around the crib of a sleeping infant they want to steal.

"What is it?" asks one of them, taking the shape of a soul that floats around Orson. "Powerful," she says.

Another orb floats to his side, a pale face growing out of the shape in a grotesque manner, smelling him as she floats past. "A great king?"

"No," replies another. "A hero?" she asks, curiously examining him.

The spirits bicker and observe, examining Orson as he resumes his footing, returning his sword to where it rested. "No," they agree. "They smell different."

"He smells . . . bad," remarks one of them.

"Stinks!" says another, floating away a little further.

A foggy hand reaches out toward him from the front, spinning a finger in the air. A strand of a white, wispy substance pulls out of Orson's chest. "His soul . . ." He lifts a hand, swiping the spirit away. The string pulls back into himself. "Mundane. But . . ."

"The smell . . ."

They nod to each other in agreement, floating back toward the recuperating mass of demons. The hole pressed into the army of the Demon King is filled as bodies flood in from all sides like blood filling an open wound. Thousands of twisted, rotting faces turn his way, the horde looking at the sole man who is blocking the path of His Most Wretched Highness—the Demon King.

Orson just shrugs and nods his head to the side. "You're going to have to leave," says the old man rather dryly, his voice carrying across the swarm, their cackling voices interwoven with the crackling of the great burning, as if the fire were laughing too.

But all of their voices, all of these noises, are overpowered as a growl fills the air, a crushing note that causes the swarm to cease their undulations, that causes the flames of the endless fire themselves to lower their burn, as if cowering. "And why is that?" it asks, amused.

The ground around Orson's feet shakes as the power of the presence, of the voice that can only belong to the master of the endless night, the Demon King, washes over the land. Limbs break off of dead trees. Stones fall into the ravine. The clouds fray and tear.

"Bridge is out," replies Orson dryly, nodding back behind himself to the bridge that is, very clearly, still there. "What can ya do?" he asks, shaking his head.

The quaking stops, coming to a slow halt. "You would be surprised," replies the heavy voice surrounding him from all sides as if he were fully immersed in it, like he was underwater in a glass tank and being spoken to from above.

The heat of the world intensifies. Sweat mats his hair and brow, the quivering air doing little to take it away, as it is so thickly humid from weeks of endless rain and fire that breathing itself feels like an almost useless effort.

And Orson stands there, amidst that deep laughter that envelops him.

"What do you think you are?" asks the voice as the carriages of the demon carnival right themselves up again by an unseen force. The broken undead all around them pull back together, thousands of twisted, rotted bones reconnecting loosely to recreate the shapes they once held.

It can sense something around him; a familiar feeling that lingers, that floats in the air like so much wafting smoke from the wildfires. How does this man have so much power in him? He is not a man of rare blood or ancient courage, a man of legend or renown. He is simply a man, alone, with a smell about him that is . . . distinct.

The flames of a thousand burn sites pull in, press in, shape in together—they move deeply, unnaturally, enveloping hordes of screaming monsters that are in the wrong place at the wrong time in a conflagration as the fires come together into a shape, into a whole mass that slowly, thunderously, walks toward him. Its steps shake the world.

Knight Errant Orson stares at the Demon King as it walks toward him, looking almost curious.

There is something residual about this man. Something familiar. It is something that the beast had once known and felt. It has sensed it once before, too, on a man it killed long ago who was preventing him from entering a city—a mayor. This fellow feeling here is akin to that one, that emotion the man had kept secret from him to his grave.

"In your way, I suppose," replies Orson, finally.

The Demon King, pressed free from his foul castle, looks at the man he wants something from; he wants his secret, a thing he had been denied before.

"Tell me," starts the Demon King, his voice carrying back and causing the legions of the damned to cower. "What are you?" he asks, lifting a great, massive hand. "Tell me, and you will be spared," it promises, wanting the beautiful thing it can sense, smell, taste—but never quite touch.

Orson stands there, looking back over his shoulder for a second at the bridge, which is now long since cleared, and then back at the world-eating beast standing seconds from him, towering above him.

He straightens himself up, his hand grabbing the hilt of his sword. "Like I said," replies the man, looking at the Demon King. "I'm in your way." He pulls the blade free again a second time, and everything cascades with white, a raging energy pressing against everything all around at the same time, while a red tyrant simply barrels toward him, waves of power blasting off its exterior as it walks through the tsunami of energy, trailing smoke and souls drifting out and away, its massive claw pressing forward and reaching him, clutching the blade of the sword as it strikes.

"Is that so?" asks the Demon King, looking down at the man, enraged at being denied, the world rupturing between them. "YOU WILL TELL ME!" roars Swain, the Demon King.

The swordsman pulls his blade free as the two of them collide—a burst of light blasting into the air like a beacon that shines over the world as they fight.

CHAPTER 10

THE MAN WHO WAS

Seldom has a light of such intensity been seen on the surface of the living world, the flash of metal sliding against demon claws showering a wave of sparks that fly through the air, glittering as would the boundless stars in the night sky to which the sparks seem to wish to ascend. Yet they all die out, glistening to lifelessness as their rising climb is met with wind and time, and they crash and fade down toward the empty void—only to be replaced by a new thousand more as metal and beast both scream.

Impossible.

Swain's endless eyes, enraged, glare at the single, simple man who stands now before him, his massive grip and claws holding the blade of the sword that he has now caught. The iron metal glows, softening and radiating a vivid orange shine as the furnace heat of the Demon Core superheats the metal.

And the man holds on to the smoking hilt, his leather gloves hissing as he stands before the beast that towers above him in everything from power to stature.

"I will not ask you again," snarls the Demon King, his legions of the damned cowering, hiding by the thousands, as they dare not lift their heads from their lowered positions in the presence of the destructive wrath of their true master. Swain's eyes narrow. He needs it; he must have it. Whatever this man is in possession of, whatever secret he holds, it is the thing he is hounding. He can smell that familiar scent, feel that familiar touch on his skin, that prickling that he cannot identify.

But he reeks of it.

It's drifting from him like an overly applied perfume, like the foulness of a skunk. The smell absolutely permeates everything around him, and it infuriates the Demon King to no end.

"Good," replies Knight Errant Orson. He lifts a hand to his mouth, his teeth biting the tip of the smoking leather glove and holding it as he rips it off himself before gripping the steaming, hissing metal with his bare palm. "Then we won't have to waste any more time."

The man twists the handle of the sword as he did before. The Demon King, knowing the destructive power of whatever ability this is from its prior demonstration, immediately lets go as the world flashes with the blinding whiteness of a day that might never end. Waves of cascading power stream over him as the sun rises before his eyes. The Demon King roars in rage, his massive arms lifting to shield his face from the shine as he barrels forward, swiping with his other arm out to strike whatever presence he can make contact with.

The night itself seems to move with him as he charges toward his incomprehensible opponent, a mere human with nothing special about him. The endless blackness of the storm and the night that never stops collide with the opposing shine of the counterthreat, of a sunrise that threatens to never end, as the Demon King and nothing more than a man with burnt hands fight.

Orson flies, tumbling as a massive, barreling fist makes contact, but saves his landing with grace that is unexpected of a man of his years, of a man who has been living the quiet life for so long. The old knight slides on his boots, his heel pressing back against the body of a dead, blackened tree which branches are on fire. Cinders drop down from above, silhouetting him with a red curtain as he bashes forward, the glowing blade cutting through the encroaching shadows and nightmares as Swain, pulling his fist together, carves a simple, elegant poem into his own flesh with a searing nail. He subconsciously recalls a familiar monster, one he connects with this scent, as he recalls a feeling that he once felt, and as he says everything he has to say from the pit of his soul with a simple, beautiful phrase.

A Thing That Hungers
Die.

A large, spiderish, skittering hand shoots out of the darkness. Each segment of the sharp thing is as long as a man's full-grown hand. Attached to its base is a long, leathery arm that drapes over the smoldering floor all the way back into the burning forest. It immediately shoots toward Orson, desperate and hungry to grab fresh prey after having been in slumber for so long now, ever since that night.

The knight errant sidesteps, his sword cutting into the palm of the shadowy hand, which grabs hold of the first thing it can. But instead of fighting it, he simply lets go of the sword, never stopping his stride as he runs toward the enraged, roaring Demon King, who catches his fist, a shock wave blasting out in all directions.

"Being a hero is dumb," recites Swain, narrowing his eyes as he looks at the man.

"Sounds like something an idiot would say," replies Orson, reaching into his belt and pulling out a knife that immediately plunges into one of the eyes on Swain's body. He screams—not in pain but because of his words.

A massive fist cracks into Orson's chest, sending the old man flying back, crashing as he slides through the ash and then farther still.

"Never call her that again," warns the Demon King, his hand pointing at the man with broken armor who lies on the ground. His arm still extended, he stops midpace.

. . . Who? Her?

Swain stands there, cinders and smolders falling all around him like down feathers.

His eyes look at his palm and then all around the world, at everything he can see, sense, feel, touch, as he tries to understand what he himself just meant, what he is trying to figure out, what this feeling is that torments him so.

That person, that girl who made him become what he is now, the one who started all of this . . . Everywhere he goes, her presence becomes stronger. Everywhere he looks, everywhere he turns, he can see her, smell her. It's like her spirit is with him, following him and mocking him every step of the way.

It's enraging.

And this man, this wretch . . .

Swain lifts his gaze, looking back at the knight who is rising to his feet, unhooking his smoldering, broken breastplate, and letting it fall to the ground.

This creature is hiding the thing he needs to identify her once and for all.

He, who can see all across the world, the terrible Demon King who can look into the fearful shadows behind the hearts of men to learn their darkest desires, their wretched secrets and thoughts; he, who can smell and taste the fear of mothers and the crying of fathers, the beast that partakes in every hunt—this last, miserable little secret is being kept from him by nothing more than a man once again.

He hates them.

The ground around Swain cracks as he steps forward in a rage. What are they, in their ugliness, to keep such a thing from him? The absurdity of it all.

The old knight picks up an old sword that was leaning against the bridge before turning back toward the king of all things foul and bleak and his legion of crawling, biting, screaming things that stretch from one end of the horizon to the other.

"You won't be able to hurt me with that old thing, knight," mocks the Demon King, readying himself to end this. The knight's old sword is being dragged off into the darkness by a clawed hand belonging to a thing that chews on metal as readily as it does bones and meat. "Your light tricks won't work anymore without your old sword," he says, a deep laughter filling the air as he moves toward the man on the bridge, the heated wind pressing past them both, swirling as the updraft from the raging river below and the heat of the Demon Core collide, creating firestorms across the landscape all around them.

Orson engages in his greatest mockery yet of the terrible king, under-going an unforgivable act as he leans his head back and laughs. All across the world, the burning of every flame there is intensifies at once.

"That?" asks Orson, looking back at the Demon King and then nod-ding his head to the side. "That was my new sword," he explains, readying himself in a fighting stance. The metal rises up into the air. "This here is my old one," says the knight errant with a smile that sends Swain over the edge, as it carries with it a repugnant, mocking shine of something so good and unearned that it worms its way down through the core of the demon's heart and writhes there like a parasite, touching and feeling around all the dead matter within.

The scream that follows can be heard resounding around the world as the true terror and a single man of no notable renown charge back toward one another. The man presses forward, clicking a mechanism in his sword as the world flashes with incredible power and glory in contrast to the raging storm of the Demon King, who comes to crash against it like the drowning tide of a great tsunami.

Fresh quakes rattle the deepest buried bones of the regions around them, far down below eons worth of turned over topsoil, as intents collide.

The grace, the beauty, the power of the things this man is bringing to the forefront against him—How? Why?

Metal and claws slide against one another. Swain presses the offensive—massive, lumbering fists cracking stones and striking with trails of fire behind them to reach the dodging knight. The firmament of existence rattles as the foundations present between heaven and the world are cracked from the force of the blows being exchanged, on one hand, into the true avatar of unending darkness and yearning, and on the other, into but a man, in which the effects of such force are visible after a few more exchanges of this nature.

The Demon King stands there, his eyes full of discontent as he stares at the man he holds aloft with one arm, his body burned, battered, and broken.

But despite all of his rage, Swain has learned his lesson after last time. After he was robbed of his chance to receive an answer.

"What is it?" asks the Demon King, trying to decipher the thing this person is painted in, trying to understand the nature of the fabric that wraps his heart and soul—those beautiful threads tickling and taunting him to know their name. "Tell me," orders the monster, the melted, glowing sword clattering to the blackened stones of the bridge. The water of the river below boils as it flows, deadly steam rising up all along the river.

What power could there be in the world—what secret force—that would allow a simple, common, nobody of a man like this to stand against the strength of the Demon King for even a moment? What does he know, what does he possess, that all of the kings and heroes of the world do not?

He must know.

He *has* to know.

"TELL ME!" orders the Demon King.

Knight Errant Orson looks at him through his bleeding vision and dirtied face, laughing as he reaches his end, the heat of the Demon Core cooking the blood within his beating heart.

Slowly, the man's hand reaches out toward Swain, the old man laughing all the while, seeming to find something quite funny as the ungloved palm touches Swain's forehead—his wordless answer to the question, which he answers truthfully, on his knight's honor.

Knight Errant Orson's fingers slip and fall away from Swain as his eyes roll shut and his body dies within the Demon King's grasp.

And while an answer was given, it is not one the Demon King can understand.

And even if the man is dead, his laughter resounds in Swain's head like that of a child looking at him and realizing something obvious, something stupid, that he himself hasn't noticed yet—like a bug on his clothes, a smear on his cheek. The Demon King's claws rip into his own face as he tries to find it, tries to understand what it is, that STENCH in the air that continues to linger even now all around him.

The sight of this particular beauty that he desperately seeks is simply hidden from his eyes, no matter how plentiful and sharp they might be.

And so, the Demon King turns his rage toward humanity at an even greater pace than before, as one million horrors of the dying world tear over the bridge, through the river, through the grasslands, as they storm toward the human capital and its defenses.

Swain looks back at the corpse of the man that even his dark tides seem to flow around, rather than over.

It doesn't matter.

Soon, the Demon Core will burst, one million souls having been collected, and then . . .

He returns to the carnival, the carriages and his gallu waiting for him as always.

. . . And then he will end this once and for all. He will find out what that feeling is when he finds the person, the girl who made him into this, and tears those filthy secrets from the heart of her ghost before sundering both the spirit and the physical domains and bringing on an era of endless nothingness, forever and ever more, in which only the thought of beauty itself can remain, uncorrupted by the ugliness that is existence.

CHAPTER 11

THE LAST PLACE THERE

Deep within the halls of Hell,
Wrestle, lost, the souls of men and their kin,
Against the weight of demonic wiles,
And away from whisper of fair, worldly willow winds,
The corridors below the shattered stone,
Ring abound with strikes of bone,
As clash thrice men and beast and forlorn things,
Along the path to the Demon's throne,
The world above does burn,
So does the world below sink in toward inner quenching,
As the fires of the King and the waters of the sorceress,
Both touch parts of the fortress, both burning it and
drenching,
But these halls are more than rock and screams,
They are made of the power of my soul,
And within their confines flows so much more than
waters,
So much more than fire burning ruddy coal,
The castle is my palace, yes, but it also so much more,
Than a den of beasts and a nest for witches,
And a hole into which we all pour
Blood.
The castle is alive, it feels and it knows, and it changes,
To the whims that it itself harkens,
as your feet its tongue estranges,
You step on its guts and onto its heart and expect not
much more resistance,

But you are mistaken in your mumblings and musings,
As you have misjudged the remaining distance,
One hundred floors to reach the king, yes,
This, so much, is true,
But what happens when the pattern changes?
What happens when the castle is made, once more, anew?
You've come so far,
You've come so close,
And paid such a high, high price,
But that is the nature of the game that we play,
We are two cats stuck together inside of a simple den of
mice,
I, a shade of damning red, and you of sacred blue,
Yet the third is a mix of slates and shadows, of stonework
cold and new,
And this third no longer wishes for scratches and hisses,
To happen within its own,
Flesh.
For it, unlike us two of meat and sinew, is a thing that
changes.
Let us begin our final act.

~ [The Human Capital] ~

It has been a most terrible season.

Lost to the maelstrom of the Demon King's wrath, nearly one million souls have been swallowed by the beast and used as tinder to bring about the true end of days: the potential collision between the living and the spirit world, both fraying and merging into a hellish brack of indistinguishable threads and mess. Should both the individualities of these constructs collide through the activation of the Demon Core, they would become inseparable from another forevermore.

The physical world would end, plagued with spirits and the damned, flooding with the blackwater contained within the well of souls.

The spirit world in turn would be damned to eternal inconsequentiality, as the souls of the dead would never depart from the physical world, becoming corrupted by the forces of life.

Both of these planes must exist separately from another in order to function as they ought to.

A man needs water to drink, but in the ocean, he will drown.

A man needs fire to stay warm, but in the furnace, he will crumble to ash.

Some things are separated by the natural order for good reason.

People run around the city in fear, mounting the walls and climbing to high towers so that they might look out and over toward the horizon, toward the encroaching end of days. A great horde, a swarm of tooth and claw the size of oceans, washes over the barren landscape like a great tsunami. Bodies of demons and the undead, of monsters both plagued and hounded by the fires of damnation, rush and surge toward them for as far as the eye can see. Hundreds of thousands of individual beasts have come together into the great tide of the end, and they flood the land.

All who remain of the world rush up to the highest ground they can find as the waters of the end surge toward the last island that exists—the human capital city, protected by ancient, powerful spells and barriers that protect the ancient city, encasing it in one of the strongest wards known to any civilizations of this world, a powerful mixture of coordinated spell casting and ancient sigils the likes of which no one truly understands, as they come from times long before today.

Seals and sigils float through the sky across the dome, like stars shooting through that endless night beyond it, in which a great claw can be seen every now and then, coming to pluck another star from the night sky and carry it off into the darkness beyond the horizon. On all sides, the city is encroached by darkness. On all sides comes the helltide, and on all sides comes the pressure that comes with it.

Here, now, begins the final sequence of the end of days. The Demon King has arrived at his destination, with only a few souls left to collect in order to destroy all that is and ever will be so he can achieve his terrible goals. The human capital is all that remains in his path; if it falls, so does all of the world now and forevermore. If it subsists, so will all of existence—at least until the next one-hundred-year crisis.

The gods can be very fickle.

Guardsmen and soldiers run in swarms, circling the city and manning posts and defensive positions inside the barrier as they watch from inside the shield as the night beyond it grows darker, and darker, and darker.

Terrible things move closer and closer toward them by the second, rampaging and rolling like an avalanche falling down the mountain of bodies toward them. Bones and flesh roll and fall over each other, the mass of monsters so great and beyond scope that there simply isn't enough land for all of them to stand and walk on, causing them to stand and trample over one another endlessly in their relentless hunger to breach the last bastille of the living.

And there, within the core, central mass of ambulating flesh and twisting sinew, roll a series of painted carriages covered in depictions of clowns and tomfoolery, hung with signs of acrobats and feats of bravery and skill—a circus, a carnival. They are pulled by throngs of hundreds of beasts turned into corrupted things and formed into a line—as if the carriages were so full and so heavy with its contents that a mere one or two of these creatures, anqas, could no longer suffice to pull it along, the weight of the sin nested inside too great, too dense. The carriages tear the world behind them up as they move, leaving deep grooves in the world that monsters plunge into, marching and screaming through the fires that spread around it as what seems to be the devil himself rolls toward the city.

Creatures that fly fill the night, screaming and shrieking. Gargoyles, stolen from cathedrals and corrupted, fly between the fabrics draped around banshees and ghosts. Witches shoot through the sky on brooms, weaving through the lesser demons with leathery wings and great bats of black, matted fur and leather. Weaving between them all are horrors that cannot be defined by classical conventions, creatures who go beyond the word of *monster* in the way an adult would use it and end up in the realm of a child uttering the word.

Monster.

True monsters.

Things with twenty-seven faces and ten thousand legs, creeping and chittering and skittering as they undulate this way and that. Beings with more teeth than eyes and more eyes than hearts and more hearts than fingers, the throbbing of their chest—coming from endless places and sources—causing their winding bodies to pulse in and out as if they were filled with writhing parasites.

Creatures subsisting on nothing but tongues and entrails, always hungry to pull in more flesh and mass into their whole, always hungry to collect more pieces of themselves before the others can take from the few unlucky living they swallow. Collections of screaming bodies that never die and of screaming, harvested minds that have no voice but feel only terror forevermore as they sit trapped within the prisons of their consumers. Horrors fill the world and the eyes of every man, woman, and child within the human city as the black tide crashes against the barrier.

On all sides, bodies press and collide against the wall like a flood surging around an island. Faces, mangled, press against the glassy bubble as an endless application of weight comes from behind them, crushing and smearing them against the glass, only for new faces to come and take their place, only to be crushed against the skull fragments of the former. Over and over, endlessly, endless numbers of monsters press and force themselves against the barrier's exterior, creating a film and a wall of meat and crushed flesh, squirting the juices of the undead and the pulp of the living in all directions as the endless trampling, the endless crowd crush, comes forevermore. There is no end to the mass outside the city. A layer of bodies piles up around the barrier a foot high, then two, then ten. More and more undead, demons, serpents, and cruel, hungry things come, only to be crushed by the endless greed coming from just behind them.

The people inside the city can only watch in horror as the bodies of the gluttonous monsters pile up moment by moment, as they rise to match the faces of men, and then the faces of those on the walls, and then the faces of those high up in the towers. Bodies pile around the dome in nearly infinite numbers, flesh leaking and cracking as they pile up toward the sky above the city. Beasts with twenty paws and demons with a hundred eyes tumble and stampede over their heads, over the tops of towers, and over the high palaces and castles of the city. The number of bodies is so great that even the endless mass of killed and crushed beings is inconsequential. The city is swallowed by darkness as people scream in horror.

The shield never fails; it never falters or cracks for even a second.

However, the feeble light that had remained, even in this most bleak darkness, now fully dies out as the sky and the horizon in all directions is blotted out—not by clouds or by storm, or by the acts of demon magic.

No, only through the pure mass of raw flesh and dead creatures moving and gnashing, trying to get in. The entire dome is covered, surrounded, and knocked on from every angle by eager hands trying to find a way inside. The pleading voices of the damned and of lost souls whisper for their kin on the inside of the barrier to step out, to let them in. Flailing faces and hands hammer against it.

And all that there is to perceive inside the dome is darkness and hell as a great quake fills the world, a horrific rumbling.

Those inside the barrier, those horrified, terrified people whose prayers cannot reach the gods through the thickness of flesh above their heads, assume the quake and the rumbling to stem from the attackers besieging them.

But those few who stand at the front, those few who have a second's long view now and then through a thin, pinprick hole of light that emerges by chance between the movements of boundless corpses and monsters, see that it comes from the carriage, from what is known to be the entrance to the Demon King's castle.

Like a man skewered by a demon, something horrific happens there, in the distance, to it. The wooden construct shakes and trembles so much that even the mindless undead animals pulling it along scream and squawk in terror. They pull and yank on their reins, trying to escape, as the wooden thing behind them bulges and shifts disturbingly, moving in a fashion that a material of this nature never should. The wood spreads and flexes outwardly like a bloating mass, like skin stretched because of a swelling cyst. The painted faces of clowns and performers shift and warp horrifically as the wheels of the carriage break and pop, shattering or flying off into the mass of demons, impaling many on the broken wood. The boards that make the carriage's structure begin to break free, popping out their nails one after the other before flying out or fragmenting apart like soaked, damp wood put under pressure.

The wet, goopy strings of sinew and pus that connect them to the rest of the carriage give much the impression that it is a thing of flesh and meat rather than a thing made of wood and metal. The inside throbs and moves, and the blackened, strange contents inside the carriage slowly appear as one board after the other breaks or shatters, as one oozing, slimy tendril after the other plants itself outside—leaking, more than moving. Like ink, a strange, black tarlike substance flows out of the rotting mass.

The carriage collapses fully, all of the wooden exterior breaking off before the sight line is closed once again by hammering fists and smashing faces pressing their broken teeth against the glass—inches away from the faces on the other side.

But beyond those wretched souls, something changes and transforms. The Demon King's castle warps and alters itself. The need for mobility is gone; the final destination has been reached. Those inky, flopping tendrils that had come out before reach into the entrance, into the opening of the malignancy—like a tumor feeding back in onto itself—and grab hold of whatever they can before pulling.

The rumbling continues, the quake shaking the world as the laws of reality are bent and warped as so much rotted, wet wood, and the mass pulls and pulls and pulls, and eventually, something bursts.

Rupturing, this rotting blood, this blackwater, shoots up into the air beyond the sight of any who live with pure soul, rising like a fountain. The castle pulls on itself, pulling its insides to the outside like a man yanking out his own stomach by forcing his hand down his own throat.

There, next to the city, black towers rise toward the dead sky. Black keeps and walls and inferno-covered walkways dripping with scraps of flesh and dark blood form out of not much more than the power of the Demon King's word. His magic forces the castle to take a new shape, a new form. The carriage and demon carnival have served their purpose. The fun has been had.

But every carnival must pack up and leave one day, and every clown must one day be buried into the same mass grave as those innocents he was executed with.

There, beyond the human capital, the Demon King's true castle begins to erect itself as walls form around the shielding bubble. Section after section, tower after tower, kilometer after kilometer, the fortress builds itself up—not as a construct meant to keep any intruders out and away from its precious insides, but as a prison. The Demon King's castle encloses the human city, his monsters drowning it and pressing over them endlessly.

Not one single life of a living creature is taken.

But, undeniably, taken are the last sparks of hope and faith. Taken are the words of the last prayer uttered by the last man to truthfully call himself a man of faith, as a hundred witches claw for his eyes but never quite reach. Taken is the last assurance of safety by the mothers of boys and girls holding their children close to breast as squelching creatures of organs and teeth loom over them no matter where they run.

What every person in this place now feels is what he, the Demon King, wants them to feel. It is the single emotion that began this quest; the single feeling that set all of this mess off to begin with. The sole reason he became the thing that he has become.

Despair.

CHAPTER 12

RECONFIGURATION

~ [The Demon King] ~

Endless is the turmoil within the souls of men when faced with the falling of the night.

In the good days of the lantern, of the hearth, of the wall, and of the firmament of faith, true darkness and night have been repelled and obscured to such a degree that when a man steps outside beyond his comforts and is faced with this distant lightlessness, he fears but does not quite know why. He sees the black moon on the horizon but does not know why it makes his gut churn. He sees the dead sun on the far side of the mountain but does not know why it makes his hands cold and damp.

He does not know that both of these things sitting on either side of him—the sun and the moon—are not two distinct, distant objects. Rather, they are, together, a pair of eyes belonging to the great creation, observing him as he stands atop a lonesome peak mired in a sea of creeping, encroaching, reaching things below him.

The natural, instinctual fear of the darkness is present and acknowledged in such a man, but the reasoning for this has been antiquated and lost to the generations. The men of the new world fear darkness, but they no longer fear monsters.

It is this folly that the Demon King has come to correct.

Monsters and darkness have been separated for too long, but the nature of darkness—in its true, primal state—is that of monsterhood. Monsters ought to permeate the darkness like too many fish in a pond. One cannot exist without the other, and in such a place, they thrive and multiply until they fill and overconsume the production of their ecosystem. However, in the modern world, reaped from generations of people with swords and will, darkness and monsters have become fully separate from one another.

The darkness is everywhere, even within the homes of happy children.

But there are no monsters save for those in the distant, forgotten places—the dungeons and the ancient crypts, the far wildlands and such obscure areas.

It is only through the reign of the Demon King that this correction—this natural readjustment, reassignment, toward the state of pure beauty that nature always tries to strive for—can be achieved.

In a beautiful world, man is not above monster.

In a beautiful world, man is the doe wildly running through the midnight forests with wolves at its heels.

Swain sits atop his throne, listening to the sounds that come from around the world—the cries of banshees chasing young children through forgotten glades. The screams of goblin tribes as they descend over hamlets and villages. The howls of beasts with too much meat for their frame, their flesh hanging off of them like sagging sacks full of teeth as they press their weight down on the screaming, struggling, kicking victims below who cannot escape their mass. It's not just here, around the castle.

All around the world, monsters hunt and kill and thrive in ways they have not done since the long-forgotten days of ancient eras in which the world belonged to them primarily.

"My lord," says a voice from down below his throne. "The castle is reconstructed." Swain looks down at Peribsen the engineer, and at the other gallu—his most trusted advisors and demons—who kneel in a line before him. "There is no way out of the city now."

All of them are connected by one singular desire: the search for true beauty, though each through their own method of creation. Painters, dancers, engineers, playful rabbits and cooks, and anything else—anyone who has the desire to achieve the creation of something truly beautiful within this world is someone who catches the eyes of the Demon King, who was once himself but a poet. Whether this desired creation is a physical thing or a construct of the imagination and soul, are both irrelevant.

"The underground?" asks the Demon King, his voice booming through the great hall, which is full of trapezing souls—the damned and lost who are trapped here, bound to the Demon Core.

"Sealed," remarks another voice. "The quakes broke every tunnel and shaft around the city," says Cartouche the dancer, lifting her gaze toward him. Her short, dark hair sways and bangle earrings jangle as she moves her head.

"If we cannot break the shield, they will likely have supplies rationed for months," remarks a voice, the spirit cook, Byblos. "It would be faster for us to leave a regiment stationed here and hunt the rest of the continent," she suggests. "We will find the missing souls we need."

The room cracks with thunder as energy condenses, all of them twitching together and bowing their heads again as Swain, the Demon King, speaks. His fist rests on the crumbled armrest of his grim throne.

"No," replies Swain, his voice echoing around the cataclysm contained within the dungeon—the Demon Core. "You should know me best of all, Byblos," notes his voice, prowling throughout every shadow within the chamber, bounding from one side to the other, like a predator waiting for the perfect opportunity to leap from cover at its unsuspecting prey. "There is a purpose to this place, and this place alone," says Swain, rising from his throne. The Demon King moves down the steps, the gallu shuffling to the side to make way for him as the giant with a kingly frame walks past them toward the rows and rows of statues of horrified, frozen faces and people who fill the throne room. Hundreds, *thousands* of them, all look toward him as he towers over them.

"It isn't about the missing souls," says a voice. It belongs to the demon painter, Abydos. "It is about the composition of the piece," he explains. "The ingredients, Byblos. We wouldn't want a subpar dish just for the sake of eating."

"I will not be lectured on such things by you," snaps Byblos, looking at the lanky man draped in a shadow that emits from his body like a fabric. It's draped over him and lifts its head, obscuring Abydos's face with its own. "You keep a human in our lord's castle," she hisses at him. "A priestess. A filthy, disgusting creature," remarks the demonic cook. "Her smell befouls every meal I create."

The Demon King stops, looking down at one statue in particular, which alone has eyes that move. It alone has eyes that turn and watch them in horror, with a body, face, and mouth of unmoving stone—a spirit condemned to only watch forever but never to touch, act, or do.

"I do not complain about your poor ingredients," remarks Abydos. Byblos narrows her eyes. "So do not speak of the tools of my craft. She is my muse, and I have need of her the same you have need of old snails and foot rot in your creations."

Byblos hisses at him, but Cartouche steps in and holds them apart from one another. "Mind your childishness in the presence of our king," she warns. The two of them share a glare and then return to their prostration before Swain, whose deep, bellowing chortle causes the flying spirits all around him to flee in terror.

"Such pettiness," says the Demon King, his words falling around the room. He turns his head toward them. "Will you let such childish things befoul your spirits, and in turn, your work?" he asks, turning back toward the statue with eyes and holding a single finger against its forehead. The quivering eyes, wide with terror, stare up at the massive nail that digs in toward its head like a bolt driven into a firm board. "Go," orders the Demon King. "Seek beauty."

Several shadows move past him as the demons leave the chamber, their essences carrying into the other parts of the castle as they return to their pursuit of the greatest prize there is to win in the carnival of games they have hosted here until now.

Left alone in his grand, horrific throne room, the statue before him cracks and begins to crumble into dust, the spirit trapped inside breaking free as the monument falls to ash. "Tell them I'm coming," says the Demon King, looking into the living eyes embedded into the rock one last time before they fade and dissipate. The soul embedded in the statue screams and rails against him until he lets it go, the single, fortunate dead thing shooting off toward a place where none of the other jealous spirits trapped down here can go. It alone dissipates, leaving the mortal coil and entering into the spiritual plane that lies beyond life.

He wants them—those on the other side of this curtain that separates life and death—he wants her, whoever she was, to fear.

He wants them to know, without a shadow of a doubt, that the life of all things living and the existence of all things not among the breathing are both limited and fading quickly. The fires of his reign burn through the world, and the sparks are soon to carry over to the realm of the dead.

None will escape the wrath of the Demon King.

Swain stares into the sea of thousands of souls flying all around him, horrified faces and expressions screaming cries that never end.

His most beautiful creation is taking shape and is soon to become manifest.

The twilight of existence has begun. The last stars begin to flicker, and soon, everything will be darkness.

"Can you hear me?" asks Swain into the void, picturing her face before his eyes as best he can. The face of the person who made him what he is. He doesn't know what she looks like, but he knows pieces—what she smelled like, what he felt when she was around, what he felt when he was betrayed—and from those pieces, he builds an image of a person, of a creature, that floats around before him, formed by the thousands of writhing souls that flow together like oils and paints, creating a muddy, blurry visage in the throne room before him that he reaches out for, fire leaking from his hands, arms, and body. "I'll never let you go," promises the Demon King, the painting of souls catching fire and breaking apart as the thousand essences he had forced together break off and flee in horror, burning to ash one after the other.

Every step he's taken, every new thing he's discovered in this new world, new life, has brought him closer and closer to her.

To beauty.

Fire fills the elevated throne room from the superheated Demon Core that now sits high in a tower which spires over the human kingdoms, thousands of souls burning to ash. The nigh bottomless pit that was once the Demon King's castle has turned inside out, and now shoots up toward the black heavens above, which sit empty with broken gates and burning thrones.

~ [The Capital Legion] ~
Location: The Demon King's Castle, Floor Negative One

As everything changes on the outside—the castle of the wretched Demon King taking a new form—so does everything on the inside shift and warp. From the precipice, the very beginning of the castle that so many thousands of boots have come to know, to the deepest pit inside of which the crusade's spear tip presses—it has all changed.

To think that everything in life will always stay the same is folly. To always reread the same line of a poem over and over, never moving on to the next stance, is strangeness.

[Section One - Lust]
Floor {-1}: The Gate to the Underworld
**The once great chasm, spanned by a single bridge and dotted with
poison fruit, has changed and turned. Like a tongue grabbed by
pinching fingers and pulled out from battered lips, the bridge now
spirals upward like a ramping serpent. Smears of poison fruit fall
down it continuously, together with a near endless rain of broken,
naked carcasses which claw and bite at anyone trying to ascend as
they themselves plummet into oblivion.**
**Room Effects: Gate to the Underworld—Anyone who enters here
will be tormented by the bodies of the restless dead, disturbed
from the depths of true sleep.**
**Underworld Fruit: Partaking of any food or drink within the
underworld will bind your spirit to it forever.**

"Shield!" yells a man as the casters to his side project their hands
ahead of themselves. Magic glows around their fingers as cinders float up
through the air, electricity and fire carrying upwards in the rising draft of
the new tower.

The Demon King's castle has become a fortress. The pit is now no
longer; instead, a tower must be ascended to reach the dark lord. The
superheated air all around the castle rises in an updraft, pulling toward
the pinnacle that everyone is fighting to reach, as if they were climbing up
the inside of a furnace pipe.

The casters at his side create a magical barrier, a shield that spans the
upward ascent ahead of them. It is a prismatic, glassy wall against which
splatter corpses by the hundreds. Messy, mangled faces with broken teeth
and gouged eyes slam against the magical wall, weighing down on it as
the assault team moves to ascend the spiral ramp against the pressure of
the corpse rain.

"Where's that damn portal?!" shouts the party commander as his people move with him, the barrier cracking somewhat as they push higher up
the ramp. The weight on the other side is becoming too great as more and
more corpses rain from above like pus from a dripping wound. "Arrowhead!" he orders as the two priests struggle.

More casters come up behind them and repeat the exercise. However, instead of a flat wall spanning from left to right across the ramp,

they project two new barriers behind the current one at sharp, opposite angles, creating an upward-pointed arrowhead. The first barriers shatter, and the thousands of piled corpses rain down against the new formation, dividing left and right as they plummet into the depths. Splattering against the black rock, their bones and limbs break and twist—though not enough to stop them from moving, from screaming, from climbing up again, now after the ascending party.

With legs twisted backward and arms pressed around in opposite directions, the undead crawl after the living while more and more rain down from above, reaching past the sides of the shield as they fall, trying to grab the stragglers as they plummet so they will not descend into the depths of hell alone.

They are the external incursion force of the human capital, who fought tooth and nail to make it into this horrific place; however, he can't help but feel like the way inside was almost too easy. It was like a tunnel was made in the mass of monsters outside just for them to move through. It wasn't like they cut into the beast that is the Demon King's castle; it was like they were swallowed by it.

Worse still, their intel about the inside of the castle is entirely wrong. It looks like when the transformation occurred, it wasn't just the outside of the castle that changed, but also its insides. All of the scouting, all the collecting of information, all of the effort and lives sacrificed for this, all of it was wasted.

"Maybe they're dead, sir?" remarks a man next to him as they watch the back line of the army, who hold off the zombies and ghouls below as they march backward, continuing up the ramp. The front is guarded by the arrowhead barrier, while the rear is guarded by a formation of tower shields and spears who continually throw the stumbling undead back down toward the ground below, which is hardly visible anymore. Instead, there are so many corpses, so many moving things, that it has become nothing more than a writhing mass of flesh and sinew, crawling—no, growing up the ramp after them with endless numbers of fingers and teeth. "If they didn't make it, the portal's gone," finishes the advising soldier.

"You shut your mouth, boy!" barks the commanding knight as they keep ascending.

That would be bad news for them. He knows the crusade has pushed far into the castle; farther than they can make it. He knows the numbers he's up against here, and how many of his own men he has. The math doesn't stack up in his favor. But if the crusade is still alive, if they're still here . . . If the gods are so kind, they'll have a shot—a chance—to reach the throne room before devastation takes the world. There's not much time left. The Demon King almost has enough souls to bring an end to everything.

The assault climbs, fighting their way through the gory rain, slipping and sliding as loose entrails and crushed fruit mash together on the ramp. Unfortunate men lose their footing, slipping and falling down into the chasm, into the awaiting mass of flesh below into which they sink as if falling into a black ocean. Others strike their brothers in arms as they fall, taking them with them down into the brink.

Worse still is the ramp itself. It twists upward in a spiral—never at an angle that isn't traversable, but in manners that make no sense to the mind. As they walk, men find themselves looking down, only to find themselves looking up. The pathway twists and turns, taking gravity with it, but only in the most unfortunate of ways. Men may walk on it no matter what, their bodies never signaling anything wrong—neither their hair, which does not fall, nor their sense of equilibrium, which does not either. But their eyes do tell them so as they look up toward what was once the ground below. Minutes later, they find themselves back upright again, the twisted magics of the castle making the impossible more than possible, making the incoherence of feverish nightmares reality.

"There!" shouts a voice from ahead. "Captain! I see it!" yells a scout, pointing out a segment ahead. A glowing rip in reality floats on the side of the ramp, hovering just next to it.

The portal.

The grand crusade, the people who began the first core assault against the Demon King's castle, had created a portal to allow a shortcut between the entrance and their current location, allowing anyone who entered to bypass dozens and dozens of floors, saving countless lives and days. It being here meant the crusade and its members were still alive, thank the gods.

"Move!" he yells, the assault troop pressing onward toward their beacon of salvation as the dead tide below rises higher and higher, the endless corpse rain continuing, the pile of bodies becoming massive and wide. The weight of so many endless bodies crush those below them into a broken paste of bone shards and mush that those who fall fresh land onto, before the churning commences, and they too go under.

Boot after boot, the formation climbs toward the next section, moving closer to the glowing rift that sits floating in the air like a tear in reality. Vivid, glowing light pours out in wispy tendrils. "Go! Go! Go!" ushers the captain, waving his men after him as the formation encroaches on the portal, the dead tide rising after them.

He turns his head, watching as the formation covers their ascent, before the scout who had spotted the portal gets the okay signal to proceed. The elven man takes a running start and leaps off the platform, reaching out for the shining light. His hands and arms press into it and reach through to the other side.

Literally.

He flies through the portal, rather than into it. The scout screams as he travels to another place. That is, downward. Hurtling into the abyss below, he crashes into the swallowing tide of faces that gnaw on him and eat him alive before pulling him under, undead mouths falling down over his cheeks and eyes as they consume him whole.

The portal flickers out, the light dying.

It was fake.

Men scream in confusion all around the formation as they hold fast, not sure what to do as the undead press from all around them. "Keep moving!" yells the captain, looking around the area for the real portal. *Damn demons. To think that they would stoop to such devilry as this.*

His eyes find it—the portal.

And then they find it again, just to the left.

And then one more.

Thousands of lights begin to flicker all around the grim chamber as, one after the other, "portals" begin to appear, floating around like fireflies in the night. Among them might perhaps be the real one, but it is impossible to tell. Hundreds of them, like eyes of a wretched beast, float all around—above and below.

Men fight and shout, disorganization coming over the ranks from the pressure they are under. These are all trained, experienced men—master soldiers of their craft. But no man has ever been faced with a threat, with a pressure of death, like this before. His cries to move carry throughout the chamber, rolling along the beast's tongue that is the ramping bridge up toward the next floor above. Somehow, the formation keeps moving; not so much because of his orders, he feels, but because of the sea of anguished, gnawing faces coming ever closer and closer from the ground below. An impossible number of the dead gnaw at their heels as they move, the back formation having almost all but broken now as men sprint onward, urging the forward casters to move faster.

Quickly, they ascend, moving toward the precipice, hundreds of men running not as soldiers in a formation but as children fleeing from a beast who hounds them through the depths of a dark wood. Spells fly left and right as desperate casters come up with a plan to test the portals by flinging magic and arrows through them, watching to see if they disappear or if they simply move through the illusion—but none are fruitful.

The dead hunt and the living run, pressing against the rain from above and below as they follow the twisting, winding path that defies logic until they finally reach the end—a door.

A closed, sealed door. A large, ornate construct sits firmly at the end of the ramp, lined with faces of demons of old and men of new days. A door made of solid gold and cold steel, warmed only by the hammering of fists against it. From higher above, from the emptiness above their heads, corpses continue to rain down endlessly over them. The pit below fills and fills with meat, the grinding that is the Demon King's castle never finding rest as soldiers scream and cry, battering against the only thing standing between them and the way forward—the only way "out."

But it doesn't budge.

The tide rises higher, the faces of the lost coming closer and closer by the minute, their reaching hands coming closer and closer by the second—so close that boots begin to crunch joints and kick against faces. Dead, grabbing hands begin to reach over the sides of the walkways, insurmountable amounts of corpse mush resting below in order for them to have risen this high.

The captain slowly finds himself hitting the door, too, the men behind forming barriers all around them like an encasing bubble as the tide begins to creep up the sides of the shields, rising over the platform moment by moment, until the dead threaten to leak over their constructed cage of magical walls and tower shields.

A great groaning, like that of a devastatingly hungry gut, fills the air, rumbling the world.

And the doors slowly swing open.

He falls down, men pouring inside with the same tempo that the dead fill the space beyond, rushing into the new place to fill it, desperate to be anywhere but where they were. He looks up, crawling as someone grabs him and lifts him to his feet. Men shout and fight, working together to close the great doors behind as the dead begin to press against them, their endless weight threatening to spill over into the next floor they have now entered.

As they slam shut, he lifts his eyes, looking at the messy brown hair and wide, strong face of the man holding him there and helping him upright. His armor is mauled and decayed, marked in the signs of so many battles and skirmishes, burnt and bent and dented and smeared and covered in gore and the bile of so many endless horrors, the same of which are all visible in his firm eyes that do not, however, betray their spark of humanity. The light behind them glows still, not as one of the undead but as a man's.

"Captain," greets the man in armor, letting him go. "Welcome to my home," he jokes.

Catching his breath and his senses, the captain goes through his memories of his briefing, looking at the man standing before him.

"Guardsman Zacarias," replies the captain, taking the man's hand and shaking it. "You don't know how happy I am to see you," he says, looking over his shoulder as the door slams shut and firmly locks in place, perfectly shutting out the noise of the hammering coming from the other side. He turns his head back to Zacarias, nodding once. This man had entered into the Demon King's castle as part of the tip of the spear, together with the woman they say the gods have chosen—Ruhr, the river sorceress. If he's alive, that's a great sign.

"I could say the same," replies Zacarias, nodding back and looking around at the soldiers.

"Where is everyone?" asks the captain, looking around himself.

Zacarias shakes his head. "I was separated by a trap from the others." He shrugs. "Last I knew, we were around floor . . . twenty?" He rubs his head, thinking. "Maybe twenty-one. It's been a minute," he remarks, looking off to the distance for a while.

"They're alive?" asks the captain. "The crusade?"

"Last I heard," says Zacarias. "But damn if I know how to get back to them." He looks around the area before looking back at the captain.

"Before this place changed, we lost . . . so many people," he says. "Just to get where we were. But now that it's different," starts Zacarias, glancing around the changed castle, "I have no idea how hard it will be catch up to them."

"If we even can," remarks the captain. "Is every floor like that one?" he asks, watching the large man walk in sure strides that align with his documented personality but not with the puzzled look on his face.

Zacarias glances back his way, shaking his head. "They're worse," is all he says, turning to face the darkness that lines the path onward as soldiers all around them fall and sit to the ground, unpacking their loads and pulling out bottles of water and provisions, tending to their wounds and sores. "How's the surface?" asks Zacarias.

"Bad," replies the captain, motioning for a soldier to give him a ration. "We're outside the capital city now."

"Damn . . ." mutters Zacarias, looking over at the captain as he holds out the ration for him to take. He stares at it for a time before shaking his head and walking away. "You shouldn't eat anything down here," explains the man before looking down at his hands. "They say if you eat food in the underworld, you'll be damned to stay there forever," finishes Zacarias before walking on ahead by himself.

The captain looks down at his ration for a moment, then back to the man, before packing it away but taking a very tentative sip of his water canteen.

CHAPTER 13

THE GRAND FINALE

~ [The Demon King] ~

What is the Demon King, really?

Swain wanders through the darkness of his grim castle, the battlements of the spire to his side, as his giant frame moves through the night that hovers over the world. Throughout history, great beasts and terrors have come and gone. Creatures with unspeakable names and conventions have appeared, only to be vanquished by the heroes of their times.

The stars that fill the night sky, shimmering with waning brightness as they try to hide in the concealing darkness of the canvas that floats above everything, flicker in and out. A great hand reaches over the horizon, over the distance where no man sits and no beast lives, reaching with an impossible length like a spire toward the heavens above. With long, witchy fingers, it grasps the pinprick light of a star in the sky above like a person plucking a berry from a stem, and slowly pulls it down toward the darkness below. The star glimmers and flickers as it dissipates into the forever darkness that lies beyond, where no eyes are present.

Great power has come to him, to be able to conjure up nightmares such as this, beyond the imaginings of any but the most fearful children who hide in their cots from the terrors of the moonlight hours.

Dead winds carry through the air, coming in from shores so distant and far off, yet bringing with them the worries and the screams of the many they have brushed over to reach this distant pinnacle. It wraps itself around him as he moves, the heat of the Demon Core sweltering and carrying with it, moving along the blackened walls he passes by.

What feels like only days ago, the Demon King was but a boy; a boy who felt and yearned for things that were denied to him—beauty, of the internal soul and world. This beauty he had designed and longed for had been denied to him, perhaps because of his own foolishness, or perhaps because of the world's cruelties. Nonetheless, its snatching from his fingers, which had desperately clawed after it, had left him with nothing to grasp, nothing to hold on to except for the emptiness present within his claws.

And he'd pressed down against that emptiness, gripping it firmly and tighter than anything he had ever held before, stronger than any fingers which had ever been wrapped within his own, and any pen that had ever stroked paper at his behest. He'd gripped that broken promise so harshly that the power of his rage and hatred remanifested itself, corrupting and twisting its way up and into his marrow, breaking and changing him, making him the physical avatar of not just his perception of such sensations but the avatar of all who had ever felt what he'd felt that day.

The Demon King is despair in its purest, most distilled form. The Demon King is but a creation of the world; a statue made manifest by thousands of sculptors, each holding the chisel of anguish in their hands. His mother who left him. His father who beat him. The girl who corrupted him. These are the easiest souls for him to blame for what he has become at the end of days.

Just the same as he blames them for making him what he is, he exists now as a construct for others to blame the state of the world on.

But what is there in this world, that there is to cherish?

If anything, those who wronged him showed him as much: the thing that he longs for most of all—beauty: unfettered, clean, simple, and whole—simply doesn't exist here. In this world, there are only things that lean toward beauty, that brush along its side, that carry a hint of its gentle scent. But the thing itself does not exist in this domain; it is an element not tangible in the physical world. True, radiant, ravishing beauty can only exist in a place where he cannot—the spirit world.

Soon, the Demon Core will be complete, and his mission, his quest, will be fulfilled.

Swain stares out over the night as witches and ghosts fly past the towers, filling the world with their haunts. The city below, which he looks down upon from above, is fully invisible, fully consumed by the ravages of millions of monsters who swarm over their protective bubble like ants over an overturned glass, desperately trying to enter it in order to devour the last, sticky remnants inside.

So, for now, until this process is complete, until the last soul reaches his heart, until the knife currently plunging toward his throne room arrives, the world will have to settle for its new lord of ashes. Until the final hour strikes, and the great unraveling can begin.

The Demon King stares out over the dead world.

The threads of life will be undone; the threads of the other side of physicality will be as well, and with those, something new will be created. Something whole and good and pure. Something . . . beautiful.

Swain stares down at the human city, closing his fist around it, allowing the shield that protects it from him to crumble within his imagination for now.

Reality will be soon to follow.

The countless eyes that cover his body look not toward his act of imagination but toward the distance in the opposite direction from whence the carnival had come. They watch as, over the horizon, crests a legion that is his own. His demon generals and knights, and their countless prisoners who are to be sacrificed as more fuel for the Demon Core, have arrived.

~ [Shaushka] ~
Elf | ♀ | Classless
Location: Near the Capital City
Level: 4

The sky passes them by as they move, the girl lying on her back and staring upward at the stars in the endless night. They vanish, one after the other, plucked away by a great, massive claw that reaches toward the endlessness. From all around her come miserable cries and sobs, screams of pain and horror, and the cold, lost emptiness present within the many faces around her who have already resigned themselves to the inevitability of death.

They march—thousands strong in number when counting the beasts and terrors, and thousands more when counting the men, women, and children in shackles of metal and spirit being led toward the bleak future ahead by demons of great stature. The death march moves on toward the Demon King's castle, the prisoners being led to their grave-to-be by the legions of the united demon generals and demon knights who serve under the Demon King.

But to her, all of that is neither here nor there.

Shaushka lies on her back, her mouth slightly agape as she watches the stars vanish one after the other. The cart she's on rolls onward, the undead beasts that pull it trampling over the mud and the bones of those who fall during the march with the same indiscriminate weight. A pile of corpses below her jostle and move with the bumps. But she isn't bothered by them, or by the unimaginable horrors all around her.

Shaushka just stares with an empty head and full eyes, taking in the sights that she sees on a visual level but not really on a deeper level of understanding. She exists within the horror all around her, yet entirely separate to it. Like a stone in a bowl of soup, she shares the space with the contents but is not a part of the creation. She is a thing that is extra.

The carriage jostles. Someone screams.

"Ah . . ." mutters Shaushka, sitting upright and looking around herself.

Life has had a way of carrying her from place to place, from moment to moment. She is a passenger of existence in every regard, more than an active participant.

Turning her head, she looks ahead of herself, toward the great, black spire that rises up in the distance—a tower, a castle, a horrific monument to all who crawl and creep and bite and tear toward the sky, the battlements and walls arching with towers, giving the entire construct the appearance of another hand—a match to the black claw that takes the stars from the sky. But this one looks as if it threatens to take the world once it closes its grip for good.

And all around it, the ground writhes, moving and flowing like water running over a riverbed. Monsters. Countless, endless amounts of monsters cover the distance, visible even in this darkness as a moving, slithering carpet rather than as distinct, individual shapes.

Next to her, people scream and wail as they're forced onward, pressed by spears and by gnawing teeth that snap at their heels and backs, but she doesn't really absorb any of their anguish. She just quietly, blankly, stares as she sits there, staring past the marching legions, past the towering generals, past the cruel demon knights who carry skewers of bodies between them—most of which are dead, but not all of which are—and stares into the distance, toward where she is being carried.

Head empty. Eyes full.

Shaushka lets out a curious sound, staring at the castle, wondering if this is where she's going to go next.

Life brings her to so many strange places.

~ [Cartouche] ~

Gallu | ♀ | Dancer

Location: The Demon King's Castle

Level: 100

Maggots and filth, dust and cobwebs, grime and gunk and goo and ooze and all manner of such things drip and seep and hang from the decrepit walls all around her. She sways alone in the middle of a dark, grand chamber lit only by the cowardly starlight that shines in through the opening from above. She moves, sliding in and out between the beams of light as if she were a creature of darkness hiding from the sun. And perhaps this is what she is, really.

But more, her movements—her feet sliding over the polished, smooth stone that glistens and contrasts strongly with the harshness of the walls and the echoing screams of the Demon King's castle—are made in the pursuit of her craft's goal. The dancer dances as she does, following the song present within herself and her corrupted, changed body as she tries to dance her way toward the towers of absolution: paradise, beauty.

Like a wanderer traveling a strange road, she jumps and leaps into crawls and slides, slipping in and out of states of consciousness as she loses herself for brief seconds to the flow of her work.

There are no viewers. There is no music apart from the song in her head. Cartouche dances, moving her body as if it were a language and she were trying to incant a spell written in forgotten tongues. A leap turns to a pirouette, but that's wrong. It is a misspelling; it doesn't feel right. Instead, she starts again, the swan step falling into a drop below a shaft of starlight, but that feels like a stuttering rather than a correct pronunciation of the forgotten spell.

And so it goes; the dancer dances, and the stars in the sky above have no choice but to watch, unable to hide from the power of the Demon King that steals them one after the other into the darkness eternal.

Perhaps in the eyes of an audience, in the context of a stage, a theater, a grand opera, her movements would be considered inspired and daring. But here, dancing below the cosmic stage and the endless eyes of the heavens above, even she can't help but feel like she is a nervous child, pitter-pattering around on a school stage in some uninspired, awkward prance with a disinterested audience.

She feels the desire to create and achieve, but feels, at the same time, the impossible weight of the goal she might never reach: true creation, perfect creation, beauty without flaw. As a human, it had been her goal to dance just the same as now, with the desires to make money, to earn a living with her craft and trade, to escape the carnival lifestyle and open a school of her own. But that was a deceit to herself—that plan, which by human standards sounds very reasonable.

After all, making money with something like dancing isn't exactly easy, so any sensible person who understands the desire of an artist would support such an endeavor, considering it brave. Dancing to open your own dance school? Wow. What a creative pursuit.

But the truth is, that even this is—in the eyes of a rabid creative—a sellout. It's an abandoning of the true dream, of the desire to touch the raw state of existence that no living entity has ever been able to reach. It was a sensible plan, a logical plan, a cowardly plan. It was her way of giving up, of becoming a "normal" person whom others would call creative because of her work, but whom she herself would know had given up the hunt halfway through.

The thin fabric of the shawl she has around her neck shoots out, together with her arm, as she dances, implementing everything she has into her dance, everything beyond the baseness of her flesh and sinew: her clothes, her hair, her bangles and jewelry that glisten as her sweat collects along the metal.

She dances and dances for hours on end. She marches and spins and springs and bounds.

But despite the kilometers she leaves behind herself, she never gets anywhere, ending up at the same spot where she began, falling to her knees and panting for breath. Sweat rolls down her body as she gasps for air; even the power of her demonic body is spent by her exertions, fighting against the metaphorical ghost in here with her as her waltzing partner.

Cartouche stares down at the floor between her knees. Even now, even in this state of power, she can't climb that ladder toward the heaven she desires. Maybe she's taken a step more than before, climbed a single rung higher than when she was a human, but it feels like there still remain ten thousand more before she manages to touch the first wisps of cloud and sky.

The heavens drift, the light shifting as the dancer no longer dances but instead lifts her gaze toward the beam of starglow that catches her finally. As if imprisoned inside of it, Cartouche sits there and stares up at the perennial glow that has dared illuminate her inadequacy to herself.

She tsks, turning her head away as if she were being watched by someone with a judgmental gaze. The click of her tongue carries around the room, echoing from pillar to pillar, carrying around her again and again like the sound of unimpressed, half-hearted clapping.

Slowly rising to her feet with a drooping upper body, Cartouche forces herself to straighten up once more, rolling her shoulders and shaking out her arms.

How does he do it?

How does the Demon King not wane in his desire to achieve the same thing as any of them? How does he not sit on his throne and falter, wondering if his tool is the right one for the job—wondering if he himself is the right one for the job?

The starlight shaft fades as clouds obscure her observer, returning her to darkness once more. Cartouche strikes her hands together, the single, loud, sharp clap echoing around the chamber again, but now with fervor. She claps again and again, closing her eyes and listening to the reverberations coming from all around her as the noise bounces back around the castle chamber over and over again. It sounds like there are hundreds of people, thousands, watching her and cheering. It is a delusion, of course, but the sensation remains as she stands there and listens to the noise and what it means.

It means something.

The clapping—it's more than just an echo. It's a representation of something. Of something she can't just . . . quite manage to place anymore. It's right there, on the tip of her tongue, but it never really reaches her mind as she stops and listens to the clapping fade. The hairs on her neck begin to fall again as the silence retakes the chamber, and she thinks.

Beauty.

She is looking for beauty, but she can't find it. She has tools and skill, but still, she can't find it. It's here somewhere, close by, but still, she can't find it. It's—

"Want me to whistle next time?" asks a voice from across the room, breaking her feverish introspection, which was on the raw edge of seeing something it had been missing this entire time—something obvious.

Cartouche turns her head, looking. She had been so lost in her work that she hadn't been paying attention. The dancer holds out a hand in a flourish, stretching her palm out as she stares at steel and coldness taking the shape of men and women.

"You've become a great problem for my lord," says Cartouche. "Ruhr, the river sorceress."

From the steps moves forward her conversation partner, a nearly skeletal woman at this point with features below her eyes as stiff as her cold gaze. "I'm happy to hear that," says the woman with azure hair—shorter now than it once was—as she steps to the front of the crusade by a good margin, between them and Cartouche. "Tell him that he needs to work on his housekeeping," remarks the half-elven woman, who carries as many ghosts now in her eyes as the castle itself has within its walls. "This place is a mess and, quite frankly, below my standards."

The crusade had really pushed far into the castle now. But it was of no matter. Even at this point, they would never make it in time before the Demon King collected his souls. Between the sacrifice to come imminently, brought by the demon generals, and the human city about to be crushed, they were within abundance.

Cartouche's laughter carries around the chamber. "Perhaps this was once true," remarks the demon, walking closer toward the enemy. The dancer and the elf stare at one another, looking into each other's eyes, both with a coldness not born of any knowing of the other but rather of being in different factions. Cartouche lifts a hand, touching Ruhr's chin as crusaders file in by the hundreds, coming from the back tunnels and spreading around the room. Cartouche listens to the sounds of their metal boots hammering against the floor from every direction, like metal hands clapping. "But I can see you're closer to me now than to what you were when you came here," explains the demon, pulling back and holding out her hand to the woman. "Would you care to dance with me? There isn't much time left, Ruhr."

Spell glow gathers from all around the arena as soldiers ready themselves for a fight. Crossbowmen arm their weapons, and knights with great shields prepare themselves for a push. Everyone keeps their distance, however, letting Ruhr and the demon hold the centerpiece of the floor together.

"I don't dance anymore," replies Ruhr dryly, looking at her.

The dancer tilts her head. "I'll show you how," promises Cartouche, the bangles on her body jostling, as does her ghostly white hair. She smiles a smile that one might not hold as warm, but for a demon, it is, and it follows Ruhr's hand as it slowly lifts up toward her, the bony fingers of the sorceress reaching up and out until they touch the dancer's. "I'd like a dancing partner," admits Cartouche. "I think it would help me, too."

"Here," says Ruhr, pulling her hand away. "For the show," finishes the half elf in a loveless voice.

Cartouche looks down at her open palm, at the single, dirty coin left there. A single Obol, the kind that was thrown at her at the carnival by the hands of the people she hated most. "Not a bad act. You're just missing some music," notes Ruhr. "If I was still an adventurer, I'd buy you back to my room." She shrugs.

The demon stands there in silence, staring down at the coin that rattles around in her shaking palm, the quiver carrying down her arm like a poison infecting her blood until her shoulders rattle and her core shakes from the inside out as memories replay over and over of people pelting her with money on a carnival stage, of people whistling and hollering and touching her as she tried to chase after that which she wanted most in life. Of people who took the beautiful, graceful act of a body moving in perfect flow and harmony and debased it, made it filthy and vile and rotten. Of carnal animals who couldn't see past their drunken hazes as they leered at her body, which was offering sacrament to the heavens.

The ground shakes. The dancer shakes. The castle and the firmaments of the world rattle and jostle, the coin melting in her grip, as she can't force herself to let it go or close her hand around it and cast it to the side. The crassness, the ugliness and the depravity of those cold, loveless eyes that she stares into while feeling that glow thrashing within her core come to rise is unbearable—the demon sensation takes hold of her.

It's not possible.

It's not possible to find, to reach, to touch and hold and grasp and know—the thing that she wants more than anything. Can it really be more than the naive delusion of a child's fevered mind? There's only ugliness. It doesn't matter where, how. There's nothing in this world but that.

The castle quakes, the stars above hiding behind a wall of clouds as everything turns dark. Fires die out from the torches, and walls crumble and crack as Cartouche screams. Pillars collapse and stones fall from above as she flings her arm out to cast the coin aside, but the bubbling metal has already liquefied and steamed, burning and singing its way into her palm, imprinting her with the mark of a single denomination, branding her with the sign of what she hates most.

It takes her now—the beast that had taken the Demon King when he was but a boy. The beast that had taken the hearts of men all around the world. The beast that knows only hunger and wrath. The great corrupter and transformer of souls. The thing that takes all that is good and pure and unmakes it into nothing more than one single feeling.

Despair.

Cartouche screams, tearing at her hand and ripping it off with untold strength, the bloody meat flopping over the floor as she clutches her stump, watching as new flesh, powered by demonic magic, regrows the missing part of her body. The blessing of the Demon King flows through her, regenerating her wound, as raw energy breaks free from her body. Pure, distilled magical power whips and strikes all around her, like maelstrom winds that hammer into the walls of the chamber.

Her sense of reasoning and desire, her feeling of normalcy and want—such things are lost to the animal frenzy triggered by the reenactment of the deepest wounds of her soul and being. Mindless, frenzied, Cartouche watches as her hand regrows, as the meat and bone and skin regenerate, and stares in the darkness with her glowing yellow eyes as the brand of the coin regrows with it.

Her scream carries out around the castle and around the world as a howl that never stops. She lashes out, her raw magic colliding with a torrential wall of water that stems from the hands of the blue-haired sorceress.

Towers of water strike out in all directions, together with the lashing tendrils of demon magic, as Cartouche's and Ruhr's spells collide.

The dancer flies, twisting and spinning and twirling in the great wave as if lost in a puppeteer's dance. She spins and spins, her eyes passing over the thousands of bodies she sees through the distortion of the water. Through the great mass of wetness moves a form, a shape. Like a sea serpent hunting a fish, something shoots through the wave toward her, hammering against her with colossal might.

Cartouche catches it, her arms spread wide as she holds the maw of a great snake made entirely out of water open apart, stopping it from consuming her. Her feet hit stone, the wave around her crashing and lessening as the heat from her body boils and bubbles the water away. The great, round chamber is filled with steam that wafts up toward the single opening in the ceiling, as if they were all within an oven. The dancer spins, dragging the great dragon with her. Its tail strikes out, lashing along the dozens of pillars and columns around the chamber, and against the hundreds of armored bodies as she whips the magical construct out and dispels it.

Her feet move along the wet, boiling stones, stamping through the water as she performs her act. Arrows and spells launch toward her as she moves, a single person within an army of thousands. Her hands and legs move around and up and down, the air around them distorting. The change is only visible because of the steam from the floor that fails to rise in specific pockets of air, as if those places had become frozen in time, separate from the laws of reality.

Metal and magic fly in all directions as they hit those distortions, rebounding in all directions. The arrows and spells fly back toward their casters or toward other groups of soldiers, crashing into the walls and the ceiling, and up toward the few brave stars that dare manage to watch through the clouds as hell fills the castle. The drumming of metal and the forcefulness of swords fill the air as hundreds of people charge toward the lone figure, who follows the only movements she knows—stomping and spinning now with forceful will, rather than with a swan's graceful touch, dancing now not in the pursuit of something beautiful, but in the pursuit of what can only really be true: ugliness.

Stones and spires of blackened, soaked, boiled rock blast out of the floor, gruesomely skewering countless of people on sharp points, causing them to scream and wail as they hold their breaking rib cages steady as they slide deeper and deeper down the widening points that tear them apart.

No, they're not stones; they're not rock—they're teeth. The castle itself twists and churns, bulging in and out in response to her movements, which hammer against it like a disruptive parasite in an intestinal tract. Cartouche dances as, all around, both fire and magic burn.

It writhes and churns. The stones become soft and pliant as the illusion of rock becomes broken. As the meat and sinew of the Demon King's castle begins to drip and leak.

Thousands of soldiers run and move in formation, trying to position themselves in the fight against a single dancer, but never finding themselves in the right places as the floors move, as the walls and pillars and columns move together with her. Teeth—long, broken columns—crush down and grind the bodies of the unfortunate screamers into mush, more often leaving them alive than killing them outright, and they crawl and scream in mindless horror, with pasted legs and flattened arms.

Despair.

Despair.

DESPAIR.

Cartouche knows nothing else as she follows her instincts—everything she knows. A flash of blue strikes near her, and she ducks, her shoulder-length white hair flowing up like water as its avatar barely misses her head. The dancer rises again, her leg kicking out in a swaying twist that connects with the gut of the half elf. Ruhr the river sorceress flies and crashes into a wall while Cartouche lifts her fist and closes it, feeling the molten metal gluing her own fingers together.

A soldier runs and dives, tackling Ruhr out of the way as the walls of the castle collapse in on themselves. Blood and gore spray in all directions as he's crushed, while Ruhr rolls off and tumbles to the side before getting back up to her feet, water casting around her hands.

A sharpened lance of blue flies toward Cartouche, who leaps, catching the needle that was meant for her heart. The stiffened, hardened stream of water softens into something akin to a rope—a sash—as she twirls it around her hand, infusing it with her demonic corruption while she continues her dance.

It changes color, and the rope of red water lashes out around her like a whip. The stream cuts through a row of knights in armor, separating them fully from their legs and leaving a screaming heap of bones and meat on the floor, which is then swallowed by the castle as the once solid floor begins to dip and break in holes and pivots that disrupt the movement of these graceless, base creatures. But the dancer simply dances as if nothing had changed, moving and leaping from one section to the other as many are swallowed whole.

Water roars. Cartouche cuts through the wave with the red sash, the water crashing violently all around them as the tidal wave breaks. The room floods, the pockets and divots filling with liquid. Gore and the dying float toward the surface; those who were unfortunate enough not to have died immediately drown instead. But now, the pockets of the room cannot swallow anyone, as they choke on water. The room itself spasms, the walls moving in and out unnaturally as if the castle itself were trying to displace the wetness inside its throat.

The dancer focuses her efforts—her rage and anger—on Ruhr, who is, in this moment, the personification of everything she hates most in this world. It's because of her, because of people like her, that she's become what she's become. It's because of people—No, *creatures* like Ruhr the river sorceress—that the world is full of nothing but such horrific, true ugliness.

She's been wrong.

She's been going about it all wrong. She understands now, the Demon King and his ways.

Cartouche whips out the red sash of corrupted water toward the half elf, who guards it with her own arm. Rather than being cut through, however, she is protected by the blue water that encircles her from her wrist down. With Ruhr holding on to one end of the rope, it being bound around her arm, while Cartouche does the same on the other side, they find themselves now in a dance, after all.

The dancer yanks on the sash, and Ruhr flies toward her from the force of the tug, her demonic strength far surpassing that of any human, elf, or anything in between.

The Demon King seeks to eradicate everyone who lives because beauty cannot exist in the same place they do. Pure, radiant, blissful beauty cannot exist in the same dimension as such ugliness. If beauty is the most radiant flower in heaven's garden, then humanity and their ilk are the pests that gnaw away the petals, the poison that rots the roots, and the miasma that withers the blossoms.

Beauty and mankind are incompatible. Neither can exist in their purest state when the other is around. She sees it now.

Red water collects around Cartouche's free hand as blue water collects around Ruhr's, and the two of them collide—bound by one arm with the sash, and on the other by fists and palms that interlock, the melted metal on Cartouche's hand hissing as it touches Ruhr's wet palm, the molten metal burning into the half elf's palm and connecting them now through both arms.

The two of them fight like that, swaying and kicking over footing, each trying to topple the other as Cartouche spins them around, dancing and leaping from platform to platform with the strength for two as all around them, broken arrows and corrupted spells fly around the arena like a light show for their waltz.

Ruhr drops down, trying to break Cartouche's footing, but Cartouche spins her around instead so that the half elf's back is now touching the dancer's front. Ruhr's hands are up and over her head, the two of them still stuck together. Not breaking the flow of the dance, Ruhr drops down into a fall, her head landing between Cartouche's feet, and the connection of their arms pulls the dancer's torso and head down, too. Two feet kick up, waterlogged boots grabbing on to either side of the dancer's head, and jolt with a quick twist to snap a thin neck—but not quick enough.

Cartouche moves her entire body with the twist, falling in its direction and causing the two of them to nearly switch positions. She slowly unravels the wrap around her wrist, allowing some distance from Ruhr to grow on one arm, even if the other is still connected at the palm by metal that is now stuck in a strange state between solid and liquid, constantly melting from the heat of Cartouche's body but solidifying from the coldness of Ruhr's water.

A foot presses itself against Ruhr's gut, kicking her off. There is a wet tearing as the skin of both their palms rip apart, the binding of one of their hands each breaking. Ruhr stumbles back, but only a step, as the remaining red sash still holds them at a body's length apart—two waltzing silhouettes at a point of exchange. As she flies back, Ruhr prepares another spell in her grasp, water condensing into a firm needlepoint that presses itself more and more tightly until it becomes a needle-honed blade, a dagger of water so tightly compressed that it is nearly crystalline.

The shaking and rumbling of the castle go on, bones of the construct and bones of the dead clattering together as the disruption continues all around them. Cartouche, rolling her back, propels herself back up to her feet as Ruhr strikes at her with the sapphire blade. Her strike is blocked by a wrist hitting hers, and the two of them stand there, before one another, water sloshing and crashing around their legs as the arena—filling with the flood—sways back and forth as if they were standing atop the surface of a violent ocean.

Soldiers and crusaders lose their footing and are thrown around, the chaotic wildfire of their attacks projected all around the space as coordination becomes nearly impossible for anyone who isn't one of the two locked in the eye of the storm. Yellow eyes and blue of the same cold depth stare into one another, a dead sun shining over a lifeless ocean. Cartouche flicks her sashed arm outward in a flourish, the half elf's connected limb moving with her as the demon power the dancer possesses manipulates the castle further

The gargling pit in which they fight spasms, the hundreds of sinkholes falling downward deeper and deeper, tearing apart wider and wider, as they connect into one massive gash in the structure rather than countless pockmarks. People scream as they fight against the raging water that pours downward into the abyss, while the arena sinks in on itself everywhere except for the center, where the two of them stand on a single pillar.

All around the chamber, the floor angles downward in a steep slant that endless torrents of water rush downward into. The entire dungeon floor acts as a circular, downward ramp. Only a single column in the center of the ring remains flat and in place; a single column that is straight and narrow and two steps wide in any direction. People scream all around the arena as they hold on to whatever they can while the ocean flushes down the pit, carrying everything with it that is too weak to hold firm to strong hands or strong stone.

The knife and the arm holding it move, the dancer ducking and weaving around as Ruhr tries to cut her, the two of them barely having more than a step to move in any direction as they fight. The clouds above cannot manage to protect the world below from the curious starlight, and the strong glow of so many thousands of eyes shines from heaven above.

Down, left, back, and forth, the sapphire blade and eyes move, trying to cut a close body that is always there but not ever where she is. Cartouche ducks, spinning around in one knee and slamming her body into Ruhr's side. The sorceress flies off the platform, Cartouche holding her arm out and letting the red sash unwind from around her own wrist.

The rope uncoils as the half elf goes over the edge, the red sash slithering down after her as she falls into the pit, together with the torrential flood of water.

Cartouche watches the rope fall over the edge, vanishing together with the half elf. Rising up to her feet to stand straight, she holds her arms out to her sides and bows with a flourish, now that the dance has come to an end.

Like a spurt of blood blasting from a ruptured artery, red splashes all over Cartouche's face as it shoots from below with violent force. The blood-tinged water, the sash, shoots back up from the abyss.

The dancer looks up toward the needle, toward the jet stream of water that is being controlled by the sorceress, who doesn't seem to be done yet.

"Anymore," speaks Cartouche, looking all around herself as another red needle rises toward the sky. Then another. Then another. Like bars of a cage, red bursts of flesh-cutting water shoot toward the clouds, ripping apart the stone ceiling as they cut through it. The dungeon contorts, spreading the opening above wider to avoid being hurt, like an opening mouth. More and more streams rise from below. She readies herself, watching the closing space all around her for movement as the room becomes obscured by a cage of water. "You said you don't dance *anymore*," says the gallu, trying to provoke a voice into speaking so she knows where the half elf is going to attack from.

A splash comes from the side as something moves through the red wall. Cartouche spins, her leg kicking out and striking the person directly in the neck.

But there is no person. Instead, only a vaguely human-shaped mass of water falls apart into itself, the golemlike construct collapsing into a puddle and splashing down into the abyss below the small platform.

Movement comes from behind her. This was a distraction.

Cartouche turns, striking out just in time with her arm, the bangles around it jangling as . . . she strikes another water construct. Her hand moves through its face, and the form breaks apart, falling into the nothingness as droplets and foam.

"Because I realized that Ruhr the River Sorceress doesn't dance," replies a cold voice from above. Cartouche lifts her head, her eyes going wide as she stares into the maw of the great water dragon that hovers over the red cage she had been too distracted to realize she needed to escape from. "I have people who do it for me," finishes the half elf, standing on a plume of blue water by the boiling dragon's maw, her arm outstretched and aimed toward Cartouche.

The demon's eyes twitch as she moves to dodge, but the dragon blasts down from above, an ocean's worth of water pressed into the form of a serpent with a maw like the great gate to the underworld that now lunges toward her.

Cartouche laughs to herself and leaps toward the beast, her arms flourishing out at her sides openly as she springs forward and off the platform to the dragon, who consumes the column and her whole. The fabric of her loose clothing, the golden bangles, all flow around her as she moves through the spray, her eyes closed but her senses open as it takes her.

It doesn't matter.

What she was looking for isn't in this world, anyway. What she's looking for is there, on the other side, where the Demon King is soon to be. Beauty cannot exist in this place, so she will go and wait there, where it does exist.

The Demon King will achieve his goal, and the world—and herself—will finally get to experience that state of true bliss when he does.

As her body and mind both dissolve, the water all around her is lit with the glow of endless starlight as the show comes to an end, the endless sound of raging water carrying the noise of what she can only feel is thunderous applause to her ears.

~ [The Demon King] ~

Large fingers tap against the armrest of the throne, a massive head resting on a fist just as large, as Swain stares down the length of the throne room. The cries of the aching castle carry to where he watches with endless eyes the skirmishes that happen around the world, the horrors that happen around his shadow, and the battles that happen within his own keep.

"My lord," says a voice from next to him—Kirsch, the ghost. "Cartouche has . . ."

Swain sits there, his fingers falling one after the other, as the eyes on his head stare forward but the eyes on his body turn toward her. The sheet-covered specter, blood endlessly dripping toward the ground from her visible legs and feet, hovers close by as he sits upright and holds out his hands. She falls quiet.

An echo reverberates around the chamber, dozens of statues crumbling at his feet, and Kirsch yelps as the force sends her flying back. Two hands strike each other, two palms colliding.

A slow, strong, thorough clap fills the superheated air around the Demon Core as his applause for the dance that has been presented carries off to wherever her soul is drifting now.

"My lord, can't you . . ." Kirsch flies toward him again. "Can't you save her?" she asks, as the power of his strikes against his own skin send waves outward that cause her sheet to billow, and the wetness on it to boil. The endless leaking of blood from her body curdles as his infernal heat causes it to evaporate, turning it into a thick, gelatinous coagulation on the ghost's body. Chunks of it fall to the floor, steaming in piles. "I liked Cartouche! She was always nice to me . . ."

The Demon King rests his back against his grim throne, looking at the ghost now. "She is already saved, Kirsch," replies the beast, his harrowing voice weighing down the air. "She finally saw it. What I saw. She finally knows the truth about what we're after, about what this is." Swirling his finger, he catches the trail of a random soul flying through the chamber, winding the screaming wisp around his claw, and staring at its distorted face.

"I don't understand," replies Kirsch sadly. "Please help her!"

Swain shakes his head. "I have helped her," says the Demon King. "And now, she's in a beautiful place; a place nothing like this disgusting world," he explains, lifting his hand. The soul unwinds from around his finger, screaming in horror as it flies off to escape to another part of its eternal prison. Something sniffles and struggles breathing next to him.

The Demon King holds out his hand, letting the ghost land on it.

"Do not be sad, Kirsch," he tells the confused, small spirit, who looks up toward him. He nods once with his monstrous head. "I promise that you'll see Cartouche again very soon," he assures her, a single claw lowering itself below her chin to lift her head somewhat higher.

". . . Really?" asks Kirsch, the sticky, gore-stained sheet lifting as she wipes her face, but only ends up smearing more red everywhere in the process.

Swain nods, looking at her, and then releasing her to fly free again before he sits back against his throne, returning to his position of wait.

"Very soon," he confirms, his thousands of eyes turning to look at the crusade that has pressed deep into the heart of his bastion, at first as a pest, but now exactly as he desires. Like a poem, like a dance, such things have a way of developing and growing while in the process of creation. New thoughts and ideas have their ways of coming in the middle of the process of making something, and now, he's had his thought. Every poem needs a leading stanza, every dancing its strongest step and flourish to cap it off.

And just the same, the demon creation that he has wrought needs the perfect cutoff to wrap it up. The last period in the poem. The last step in the dance.

The Demon King stares feverishly through his ten thousand eyes at a blue-haired, half-elven woman, who will serve as the tide-colored ink for his last poem in this terrible world.

"Very soon," he repeats after himself, his deep, echoing laugh carrying off down a thousand corridors of endlessly screaming and clawing shadows and horrors unimaginable.

CHAPTER 14

A GRAND SACRAMENT

~ [Ruhr, the River Sorceress] ~
Half Elf | ♀ | Sorceress
Rank: SSS
Location: The Demon King's Castle, Floor Negative Ninety-Four
Level: 100

Why are we even here?" asks a man from the side. "I could've been in the city. She can clearly handle this by herself," he says, gesturing to Ruhr as she walks past.

The crusade has recollected as best as they can after the encounter just now with a corruption far stronger than any monster she has faced so far. This wasn't just a creature or a beast; this was a truly twisted and changed soul picked by the Demon King himself as a servant.

Ruhr turns her head, looking at the man. "You're here to carry my bag," she says dryly, snapping her fingers once and nodding her head back to the entryway, where a pile of gear lies. "Don't get blood on it," warns the sorceress with a stern tone as she walks past the wounded and injured, covered in water and sedimentary slosh.

"Ruhr!" yells a voice, running toward her. Ruhr hisses between her clenched teeth, flinching as she turns her head. A priestess of the Holy Church runs toward her.

"Hey, hey!" snaps Ruhr, looking around as she's grabbed and held by a worried person. "Take it easy," she warns as Springer holds her. "You're ruining my image," says Ruhr, trying to walk off and pulling the priestess behind her, whose heels drag over the damp stonework. The castle, which had been previously moving and twisting with the dancer's corruption, has now become stiff and static again. The slanted room returned to its former state, the signs of battle—other than the many scars—healing like a body would with fresh wounds.

Springer looks up her way, her messy hair covering half her face. "What are you even talking about?" asks the exasperated priestess. She shakes her head. "You're always 'my image' this and 'my reputation' that," she starts, standing up straight and looking at Ruhr. "But before this, I'd never even heard of you. What image?"

Ruhr flinches, her eyes twitching as she lets out a gurgling noise in the back of her throat. The river sorceress clears her throat and look down at Springer with a cool gaze. "That's because you live a sheltered, lonely little life," replies the sorceress in a harsh tone. She plants her hands on her hips, lifting a leg to set it down on something. "Everyone has heard of"—Ruhr lifts her voice—"Ruhr! The River Sorceress!" proclaims Ruhr, holding her hands on the sides of her hips, with her boot resting on a box that Springer looks down at in confusion.

"Where did that box come from?" she mutters as Ruhr kicks the hollow crate to the side.

"Don't worry about that," replies Ruhr. "I'm good; you're good." She nods her head. "Let's keep going," she says, marching onward toward the next door to the next floor of the castle. "Before this place changes again."

"Ruhr . . ." mutters Springer, pulling on her sleeve again. Ruhr stops with a sigh, rolling her eyes as she looks back.

"What?" asks the half elf.

Springer softly nods her head to the side, lowering her voice. "The wounded . . ." whispers the priestess quietly. Behind them lie rows and rows of people who were injured in the fight.

Ruhr stares at them and then at her. "You're right, froggy," concedes Ruhr, hitting Springer on the backside as she walks back. The priestess hits her on the shoulder, muttering her way.

"Everybody, get the fuck up!" yells Ruhr, her voice echoing around the chamber as she looks at the wounded and injured. The soldiers look her way. "If you can't move, you're getting left behind here and now." She narrows her eyes. "Let's go. You! Bag!" barks Ruhr, the leader of what remains of the grand crusade, snapping her fingers at the soldier from before as she goes.

"Ruhr!" hisses Springer, running after her as the crusade—some begrudgingly, others silently—begins to move again. "Everyone is hurt and tired."

"I've been here longer than all of you," says Ruhr dryly, walking on without looking at Springer. "If you stop, if you wait, this goddamned place is going to eat you like an owl swooping down from a tree," explains the half elf as she walks into the darkness that is waiting for her. "You can stay there with the dead, or you can come with me."

"I get that," replies Springer in a frustrated, lowered tone. "But you could be a little more reassuring with them."

Ruhr shakes her head, her short, wet hair clinging to her nape. "This is me being reassuring," says the half elf with an empty gaze as she walks deeper into the heart of the Demon Core. "If I ever baby you, that's when you should worry." She waves Springer off and walks onward by herself.

Springer stops, watching her, and then turns back to look at the crusade, who do their best to march on. The wounded who can walk do so as best they can, and those who can't are given assurances and promises that they will be back.

But everyone knows that isn't true.

Nobody is coming back from where they're going.

Springer looks back toward the darkness ahead, expecting to see Ruhr there, but she is already too far gone. Gulping, stuck between two groups, the priestess runs after her.

~ [The Demon King] ~

Dungeons, adventurers, monsters, gold, and drink—such things have intoxicated the hearts of the people of the world for generations now. Great stories of men and women of notable renown who plunge deeply into the darkest regions of the world in search of treasure and glory fill the hearts of every young boy and girl. Despite the horrific lifestyle that adventuring really is for most, full of poverty, despair, and danger, it has become so deeply romanticized that the truth simply can't live up to the fable.

In this world, places called *dungeons* exist. They are deep holes below the ground in which monsters breed and treasures are hoarded, all guided by an entity known as a *dungeon master* or a *dungeon core*, depending on your era of life and region. These are places of deep, old, primal magic where the forces of the world collide far below the ground in order to foster the creation of such places. They are in essence anthills that, rather than being created by ants, create the ants themselves.

The humans of the world first feared dungeons, in days of long forgotten antiquity. Back when men huddled around fires to keep safe from the monsters who lay in the darkness only ever beyond the fading flickering of red, they whispered and told stories of such places. They spoke in quiet voices and hushed words of dark holes full of teeth and claws, always silently, lest these places heard their uttering. Some beasts should never be called by their name, for that would get their attention.

But as society grew out of the shadows and people grew in numbers, as their walls became stronger and their doors thicker, so, too, did their fear of the darkness below the world lessen. Dungeons quickly changed, turning from dens of horror into captives of their own making. The very terror that dungeons produced in abundance—monsters—became their undoing. Like an old growth forest, like a shaft in a cave full of rare gems, humanity and the ilks of all races saw fit to not squander this resource as well. Dungeons became walled in, with people building their cities around them rather than as far away as possible. They became, in essence, domesticated by force.

In legions, humans and elves and all such people would now fight in the dungeon, abusing its nature as a monster creator in order to acquire nearly endless resources—meat and reagents and all manner of precious things that could be found below the world.

These people, these "farmers" of dungeons, who do nothing but plunder dungeons to earn their bread and water, are what society have dubbed *adventurers*. While in days of old, the word would have implied someone who took it upon themselves to wander and explore the world in its breadth and beauty, the adventurers of the modern age are nothing but miners, but loggers, at the end of the day in this new era.

There is no romanticism left in the nature of their work.

An adventurer rises in the morning in their grubby, low-cost accommodation, and picks up their tool of the craft after eating a gruel of porridge and low-cost monster meat—often self-harvested—before trekking down through a city that lives in abundance in order to risk their lives again to harvest a new pound of flesh from kicking, biting, screaming things, in the hopes that they, too, might one day become one of the rare and the powerful; one of the loved and beholden people of spectacle.

There are some adventurers who take on a nearly celebratory, nigh-deistic status among the population, akin to the greatest kings and heroes of legends—literal champions of the people who walk the street, their titles given because of their good fortune below in the underworld. This is where the sickness of the game is at its highest peak, for of the hundreds of thousands of adventurers across the world, only a fraction of the total population, only a *handful* of them, will ever know anything close to such luxury. The majority will die, kicking and howling, as they are torn into the shadows by a noose made out of their own entrails. Sons and daughters of countless families die every day in order to provide the world above with precious tokens and gems, with meat and flora, but none of them will ever have a name of note outside their circle.

But it isn't that they don't think they will.

These deluded, young, eager, excitable faces will look at the greats of the world, the legendary folk and adventurers of bygone and current day, and promise to themselves that they, too, will be one of these names shortly, in only a little while longer.

Day, after day, after day, they will parade around from one darkness to the next, always just escaping the reaper's scythe without ever really knowing it. Day after day, they promise themselves that their real life will start soon, that their real existences will start soon, that all of this mud and gore is just the developmental stage that they are in. Only another month. Only another year. Faces wrinkle, and around the table, the owners of seats are exchanged, as every so often someone just doesn't make it back, though there is always a new body to fill the spot. There are always more young people who can be told that they're going to be great. That they're going to be the one.

And night after night, the people feed on the creations of the dungeons, and the dungeons feed on the people. The serpent devours its own tail, regurgitating around and around endlessly as the same flesh is tossed back and forth between two vomiting parties until nothing is left between either of them except a strange, unidentifiable mass.

Such things are evidence of society's sickness. Dungeons and adventurers are only one such example of many countless more.

To think, he himself had wanted to become an adventurer once.

Swain, the Demon King, sits on his throne and stares into the fires as he tries to rearrange them into the features of a girl. He remembers some things now and then, but only ever barely, only ever whispers. He remembers that he had promised himself to become such a man, such a person, who would carry a sword and plunge it into the breasts of beasts day in and day out, if only he could provide for her, if only he could be reassured that she would stay with him forevermore, in times of squalor and in times of fortune.

What was her name?

What had she said that had captivated him, had placed him under her spell? Was it witchcraft? Or was it the foolishness of his young heart, having been so easily swayed and moved by things as gentle as the wind. These young folks who lifted up the sword were deluded by their society and world, but what had overtaken him?

The Demon King, in all of his wrathful power, sits there in silence and puzzles as around him scream the tormented souls of nearly one million dead, always burning in the inferno of the Demon Core but never reaching the satisfactory point of ash. Was she a demon, sent to corrupt his soul from the other side, meant to guide him down the path he had taken? Or was she an angel of the heavens, having failed her attempt to avert the destiny of the world?

He doesn't know.

His claws rest against his face as his other hand lies on the armrest of the throne. His burning eyes stare through the gaps at the leaking of souls all around him as he puzzles her together.

He has to remember everything.

He has to know, when he breaches through to the other side, where she is, who she is. Everything will burn; everyone will be wrought to nothingness—but he has to find her first so that she can be last.

Through his visions, he sees walking inside of his castle the blue-haired river sorceress. She is perhaps the perfect example, being herself what those many thousands of dead boys and girls had dreamed of becoming: an adventurer.

Swain stares at the vision of her parading forward like a cockatrice as she marches toward his throne room, climbing ever higher and higher into his castle as the last piece of the puzzle clicks into place. He wonders, how many?

He knows how many people he has killed.

But does she know how many she has lured into an early grave? Does the half elf know that she acts as a shining beacon hovering just above a bottomless pit? Does she know how many desperately reaching arms have grasped out toward her in the hopes of becoming wealthy, renowned, known—only to fall into the deepest oblivion imaginable as her unreachable light becomes more distant and distant by the moment?

Demons come in many forms.

Not all of them are so obvious as him. Others are hidden and live in plain sight, masquerading as the endless desires of men and women.

Some demons write poems; some write songs. Some demons dance, and some demons build. Some cook, and some play—but there are other demons who do not engage in such pursuits. Rather, they fester and nest and rot deep inside the hearts of the living like a mold, their unseen roots spreading further and deeper throughout the will of a creature. And while they might think they are growing—they are healing—as the years go on by, the truth is that they are, but not toward an organic, natural direction. They are being guided by the whims of the unseen demon, pushing them this way and that, so that when the last hour strikes and the last breath leaves their body, they will realize in a final moment of pure, radiant despair that this life they lived in pursuit of their "real" life was everything they had all along.

To live only in pursuit of a singular goal is a mistake; it's a trap set by demons.

The world is ending; everyone is going to die in hellfire. So have a little fun and do some other things, too, instead of being an obsessive creature, beholden to only your aims and desires.

"Are you done yet, Abydos?" asks Swain, looking down at the demon painter who stands below his throne with a canvas, working.

The painter and his shadow look around from behind it. "Just a little longer, my lord," promises the gallu with a crooked smile on his face. Behind him giggles the voice of a pleased ghost as Kirsch floats next to him and peeks at his work. "Please, hold still."

Swain obliges, leaning back against his throne and resuming his dramatic pose as he models for the painter's work—a portrait of the Demon King.

What he does not know, however, is that within the painting, all around his throne, are dancing clowns and acrobats wrapping chains with smiles on their faces around a screaming, tormented, warped shadow.

But it does have a big, funny, red clown's nose that one of them is about to squeeze.

So, that's something.

~ [A Slime] ~
Location: Somewhere Not So Far Away

Plap. Plap. Plap.

The wet, gooey monster jumps from one burnt stone to the next, its gelatinous body slapping against the scalded, cooled rock as it hops onward toward the inexplicable desire that it feels. It's not a very clever creature, nor very wise. It does not know why it does things on a very deep level, but it does know that it does them. It knows that it is hopping and hopping, just as it has been doing for a very long time, but that really is about it. It has come very far from its meadow, the one-eyed slime sustaining itself on a diet of smoldered worms and burnt field mice as it follows the calling.

Sometimes, it will stop here and there to engage in the practices of slimes: wobbling, wiggling, or jiggling at things that it might perceive to be a threat to itself—big, scary rocks; big, scary trees; big, scary clouds.

But all of these horrors are repelled by sufficient wiggling, waggling, bobbling, and goggling, and so the little slime then hops onward, victorious in its conquests.

The wandering undead that prowl the wastelands, the screaming ghosts that howl in the skies above—none of them pay it any mind, as it is entirely inconsequential. The Demon King's legions hunt people, not monsters. Most wild monsters of the world have fallen under the Demon King's control, and so, the little one-eyed slime just hops on forevermore—beckoned, perhaps.

Or not.

It's quite difficult to say, really.

~ [Peribsen] ~

"Magnificent," mutters the gallu to himself, standing atop a high tower of the Demon King's castle and staring out at the ramparts and embrasures, staring at the crisscrossing bridges and the impossibly high walls and keeps that defy the logical reality of material sciences.

Stones are stacked so high that they ought to crush the lowest ones below. Beams are strung so long that no tree in the world should be tall enough to produce such singular struts of wood. Staircases wind and loop in impossible manners, stretching across abysses and chasms, somehow allowing one to walk upstairs to a lower floor, and downstairs to a higher one.

"Simply magnificent," he whispers to himself, watching closely as he sets down a marble onto the stonework.

The small glass sphere, the size of a coin, rolls along the uneven ground as if it were going down a hill. It picks up speed, and he follows it as it rolls along a long walkway and strikes into a stairwell leading upward toward a tower.

And the marble keeps rolling faster and faster, as if it were plummeting, as it rises up the staircase. The demon reengineer huffs as he runs after it, climbing the railingless stairway above the cataclysm in a hurry as the marble outpaces him.

He runs into the tower, looking around for it in the darkness, his hand resting on the arch of the doorway as he steps inside.

"Now, where did you go . . ." he whispers.

The castle's redesign is truly something to marvel at. While before, it was an impressive construct that defied everything he had ever learned; now, it is something beyond what he knows. The inversion of the structure has, in a sense, also inverted the rules of reality present within it. The power of the Demon King is to create things that aren't there through his words; things that are of a . . . less tangible and grounded nature. The dungeon has, until now, followed the rules of reality quite firmly, acting as a dungeon in the classical sense of the term. It was something people knew and understood and, while being more horrific and darker than most, was still nonetheless a dungeon at the end of the day.

Peribsen lifts his head, looking up toward the ceiling, which is actually the ground of another floor. There, above him—or below, depending on where you are—marches the human crusade.

He tilts his head, his hair hanging upside down—the same as theirs does toward him—as both parties stand on the wrong side up but never fall.

Very peculiar.

~ [Demon General Sieben] ~
Terror | ♂ | Demon General
Location: The Ashlands

It is a new age. An age of turmoil, which the peoples of humanity might never have come to know the depths of in their days of sanctuary and peace if not for the boundless grace of the Demon King. Thanks to him, the world will know of a new day and age in which the pointless trivialities of what came before are all but erased.

The seven demon generals march at the head of the legion, some with two feet that step one after the other, and others with skittering, chitinous movements; some who glide on clouds of dark magic, and others who lurch and undulate unnaturally as they move. Each of the seven is blessed in their own unique way by their lord, the Demon King. No two gifts are the same, as every creation of their master is fully individual in its purpose and design. No two artworks are ever truly alike.

"We should eat them," whispers a voice into the communion. "Crawl down their throats and chew through their tongues," it suggests.

"No," replies another, harsher one in a crawling, slow whisper that moves on a centipede's legs through the air. "We should fill their mouths with oil and blood until their bellies rupture," it says.

"We should hang them all as banners of our flag," considers a third. "We'll break their arms and legs and tie them together into one tapestry of flesh," it demands, its voice slithering between the lurching, shuffling feet of the weary.

Tens of thousands of prisoners gathered from around the nation have been transported here for the purpose of presenting their souls to the master of all beasts and lord of all bones—the Demon King.

Yet, the exact process is still under dispute between the many benefactors of his endless might.

"We will feed them to the beasts of the wild," suggests another general. "Let a great ravishing take place; let their bodies be descended upon by wolves and fangs."

The Demon General Sieben marches on silently, a contingent of mind-controlled Vildt from the other continent marching behind him as his horde, many of them holding firm to the shackles of the prisoners who have no tears left to weep. He lifts his gaze, his hollow face staring toward the castle they face toward. On this side of it, there is nothing but ash and forsaken dirt. On the other side is a legion of monsters so plentiful that their stack of bodies rises over the castle exterior, giving it the impression of enclosing itself around a writhing, black core.

They've arrived.

It's been a long time since this all began, since he—*they*—were created.

Countless monsters and beasts come to a stop as the generals cease their death march. Seven silhouettes of ghastly form and shape—some in armor, and some in drabs of flesh and leather; some in a form akin to a broken giant, and others in indescribable shapes made of more limbs than core—stand there, their bodies forming the same contour on the horizon as the lightless towers of the castle.

And then, one after the other, they fall.

Each demon general, in accordance with their order of birth, falls to a knee or a bow or whatever form of prostration works best for their broken husks and mangled, wrong frames. Perhaps they do so because it is their place, or perhaps they do so because they have no choice.

Power is in the air—power so indescribable and heavy that everything seems to carry an unbearable weight to it. The generals, the knights, the monsters, and the prisoners all fall, the stronger to where they can hold, and the weakest flat and violently against the dead ground to which they seem almost attached now. Weak, brittle bones break, and the strongest ones hold firm but bend and give. Metal buckles as if by itself.

A heat fills the air, fills his core, as the spiritual presence of the Demon King is unmistakable. The ground cracks, the air itself seeming to contract in and out, the contortions visible through the distortion of sight within it.

The colorless horizon breaks open—a slit emerging, and then a rip in reality. The castle wall opens ajar as a great, massive gate that spans impossibly high, from top to bottom, swings open wide.

A thunder captures the world within its roar again and again as a supermassive pressure moves toward them, each step shaking the firmament of reality, each stride threatening to rip a metaphysical thread of the world that was already only just barely holding on. The Demon King approaches.

Even if they have seen all the horrors the world has to offer, even if their souls have been picked clean of concepts such as agony and suffering and fear as they have all accepted their fate—now, after so much marching, new screams and cries fill the air. A fresh terror, a new terror, arises. One that draws from a well so deep within the core of the living that even in their darkest hours they had been unable to pull from it. But now, here, as the steps grow louder, as all of their senses are crushed by the weight of his arriving, the same as their bodies, the prisoners once again know what raw, instinctual fear is.

"We have come," speak several voices in unison as the demon generals all speak at once, the voices coalescing like the buzzing of a hive into one uniform drone.

The massive silhouette of the Demon King stands before them, flames and power arching from his body, emanating from the catastrophic core of his heart as he looks over them all and their bounty. "Well done," he compliments, his crushing voice pressing down over them all like further blows of a hammer against their already quaking frames. The giant moves toward the group of prisoners, who have nowhere to back away, pressing their harrowed, skeletal frames into one another as they each try to hide further in the mess of their bodies. A massive hand reaches into the heap of wretches, grabbing an unfortunate wrist and yanking it into the air with a body attached.

The young boy with black hair that he pulls out of the pile kicks and screams, dangling toward the ground as if he were suspended from a meat hook. The superheated rock and soil hiss as droplets of urine strike it.

"Boy," growls the Demon King, looking at the defeated, ugly thing he is holding. Two eyes look at him in terror, opening wide not at their own will, but at the behest of his command, of the power of his words speaking to him. "Tell me," he starts, the body in his grasp rattling from the strength of his voice moving through it like a scream through a wall. "What do you want the most?" asks the Demon King. "Out of anything in this world."

"I . . . I . . ." stutters the terrified creature, unable to pull air into its lungs without cooking them. The grip around his arm grows tighter, the single, massive fist holding him from hand all the way to shoulder. "I want to go home!" cries the young man, the signs on his face which hint toward his progression to adulthood all reverting as the expressions of a crying boy overtakes him and turns back the years of development and change of character, of maturation.

"Ah, a pity," remarks the Demon King, shaking his head. His other hand rises up, a massive claw attached to one large finger pressing against the boy's ribs. "They say that home is where the heart is," ponders the master of all things rotten and foul. "So I wonder, if you aren't home now, then where is your heart?" he asks, his nail pressing against a rib that snaps like a frail, thin bush's branch. An unimaginable writhing and screaming fills the air as the tip of a nail touches right against the edge of a heart that beats and strikes and hammers. "Oh . . . there it is," says the Demon King, his finger touching the living organ, lightly scratching it as the creature he holds screams and fights an animal fight. "Good." He drops him.

The boy lies there in the ash, a cauterized hole in his chest leaving his beating heart clearly visible to the world all around him, to the eyes of the many thousands of prisoners. His arm is scalded and blistered from top to bottom.

Had the young man wished for something more pure, more beautiful, such as the freedom of another, mercy for another soul whom he loves or knows—or perhaps even doesn't—for a horrified face of the many to be spared the terror to come, then the Demon King would have granted that beautiful wish in truth. A life, maybe even many, would have been spared.

But instead, the pleading for one's own self, for one's own hopes and desires in a time so cruel and desolate such as this one . . . that itself was what brought humanity into this situation to begin with. That is why the Demon King is what he is, isn't it?

He cannot grant such an ugly wish.

Two knights, walking on their spindly, sharp legs over the wastelands, escort the Demon King as he walks past the generals and returns to his castle.

"Prepare the sacrifices for the final event," he orders, looking over his shoulder at his many trusted delegations. They lift their heads toward him. "Do so as you see fit yourselves," he instructs, before returning to his seat of power, his back turned toward countless horrific atrocities that happen in his departure. The cracking of bones and the ripping of flesh fills the air, the wetness of so much blood soaking into the dry land and turning it solid and firm as the superheated air cooks the mud and solidifies it into black-and-ruby brickwork, against which the bodies of thousands are mushed into pulp.

And these tens of thousands of souls carry into the Demon Core, empowering it.

And as for what is left of them, an indistinguishable heap of flayed meat and grounded wetness is piled into a steaming mound, inside of which somehow—impossibly—continue to beat thousands of hearts attached to nothing more than flays of sinew and cut arteries.

Unstopped and unhindered by anyone, a confused elf wanders off in the vague direction the Demon King had gone toward.

CHAPTER 15

BEST SERVED HOT

~ [Byblos] ~
Gallu | ♀ | Spirit Cook
Location: The Demon King's Castle, Floor Negative Ninety-Five
Level: 100

What is the essence of a creation?

How does one work their way down to the purest, deepest point of something in order to reach the cleanest, most distilled purpose of its existence? The obvious thing one would think would be to lessen, to strip away pieces. One would think that in order to reach the core of a piece, one would need to peel back the skin, cut through and off the meat, remove the bones and the organs that are in the way until one finds the specific thing inside of the mass that one is looking for.

But there isn't anything there, is there?

If one cuts into a body and removes everything that makes it so, there is no single raw core element, no essence, left behind. All that one has is a heap of meat and a messy table.

The essence, then, is not a physical thing.

There is no "core" inside of a person, animal, or flower. There is, poetically speaking, the heart. But this in reality is no more than another lump on the table.

No, the essence, then, as one would think of it—the purest, truest point of an existence—must be something else. Beauty is something else other than a single thing.

Beauty is the many lines that make a poem, the many colors that make a painting, the many ingredients that make a dish.

This is the great deception of life. *Essence* as a word implies something simplistic and truly raw on a base level, but in reality, to reach such a thing, one must combine. The essence of something beautiful is achieved only through the act of combination.

The demonic cook, Byblos, works, flattening out a screaming soul with the back end of a knife and sprinkling it with salt as she works toward her craft. Somber sobbing comes from the side of the room, hardly audible over the bubbling and the hissing of the many cauldrons and stoves out of which unnatural fire spews like a dragon's breath. All around her rattle lids on overboiling pots out of which flow and bubble frothing liquids and tepid sludges that she has been ignoring in her pursuit of a new creation—those old ones having been deemed as failures in the midst of the process by her testers.

It's all not right.

She frowns at the flailing spirit before turning the knife around and taking to it, cutting this way and that with precise movements and cold, focused eyes. Just like back then, when she was working that stupid job at the roadside inn full of people who didn't appreciate her creations, she drowns out the noise of the crying and wailing ungrateful wretches she's forced to share this world with. Those base, simple creations who don't understand what a real culinary creation is, what it means to nourish rather than simply consume.

The gallu works, cutting and slicing, before taking the pieces of the still "living" soul and dropping them into a light pan, moving gracefully around the chaotic, dangerously volatile mess of a kitchen like a doe through the woodland as she grabs oils and vinegars, salts and sugars, alcohols and all manner of tools and implements as she works, throwing in a dash here, stirring a little there, adding in a pinch of this and that—and so it goes. Like a ghost haunting its final resting place, she flows around with haunting grace, entirely lost to her purpose, as everything around her rattles and clanks, shaking like the chains binding a tormented spirit to its gravesite.

And then, after a time of such work in which she feels like she is climbing a mountain that never ends, she plates her newest creation.

But the act of cooking is not over.

There's more to it than just dumping a mess from a pan onto a dish. The eyes of a person eat just as much, if not more, than the mouth does. She adjusts the food she's made, forcing it back into place as it tries to move away from its designated corner over and over. Byblos drizzles oils and colorful sauces here and there in vivid patterns, adding in more color with greenery and such things, until eventually, what she has before her looks just as vivid and colorful as any painting of a grand master—only rising higher than what could be done on a flat canvas.

It offers so much. Smells rise into the air from the creation that emanates heat and warmth; textures are present within the dish that the mind can savor, and with all of this—the taste—can connections of memory and heart come which are deeper than what any other form of art can make. She's sure of it. Cooking is an art more true and powerful than any other, as it touches every sense there is. The sight of food, the smell of it, the texture one can feel, the sizzling and bubbling one can hear—the taste. No other act of creation comes close to what cooking offers. She's convinced. Everyone has their own way forward in life, yes. But her art, compared to that of even the Demon King, is the true pathway to finding the raw essence of creation—beauty.

Her breath leaves her as she looks at her newest creation.

Smiling, she grabs the plate and lifts it expertly with one hand, walking over with a confident saunter toward the table by the kitchen, looking at the people present there. Many of them have deadpan gazes and fractured spirits, staring with mouths agape blankly ahead of themselves as their legs are shackled to the chairs they sit atop. The newest one sobs. The ones who have been here longer are simply quiet, having eaten their share.

She likes to let them get hungry first so that they appreciate the food a little more.

There's something to that, to the . . . *desire* one has when seeking something out in life. The desperation adds a spice to it. Seeing a beautiful tower on the horizon is a much grander experience if one has been wandering lost in the desert for days before. Feeling alive is so much cleaner and stronger if one has almost died and now knows what they almost lost. There is an appreciation to things that those who are content with their existences simply do not know on a deep level, and she thinks that this appreciation is just another bit of spice that adds to the dish.

Byblos sets the plate down before a sobbing man, the clacking carrying out through the room like the fall of an executioner's axe. "It's ready for you," she presents with a one-handed curtsy. He's a new person, captured from the crusade. She needed a new one. The old ones have stopped talking. They're all just kind of . . . full. Byblos' eyes turn back from down the long table, back to him as he sits there, trying to fight against the chair. But just the same as he is bolted to it, it is bolted to the ground. "Please eat before it gets cold," she insists, gesturing to the table. The sobbing man looks at her.

"Oh!" says Byblos. "I'm terribly sorry." The demon shakes her head as she strikes herself. The gallu hurries over back to the kitchen, grabbing a set of a fork and knife with a fabric napkin, bringing it back to him. "Please," she insists, setting everything down before him.

He shakes his head.

Byblos purses her lips at his refusal, looking at him and forcing a smile as she glances at the dish, which is beginning to squirm. The flayed, cooked, and spiced soul of a person begins to try to crawl away, having never truly died.

"No, I don't . . . I won't," he says, breaking down and crying as he looks around the room and then at the thing set before him. "Gods help me," he pleads. "I w—"

"EAT!" screams a banshee cry directly at him, the man's head yanked to the side so forcefully by his hair that his neck threatens to break from the speed of the tug. A contorted, sharp face is inches away from his.

"Be—Be gone, demon!" cries the crusader, clenching his eyes shut.

Everyone else at the table is quiet.

Byblos takes a deep, long breath. "I worked for hours on this," she explains, letting go of his head and folding her hands together in front of her chest as she collects herself. "I've been standing here in a steaming kitchen to make you this." She exhales very slowly as she opens her eyes to look at the crying prisoner. "I would really, very much, appreciate it if you please tried at least a bite," she asks in a tense voice, finding that she is being very reasonable about his horrifically rude behavior.

The dish isn't ruined yet; it's not too late. Even a terrible atmosphere can serve as the soil in which beauty can thrust out of as a verdant sprout, becoming a single, perfect flower over a sunken grave.

"Here," she says, picking up his fork and knife and cutting a piece off. Holding it above her hand, she reaches out toward him to feed him like a mother would her stubborn child. "It's hot. Careful," she warns.

"NO!" screams the man in a loud, bellowing voice as he strikes out with his free hand against her, knocking her arms away. The fork flies off, and with his free hand, he swipes over the table. Byblos screams the same cry he had done a moment ago as the plate falls toward the ground and shatters into a mess of warm porcelain and writhing chunks. "I WON'T BECOME LIKE THEM!" he yells at her, fighting against the restraints holding his lower body to no avail. He looks at the other people at the table, the other guests who had dined before him.

Their eyes are blank, their heads drooped as they sit in silence.

Their bellies and guts and ribs are ruptured from the inside out, whatever they ate eating them in turn as it tried to leave again—as the souls they were fed broke out through them forcefully in order to reconnect with their missing strands. Blood and organs hang down over their legs like set napkins, their arms hanging limply at their sides.

Byblos screams a feral scream, feeling an anger in her that she hasn't felt before. The others ate; they didn't like it, but they at least ate, and she appreciates that. Not every art piece is a masterwork, but if it finds even a viewer, that is often enough to keep an artist's soul content as they try once more.

But to dismiss it from the get-go, to not even give her blood and sweat and tears a chance, isn't just a dismissal of her art: it's a dismissal of her as a person.

She crashes down over him, lunging forward. The wooden legs of the bolted-down chair break as the strength of her charge crashes against him, causing him to fall to his back, his head striking against the stone floor. The demon cook sits on his chest, strangling him as he tries in vain to fight her off.

"EAT IT!" she yells, picking up a handful of the slop on the floor as the man turns his head away, fighting in vain to get her off of him. "EAT IT!" she screams, demented, at the refusing man. Her free hand grabs his face, wrenching it up to look at her. Her fingers force themselves into his mouth, ripping it open. His jaw cracks and breaks from the force, and he screams in pain, his eyes watching in horror as she shoves the mess of food into her own mouth so that at least somebody here can appreciate the work she put into it. Porcelain and goo mix in with her spit as she swallows and then hangs over the man, wrenching her gut so that she can vomit it back out into his mouth.

If she can't feed him like a person, then she'll feed him like a bird.

"Man, what the fuck is this place?" asks a voice from the side as Byblos hangs over him, a string of undefinable, off-colored slop already hanging out of her mouth over his as she turns her head, looking at the woman standing there and looking her way.

"Guests . . ." mutters Byblos to herself as the spew of off-orange bile disconnects from her.

Her hand flicks, and the man's head snaps to the side, the light leaving his eyes as she rises off him, pulling the napkin from the table and wiping her face with it. "Are you hungry?" she asks. "Please, have a seat!" offers the gallu, gesturing to the table as people move into the room. "I haven't had a crowd in a while!"

"You know what?" starts the blue-haired half elf, walking forward and looking around the area. "I'm kind of lowbrow about food," she explains, picking up a very fancy fork with the tips of her fingers before letting it drop back down to the table in front of a blown-out corpse. "Do you have any, like, plain bread or potatoes?"

Byblos claps her hands together excitedly. "Why, yes, actually!" she replies with true joy in her eyes. This is the first time someone has directly asked her for food in a while. A simple palette isn't a make-or-break happenstance in regard to food. It's something that can be expanded and trained upon, like a person who can only do one push-up. With some effort, this can be raised to two, and then three, and before you know it, the dishes become more and more exotic until—

Byblos crashes against the stove, thrown violently by a wave of raging water. Pots and pans fly in all directions, clattering against the walls with her as sauces and crèmes splatter and dilute in the wash. Lids fly all around the room, and the fires of hundreds of stoves are quenched, washing out the bones that had been crackling inside of them.

The demon's yellow eyes glare through the water, casting into her mind the distorted image of a woman standing across the room from her with her arm outstretched. The bolted-down table breaks free from the floor and crashes on its side, fully obscuring her vision.

The spell stops, and the room falls quiet, apart from the dripping of water and the clattering of metal. "Well," says a voice, "that handles that. Come on, let's go," orders Ruhr. "You. Go look for that brea—" The heavy table breaks as a hand tears through it from the other side. "Ah, fuck."

The wooden construct falls over as Byblos, drenched, rises to her feet with fists clenched and looks around the room. "My kitchen . . ." she mutters to herself, stepping forward in a daze with a hand against her head, her other hand running over the nearby cooking surface, puddles splashing beneath her feet. "My . . ." The gallu's eyes wander over everything that drips. All of her fires are out; all of the pots and pans and dishes are broken and scattered. Messes lie everywhere, as everything has been destroyed in the chaos of the spell.

Her work, all of her work . . .

Byblos cries out in pain, not at any injury but at the desecration of everything she's put so much hope and time into.

Chest heaving with anger as she stands there—water dripping down her soaked apron and wet hair—Byblos's hand slaps against the counter, grabbing hold of a chef's cleaver.

"LOOK OUT!" calls a voice, and a figure dives past, shoving Ruhr out of the way as the cleaver flies through the air. A loud metal clanging fills the air, and the man who stood behind them falls to the ground, his head split in two. The man behind him cowers behind his tower shield, into which the bloody cleaver is embedded. Ruhr lifts her head, looking over the priestess's shoulder at the raging demon.

Everything within the chamber begins to rattle, shaking and vibrating as the demon howl carries around the dripping space. The stoves crash into one another, rattling over the floor, and spill out their contents like vomiting maws in all directions. Doors fly open, and hinges break. Shelves collapse from the walls, and the furnishing all around the room falls apart and shatters as porcelain and metal alike both fall and both break—unnaturally—as they hit the ground. Raw and spoiled ingredients, meat and sinew, bone and grain—they all come together, flopping out of open pantries and sacks that tear open like eviscerated chests, as everything flows together into a mess.

Byblos screams, rushing forward in a blind rage toward the people she can't view as either guest or intruder in her kitchen anymore—they're less than vermin.

The crusade. She knows them and of them, and how they play into the Demon King's plans for the end of days, but he'll have to make do without them now because she will not stand for this disregard for everything that is sacred to her, this sacrilege against the true essence she has been after; it will not be overseen.

All around her jut out broken pieces of metal, broken glassware, and bent knives. Fractured plates and smoldering, jagged wood bursts out together in all directions like a gnashing mouth. In an instant, prismatic magical barriers—cast by the holy people of the crusade—form all around them, just as the broken teeth she has formed with her demon magic crash closed together. Splinters and shrapnel fly in all directions as they break on the shields on both sides of the wretches. The fracturing, cracking barriers move, pressing inwardly, as the force of her rage pushes against them from both sides, squeezing some back into the passage from whence they came, and others onward toward her like the flow from a punctured pustule.

And at the head of the movement is a blur of blue.

Byblos lifts an arm, thrusting out a fist and breaking the chair that is flung her way. Her other hand grabs a broken knife from the counter as she slashes, aiming for the gut of the river sorceress, which she intends to cleanly empty out from top to bottom. Maybe then there will be some space in the half elf for anything but such heartless cruelty.

The two of them collide, stumbling over a ruptured corpse that sits strapped to a half-broken chair.

The knife plunges toward Ruhr's core, but stops firmly when it strikes against something rigid, cutting through it but with a shrieking screech of metal against metal. Byblos looks down, glancing for a second at the pot lid that has blocked the blade. Twisting the lid in her hands, Ruhr tears the knife out of Byblos's hands.

Nodding her head to the side in that same moment, the massive collection of sludge and metal in the room moves at Byblos's behest. All of the broken furniture comes together and writhes, undulating like a worm. Stoves held together by pastes of meat and flour stir and scrape along the stone floors, disturbing the wet puddles as they tear along cabinets of broken wood, which pierce the scattered corpses and limbs around the destroyed kitchen. Like a serpent, it rises and then crashes down toward them both.

Spells fling from the crusade, blasting into the distorted monster as people file into the arena. Not everyone makes it, as the shields finally fail, giving in to the crush of the jagged maw. Blood spurts out in many directions as dozens of people are skewered in the mess that seals off the room. Those who are inside are inside, and those who were pressed back or never had a chance to enter are blocked by the writhing mess. Worst off are those in the middle, not all of whom have the luxury of a quick death.

Soldiers scatter all around the arena, running as they try to position themselves. The coagulation, the strange amalgamation of living and dead material, writhes as it moves after them. The giant smashes into the walls, roaring a wet roar as it flails around like a blind dragon.

Byblos's eyes twitch as she stares around her kitchen, looking at the rats scurrying all around it in many directions, looking in disgust until her eyes meet the ones of the avatar of all of her problems.

She's wasting her time.

For all of her life, she's been trying to perfect her craft, to perfect her recipes and techniques, so she can reach a point beyond the normal experience of living beings. For all of her life, she has been practicing and learning, spending her rare and preciously small cook's wages on recipes and foreign, exotic instructions on skills and concepts—all so she could get better. She's done nothing but suffer for her passion day after day after day in her pursuit of something pure and whole. And what does she get for her trouble? What has she always gotten?

Fetid, rotten ugliness.

The demon holds out her arms, an unseen force pulling objects from around the space toward her. The dripping walls of the kitchen tremble, like the lining of a stomach filling with acid, and the castle shakes, quaking in a rumble as the serpent crashes down onto a crusader, crushing her whole with its weight. Indiscriminate spray splatters out in all directions as the dust settles, spells blasting against the monster. It lifts itself up, roaring, and imprinted into its belly is a new addition of flesh and metal. The coagulation writhes, the terror—born not of the Demon King's magic but of the magic of a gallu—working to collect every last piece of scrap meat it can from the living, who are unable to repel it for more than a few moments at a time.

Water surges over her head, a needlelike jet stream cutting through the mass of flesh behind the demon, whose hands are filled with implements of her trade.

"You know what?" starts Ruhr as the two of them make eye contact again. "Forget the potatoes."

"Oh?" asks Byblos, shaking a little bottle of spices in her hands. "Really?" she says, soldiers screaming all around them as they fight the creature. "But the oven's just started getting hot," she remarks with a cold glare, throwing the red spice into the air.

The chamber all around them erupts, exploding with fury, as spontaneous fire fills the space, a great heat coming from almost nowhere at all, empowered by nothing but the demon's rage. The coagulation—its body made of just as many broken ovens as it has bones inside of it—bursts into flame, fire shooting out of dozens and dozens of metal doors, spewing in all directions, as the raw monster cooks itself. Flesh sizzles and bubbles as it turns, crashing down directly toward Ruhr.

The sorceress spins, blasting a stream of water directly into its lunging maw, and flinches at the burst of nearly boiling steam that comes from the collision of their magics, which blasts directly against her face. The half elf stumbles, clutching her face for a moment as Byblos considers her options.

The recipe has substance, and now it has a little spice. But it's missing flavor. A good flavor profile can be brought out through a reasonable level of fats and oils.

Casting out her hand, Byblos grabs a bottle and swings it outwardly, oil splashing across the area as Ruhr holds out her hands a second time, water leaking from her fingers.

A man screams as he's thrown against the wall and skewered there by a broken piece of wood layered in meat. The acid, which runs down the walls perpetually, drips and leaks over his spaulders and armor, leaking into the gaps between the metal plates. It runs down into the spaces between, into the fabric and against his body, which it slowly begins to eat away at.

Ruhr blasts out another spell, water flying toward the burning terror that now begins to drip and secrete oil from itself like a slime.

And then it all comes to a head.

The oil and water mix, carrying fire out in all directions. Rather than extinguishing the flames of the monster, the fresh grease fire carries down its body, out in all directions, as if she had projected a blast of incendiary fuel. Half of the chamber is engulfed in a massive explosion, the castle quaking and shaking. The walls ripple in and out unnaturally, acting in response to the explosion less like a rigid, stiff construction of brickwork and more like a soft, supple giving of pliable flesh. People scream everywhere in horror, running and rolling through the fires as they're soaked in burning fat.

Ruhr stumbles back, still clutching her face, as the blast wave presses against her. She falls down, splashing into a puddle, while anarchy takes the room.

Her dish has everything. It has acid, it has fat, heat, texture, flavor. But even this, even all of this, isn't enough to reach where she needs it to be. She can tell as much as she looks and listens and feels the many experiences had by many souls as they partake in her work.

Nobody is enjoying her food, her work, her creation. She can see it in their eyes, on their faces. She can hear it in their voices as they yell and howl and fight and run.

They hate it.

Byblos screams and screams and screams, holding her head as everything all around her breaks down. Her nails dig into her skin, pressing through her scalp and all the way to her skull, which she can feel being scratched as she vexes and curses and lets everything she has in her out.

She was too arrogant.

She had assumed that she was on the right path, but was she really? She had assumed her craft would get her to that place, to that elevated state of existence that she desires in her core. But she was half wrong.

Perhaps she has the tools. Perhaps she has the ingredients. Perhaps she has the skills. But the environment, the setting, is entirely wrong. She's trying to create a banquet for the soul while sitting inside a collapsed ruin. The eyes eat just as much as the mouth. But the eyes wander. They don't just look at the plate and at the bowl; they don't just look at their table partner—they also gaze all around them at the space they reside in.

And in this world, in this wretched, disgusting physical world filled with nothing but base, disgusting souls of the same low caliber, there is nothing to look at except mud, filth, and ashes.

There is no beauty to be found here, and just the same, trying to create it in a place like this—in a world like this—is a fool's endeavor.

All there is to do, in order to come even a step closer to that place of paradise, is to erase it all. The Demon King really is right in his decision to remove the overpowering weight of the festering rot that is physicality, to purge all of reality in order to wipe the table clean and provide a sanitary, pleasant table where all can feast in the sight of true beauty.

It all just needs to go.

Hellfire fills the chamber as greasy, burning water runs down the walls and bodies that line it, the flames hissing high toward the ceiling like claws trying to dig free from the dirt covering a heavy grave. Byblos grabs a broken cleaver, swinging it out. The serpent of metal and flesh rips apart as if she had cleaved it herself, the head splitting down the middle in a jagged fashion, first in two, and then in four, the hydra thrashing around within the blaze as magic erupts all around the crackling chamber.

She's put everything she has into it, and it's all still not enough for these people. It has never been enough: she, her work—it has all simply never been enough.

It's time to put an end to all of this.

Byblos lifts her hand, holding the cleaver as she adds the finishing touches to her creation.

Something grabs her from behind as she swings the cleaver in a forward arc, the disrupted movement guiding the serpent to crash against a nearby wall, which it shatters. The gallu falters, stumbling as a person wraps their arms around her shoulders from the back, the two of them rolling across the puddled water where fire spreads through like food poisoning through an inflicted body.

The demon screams, fighting with the other, turning and rolling around to press off the weight of . . . somebody.

A crusader has latched on to her, their robes and armor burnt, their hair wet and matted with grease and old blood. "NOW!" yells the man, pressing down against her with his forearm as she easily starts to lift him off her with her raw strength—even all of his mass and metal armor weighing down on her is nothing for the power gifted to her by the Demon King. "DO IT!" screams the crusader as he claws against the ground, trying his best to pin her down in vain.

Until her lifting comes to a stop.

Byblos's eyes are filled with light as a greater shine comes to eye, her arms unable to leverage anymore as the man above her, whom she had been pushing toward the ceiling, can be pushed no further. "What the—" Her eyes go wide as she looks around the arena, where, in the fire, stand many people of the holy faith holding their hands out and projecting barriers—not at her sides, at the left or the right, but directly above her, creating a new, much lower ceiling only a foot above her face where she lies on the ground. The man's back presses against it.

"GET OFF OF ME!" screams the gallu, trying to force him, but there is no space. She succeeds in crushing some of his armor, some of his bones, but the man who coughs out a spurt of blood over her face holds firm as water soaks into her back.

"No," replies the unremarkable crusader, no more than a man like any other. He's not a man of distinct title or rank; not a man of famous history or of unique power. He's simply a man who put on some armor and marched in the direction he knew he had to go. His hands grab her, despite the breaking of his ribs and core. Byblos's eyes look around at the greasy water that moves toward them, the fire that claws its way closer and closer as it spreads around the grease.

The serpent dives in, hammering from above on the barrier, breaking only one of many, as there are stacks and stacks of them layered over her, like the layers of a pastry dough.

And as her head turns toward the side, her eyes stare at a single, colorless silhouette hidden by the shadows and light of the chaos, its slender, bony form rising up to its weak feet and holding its arms out toward her prison one last time.

"GET OFF!" yells Byblos, perhaps more instinctively than anything, as she knows it's already over. Her eyes stare at the one who has prepared this creation, *this*, for her. As the hands point her way, taking the same position as all of those around her, Byblos understands the problem with her technique.

They say that too many cooks will spoil the broth, but too few can leave it weak.

Her desires were too large for her hands alone to hold.

"Cooking together is more fun than alone," jokes the man, knowing they're both about to die. It's not that he can read her thoughts; it's just that he's making a morbid remark about their death to come, and it just so happens to fit with exactly what she's thinking now. Some might call such a thing coincidence, or perhaps synchronicity, if one were to go a stage deeper. Some might imply that the universe is watching and guiding her life, the same as it orchestrates all events that happen within it. Or maybe it really is just dumb chance.

Ruhr the river sorceress lifts her hands, a stream of wild water propelling the grease fire directly toward the trap that the gallu and the crusader with no name are inside of.

"Yeah . . ." concedes Byblos, the demon cook, as her hands grab his sides and hold on to them while the fire propels toward them both, the greasy, burning water shoving its way down beneath the glassy magical barriers into the trap and consuming them both whole.

~ [The Demon King] ~

And so, comes to an end the artistry of another passionate soul.

Swain sits on his throne, like he always does, as he watches and observes the happenings of the world all around him; as he watches the steam and smoke rise out of the furnace, together with the tufts of soul that drift and fade—not toward his collection, but toward the other place, the distant place where he is soon to be himself.

It's not that the Demon King doesn't cherish and care for his gallu, his most loyal and devoted servants, the ones whose souls are the closest to his own. Each and every one of them shares with him the true heart, the true yearning.

Yet, he sits here and watches in silence, not feeling much of anything stir inside his chest as he does so. Not a tug, not a pull, not a weight— nothing. The Demon King feels nothing as Byblos, one of his own and his first and only lover, dies.

Because the truth is, that while he is watching, while he is listening, he really isn't.

His eyes might stare, but his inner sight wanders from feature to feature, from smell to sense, as it tries to piece together the face and wholeness of the person he has—in any life of his—sought after the most. As screams fill the air and fall silent, the Demon King has nothing on his mind but the destruction of this world so that he might finally return the rot inside his soul to the one who had set it there to begin with.

And by the time he returns to focus, the fires have died out, the smoke has cleared, and the chamber where the gallu, Byblos, had been is nothing more except an empty room filled with puddles, soot, and some leftovers that nobody wants to eat.

But who needs food at a time like this?

Tomorrow will be a new day, after all.

At least, it will be if he doesn't get his way.

CHAPTER 16

IN THE EYE OF THE BEHOLDER

~ [Zacarias] ~
Human | ♂ | Royal Guard
Location: The Demon King's Castle, Floor Negative Three

What happened to him?

Zacarias marches onward, toward the chamber further ahead, the troops marching at his back.

He was with Ruhr in that . . . puppet chamber, or whatever it was. He remembers. But then . . .

The man holds his head as he walks, metal armor rattling all around him.

But then something took him, grabbed him. A trap?

He's not sure, but the next thing he knew, he was back at the beginning of the Demon King's castle all over again. What is this, the third time now? At this point, he's going to know this place inside out like his own house.

His house . . .

The man stops, lifting his gaze toward the darkness above his head as he tries to picture that place in his mind, but he just . . . can't. His house, his home—whatever was before this place simply isn't anymore. It's gone. There's no going back to it from here. He is himself one of the souls who is now destined to be bound to the underworld forevermore. Of this, he has no doubts.

"Guardsman Zacarias?" speaks someone at his side. He turns his head to look at the captain of the troop, who is nervously following his gaze toward the ceiling.

"Nothing," replies Zacarias, shaking his head. "Just lost in thoughts," explains the man as he marches onward. "Come on. We've made good progress so far; let us make more. Time is short."

The captain nods, the legion marching behind them. "We'd be lost without your guidance," he remarks. "This place, these designs . . . I've never seen such nightmares before."

Zacarias walks on in contemplative silence for a time before shaking his head. "You get used to them. These patterns—They've changed the floor layouts since we were here last, but . . ."

"But?" asks the captain.

Zacarias rubs his chin as he walks.

"It's . . ." He thinks for a time, trying to find his words. "It's the same creator."

The captain looks at him with a puzzled look as Zacarias holds a hand against a wall, letting it slide along the surface while they move. Seeing that he doesn't understand, Zacarias goes on. "It's like a different song, but sung by the same singer," he explains. "You know the words are different and everything, but the foundation of it all is the same as it was before. It's new, but it's not."

While he and the captain met up on the second floor of the castle, they're making rapid progress nonetheless toward the higher floors, which used to be the lower ones during his first two runs of the Demon King's dungeon. The rooms and chambers really are different in many ways, the layouts and designs having changed; in many cases, the monsters and traps as well.

But the fundamental idea and threat behind each section is still essentially the same as it was before. If he didn't know better, he would have said the creator—the Demon King, or whoever else made these places— isn't quite as creative as they thought themselves to be. The secret mechanisms, the locks, and the hidden doors, all such things are still what they were before, just painted slightly different or put in a different place. The changes of the great creation that is the Demon King's castle are, to put it kindly, cosmetic and surface level.

Inside, deep in the core of the beast, the same heart beats as it did before.

If this keeps up, he's going to have a chance of catching up with Ruhr before she makes it to the throne room. They have to—*He* has to. He knows she can't be dead; she's too much of a stubborn jackass to die, but she doesn't know that he's still alive. Him and her, they're a team. She needs his help, and he won't let her, after everything they've been through since this all began, fight the Demon King alone.

"Perhaps we might live to see a new day yet," remarks the captain. "I dare say that you are giving me hope, Guardsman."

Zacarias walks onward. "I wouldn't," is all he replies with as the legion moves on to its next point of conflict.

A strange light comes from ahead of them. It is different than the orange torch glow that illuminates their path. Rather, it is a cool, moonlight shine. The light is almost unnaturally white and soft.

The legion stops, looking into the chamber.

A bridge lies ahead of them, wide enough to easily cross in groups. However, below it is a deep chasm on either side, in which only blackness can be seen. It spans toward a large, flat, fully featureless rectangular platform that is free on all sides. On the far side of the mostly sterile room is a second bridge just like the first that leads out through the other side. Given the odd lightfall, the core platform seems to be painted almost vividly white, in contrast with the dark frames of the bridges on either side.

And in the center of it all, strung up like a puppet, is a single human woman—a partially disrobed priestess of the crusade. Her arms are splayed to her sides, with a single bundle on either end binding her to the far-off walls, her feet hovering above the ground, just barely over it, so that her toes occasionally scrape the stones by just a touch, but never enough that she could stand. Blood stains the ground below her. She's muttering something to herself, but her words never carry far enough to be clearly understood.

"What is this devilry?" asks the captain.

"A trap," remarks Zacarias, dryly, as if this were the most obvious thing in the world. He eyes the woman, not sure if he recognizes her or not from this distance. Although he thinks that he does recall seeing glances of her here and there during his march together with Ruhr and the crusade. The priestess has very recognizable and unique facial features, which make her easy to remember.

The men watch uneasily from the distance.

"It seems to me that we have no choice but to spring it," remarks the captain.

Zacarias nods once, gesturing for them to stay back as he lifts his massive tower shield—covered in marks and scars to the point of it being nigh unrecognizable—and walks on ahead by himself toward the muttering silhouette suspended in the air; a lone figure within the massive chamber.

The ceiling is giant and vaulted, the walls plain and smooth, as if there was intentionally nothing here to see except her. As if she were a piece on display within a gallery.

The ground rumbles, quaking, and Zacarias stops, feeling his legs shift somewhat but then steady again.

"Stay back!" he barks, gesturing to the soldiers behind him, some of whom had started walking forward.

The ground, the central platform, has begun to sway left and right.

The bridges aren't bridges—they're pivots. The room is a rectangle in the middle attached on either side to a pivot point. Zacarias watches the platform's edges slowly shift again. Like a waterwheel, it threatens to tip to either direction, given enough weight on any particular point.

The muttering grows louder and louder as he approaches the centerpiece, looking at the woman. Her arms are outstretched and bound by what looks like a black cord on either end, but of an oddly wet and slick material that he can't identify immediately. Like ropes made from bundles, they are wound together and woven into a single, thick cord that catches at her wrists and attach to two pillars on either side of the platform.

"—eautiful. I'm beautiful. I'm beautiful," mutters the woman to herself over and over again, her shaky words carrying across the space toward him now as he comes closer and closer to look at her.

"Hey, hey!" calls Zacarias in a half-hushed voice that doesn't seem to reach her. She just keeps muttering to herself, her eyes staring down at the ground as if imprinting on it, her mouth just muttering the repeated affirmation over and over again. The blood that runs down her legs splatters against the floor; it has left a slight trail, as the swaying platform caused it to run down toward the left for a moment. "Look at me!"

The priestess stops muttering, her mouth still somewhat agape as she lowers her eyes, looking at him in silence for a moment.

"What happ—"

"DON'T LOOK AT ME!" she screams in a banshee shriek, spit flying out of her mouth as she writhes, kicking and howling, pulling at her arms and legs as she dangles there above the ground at the cords that, Zacarias realizes now, aren't around her wrists. They're in them. Bundles of veins and arteries have been cut free and pulled out to be wrapped delicately around wire that suspends itself from wall to wall.

"DON'T LOOK AT ME! DON'T LOOK AT ME!" she screams and howls and cries, her legs kicking out toward him. Her flailing puts tears and rips in the binds that hold her aloft, blood spurting out of her body as veins rip because of her fighting. Zacarias grabs her, trying to hold her steady as her fighting and movements send vibrations along the wire toward the posts on either side of the rectangle, causing it to start swaying.

"STOP MOVING!" yells Zacarias, looking behind himself to judge the distance. It's too late to run back. It's too far. The platform begins to shift to the side, his feet starting to angle. The woman screams like a haunting banshee.

The platform stops, locking in place as the tilt ends.

The soldiers behind him had thought quickly and moved in to counterbalance, several of them having gone up toward the lifting edge so that their weight would push it back down again.

"Don't touch me!" she yells, a knee striking him on the side of his face, causing Zacarias to stumble back and hold his jaw. "I'm beautiful . . . He told me I'm beautiful," mutters the woman, who clearly isn't all there in her mind anymore, as evidenced by her eyes, which stare around, looking at things that he can't see, but she can.

"I'm art. I'm beautiful. Only he can touch me. Only his hands . . . him . . ." she mutters, the blood that falls down her legs leaking toward the puddle. The streak of blood that has hit the ground goes farther and farther, creating a line that runs almost perfectly toward the edge of the space, until it begins to drip over the side. "He made me feel beautiful," she says, staring with not madness or uncertainty but warmth in her eyes. "I can still feel him. He's still here."

She's too far gone. This woman can't be saved. The safest thing to do is to put her out of her misery so they can cross safely. If she has another episode, it could send all of them down into the pit.

"Close your eyes," says Zacarias, reaching down with his free hand for the knife on his belt. "I'm going to cut you down," he lies. "It might hurt."

"NO!" she screams, flailing again, stronger than before. Zacarias stumbles, falling over sideways as he, in his heavy armor, loses his footing when the platform shifts. He slides toward the edge, his hands gripping the stones as he falls toward the pit and falls off the edge.

But he doesn't plummet.

A chain wraps itself around his torso and pulls him back, the casters of the legion—still standing on the entryway bridge—working together to form a bind that catches him at the last second. Together, they tug and heave him back up toward the wobbling platform.

Panting, he crawls forward, smearing over the blood that drips over the edge with his armor as he waves to them once briefly as thanks before looking back up at the muttering woman, who has returned to her self-affirmations and vacant staring.

Okay. They'll need to just shoot her with a crossbow. It's grim, but there's nothing else to be done here.

The legionnaires seem to have come to the same consensus, as the captain has three men ready with their weapons—enough to ensure that her death will be quick, even at this distance.

Zacarias gives his nod of approval, crawling back to the center and rising to his feet.

Three clangs fill the air as crossbow bolts fly free from their weapons, propelled through the air at a speed that is almost too fast for the human eye to follow.

The priestess's shadow, cast down as a single dark splotch on the moonlight-white platform with stripes of red, reacts fully unnaturally, entering the dimension of height from its flat base. A projection of light-lessness bursts out from below her, all three crossbow bolts striking it and stopping unnaturally in the air only inches from her face and heart.

"Please," speaks a voice from the shadow. "Mind yourselves," says a man whom Zacarias can't see. The priestess lifts her head, stopping her muttering as she smiles a delusional, vivid smile. The bolts all clatter to the ground, rattling as they roll away, having done no harm. The unnatural shadow they had struck simply regenerates its form, as if nothing had happened.

"The artistic process is very . . ." A man steps out of the shadow as if it were a doorway. The priestess leans forward against the restraints that pull through her marrow, tugging tight against her own extracted blood vessels as she tries to move closer to him, to the gray man who appears and looks back at her. The demon turns, lifting a hand and holding it against the side of her face. She smiles and closes her eyes, resting her cheek in his palm. ". . . *delicate*."

Zacarias whistles.

Without much talk or explanation, a full volley of crossbow bolts and spells blasts out directly toward the creature, who is unmistakably a powerful demon.

He doesn't have time for whiff-whaff and posturing. He has to get to Ruhr.

Standing in the middle of the platform, between the smoking center and the legion, Zacarias lifts his shield, as he knows it's never that easy in this hellhole.

The smoke begins to clear, and as it does, the silhouette of a man and a woman—a demon and a strung-up, broken-minded person—becomes visible, both of the haunted souls locked in a kiss with ash stuck between their lips.

Zacarias grips his shield tighter as the demon lets go of her. "Please . . ." she begs, a tear running down her face. "Make me beautiful," she pleads to the gray creature as his hand leaves her face, his yellow eyes parting from hers as they turn through the smoke toward the intruders.

"Even I wouldn't dare try to change such perfection," he tells her, swinging out a brush toward Zacarias like a fencer would a blade. He stands with his back to the priestess, like a knight guarding a princess.

But the black ink that flies free from the tip of the brush streaks behind him, not toward Zacarias, in a perfect, straight line that falls over the strung-up priestess from bottom to top. The platform begins to rumble and shake as the priestess jolts once the ink strikes her, the black, tepid mess splattering over her body like a dividing line—to which her flesh acts accordingly.

As if pulled on strongly from both sides, she rips in half cleanly down the middle. Her arms are pulled further apart as the snaking veins and arteries crawl down along the metal wires, like snakes. Her skin rips open, her muscles rip open, and even her skeleton cracks jaggedly as if someone had simply taken hold of her with two massive hands and ripped her cleanly apart.

Gore and bile and sloppy entrails fall out of her into a steaming heap on the ground. But her body doesn't break apart into two pieces; instead, the wire runs through her, holding her together. It hadn't just been fed into her wrists; it had been pulled down her arms, her shoulders, through her core over and over again before exiting out the other side. The metal coil pulls through her like a single, massive parasitic worm that has overtaken its host from head to toe. Organs stick to it, as does one of her eyes. The other carries away as the coil moves, taking chunks of her further and further away. The unbalanced platform wobbles as the demon arcs his brush out again—but only just to barely touch the tip of Zacarias's shield, who has already charged toward him.

But he makes contact with nothing except for a red wire.

Zacarias looks around his tower shield, expecting to see the demon there, but he's gone. Instead, he's rammed into the bloody spool.

"Yes, continue!" says a voice from behind him. Zacarias turns, his armored wrist striking where he expects a person to be. Instead, it simply collides with stone. Rocks crumble and fall as Zacarias stares in confusion at the square stone column that appeared behind him silently, instantly, as a single disruption atop the perfectly rectangular arena.

He charges around it, the platform shaking and wobbling as the soldiers move, running along both sides at the same time in order to force a balance. On the other side is the demon, holding his brush, standing on a string of metal wire that . . . just can't be here.

Zacarias looks in confusion, staring at the wire that is behind him, and the wire that is front of him now—a new one. But the same pieces of the priestess slide along it, some chunks of meat draped like old, wet laundry. The man grabs his knife, throwing it from his belt at the demon, who dodges with almost childish ease, the blade flying off into the distance and rattling into the pit below.

"More," demands the creature, holding the brush in his hands between his lips for a moment. "You're just what I've been waiting for," says the demon painter, casting a new arc all around him. Black paint flies in all directions, from the tip of a brush that never seems to dry or run out of color. Like shadows, the color holds stiff and firm in its lightlessness everywhere it lands—impossibly so. Black ink clings to invisible corners in the air. Black ink hangs and floats as it drapes over unseen ledges and stairs. Black ink drip and drops as it flows down through grooves that don't yet exist.

But then they do.

Wherever the ink touches, the flat arena changes and shifts to meet the expectation of the artist. Brickwork rises and holds flat, forming platforms and walkways all around them in seconds that ruby wires crisscross between. Zacarias runs as the ground beneath him wobbles, climbing up a staircase that comes into existence as he charges up toward the demon painter. From the painter's back emerges a shadow that clings onto a wire one stage higher and pulls the two of them up, out of Zacarias' reach. He's too slow. If only Ruhr were here.

"Mind the paint," remarks the demon, looking his way. "It's still wet," he says, biting his tongue.

"Beautiful, beautiful, beautiful," comes from next to him. Zacarias watches as a broken chunk of meat, once half of a lower jaw, continues to move, sliding along a copper wire, and somehow still speaking over and over and over again that which it wants most in life. Teeth hang out at their roots, dangling like jewelry as he runs past the red chunk, chasing after the demon.

The platform tips, too much weight added on one side by the constructions that come into time and space from nowhere at all except a twisted imagination. Crossbow bolts fire in rapid succession from below as the legionnaires do what they can, but the painter can't be touched, between his nimbleness as he dodges everything with almost lackluster ease and those shadows that he emits from himself, which steal the bolts that come too close.

Zacarias leaps across a gap as a new platform emerges below him. "Fight me, demon!" yells the man at the entity, who seems to be doing nothing but fleeing, yet still creates more and more walkways and platforms and pillars through which the wires connect.

The demon stops and spins, ink flying toward him. Zacarias holds his shield up, the streak cutting straight over it. A second later, a clean, diagonal piece of shield falls off toward the ground below, which he only now realizes the distance of.

The painter laughs, working on some unseen strategy that Zacarias can't identify as he occasionally attacks a soldier with his ink, rendering the victim into nothing but a screaming heap of red, or creates new platforms and walkways. Before long, the arena—which had been entirely flat, suspended between the two bridges—is a fully chaotic mixture of walkways and paths and stairs that lead in all manner of impossible directions.

Zacarias leaps toward a ledge, barely catching it and even less barely being able to pull himself up it thanks to the weight of his armor.

As he rises, he finds himself standing on a single straight walkway. On the far side is the demon painter. The guardsman readies his shield, seeing nowhere else to go from here, this high up in the chamber. They're coming closer and closer to the dungeon's ceiling.

"It's not enough . . . It's not enough!" cries the demon, almost distressed, as he clutches his hair. "Unless . . . Yes . . . Yes!" he shouts, holding his arms out to his sides and turning around. The platform wobbles and shakes, the balance of the whole thing becoming far more than precarious at this point. The demon painter looks at Zacarias, who stands opposite him a good ten paces away. "Do you know what separates a good artist from a great one?" asks the servant of the Demon King.

Zacarias takes a step forward, feeling the arena tilt ever so slightly as the balance shifts, causing him to almost fall forward. The demon, standing with his back to the ledge, holds his arms out wide.

"Expensive paint?" asks Zacarias.

"Yes!" replies the demon, shaking his head. "Good paint is very expensive," he concedes. "But more than that," says the creature, taking a step back toward the edge of the ledge.

The arena tilts.

"Unconventionality," finishes the demon, as the floor, the entire arena, begins to rotate on its axis at an unrecoverable angle. Ink, blood, and color run in all directions as people scream and grab on to whatever they can. Zacarias, being up the highest, has nowhere to fall but straight toward the demon waiting there with open arms.

The arena shifts; Zacarias feels a lurching in his gut as the entire space rotates a full ninety, and then finally, a full one hundred and eighty degrees, leaving the arena upside down. His hair, his weight, and his blood all press downward, threatening to fall—but they never do. Zacarias looks down at his ankles, staring at the magical chains that tether him to the walkway—the same kind that the legionnaires had used to catch him before, when he almost fell off.

"Isn't this better?" asks the demon, walking toward him, both of their hair hanging upside down. "I find it so much easier to work without a roof over my head," he remarks, the shadow that permeates him tapping the side of his head for him. He stares up toward what is below, at what might be an endless abyss that they hover over.

"There's nowhere to run now," remarks Zacarias, ready to give his life's fortune to whatever quick-thinking caster came up with the idea for this spell just now. He watches the legionnaires out of the corner of his eye, as they latch on to walls and platforms, clinging to upside-down stairwells and climbing to sit on the back sides of them, where they can be right side up again.

The demon's smile comes close enough to be clear, but not to reach with a fist. The brush, tipped with black ink that never dries, extends toward him. "No, my good man. You're wrong," replies the demon. "There's nowhere to go but up!" he exclaims with a flick of his wrist, droplets of ink splashing toward Zacarias, who catches it with his shield, which falls apart entirely now—except for a small drop that strikes the magical chain.

"SH—"

Zacarias plummets, falling directly into a nest of wires, grabbing on and holding to the slippery mess, his fingers pressing down around a calf muscle that has been stretched apart and woven around the piece like a spider's silk. He clings on for his life, his arms and legs wrapped between many different pieces of copper.

Below him emerge more and more platforms as the arena continues to grow, now spreading deeper toward the endless darkness, since it cannot grow higher.

"We're almost there!" calls a voice.

Zacarias swings on the cables for a moment, to try and put some momentum into them, until his hands reach a new wall that wasn't there a moment ago. He crawls over it, not even sure anymore if he is upside down or right side up. His senses are entirely off now. But out of the corner of his eye, he sees bolts and magic explode as they hit the spot where the demon was. An arc of black ink flies out of the smoke, drawing a clean line across a man with a crossbow, who stumbles back, clutching his chest in fear as he looks over himself, knowing what happens to anyone who is touched by the mess.

Nothing happens.

He looks around in confusion at his compatriots, who watch him already, expecting him to die.

"Just kidding," says a voice from behind the marked soldier, who never falls apart.

Instead, two shadowy hands plunge out of the wall and shove him off the ledge. He falls, screaming as he vanishes into the abyss, the magical chain around his leg holding firm as it drops after him as if he were an anchor flung from a ship. Unfortunately, there is a little too much give in its length, and he plummets with such speed and force that the wrap around his ankle tears his foot cleanly off as he strikes the breaking point, and the rest of him is taken by the abyss.

Zacarias moves, noting that the shadow and the demon itself can separate and move as individuals.

But the painter isn't even really fighting him; he's just moving and dodging and creating new places to run. What is this?

Catching his breath, Zacarias looks around himself, trying to find the enemy, His eyes wander down, expecting to see the floor of the arena, but he doesn't. A new disorientation, if even possible at this point, runs through Zacarias as he stares toward the heights below him, where he cannot even see the flat origin from which he came.

"Here," says a voice from behind.

Zacarias turns, lifting his arms together as a wrist strikes his. The black ink flies over his head, splattering along the path as he guards the painter's arm. The heavy man lunges. The nimble painter dodges. Zacarias swipes and strikes with his fist and remaining shield, only for the thin, bony demon to shoot from side to side, up and around, with the brush flying this way and that—the ink never hitting him, but hitting just about everything else as he keeps the enemy on the ropes and never lets him get a clean shot in. He's not as fast as him, not fast enough to get a fistful of him, but he's fast enough to keep the pressure on.

The two of them fight like this, carrying their exchange from walkway to walkway, platform to platform, as bolts rain down from above or below—he's unsure—always caught by the shadow that acts as a shield as the two of them perpetuate this odd chase of theirs.

"This is it!" says the painter, the demon looking almost through him as he dodges another strike, blocking it with a wrist. "Just a touch here, a stroke there—!"

"What are you talking about?" barks Zacarias, sweat running up his blood-rushed face as he holds out his hands, preparing a spell.

(Zacarias) has used: [Royal Barrier]

A wall appears behind the painter, blocking his retreat, as Zacarias arcs his arm back for one final, solid punch.

The painter holds his brush out between them, Zacarias's arm stopping as it comes close to hitting the inky tip.

"The final stroke is yours," says the demon. "Make it beautiful."

The brush, held gently between his fingers, is allowed to rotate freely, and so it does—turning toward the ground on which they impossibly stand. The ink drips up the brush, against gravity, as if it were moving with it, a single droplet striking between their feet.

Below them, the platform shoots straight toward the abyss. Copper wires, strung in all directions, spool and hiss as they sit attached the pillar. Pieces of meat and organs carry around, the impossible mess contained within a single human body stretching further and further like an ink that never dilutes.

Zacarias grabs the man's wrist as they fly, tearing the brush from his hands and slicing a clean streak across his face from left to right, above his smile and below his nose.

The painter's face cuts cleanly in half, following the line. The shadow behind the painter drapes around him like a mantle, holding his severed head in place so that the cutoff piece doesn't fall off just yet—just so he can see it once before it's over.

His masterpiece.

The platform stops moving, and Zacarias, confused, follows the demon's gaze, looking back down at the rectangular arena they left behind as the two of them hover in the abyss.

The perforations, the platforms and stairwells, the copper wire, the organs and smears and red and bloody streaks, the ashen marks of spellcraft, and the broken chunks where the painter had dodged and guided attacks—all come together into one whole construct.

Zacarias stares down from the tower on which he stands at the grim mess below him, a copper wire running parallel to him with an eyeball stuck to it.

From up here, from this perspective that nobody except him, the painter, and a single severed eye share—all good things being a part of three—is visible a single, great, colossal painting, the moonlit-white stone acting as a canvas, and all of the colors of their work just now smearing and coming together. The stone, the constructs—all of these give depth and shadows and texture to what may be the greatest work of a truly demented mind.

Zacarias stares at the picture.

"Is that a . . . ?" he mutters to himself, looking back at the painter just in time to watch the killed demon fall apart into two pieces and plummet into the abyss, taking his shadow with him.

What even is this place?

Zacarias shakes his head, getting the image out of his focus and mind, as he instead tries to figure out how he's meant to get out—or more promptly, up or down from here. He's still not entirely sure which way he's standing.

Presented there, for no eyes other than his own now to see, is a single, nonsensical picture of a silly goose, sitting by a pond in a ruby sunset.

He doesn't really understand.

But they say that artists tend to be eccentric types, after all. It probably doesn't mean anything, really.

CHAPTER 17

THE GRAND TERROR — PHANTASMAGORIA

~ [The Demon King] ~

There isn't much time left.

All of this, everything, is going to come to an end very soon. The world is now filled with nothing but fear, darkness, and death, bringing it much closer to the truth of its nature than it was before. Before the demon era had begun, men lived their lives below the sunshine of fresh days, keeping themselves occupied with trivialities in order to convince themselves that the passing of their idle lives was a noble and good thing; occupying themselves so that they would have no choice but to ignore the horror that festered within the world for decades and centuries—the ugliness.

Perhaps once, in a day now long since forgotten, in times when men and their souls were in likeness with one another and not in such discordance, sisters and mothers and brothers and friends and neighbors all knew their truth in the world and the purpose of their creation. Perhaps such a time had once existed in a long bygone era; who can say for sure? But those times, if they ever really were, are long, long gone.

And ever since those fables of a world of old, there has been a plaster, a wrap, pressed around the festering rot. If one had intervened sooner, if a fire hundreds of years ago had burned brighter, perhaps it could all have been prevented. Perhaps none of this would have had to happen.

But it did.

The rot that overtook the world, and the decay that defiled the last remnant of pure beauty, have long since consumed everything of wholeness and value, leaving only a broken, dead world for the inheritors of future generations, to which he himself belonged. And because of the cumulations of the past, there is only bitterness and ugliness left to reap by the people of his day, who, knowing nothing better, assume that the bitter flowers they smell are the roses spoken of in angelic texts and forgotten historical whispers.

But they are so, so far away.

And this is why a Demon King is necessary; this is why he and his pursuit are both not just noble but good.

The people of this world cling to it and life so desperately, but they simply don't understand the ugliness that has overtaken from soul to their flesh. They know nothing other than he depravity of this existence, having never known another world and another probability. And so, they cling to the rottenness that is ever present and bite it like nesting pests attacking a logger who must fell the rotting tree in which they reside.

His precious few, cherished souls knew this the same as he does.

Cartouche, Byblos, Abydos—their journey together in the physical world has been all but brief, far, far shorter than he would have wished for in any other time and age. But there is no mourning in his black heart; no weeping in his terrible chamber apart from the howling of tormented souls. Their deaths were necessary, beautiful things which they chose in their own way, knowing a simple truth that floats through the Demon King's castle in a whisper: life and death in this physical world are, in and of themselves, creations of art that one must guide and craft upon, the same as any dance, any dish, or any painting.

The exact path one takes can either be ugly or beautiful; as much as can be in this world, at least.

Other gallu still remain, such as the rabbit, but of his cherished core creators, only Peribsen remains alive in the physical realm, and he wanders the castle, studying and learning from its ways with keen interest. Knowledge is for him as much of a tool of beauty as paints for Abydos or spices for Byblos, and so he hones his craft for the time of his great creation.

Swain looks around his crumbled throne room at the decayed, broken statues that had once decorated it, which the weight of his grown power crushed into rubble. His eyes scan the table at which he and his fellowship had sat for many meals and stories. They wander further, toward the corridor in which the gallu housed and lived—toward the hallway in which he often found them while they played games together and learned of each other's names and personalities.

Those times, as strange and short as they were, were for a creature as odd and confusing as the Demon King . . . beautiful.

There isn't much time left.

The city will fall very soon.

The crusade will finally arrive in his chambers very soon.

And he will break through everything that separates him from the spirit world, shattering it violently with the force of one million souls so that this will be over very soon.

"Paper," orders Swain, a tormented soul flying over and delivering a sheet that begins to crinkle at the edges as it smolders black from the heat of his body.

He can sense her, feel her—the creature who made him this way; that entity who only ever needed to speak but one word to captivate his heart in those young days.

He can feel the souls of his compatriots there on the other side, not far now.

His hand reaches out toward the empty chamber ahead of him, in which cinders fly and spirits dance in their haunting waltz to commemorate the end of days.

But it grasps nothing as it closes again.

And the Demon King sits in his empty throne room, staring at the paper with his ten thousand eyes as he writes the poem to bring upon this world one last final terror. The paper charcoals and folds in as he writes, and it burns away to ash as he holds it.

Let it be so.

By the time he sets the last mark, the paper has all but fully combusted, the poem crumbling to ash down in his lap, only to be blown away by the rising heat of the Demon Core, the spirit and the spell of the poem carrying off and away and out into the world, toward the place it needs to be.

~ [The Human Capital] ~

All around the city, the dome perplexingly begins to uncover. Claws stop scratching, teeth stop gnawing, fists stop hammering, and wings stop beating as monsters of all ilk slowly, one after the other, begin to fall away from the protective shield they cannot break.

A piece of sky becomes clear, and then another, and another.

Soon, the few brave stars that remain in the night sky can be seen peeking through once again—a relieving sight for some, and a horrific one for others, depending on one's take on life.

Within the hour, the dome is clear, and people stand within the city, staring up and around, unsure as to what is happening. The castle remains where it is, imprisoning them, but every beast draws away into the darkness which none of their lanterns and spells can reach.

Confused and on alert, this city watch and soldiers run and prepare for war, assuming some trickery is afoot. What else could it be?

Those with sharp eyes in the center of the city's market might look up and see the first smear.

Red pulp, a finely ground paste of mush and rotting corpse, drips onto the dome: the finely ground and mashed prisoners who had marched all this way under the guard of the demon generals, sacrificed to become nothing more than paste. All of their flesh, all of their lives, hopes, dreams, and memories add up to nothing more than a smear of dark, off-brownish red that now slides over the top of the shield protecting the human capital.

People murmur and whisper, shouting as they watch more and more such droplets appear over their heads. The red runs only ever so slightly until an unseen force, like a finger from above, presses down on it and begins to write one letter after the other, one line after the other, over their heads on the shield. The creation spans across the barrier, each letter as large as a house and each word as long as a street, as what can only be the devil's own hand continues to scrawl over their heads, like a hand writing their gravestone while they are lying below with eyes wide open, their calls unable to reach all of those around the open grave watching them being lowered deeper into the darkness.

The Phantasmagoria
Lantern light may dim down low,
To hide the shine of man-made glow,
Below the drape of heaven's shield,
And below the weight of demons' yield,
Men may run and men may crawl,

Through tunnels and homes and wall to broken wall,
Yet upon them, projected, will be horror untold,
From midnight—protected,
But from terror—beholden,
Upon the firmament canvas high above their heads,
Projects phantasmagoria down into their simple old
beds,
The illusion outside becomes the monster within,
The mind of man is taken from both his mother and kin,
And each to his own is brought up to the height of his
head,
As he stands below what is above,
And above what is dead,
For Phantasmagoria is a beast most unique,
In that it does not need enter,
To touch what it reaps,
For it is not there within the dome of the last men,
But rather within the eyes there, trapped, therein,
It suspends,
They see and they fear and they might know it does
grasp,
With long creeping stalks, and prods long like masts,
Because they see and they fear,
And one sight becomes two,
Two sights become three,
Before the night is over,
Phantasmagoria will be complete,
And all will become,
Dim.

Everything becomes dark.

Every lantern is extinguished, every candle is snuffed out, every hearth smothered, and every forge light killed in an instant as a gust moves through the city. People scream, howling in fear and running around in panic at the sudden onset of full darkness. Only one or two rare stars still manage to remain, but not enough to give them light to see. The darkness is the point; the darkness is the reason that the stars had to go.

The people of the city run and writhe in panic. Spells try to illuminate the nightmare as casters make use of their abilities, but these sparks never last for more than a brief second, as all of their efforts and attempts are rendered inoperable by a power far, far greater than their wills.

Fear.

Nobody knows, nobody senses, nobody hears anything other than the screams of those around them and the cries of pain as people strike each other, grappling and grasping and fighting, as they seem to be unsure whether the thing they are holding is their neighbor or a monster who has come in through the shield, which no eyes can see any longer.

Is it still there? Or has it fallen?

Nobody can say, and so, everybody acts as if it has, running and screaming as anarchy breaks out within the darkness.

Such a state, such a time, is an opportune moment for . . . *unfortunate* happenings. If people were to go missing, well, nobody would really notice.

And so, they begin to do so.

Not that they would know it.

The Demon King watches as his plan comes into fruition. Something long, sharp, and sleek—like a spider's leg—begins to crack as it moves for the first time, slowly, quietly, reaching down toward the city below.

~ [Shaushka] ~
Elf | ♀ | Classless
Location: The Demon King's Castle
Level: 4

"Ah . . . ?" mutters the elf to herself, blankly staring around the chamber.

She lifts her head, looking up toward the long, spiral ramp that leads up into the distance. She's inside of a building now. A very big one.

Shaushka looks around herself to the left and to the right before looking back ahead, and then just walking as she always does.

Her bare feet strike the stones as she walks leisurely up the ramp and around its spiral bends one after the other as she rises higher and higher and higher still, just moving in silence.

Something falls from above, spattering down on the distant ground below.

Leaning over the edge, perhaps somewhat carelessly, she looks down at the corpse that lies splattered against the stones. No more come after it.

"... Ah ..." says Shaushka, quietly turning as she continues to walk, one step after the other, taking in the sights but never really thinking about them. The elf moves, wandering and climbing with full eyes but an empty head, until she reaches a large, golden door that sits shut and closed.

"Ah ..." says the elf, staring at it.

The door stares at her.

The two of them get along as well as one would expect, given the circumstances.

As if by itself, the door opens. The heavy metal hinges creak and groan as it swings open slowly, letting her move forward.

Shaushka lets her hand glide over the door as she continues in the guided direction, following that tug in her heart.

She climbs higher, further, without ever really thinking about why.

It's just not really that important.

~ [Kedora] ~
Half Elf | ♀ | Shopkeeper
Location: The Human Capital, Kedora's Kennels

"There's something here," she whispers in a hush, shushing the boy next to her.

Ever since the darkness and the panic, the city has fallen into a quietness far heavier than what was before. It's so dark, so oppressive. There's nothing to see. The rare starlight that remains isn't enough to reveal the city to them anymore. Now, everyone is hiding; everyone is locked in wherever they could lock themselves in. Not being able to find their way home, many people gathered into whatever nearest building they could guide themselves into that hadn't already locked its doors.

"There's not," replies the boy in a whisper nonetheless. "If there was, people would be screaming."

She can't deny the logic of what he's saying. Even if people couldn't see the monsters, they would at the very least start screaming when they were ripped into the darkness.

Given the quiet that has fallen all around the city, it stands to reason that the shield is still intact, and no monsters have gotten inside. It's dark, yes. But they're still safe. It makes sense.

. . . But she isn't ready to test that theory herself.

She sighs, rubbing her face for a moment. "Okay," she speaks affirmatively. "Then you can get out of my store," says the shopkeeper.

When the darkness fell, she retreated down the road she hadn't gone far down yet, and which she knew in and out from years and years of walking it day and night. Since people followed each other, nobody wanting to be left outside alone, a few stragglers had managed to stick to her.

"What?" asks the boy. "No, I'm not going out there!" he says in a hiss.

She rolls her eyes, perhaps instinctively. "I thought it was safe?" asks Kedora, the shopkeeper, sarcastically. Years in this profession have given her a sharp tongue and a short temper in regard to people wasting her time. It's almost as valuable as money, after all.

Most people who profess to be wise will say the opposite is true, but she sees it differently. If she could speak to the gods and have them trade her remaining hours for cold, strong Obols, she would take that deal right away. With that money, she could live a much more fulfilling life in the hours she had left than if she struggled for her full duration for a pauper's wage. For her, it's better to die young and flamboyantly in exotic experiences than old and poor and having only ever known bread and broth.

"It is," he insists. "But . . . you know, it's dark," argues the boy. She doesn't know how old he is, but given his voice, maybe a young man who has just only entered his teenage years. "I won't find my way."

"So?" replies Kedora. "This is a business. If you aren't buying anything, please leave," she says, repeating the old mantra even at a time like this.

"What do you sell?" he asks.

"What? Read the si—" She tsks, stopping herself with a sigh. "You're in Kedora's Kennels. I sell items related to monster taming, pets, and so on," explains the shopkeeper. "Leashes, food, manuals, everything you need to train a little beast of your own."

"Do you have any pets?" asks the young man.

"Listen, boy," snaps the shopkeeper, still speaking in a tense whisper. "Buy something or get out."

"I don't have any money," he replies.

A third voice chimes in. "I have some money," speaks an older man. "Do you have any people food?"

"No," snaps Kedora. "Unless you want biscuits for hounds."

There's the sound of two coins striking against the counter, sliding their way over to her. Just by the sound the metal makes as it moves over the wood, she can tell they're two ten-Obol coins. The woman mutters to herself, turning around and taking the money as she feels her way through the room to the biscuits. She stumbles over something, letting out a yelp as her foot feels like it snags on a root. She catches herself on the counter.

"What the . . ." mutters the shopkeeper, having walked along behind this counter more times than she's walked home. With her boot, she feels around for whatever she just tripped over, wondering if a broom or something had fallen. But there's nothing there that she can feel.

Maybe she snagged her foot on a loose board or something?

Confused, she grabs a small pouch and fills it by weight that she judges in her hand before bringing it over. In order to make sure she isn't cheating the customer, she added a little extra. It's better to take a slight loss in profit to be safe from damaging her reputation as a vendor.

"Here." She slides the bag over the counter.

"Thank you," replies the man, taking it. Not that she can see him, but she hears the rattling of the dry dough as he picks up the pouch.

"Please leave my store now," insists Kedora, her hands tapping the counter.

"Miss, please," speaks the man who just bought something. "Where are we to go? Other than to rest with our backs at your door?"

Kedora groans. "This is a business. *My* business," she remarks. "It is not a house for those seeking refuge from a little darkness," she says coldly. "For ten Obols more, I will sell you each both a candle, but I cannot promise they will work."

"Surely, this is an unusual time, ma'am," argues the young boy. "The Demon King is he—"

Two loud thuds ring out as something finally breaks the silence. Kedora's fists slam onto the counter. "You think I don't know that, boy?!" she shouts across the room in his vague direction. "I've lost more to that creature than you have ever known!" she yells, her loud voice carrying unusually far across the dead-quiet city, echoing and reverberating around and around again. "My husband, my son!" she yells, swiping her arm over the counter. The two Obol coins fly and clatter against the wall, falling off and rolling across the wooden floor until they strike the wall by the door. "Both were taken from me. So leave me my peace! If I die, then I would like to do so in the last place of familiarity I have!" explains Kedora, with venom in her voice. "Alone!"

The room is quiet for a time, apart from the rattling of a coin as it slowly vibrates its way to rest.

There is no sound—not from breath or from word—as she stands there, collecting herself, her hands resting on the counter as she holds her palms firmly against it.

"Are you scared?" asks a voice.

She doesn't bother replying, clenching her eyes closed to make sure they are shut, as she was unsure before.

The shop is quiet for a time as everyone just stays in their place. It has been a hard, long journey for everyone these past few months. She understands that they don't want to go back out, but—

The front door rattles, shaking violently as something grabs it. Kedora curses, jolting upright.

"We're closed!" she barks, almost instinctively, as someone continues to pull on the door. She'd locked it after coming in. "Fuck's sake . . ." mutters the shopkeeper. The tugging continues, the person on the other side pulling harder, the hinges rattling. Her voice carries out into the full quietness of the world, and she stands there, listening to it as the rattling continues. A spark in her, trained from years and years of doing this work, tells her to yell again, walk to the door, and tell whoever is there to get lost in person.

But the echoing chasm that fills the city in which not one single person seems to be talking right now tells her on a deeper, more human level that she should shut up. It's inexplicable, but that's what she feels. Call it a woman's intuition or a gut feeling, or maybe just life and work experience, but one of these pinches her tongue.

Kedora's palms slip over the counter as she listens intently. The door is strong; it's secured firmly into the frame of the building. She paid extra to have the shop safe and locked down back during the good days. It seems that's paying dividends now in some way, at least.

The rattling stops.

Quietly, she grabs an unlit candle from her stack and creeps around from behind the counter, feeling her way through the store. "Are they gone?"

she whispers, creeping toward the window as if she could see something through it other than the blackness that has consumed the world.

"Not sure," replies the man in the room. "Biscuit?"

She reaches out, realizing the curtain is drawn shut. "Very funny," she replies dryly.

But even then, after she peeks through the gap she pulls apart for a brief moment, there is nothing to see on the other side, of course.

"Gods, I hate this," mutters Kedora, feeling around herself as she walks. "Hold on. I know I have some flint here somewhere," says the shopkeeper, squeezing the unlit candle in her hand.

"I thought we had to go?" asks the boy from across the room.

She stops in her tracks, her hand resting on a shelf as she stares . . . somewhere; she's not sure where. "I guess it's fine . . ." mutters the woman. "People are probably getting weird out there." One of her hands runs along the wall as her other searches the shelf until her fingers bump into a woody root. "What the . . . ?"

A familiar touch meets her skin. The flint.

"Ah, got it. Hold on, I'll try to get some light going," remarks the woman, striking the flint a few times. The candle bursts to flame, the light burning almost blindingly bright as she holds it in her hand and looks toward the wall where she felt something.

There's nothing there. Did she maybe just touch the shelf?

It's so disorienting in the dark. You think you know a place, but then—

The candle blows out as if by itself.

"Fuck's sake!" she snaps.

"It was a good try," says the man from nearby, maybe back where she stores the grooming tools, it sounds like. "But I don't think that'll work anymore. We should be quieter."

Kedora curses, her mind racing. She hates this. That damn monster, that beast, the Demon King—he stole everything from her. Her family, her life, her business, and now, he's even taken something as simple as the light from her eyes. She won't just let him get away with it. She can't do much; she's just a small woman with a small shop. But if she can poke his eye even once, it'll be worth it.

"I have a barrel of grease upstairs." She feels her way around the room as steps come from the side. "Candles might go out, but I'd like to see him try putting out that when it gets burning."

"Isn't that super dangerous?" asks the boy, moving around the store.

She can't really argue against that, because it is. "Yeah." But she's at a point in life where she doesn't even care anymore; at least she tells herself that. The moment's distant terror of the door being rattled is now already forgotten as she thinks about the possibility of getting some light going. It's not that she's afraid of the dark, but not seeing anything at all is just . . .

"I'm going upstairs," she declares. "Don't steal anything."

"Can I come with you?" asks the boy from nearby. "It's scary down here."

Kedora fumbles her way to the counter, and then walks around it. "Stay with him," she remarks, vaguely gesturing toward where the man is possibly standing, not that she knows.

"Actually," he starts, "I'd like to go too."

"Tough," remarks Kedora, grabbing the door to the stairway. "You can stay in my store, but not in my home," she says, opening the door. Her eyes look up the stairway, she's sure, but she doesn't see a damn thing. The hairs on her neck stand on end as she peers in a familiar direction but doesn't see a single familiar thing.

". . . Please?" pleads the boy.

"Fine," relents Kedora, changing her mind quickly once again, suddenly feeling perhaps relieved at the concept of not moving alone through this place in the dark. Sure, it's her home and she knows it, but . . . things change in this sort of darkness. Things she wasn't expecting. The perceived distances between things, places; her heightened hearing that picks up every crack and groan; her wild imagination which places monsters and ghouls in every corner and crevice. "Come on."

Steps come from behind her, following after her in the darkness as she moves, carefully shuffling forward until her feet meet the stairs, and then slowly, she begins making her way up.

They reach the top floor, and she feels her way forward, stumbling her way toward the storage room. A small grip has grabbed hold of the back of her shirt, presumably to not lose her in the murk.

Now, where was it . . . Ah! Kedora wraps her hands around the rim of a large barrel, tapping on it with her knuckles. "Here it is," she says. "Hey, help me with this. It's pretty heavy."

Someone grabs the bottom end of the barrel. The man, she presumes, given the height to which it is lifted.

"We're going to the roof," she explains, starting to shuffle forward, pressing the barrel against him as she holds her end of it with both hands.

"The roof?" asks the boy. "To make a fire? Isn't that dangerous?"

"Starting a grease fire is always dangerous, boy," replies Kedora as she moves through the doorway, slightly pinching her hand between the barrel and the doorframe. "It doesn't matter where you do it. But we live in strange days."

They move, rather effortlessly, toward the secondary staircase and begin, in total darkness, climbing up. Kedora doesn't say anything, but she does wonder how come neither of them have stumbled or tripped yet. She at least has a vague mental layout of the place, but they shouldn't have anything.

Something tickles on the back of her neck.

The door above them creaks open as they reach the top of the stairs. A gust of "fresh" air flows down into the building as evidence that they have reached the outside world—since there is simply nothing to see out there. There isn't a single glimmer more of light anywhere at all. It's all just as dark as everywhere else.

"Over here," she says, and they set the barrel down. She tips it and rolls it on its edge by herself toward the corner of the structure. "Stand back."

"Are you sure about this?" asks the man as Kedora stands there with the flint and striker in her hands. "Look around you; everything is so . . . dark. It's quiet."

"Yeah," mutters the boy nervously.

"That's the problem, isn't it?" Kedora replies, looking back at them.

It's silent for a time, the wind pressing over the rooftop. "Is it really wise to be the first light to break that?" asks the man. "What if . . . What if there's something in here with us?"

"Nonsense," remarks Kedora. "If that were true, we'd hear screaming, because people tend to scream when they're getting eaten, as we already covered."

They all stand there.

". . . Don't you want to get back at him?" asks the shopkeeper. "At the Demon King?" Her voice carries around the night. "He stole everything from us. Our lives and futures. Are you really going to let him have this, too? Or do you want to light this fire and shine it right back in his ugly face?"

The man sighs audibly with an annoyed hiss to his exhalation. A moment later, there comes a tapping as he moves closer her way. "I had a family too, you know," he says as he reaches out, his fingers fumbling over her shoulders as he tries to grab her hand to take the tool in it. "Sorry."

"It's okay," she replies, knowing his intentions and giving him the flint and striker. "Did he take them from you, too?" asks Kedora as metal and stone click together and hold there for a moment.

"I don't know," he replies, standing there next to her with the smell of grease in the air. "I never heard anything. They left the city before this all started. Business to the south," explains the man. "And then . . . I don't know."

"Maybe they're still out there?" she asks, perhaps intending to give him a little hope.

But the man shakes his head. "I hope not," is all that he finishes with, striking the tool together to create a small spark, and then he does it again a second time, and then a third, until the fire catches and the barrel erupts much faster than he had expected it to.

Yelping, he pulls his hands back, shaking them out with a nervous but almost happy laugh as the raging flame breaks the night. The red and orange glow carries off far, far into the oppressive darkness like a rebelling spirit determined to continue onward forevermore—the spirit of hope, lost within a sea of bleakness. Drowned, but never dying.

He sighs, almost relieved. "What's your name again?" He turns his head to look at the woman, who is still holding the side of his sleeve as if to steady herself. Their eyes meet, and he looks not at a face he knows or ever knew, but into two gaping black, empty holes that sit as her eyes, her mouth filled with the same ink, and her jaw dropped down unnaturally far past where any bone could go—dislocated like a snake's. Within it is only more blackness that the light of the fire can't seem to break into.

All around the dome, inside of the sphere, hang long, sharp, straight protrusions—stiff like wood—like the spindly legs of a spider standing over them all. They reach down through windows, through doorways and openings, pressing in through cracks and holes, to only ever just wait and sit for someone to partake in its spectacle.

The fire, massive and large and blazing so brightly, snuffs out in an instant, and he screams as something lunges at him, his horrific cries carrying out into the city as something kills him, but seems to take a long, long, long time to do so.

~ The Phantasmagoria ~
- Summoned Entity -
Cost: 100% SOUL POINTS
Drawn from the deepest imaginations of the living, from the darkest, most hidden crevices of the mind, Phantasmagoria is a creature who exists now as it has always done—always within the mind, but never in sight. The fear of the dark, the fear of the unknown, the fear of what lies around the next bend and below the bed and up in the dark attic—Phantasmagoria is the avatar of all of these things.
The beast hunts through a terror drive, not being able to—or wanting to—strike and kill until a living being is full of nothing other than raw horror. Perhaps it likes flesh most when it is saturated with adrenaline, or perhaps it is simply wicked, or perhaps it is nothing at all.
It lives within all men, as it has always done since their first peeps into the darkness as young boys in their cot, when they began to first wonder if there was something there in the night.
It can only ever hunt in darkness, for in the light, it is dispelled and pushed back into the deep crevices of thought, waiting for a new night so that it might come fresh as a nightmare once again—day after day, year after year, forever.

Class: MONSTER	Element: DARK
Type: Nightmare	Category: TERROR*
Rank: SSS	
Level: ???	

*TERROR is a classification term used for all monster types that do not fall into traditional monster categories such as UNDEAD, GOLEM, GHOST, etc. Terrors tend to have unique makeups and behavior patterns, and lean toward hyperviolent tendencies.

The boy, Akrasia, stands there, watching Phantasmagoria work, as someone comes up from behind him and places two hands on his shoulder. The limping sound and the striking of a crutch gives credence to their identity, but he can't look away from what is happening ahead of him. He's not really confused as to how she got up here; she can go just about anywhere she wants to.

"Such a lucky, lucky little boy!" exclaims the black rabbit—the Demon King's gallu and infiltrator into the city—standing behind him and holding him in her grasp as they look at the man being torn apart by long, sharp, impossibly massive legs that drop down from above, but end in tiny, pinprick needle points that can touch and grab anything on the human scale. "I always knew you were!" she remarks, pleased.

They watch as the man screams as he's slowly and almost methodically taken apart, not in order to preserve anything of him except the length of his suffering.

"What . . . What's happening?" asks the boy nervously, swallowing his terror, as he had been warned to do. It knows terror as a feeling and targets it specifically, like a wolf that hunts by the smell of meat.

Hands move down to around his sides as she bends down and rests her head on his shoulder. "Watch," she says, her arms wrapping around him.

As the man screams and howls, his voice the first to break the heavy emptiness of the night, lights and flames start to emerge all around the city, as people, triggered by his calls, give in to their fear and desire to understand what is happening around them.

Living in darkness can be perfectly fine when one assumes safety, but the screaming destroys that feeling. The screaming implies that there is something they need to know about; something they need to see.

With every flame that rises up into the night, illuminating a new segment of the city, more screams come once people see what is really around them. Who is really around them.

The dead walk among the living, their broken faces and soulless eyes hidden by the cloak of full darkness, their words and touches mingling in with the living, the rooms of which they share in.

And as they scream, as they cry out in shock and horror once they see the faces of the dead they have lost along the way—their sons and husbands standing next to them without them even knowing it—they wrench in terror, and Phantasmagoria reacts, cutting down from above at those who twitch and scream and writhe.

A humming comes into his ear, the rabbit and him watching.

"Is this . . ." starts Akrasia. "Is this happening because I helped?" His shaking body is held steady by the hands that fold over his stomach from behind. "Because I helped him get inside?"

"Yes!" replies the rabbit excitedly, not skipping a beat. "Such a lucky, lucky boy you are." She sighs, standing back up. "I just can't stand it!" She leans against her crutch as her one leg stomps onto the ground repeatedly. All around the city, screams and horror fill the air as people are broken and cut and torn apart in order to create even more screams and more terror, the cycle of horror perpetuated because of their responses.

"Can I have my favor now?" asks Akrasia in a weak voice. "Will the Demon King give me my wish?" He turns around to look at her, seeing her in the light of the neighboring houses for a brief moment.

"Your mother?" she asks. "You wanted her back, right?"

"Please!" begs Akrasia.

A hand grabs the bottom of his chin. "Our friend keeps all of his promises," she says, turning his gaze to the side so that he can see the total emptiness and blackness that is there. He expects to see a ghost like the others, but there is simply . . . nothing. "To me, and to you."

". . . No . . ." pleads the boy. "You promised . . ." he mutters, the weight of what he's done running through his head. "He promised."

"Yes," agrees the black rabbit as she grabs him by the wrist. "This world is dead," she explains. "It's gone. It's over. But you can come to mine with me." Her gallu eyes shine with noxious yellow firelight. "You can live in the garden forever with me. Just us two, forever and ever and ever," promises the rabbit, her free hand tapping against the tip of his nose.

"The . . . The garden?" asks Akrasia, remembering the pocket dimension of sorts in which the creature lives. A small plane that resembles a garden which sits in between places and time. It's a room, a chamber, hardly big enough to spend a day in, let alone a life. "But my wish—"

The wall behind them begins to crackle as the brickwork crumbles, and vines begin to grow in all directions, ivy crawling this way and that as a hedge appears with unnatural speed. She begins to step back toward it as every last fire within the city dies out one after the other.

"I'll be your mother now," she promises, pulling him after her. "And this will be your new life. Both wishes are kept, as promised, forever and ever and ever," says the rabbit as he tries to pull away from her strong hand around his small wrist. "Lucky, lucky boy!"

He screams as he's yanked back into the hedge and taken to another place and time, where he and the rabbit spend all of eternity together—separate from the horrors of death and dismay of this world or any other. "I just can't stand it sometimes!" says her voice as the hedge closes again, the leaves wilting and dying as the exit breaks and seals itself from such a terrible reality as this one.

And should anything horrific happen within such a place, well, it is never to be known outside by those who are lucky-lucky enough to have never heard of such an area, in which a demon lives with a captive soul for all eternity.

One after the other, as the screams begin to fade, souls fly up toward the sky, toward the stars that they never reach, as a power pulls them in toward the black castle.

PUT THE PEN DOWN

~ [Ruhr, the River Sorceress] ~
Half Elf | ♀ | Sorceress
Rank: SSS
Location: The Demon King's Castle, Floor Negative Ninety-Nine
Level: 100

We're almost there," says Ruhr, walking onward through the darkness. Behind them lies yet another broken and destroyed chamber that she has forced her way through, her desire and enjoyment of games having come to an end now. The Demon King's castle is a plaything for that beast. A joke, as presented by the optics of the carnival. But she's had enough fun, enough of the sights and sounds of the circus of life.

She looks around herself, realizing that nobody is next to her. She's muttering to herself.

The half elf shakes her head.

She's going to put this to an end. She can feel it. They're almost there. The pressure in the air, the heat—it's making it hard for even the most powerful and trained of the crusade to keep up pace with her. Perhaps it is her access to blessed magic that makes this easier for her, or perhaps there is simply a fire burning in her gut with an intensity that isn't present in theirs which makes this possible for her.

Maybe it's hate?

Maybe it's just something that simple. While everyone here is suffering, and everyone in the world has their gripes with the Demon King, she can't help but feel that this is almost personal now between the two of them. They've never met, never spoken, never interacted—but she's spent so long inside of this place, so long playing his sick games, that she feels as if they've already spoken a million words with one another, and she's reached the point where there is nothing left to say.

This conversation, this game, and this song and dance of theirs are over as far as she's concerned.

Ruhr looks behind herself at the crusade, which is lagging behind. The air shifts and swelters in a way it hadn't before. It's heavy, almost. Every step feels like it will force one's ankles to break and one's boots to crush through the stones beneath them. The air feels like it gets stuck inside one's lungs, being too heavy to exhale again after it has entered, as if it had solidified inside of them.

Purified water runs down her arms and fingers as she walks, the weight of this demonic presence feeling like its squeezing her out like a sponge, compressing her essence as she walks onward, keeping count in her head of how far they've come.

Through all of the illusions, all of the terrors, monstrosities, and fakes, all of the horrors, trials, and tribulations, she's been keeping track of every single floor.

The hallway comes to an end, opening to a grand chamber, but Ruhr keeps walking as she looks around herself at the space. It's a graveyard. Broken, crumbling walls of what looks to have once been a labyrinth of sorts line the space all across it, but they've all shattered and fractured into heaps of rubble, rendering the labyrinth useless. Most likely, the same pressure that is pounding down against her and them all is what tore this place down.

The Demon King has become too strong for his own castle.

Tears and cracks run through the walls and the floor, like scars that all lead toward a single gash in reality: a great door that sits at the end of the room. It is marked and scarred with the imprint of claws and fangs, of inferno and chaos. Decorating the great gates are thousands of depictions of faces and bodies, of people climbing and scrambling over one another toward the pinnacle of the door, more than ready to trample the thousands below them to be the one to reach the highest point there, which, for some reason . . .

Ruhr stands there, staring up past the thousands of broken graves and heaps of cracked and fractured bones as she stares at what promises to be the final door, the final gate.

He's here, just there. Just a little further. She's almost done; they're almost done.

The half elf clenches a fist, grabbing hold of a hand that isn't there as she stares at the nonsense that has welcomed her to her final confrontation. Her fingers grasp for the ones that had promised to be here, but that are not—Zacarias's.

Instead, she stares with quiet rage boiling inside of her at a depiction of a goose at the top of the doorway, standing over the bodies of the endless dead, the depiction of its honking the last drop of absurdity that she can handle.

Enough.

This has all been enough.

Ruhr lifts her hands, aiming them at the door. She contemplates if she has the energy for a one-liner while water collects around her fingers, spiraling in a violent maelstrom, the superheated air boiling the water around her hands as it moves.

No, she doesn't.

The dragon of blessed water rushes out, roaring as it strikes headfirst like a battering ram come to break a siege, the door buckling and caving and breaking in with the first strike of the spell.

Water drips and runs down the walls and columns as a backblast of heat and fire launches her way, the flames washing over her body and hair like the hands of the dead come to drag her into the final hell in which she may rest after a life now lived.

The final chamber shines with hellfire as she marches onward, her posture strong and her eyes focused as she glares directly ahead, down the lines of rubble and broken columns, down through the weaving of nearly one million souls, down through the ruins of the nightmare king who sits atop a strong throne, idly resting as if in leisurely wait, no alarm and no surprise on his horrific body to be seen. All over his gigantic, red mass sit dotted thousands of eyes that blister and boil in the heat, all staring directly at her as she walks in through the broken gate, the bent hinges of which have now failed, the decorative metal that separated the world from this deepest layer of hell fully destroyed, the seal having been broken.

Stone faces, stone hands, and stone people all lie there, broken and crumbled, facing her way as she enters the throne room, as if the destroyed statues were the many dead, pleading with her to pull them out of the mire they're stuck inside of. Stone fingers crunch as her boots step over them as lovelessly as they can.

And her arrival is marked with nothing. No grand ceremony. No great chant and cheer and jubilation. With nothing but a single, strong, loud, and slow clapping as the ruby beast atop his throne strikes his hands together.

"Ruhr, the river sorceress," growls the voice of the beast above all beasts, the true demon, who slowly rises from his throne to stand. "I've been waiting for you," says the Demon King, his voice rattling her core as if it alone had taken hold of her soul and begun trying to wrench it free from the pit of her gut in which it firmly rests.

This is it. This is him. Everything that's happened—every terrible, horrific thing that's happened to her—is because of this creature, this . . . monster. Water leaks out of Ruhr's fist, which tightens with every unceremonious clap, as the sound of him, having said her name only once, continues to crawl around inside her head over and over and over again, like a fungus trying to break its way into soft tissue, feeling its way around the sediment.

"Build a smaller castle next time," replies Ruhr, lifting her hands together.

Sacred, spiraling water swirls in a torrent just as before and then blasts forward, the dragon of the heavens, brought down to this world through such holy rains as her own, launching toward the heart of the Demon King with more force than she has ever put into it. It propels forward, the scream of the water tearing through the stones and the rubble, tearing through everything like a predator ravaging the forest floor as it charges its prey. The water collides, the dragon sinking its teeth straight into the monster, who vanishes behind the superheated steam that shoots out in all directions like a wall of fog on a grim morning.

Steam rushes out everywhere: left and right and up and down. The inferno chamber becomes opaque and hidden behind the nebula, but the sound of clapping does not stop.

No, it isn't clapping.

The ground shakes, the chamber quaking as one step after the other comes closer and closer. Ruhr screams, holding her arms out and putting everything she has into the lance that bores toward the demon's heart. The steps come closer and closer still until water splashes back in her own face from the giant who now stands before her.

The spell dies out, and Ruhr looks up, staring at the Demon King as he towers there—a clean hole visible through the off-center of his chest.

His head is turned toward her, but the many eyes in his body look at the gaping wound that he doesn't seem all too fazed by. His massive hand, the size of her core alone, reaches up and rests next to the spot where his heart ought to have been.

"I lost that a while ago," says the Demon King. "It only caused me trouble," he remarks.

A cracking fills the air as the chamber spins. Ruhr flies, rolling back over the stones violently, landing on a cushion of water.

"Ruhr!" yells a voice from behind as hands grab her and steady her while she rises again, holding her arm. Ruhr looks over her shoulder at the priestess, Springer, who has begun casting a healing spell. Crusaders move, flowing into the chamber like water by the hundreds, while the Demon King stands as the centerpiece of a great masterwork, his arms spreading wide and far as if to welcome them all.

"Ah, love . . ." growls the voice of the Demon King as he watches them. "It's funny, isn't it, Ruhr, the river sorceress?" he asks. Ruhr hisses between her teeth as he befouls her name again. If he does that one more time, she might never ever want to hear it from anyone ever again. "How selfish the heart is. How quickly it will latch on to something it wants when an old want is discarded."

Ruhr pulls away from Springer, pushing her back as she steps forward again.

"Tell me, if you could choose," starts the Demon King, stepping forward another step. Then one more. His arm gestures out to her. "If you could choose between you, her, or your old friend Zacarias," he says. "If you could save one of you from me, who would it be?" questions the Demon King, walking toward her, step after step. "I can do it," he promises, lifting a hand with an open palm. "I can bring one of you to a state of merciful release."

What? Ruhr's eyes open wide. *Zacarias . . . ? He's still . . . ?*

"There is no such thing as mercy in this world as long as you live, beast!" yells Springer, her voice carrying around the throne room. Above them fly close to one million souls, more and more pouring in by the second, while around them, the crusade prepares for the final battle.

A harrowing laughter fills the room, which begins to glow with spell-casting on all sides as commands and orders are given by the leaders of the grand crusade.

"What's the matter?" The Demon King's eyes look toward the priestess who stands behind the half elf. "Afraid of what her answer would have been?" asks the Demon King. "I received such an answer once, too, myself," he explains, fire condensing all around him. "It turns out that love is a very . . . fickle thing," assures the horrific creature.

He flicks his hand.

Springer screams, yelling as something swoops down from above and grabs hold of her.

"SPRINGER!" shouts Ruhr, failing to catch her as the priestess is hoisted into the air by a blood-soaked spirit who swooped out of the darkness and is holding her aloft, flying over the Demon King and his presence to dangle the priestess next to him. "GET AWAY FROM HER!" yells Ruhr, rushing forward.

"Ah . . ." says the Demon King, a claw touching the priestess's neck as she fights to try and get away from the ghost holding her captive by her arms. "I can feel it inside of you"—he leans in toward her—"writhing, squirming in your gut like a worm." His claw moves down toward her stomach from her neck. "You poor wretch; you've been tricked, just like I was," he says, slowly shaking his massive head.

A sharp whistle cuts the air as an officer gives a command. All around the chamber, spells blast out toward the Demon King; hundreds of shines of fire and ice, of arcane magic from old, forgotten schools, and amalgamations of nature and stonework rush toward them in a concentrated blast. Water and electricity, darkness, and the lights of so many holies of holy fill the air in a split second.

"Love isn't real," says the Demon King, looking at Springer in the eyes. "It's just an ugly lie," is the last thing he growls as the light of a thousand explosions envelops him, her, and Ruhr as they all come to a point of convergence.

Ruhr groans, her body aching. She opens her eyes and pushes herself up and off the ground as all around the chamber rings anarchy.

"There's nothing quite so ugly as a lie," echoes all around her as people scream. Ruhr holds her head, wobbling up to her feet while she tries to orient herself.

The Demon King and the crusade fight, if it can be called that.

It's a slaughter.

Spells and arrows blast against him, every strike simply absorbing into the unfazed tower of muscle and spite whose fist crashes down onto a soldier, splattering him into a flattened mush. Organs and guts spill out in all directions, turning black in an instant as the heat of his core cooks them immediately.

The half elf walks, falling down again before crawling toward a singed, burnt heap that was once a robe filled with a person. She screams, grabbing the fabric and pulling it toward herself, feeling a chunk of what is left inside as a counterweight to her tugging.

"Except for the person who lives it," says the Demon King, his thousands of eyes turned toward her as he stands upright, holding out an open palm toward a group of casters preparing a combined spell to attack him with. "And you are the ugliest creature I know of, Ruhr, the river sorceress."

Ruhr rises back up to her feet again, failing to hold what she grasps against herself, as it all falls apart into an uncollectible mess.

He closes his hand. Below the casters, the ground glows alight. Words that had been carved into it by a massive claw shine as magic flows through them. Stone spires break out of the floor, rupturing their bodies through the soles of their boots, pressing and forcing with such might that it forces the bones of their shins and knees out through their arched backs and screaming mouths.

"You know nothing of love and beauty. You only play games in their name," he accuses. "I can see it in you; I've always seen it in you, from the moment you breathed in my direction for the first time." An onslaught of shield-bearing soldiers charges his way, their push protected by a series of magical barriers and walls that start to enclose the Demon King like a prison.

Commands are given, and spells form above his head, one after the other, as the crusade plans to crush him from above with magic and force of will. The crusaders press against the barriers, holding them firm with their own tower shields so that they might not budge an inch if he hammers against them.

But he doesn't.

Instead, his claw lifts and scratches against the glass, writing and carving a few simple series of lines—a poem.

The magical walls that enclose him bulge outwardly, growing faces like gargoyles that lash out in torment toward the outside, grabbing hold of the shield bearers in their mouths and cutting them cleanly apart where they bite and chew. A swordsman rushes in, screaming, as the Demon King pushes a wall to the side and steps out back toward the throne room.

One after the other, souls collect and gather. From every dead crusader, another soul comes to his collection; from every dying person in the falling human capital, another soul comes to his collection. The room swelters and surges as the pressure inside continues to grow stronger and stronger, making it harder and harder to move than it already was.

The swordsman and the Demon King clash, the knight of no particular name or renown holding strong. His blade connects against a massive wrist, which pushes back as the edge sinks toward ruby bone. The beast lashes out, the knight counterbalancing and striking again and again, the two of them entwining in a mismatched dance as one partner towers over the other but neither relents from their pursuit.

Ruhr tries to fight against the pressure, to stand up again, but something in her is just wrong. Her shaking hands squeeze the robe, succeeding in nothing except pressing more red out of it than before. It oozes out through the fabric and over the floor.

A voice comes from its insides. "You know nothing but love for yourself, creature," it accuses in a voice that belongs to the dead priestess. "You've never been able to love anything except for yourself, ever," it says, perhaps rightfully so. "It's all an act; all an illusion."

The half elf screams as the armored body of a knight flies, broken, past her and crashes against a column, every bone in his body breaking in an instant. "STOP!"

"No," replies a voice, dryly, from next to her.

With wide eyes, Ruhr stares in terror that she doesn't want to feel at the giant towering over her.

"You blame your damage for the ugliness you create," he says. "You justify your vile existence and the terrible lies you tell because of where you came from and because of how you wish to escape it." He grabs her and lifts her into the air, his hand wrapping itself fully around her torso as her feet begin to dangle off the ground. The Demon King's face comes closer to hers as its true eyes stare through from the darkness that covers them. They look at one another, her body hissing as the heat evaporates the water and boils it on her skin.

"Ugly creatures like you are what I hate the most of all in this world," growls the Demon King. "Ugly, lonesome, lying little schemers who act in the name of righteousness and goodness but seek nothing at the end of the day except masturbatory validation," he accuses, staring into her wet eyes, which reflect ruby firelight and blood in all directions. "That's why I chose you to be last," he says. "You will be the last to die; the soul to trigger the eruption. As you deservedly lived, you will also die. Alone, Ruhr, the river sorcere—"

Water explodes in all directions, steaming and quenching holy water shooting out with a pressure strong enough to cut stone, jetting out in horrific force. People scream and shout as the off sprays blast them, holy water filling the room.

He laughs again as her defiance fails to do much, his strength being far beyond that of even her blessed magic alone.

"That's the problem you artistic types always have," snaps Ruhr, her tiny hands grabbing hold of the massive wrist that clutches her. Her fingers don't even come close to reaching a quarter of the way around it while she glares into the thousand eyes that bore her way through the fresh steam that fills and clouds the chamber. "You can never just shut up long enough to pull your head out of your ass and actually get some work done."

She lifts her hand toward him.

"That won't work, fool," he says, his hand starting to crush her body as she aims at his head.

"It'll work long enough," Ruhr replies, looking at him. "Ugly people like us need to bathe regularly." She narrows her eyes, then shouts, "NOW!"

All around them, a new series of prismatic walls appear in all directions, a fresh cage forming as the remaining crusaders gather together, their spells collecting around them. Ruhr's blast of water shoots out, the Demon King roaring in anger as it strikes him. It's not enough to hurt him alone, but it collects and pools in an instant in the tight space the two of them are enclosed in.

Sacred water rises in between the glassy walls, flooding up to his ankles, his knees, and then to her in seconds' time. The Demon King screams and strikes in rage, his blows bashing against the walls that hundreds of people work together to hold in place, his strikes becoming further muffled in their power by the dampening of the water as he tries to hit it. It bubbles and boils as the superheated aura of the Demon Core cooks it, and her.

The cage becomes filled with an opaque mess of bubbling, red water as everything inside of it stews, the sacred holy water that the true demon is suspended in roiling into a boil that glasses the stonework beneath and the ceiling above. A massive arm shoots out, trying to grab the edge of the barrier, only to slowly sink back down again into the broth.

The remaining crusaders who are still alive pant and gather themselves, holding the barrier strong with sweat and screams. The plan was on the fly, but they know Ruhr well enough at this point to know this is what she wanted. The Demon King can say what he wants, but all of them know that she was more than willing to give her life if it meant killing him.

Perhaps they do not really understand the reasons for her desire at the end of the day, assuming it to be the same as their own, but does that matter? Does the reasoning matter if the end result is the same?

It is difficult to say.

What can be said, however, is that the heat begins to fade after a few minutes. The splashing, writhing, and hammering from inside the prison begin to fade away, and the bubbling water stops roiling and spraying as the heat begins to die out.

Looking at each other, unsure, the men make their choice. They don't have much of one, anyway, as their reserves of power and strength are drained. After this long, this much terror, this much running and fighting and struggle, this was the last sprint: this was everything they had left inside of themselves. This was every last drop they had to give, every last power of essence and soul.

The barrier begins to falter and wane, with red water running out of it in leaks and then in flows, and soon, the entire thing breaks apart. The cage of glassy, magical walls fades, and a torrent of boiled water splashes out in all directions, carrying with it indistinct chunks of goo and meat, boiled eyes and claws, and the goop of everything that is left. An indescribable stench fills the chamber as the steaming pool collects around their boots, the odor of wafting gore and bile rising to their nostrils as people gasp and mutter prayers at the sight they see.

Encased in the mess is a single, round, golden sphere—like an egg laid by a bird flown down from heaven.

A shield envelops a single figure. A half elf sits there, huddled together into a ball, as around her glows the golden magic that she is fully encased in.

Ruhr, the river sorceress, opens her eyes as it fades, and she splashes down into the messy water, the blood and gore of it staining everything she's wearing.

(Zacarias) has used: [Royal Barrier]

"Typical," says a voice from the doorway. Ruhr turns, her head shooting toward it faster than it ever has before as her eyes open wide like an owl's. "Always stealing the glory for yourse—"

Zacarias is interrupted by a great splashing and thrashing as the half elf scrambles toward him like a hound who hasn't seen its master in a decade. She latches on to him, howling with the same tone as such a creature.

"ZAC!" cries Ruhr, grabbing him and holding on as tightly as she can. Her stained, red clothes smear over him as she latches on like a parasite with a firm, strong grip. "You're alive!" she says, looking at him for the brief second that she pulls back for before she holds him again so that he can't see her ugly face.

Water splashes everywhere as legionnaires of the group that came with Zacarias march in, rushing to the aid of the wounded. "Course I am," he replies, his hand resting on her back as he looks around the chamber. "I thought we were going to do this together," he remarks, looking at the mess. A fist strikes against his shoulder, hard enough to dent the metal inward. "But I guess I should have expected as much from Ruhr, the river sorceress."

Ruhr flinches, standing there quietly for a moment.

"Can . . . Zac," she says, looking up at him. "Can you just call me Ruhr from now on? I think I'm going to retire," admits the half elf.

"Really?" he asks, looking down at her eyes and the emotion locked down deep inside them, even now, after their victory over the Demon King. He can see it inside of her—some kind of hurt and confusion that can't be named in any good fashion. He nods his head to the side, down across the room. "Before the river sorceress retires," he says, "I think she'd want to sit on the throne at least once?"

Ruhr's lips tremble as she looks at him.

He knows her so well.

The half elf grabs his hands, her heart overjoyed at seeing someone so deeply connected to her again, as she runs across the red pool, her boots sloshing the water and the fabric that floats around her ankles as she runs to the ascension on top of which sits the Demon King's throne.

After everything, she's earned this.

Fuck the Demon King and his castle. Fuck being an adventurer. Fuck all of this. She's going to use her money and fame to buy a little house by the ocean. She'll buy a few ducks and chickens and maybe a couple goats, and she'll live there in quiet until the end of her days. No more fame, no more adventure, no more glory, titles, or prestige. She's done. She's had enough. She's eaten her fill.

Perhaps when they get out of here, the name of Ruhr the river sorceress will be one spoken by every child and king in the world, but they'll never speak it to her, because she won't be found by anyone she doesn't want to find her.

After this.

Ruhr drags Zacarias up the stairs, and without more grace and introduction than needed, she sits down on the grim throne and looks down over the mess and anarchy that fills the space.

It's quiet as the two of them stay there, their eyes wandering the chamber and then back to each other.

"So, what do you think he did all day while sitting here?" asks Ruhr, wanting to ask him so many things and tell him so many others, but the shield of her personality being what it is—having risen again after being separated from him for so long—prevents her from speaking so openly and truthfully.

Zacarias looks around, grabbing a piece of paper that's resting there, as Ruhr's eyes wander the chamber until they move up toward the ceiling.

"I think he . . . wrote poems?" guesses Zacarias.

"No . . ." mutters Ruhr.

"Really," he says, holding out a sheet of paper for her to look at. Ruhr jumps to her feet.

"ZAC!" she yells. His eyes follow hers and see what she sees.

Only somewhat less than one million souls fly and writhe high, high above their heads in the darkness that is the chamber's ceiling. The tormented dead waltz and float, spinning between each other in a complicated weave of motion.

They're still here. Still trapped.

Her eyes reach the paper as she jumps to her feet, screaming to warn the crusade and the legion still down below.

Our dance has come to end,
The dish—now consumed,
The painting is made,
And the crypt is exhumed,
Arts of all manner, have been seen and partook,
As come within minds, the lies of joys—mistook,
For you think you are safe,
You think you are clear,
But you know as well as I do,
That you are not close to near,
As inside of you flows the poison,
The rot, the same as I, my own,
As atop my broken, wet bones,
Sits but one emotion, one that the two of us know,
And it is what you and I share most of all,
My sister in ugliness,
The one on my throne,
The one in my hall,
Despair.

"RUN!" screams Ruhr at the top of her voice, her words carrying around the quaking, echoing chamber as the bloody water that fills the entire space below the throne's pedestal begins to slosh and move, splashing as if by itself over the rubble and broken bodies and bones. Ruhr shouts, running, but a hand grabs her, holding her back. "RUN!"

In an instant, the water rises to life, thousands of hands and thousands of claws and teeth surging out of it, the mass an indescribable form and shape. Armlike protrusions reach out, grabbing hold of ankles and legs, with teeth growing from their wrists, and eyes bulging from their elbows. Screaming faces pull out of the wet slop, their tongues replaced by centipedes, and their screams replaced by howls.

Broken bones of femurs and arms jut out like spears, impaling people through their guts and chests, lifting the screaming wretches up into the air. Crusaders and legionnaires scream and writhe as their impaled masses are hoisted up, their blood running back down into the pool as they kick and struggle, only ever falling deeper down the skewers toward the waiting, gnashing mouths that bite into their faces and chew through their jaws. They snap their fingers and bite through their wrists as hands pull them down into the muck that begins to coagulate and reform in the center of the chamber—an incomprehensible mass of flesh, sinew, and bone.

It grows and grows together without coherent shape or form, teeth collecting over eyes, and tongues lapping over flaps of soggy, loose, pale skin that hangs around its frame of broken, knifelike bones. Like a teratoma that never stops festering, the malignancy swirls and pulsates in the center of the chamber, pulling in more and more corpse meat, both living and dead, into itself. Screaming and howling men and women are pulled into the torrent, their nails and fingers breaking as they try to claw into the stones of the submerged floor.

Ruhr screams as the Demon King reforms and returns in a shape that is fully other and foreign to what he was before, consuming the flesh of the many. The castle quakes, and the world quakes as more and more souls flow into the beast that never finishes feeding. Crisis windows appear all around her, warning her of the impending end.

Nine-hundred thousand.

Nine-hundred and fifty thousand.

Seventy-five.

Ninety.

"Ruhr! Run!" barks Zacarias, pointing down a passageway off to the side of the throne room. "I'll hold him back!"

Ruhr pulls her wrist out of his grip as she takes his and yanks him down after her, jumping down into the red, water splashing in all directions as the disturbance of their motion catches the beast's eyes—tens of thousands of which squirm and twitch and look their way, many of them belonging to the people they had marched here with, as is clearly visible in the colors and the horror present within the many irises.

"Fuck retiring. Fuck chickens, and fuck the ocean!" yells Ruhr over the chaos, souls swirling down toward the consuming whirlpool. "Ruhr the river sorceress doesn't run!" she yells, water collecting around her hands as she charges toward the demon, which has a scythe of bone ready to swing her way.

That would all be terrible for her image, after all.

Laughter fills the chamber as chaos takes to the air. The castle rattles and shakes and crumbles while meat grows through the walls, the domains of reality and physicality beginning to crack and falter as the demon empowers itself by the second. A massive shadow swings her way, bones and fragments flying as she leaps, her feet making contact with the flat side of the blade of the massive scythe that arcs her way. Following its momentum, Ruhr runs over it and leaps, propelling her movements with a burst of water against the ground. A tendril shoots from the mass straight toward her heart, but a shattering fills the air as it strikes against a barrier, the meat compressing as it hits glass, eyes staring at her in rage as they try to reach, try to touch, but never come close enough to satisfy their desire.

Holding out her hands, Ruhr runs to the edge of the platform and jumps again, just as massive hands formed out of corpses slap down against it, trying to crush her. Holy water surges from her palm in the shape of a winding serpent, the fangs of which plunge into the warped, changed demon, a great hiss filling the world and carrying all around it once the graceful water touches the demon's raw flesh, soaking in through the gaps in its mass. She lands on the far side of the monster, her feet striking one barrier after the other that's been created for her by Zacarias, who strikes out himself, pushing back with a broken, cut shield against the weight of the mass that has thrust against him, trying to consume him whole.

A serpentine flow of water moves in all directions, spiraling around and around the chamber like a hurricane, ripping it apart, as the power of her magic is forced into motion by the sweltering heat of the radiating core that is all but fully gorged now. The presence, the power of it, distorts the body of her creation, pressing it out in all manners like bent bars of a cage being pried apart by hands that are too strong to be held by such simple things.

One after the other, spews of water break out of the deep reservoirs of the world below. Her mind races as she slides along a glass wall, ducking down below a tentacle of broken arms and legs that tries to whip her from straight ahead. She drops down, red water splashing as she lands next to Zacarias, holding her back to his.

The two move together, their steps and arms flowing in synchronicity with one another as she ducks and he blocks; as he pushes forward and she steps back to match him, neither needing the guidance of the other nor instructions, words, or even sight to know what the other is doing, to know how to flow together like two streams heading toward a single ocean, like two partners who have trained one another in their own shared dance, as their bloody, gore-soaked boots waltz over the graveyard of one million souls. Roaring fills the air, indescribable roaring, from all sources—from the beast, from the water, from her, from the torment of the world as they move and fight.

One after the other, barriers appear all over the chamber as Zacarias summons them with his magic, and one after the other, more and more serpentine flows appear everywhere, crisscrossing each other like the threads of a single weave. The chamber floods, water rising first to their ankles and then to their chests. The two of them move, ascending over the pool as they fight, running and dodging atop glassy platforms as meat and bone strikes toward the two of them—the two whose eyes never falter and whose heartbeats never stay out of pattern. With the stepping of their feet, they form their grand creation.

She doesn't know anything about art. Not the first goddamned thing.

But you don't have to be an artist to make something. You don't have to be an artist to appreciate a good plan, a good design, and a good state of flow. To appreciate something beautiful in its simplicity.

Nine-hundred and ninety-nine thousand.

Zacarias grabs her arm, Ruhr spinning with a spell in her hands as he hurtles her across a gap toward another platform.

Ruhr aims her hands at the Demon King's glowing, massive maw, which is gaping wide open. All around the chamber, dozens of shields and dozens of reservoirs of enchanted, glowing water have been collected, filled with the shine of everything she has in herself and of everything the dead have in themselves. Yes, they are prisoners of the Demon King. Yes, they are not with body or form, but that does not mean that they are without.

As they plummet toward the endless hell that awaits them, each and every soul does its part, leaving traces of their essence in the suspended pools of water. Each and every soul leaves the mark of its passing in this world. No matter what manner of life they lived—ugly, good, beautiful, wretched, full, or wrought with nothing but horror and sadness—they all leave a mark. They all leave a piece of themselves in the baptizing pools that glow like a million lanterns held up toward the eye of God in order to get his attention once and for all—not to ask for the aid of such a power, but to prove to it that the men and women of this world are capable of living alone in the shadow of such a presence. That they don't need its protection like a child would its parents. That they are—even in times of blood and bone—capable, strong, beautiful.

The power of one million souls collects in her hands, drenching her with their presence, quenching her, and drowning her as she flies and aims the final blast.

And out of the corner of her eye, Ruhr sees a massive spire falling down over Zacarias that he simply cannot guard against.

Her aim shoots to the side, the spell blasting toward the man instead of toward the beast, the torrent crashing against the thing that would have killed him, the spell—the likes of which can never be made twice—wasted.

Something crashes against her, and Ruhr tumbles, splashing and rolling through the water, her body cracking as she hits a pile of broken rubble. Zacarias lands next to her as the platforms break under the pressure of the Demon Core, as it all comes to an end.

Ruhr crawls back, her back pressing against the wall as she lifts her arm, holding it over Zacarias as she tries to shield him, her legs trying to get her to stand up again but not listening. "I'm sorry Zac," she says.

He reaches out, grabbing her arm, not to pull it off of him but to pull her to her feet as he tries to rise himself, but he stumbles and falls back down, the two of them falling over each other as they look at the encroaching, clawing mass that has but one word for them. A needlelike bone presses toward her heart, which has nowhere to go anymore. Zacarias grabs it, pulling as hard as he can, but he cannot make a single inch of a difference with his remaining strength, and it plunges through the fabric of her stained robe and pierces the layer of skin below.

"DES—"

Nothing.

The demon corruption, the beast who rules over all beasts, the lord of hellfire, and the nightmare that plagues all men, falls silent and still.

His pulsating, writhing, rippling mass of a body squirms and shifts as ten thousand eyes and then ten thousand more stop looking at them, and instead, look around the chamber in which something has changed. Something . . . odd.

Ruhr grits her teeth, her hands bloody as she cuts them while trying to pull the needle that is a hair's breadth from her heart away, but not succeeding. Her eyes follow the beast's, follow Zacarias's gaze, as they stare toward the entrance of the room, where water flows out of and into the rest of the chambers beyond, flowing down endless staircases and flights of many towers as everything leaks out toward the world below.

There's nothing there?

He's just staring at some ghost or something.

"Zac!" hisses Ruhr, now that the demon is distracted by whatever, and the man does his best to help her.

~ [The Demon King] ~

~ [Achievement Unlocked] ~
"The Great Deceit"
Unlocked By: Playing a trick on someone mean enough to make them lose all hope.
Reward: You're already mean enough; there's nothing else you need.

The endless eyes of the end of days stare, shaking and quivering, at what they see. Eyes that have both witnessed and projected untold, infinite horrors into this world look at the intruder inside their domain, gazing at the oddity, the . . . impossibility.

"No," it says, pulling together as a vaguely confused elf stands there with her mouth only slightly agape. She slowly blinks, looking around the chamber and then at him. The two of them stare at one another as he feels her, feels the familiarity of her, senses what she is, who she is. "It can't be . . ."

She hits her hand into an open palm, staring at him as their eyes lock. She steps forward, the demon compressing, heaps of flesh pulling away from her as a smile grows over her strangely placid face. A smile of familiarity. She nods, having reached her destination after all this time, after all of this journeying. The power of the spell had led her this way. The power of the poem.

The demon looks at her, knowing and understanding. It recoils and pulls itself together, readying to strike, readying itself to unleash the end. All of the horror, all of the ugliness, all of the despair, and all of the rot and decay to come have to come now, or they might never do so within this twisted world of theirs.

The Demon King, Swain, roars in a terror that he knows from his young days as a boy, before he became what he became, before this all took hold of his soul and made him what he is—what he chose to become. He feels a deep, primal fear in his black, wretched heart, wherever it might rest, which one would think to be impossible for something as cruel and malicious as him. But there it is, nonetheless, at the sight of her standing there with that smug, knowing smile on her face. That knowing look gazes down toward him from where she stands next to the pond as she towers over him—perhaps not in physical body, but in his own mind's eye—as he stares up to that horrific shadow of a monster, of a creature, of a beast in his memory who threatens to devour even him whole, leaving nothing in its wake but screams.

The Demon King cries out in horror as she spreads her arms out wide, looking at him, saying the single thing that she has journeyed for weeks, for months, through horror and mud, to say. The single imprinted word that carries with it the only blade that can cut his rotten soul. The only knife sharp enough to wound him and all that he is and has become, all that he represents, from the deepest pits of despair buried within the hearts of the living to the shadowy nightmares held in every child's thoughts.

It is the only power strong enough to rot what is rotten; the only light bright enough to kill the forcefully encroaching darkness of the Demon King that has plagued this world since his inception as a boy. It is not a sword or a pen; it is not a fist or a power held by any in times such as the ones beings as himself create. By design of his birth, such things have been fully removed from the world so that they might not ever come to harm him, to stop his quest to end the last day of man.

"HONK!" screams the girl into what might be his face, lowering her hand and pressing her eyes toward his. Her voice cracks as she shouts. Swain yelps, not as a demon but as a boy, faltering and recoiling further. She laughs.

The Demon King screams, roaring and raging in fear, his tendrils and mass flailing wildly all around himself as she looks at him.

"HONK! HONK! HONK!" yells the giddy woman, barely able to contain herself and her voice as she walks toward him almost tauntingly, mockingly, with that *LOOK* on her face, that look he's never forgotten. It's been imprinted into him, into his mind, ever since that day when he first met her; that day when that girl first stole him from his life and his path and made him what he became. Made him what he—

"HONK!" honks the woman, and he recoils, his poisonous thoughts breaking and shattering as she laughs and laughs and laughs and laughs. Her laughter fills the chamber of souls, of blood and marrow, as she holds her gut and falls to the wet floor, kicking and howling, splashing water everywhere. It carries all around him. Her laughter at what he is, at what he's become, at what he's created. She's laughing, laughing—she's always been laughing at him ever since they met; ever since the first time they met, she laughed at him.

The Demon King roars, thrashing, the castle cracking and breaking as he hammers against it, tendrils and fists and faces smashing against pillars and walls, breaking everything apart. Water splashes and stones fly. Guts churn and sinew snaps while his eyes bulge as he hits absolutely everything except her, the one person he cannot ever touch or reach—because she isn't real.

She doesn't exist here.

She only exists in his mind.

The girl whom he himself had created with a poem all of those days ago can barely look at him straight in the eyes as she points and opens her mouth to speak, but then just breaks into deeper laughter still as she tries to speak in between her bouts of it. "Ho—Ho—!" she starts, gasping for air and hammering against the wet ground with a fist as she looks at him. "HONK!" howls the girl who had marched all the way to the castle from where this all began. Had marched all the way to him, following sign after sign after sign, from that graveyard where he'd first left her.

Swain screams a howl that never stops, the cry carrying around the world over and over and over again, the walls of men and the halls of all that live, the hearts and minds of everyone and everything that remains upon this world partaking in the wretched scream he releases now, the same as he had done then.

It's a joke.

It's always been one big joke—him, his life, everything he does, wants, and makes. It's a joke, an absurdity. It's nothing but an illusion!

"HONK!" she screams, holding her hands next to her face as she presses it close to his bulging, quivering mass, which begins to falter and fall apart as he screams the poem that he had written back on that rainy day aloud, as the trickery of his own creation becomes apparent to him.

"Do not remember me," howls Swain, his tendril lashing out and trying to grab her, grab hold of her. "For that time, which we had shared is not now yet gone, passed," he recites, calling the poem he had written once on a grave, her grave, to the world once more. "It remains in present, in future," says the Demon King, the words becoming as clear to his eyes as she herself is. "My body has died," chants the final beast. "But my spirit will last—strong enough for us both together," he finishes in a scream as the appendage that tries to grab her squeezes shut in a crush.

But it crushes nothing.

As if she were a ghost, a specter gliding through a wall, the girl just points at him as she steps to the side. She is the spirit that lasts. She has no body, no physical presence in this world anymore, but she is what remains—the speck of her, the shadow of her that has been left behind since her departure from this world.

He's been a fool. He's been playing a game; he's so stupid and ugly and dumb. He's such an idiot; he's so foul, rotten, and broken. He's nothing but a joke.

"HONK!" she yells at him, as loud as she can, holding her arms out to her sides.

The elf smiles, shrugging, as she looks into the eyes of the beast who quivers in fear of something so simple, so plain and clear. They quiver in fear of the only weapon that could disarm a spirit so egoistical and contentedly locked into its own desires as his own.

Absurdity.

She parades around him absurdly, indifferent to what he is, what he's done, what he looks like, and what this place has come close to doing. She parades around him like a honking bird, marching over a freshly filled mass grave. She honks and chants and laughs at him like a teasing child, cutting him with a weapon that no member of the crusade, of any order of faith or military might, that no guardsman of a wall, that no fleeing man or woman had ever dared hold against him. Bravery, fearlessness, honor—all such things broke below the crushing weight of the Demon King. All such things faltered against him; all such things except this one, single thing.

The darkness fears laughter most of all; it fears not being seen or acknowledged. The heart of an artist fears nothing more than for their creations to never be noticed by the world in any capacity, just as the heart of a person wishes so deeply to be seen by those around them—but not like this. The darkness feeds on terror and fear; it thrives on it. But . . .

And as she does so, Swain, in his terror and fear, sees nothing else but her. Just like back then, just like when he was a boy and lived for nothing else, wanted for nothing else, knew nothing else—his eyes and imaginations, as endless and wide cast as they might be, see nothing but her.

They do not see the half elf. They do not see the human. They do not see their conspirings, actings, and schemings, as he has nothing but vision and mind for her . . .

". . . Goose . . ." calls the voice of the Demon King, faltering as it barely finds the strength to utter the absurd name of the absurd girl, of the one person who had never known him as anything but what he is.

She stops her parade, her hands held below her shoulders where she was flapping with imagined wings, turning her head toward him.

"Gods," she mutters. "You're still such a hopeless dweeb," says the blonde woman, shaking her head with pursed lips. "Get a grip." She rolls her eyes. "This is all just really sad and pathetic," says Goose, looking at him. "Because of a girl? Really?"

The Demon King screams his final scream as, from behind him, a great funnel of raging holy water arcs, a great syringe of sacred flow that shoots through a tightening tunnel of magical shields toward his core.

Red mass lurches as blue power blasts through it from one side to the other—the knife, the needle of water that the two surviving members of the assault had formed while he was distracted. It cuts through him like a sword plunging through a dragon's heart.

And perhaps they think it is what does the job. Perhaps Ruhr the river sorceress and Zacarias think they themselves have slain the beast, as they see nothing more than what they see, not having the eyes for such matters and details. Perhaps they will think so for the rest of their days—that they are what killed the Demon King, the two great heroes of the world to come after this long night has finally ended.

But they're not, really.

The final blow comes not from them but from her, from within the monster itself.

"Swain," finishes the phantom, her hand touching him as they stare at one another. She winks and tsks once with her mouth as she does so. "You diva," she says. "Come on, let's go together then, if this is how you're gonna be."

Everything shakes, rumbling and rattling, as the mass of meat and sinew bubbles and boils, the water pressing it apart from the inside out, rupturing him apart. Blackness takes everything he sees, then light takes everything he sees thereafter. Close to one million souls burst forth in a great flood that shoots toward the heavens, blasting out the broken castle toward the sky, filling it once more as if they each were the missing stars that had been taken from the heavens.

As the sky glows alight once more, shadows retreat, and monsters run in all directions as they pull away further and further into places that remain within the reaches of the fading night. The world below the castle begins to shake and quake, System windows appearing all across the landscape, within the vision of every man, woman, and child who still graces the world, who stare out in confusion at the brightness that slowly returns to the world outside their homes, second by second, moment by moment.

The Demon King was here, and their world was plunged into darkness and anarchy.

And then he wasn't.

! [Critical System Notification] !
THE ONE-HUNDRED-YEAR CRISIS - THE AGE OF DEMONS
The Demon King has been slain. The one-hundred-year crisis is over.
Difficulty: IMPOSSIBLE
Surviving Members: Ruhr, the River Sorceress. Guardsman Zacarias Montero

Really, it's almost absurd how fast things can change, isn't it?

And as for the heroes of humanity, as for Ruhr and Zacarias, who stand in the chaos, in the mess of the people they fought with and proclaimed to know and care for in so many different ways, the two of them look not at the beast but at each other.

And at a poem inscribed below their feet that they observe in horror as the very last droplet of corrupted, foul, demonic magic is expelled into the world as one last, cruel, *wicked* spell.

Ruhr and Zacarias,
Sitting in a tree,
K-I-S-S-I-N-G

The two of them vanish and are teleported away.

And the castle falls apart into nothing but rubble.

The era of the Demon King comes to a close. The carnival, the games, the artistry—all of it comes to a full stop, the pursuit of beauty having never been fulfilled in the context of the Demon King's twisted desires.

But those were nonsense to begin with, and he always knew it to be so, hence the presence of the carnival all of this time.

True beauty is such a fleeting, distant thing, that it is impossible for it to exist in any plane—either in this physical world or in the spirit world. Beauty, like words such as *love* or *faith*, is so flexible and malleable that it can mean entirely different things to entirely different people. What the dancer perceives to be beautiful is not what the painter might desire, and what the painter desires is not what the cook wishes to create. What the man sees when he stares at a long sunset from his home is not what the woman sees when she stares at the same sun rising in the early morning. The hearts of people are so different—some dark, some light, some wicked, and some kind—that their individualities simply make it too impossible to ever arrive at a homogeneous point of beauty that everyone agrees on.

Something like a "raw," undistilled essence of this concept can't exist. That's nonsense. Beauty is not an alchemical product; it is not something you can make through any form of creation. Beauty is a natural occurrence that happens when the presence of the universe in some specific place aligns with the perceptions of those there in that moment. Horror is a graveyard to a mother who stands over her sons, but a sign of honor to a general who looks at his fallen brothers. Poison is to an alcoholic what a remedy is to a man who ails in pain of the soul that never seems to leave him no matter what he does.

And so, the same, is beauty.

Do not seek beauty. Do not live your life in pursuit of it, and do not be so silly and childish as to proclaim that it is what you hope to create before the end of your days.

One does not create beauty.

One arrives at it.

CHAPTER 19

THE DAYS YET TO COME

~ [Ruhr, the River Sorceress] ~
Half Elf | ♀ | Sorceress
Rank: SSS
Location: The Graveyard of One Million
Level: 100

~ [Months later] ~

I'm not a good person," says Ruhr, snow falling all around them as they find themselves in a place that is full but empty. "I'm a monster," continues the half elf, kneeling down over a stone with her hand resting on it.

"No, you're not," replies an affirming voice from behind her, a hand resting on her shoulder as the two of them stand in a graveyard.

It's quiet.

Ruhr looks up over her shoulder to the man standing behind her, lightly pursing her lips. She doesn't manage to fully shake her head for more than a slight budge. "She thought I loved her, Zac." Her gaze turns back toward the grave. "I was just . . . She thought . . ."

Ruhr's eyes read over the name on the stone, one of the many thousands and thousands of dead who had fallen in the fight against the Demon King.

"What does this make me?" asks the river sorceress as she reads Springer's name out on the tombstone. Two small statues of a frog and an owl sit on top, which sets it apart from the many others adorned with flowers, candles, and such things. "I killed the Demon King," says Ruhr.

"We," interrupts Zacarias quietly.

"But . . . she thought I loved her." She doesn't look at him. "What does that make me?"

It's quiet as her hand rests on the grave of the priestess whom she didn't dislike. Whom she maybe even liked. Whom . . .

"A mess," replies Zacarias plainly, squeezing her shoulder.

Ruhr snorts, hating him for it, as she wipes fresh wetness from her eyes.

"Life is messy," he remarks. "If you want to think that you did bad, okay," says Zacarias, "then you did bad." His hand lets go of her shoulder as she rises back up to her feet, not looking away from the grave. "Do better next time. That's all we have."

Ruhr looks after him as he starts to leave. "Next time?" asks Ruhr. "Zeezee, baby," says the half elf, straightening her posture and swiping a strand of her regrowing hair out of her face. "There's no *next time*," she notes. "One-hundred-year crises happen once every hundred years. We're done," Ruhr declares. "I'm done. The next one isn't my problem."

Zacarias stops, his hands in his pockets. It's strange seeing him without armor.

Looking back over his shoulder at her, he extends his elbow outwardly, and Ruhr grabs hold of it and his upper arm as they walk away together. "*Our* problem," remarks the man, looking down at her. "And you and I both know that's nonsense." He shakes his head. "There's going to be plenty of problems before that one comes around," assures Zacarias as they leave the graveyard. "And the world will, as much as I hate to say it, need someone like you to handle it."

"Like whom?" asks Ruhr.

"Like—"

"RUHR!" shouts the elf, her voice carrying over the graves of ten thousand dead as he looks down at her. "THE RIVER SORCERE—" Ruhr's voice is gagged and muffled as he holds his hand over her mouth, looking around them at the graveyard.

"Not here," he says. "Show some respect for the dead."

Ruhr pulls his hand down. "—ess," finishes Ruhr quietly, narrowing her eyes as the two of them look down at the box one of her feet is resting on.

"Where did that even come from?" mutters Zacarias.

Ruhr shakes her head. "Don't worry about it, Big Z," she says, pulling his hand down from her face to her throat. "You can keep your hand here, though."

"Graveyard," reminds Zacarias, sighing and pulling his arm away from her, shaking his head as he walks off.

"Come on, Zac!" yells Ruhr after him, laughing as she hits him in the back. "Let's take a break," she encourages, turning back one last time to look around the graveyard before walking after the man and a new life.

Zacarias and Ruhr the river sorceress go on to those new days that await them together, separately together at first, as always, and then together-together, as was prophesized by the grim poetry of the Demon King that teleported the two of them out of the castle, the text of which neither of them ever spoke about until, during an adventure of theirs, they crash off a cliff in their carriage during a mission to capture the last escaped gallu of the Demon King and into a large tree, where they are stuck together for weeks during a strange, very abrupt storm that never seems to end, until it suddenly does.

Later, the mission is successful thanks to their efforts, and the last escaped demons—a former engineer and two strange, monstrous knights—are taken into custody. But she never follows up after that, wanting to wash her hands of the whole Demon King matter once and for all.

And then, one day, Ruhr does find herself sitting in a house by the ocean with some chickens and goats, as well as with Zacarias.

All of the fame, fortune, and glory became too much after all, after decades of it.

She's retired now, and happy.

Monsters still roam the world, as do many of the Demon King's terrors, but they are slowly being hunted down one after the other by the restored legions and cities of men, elves, dwarves, Vildt, orcs, and fairies. And honestly, such things aren't really her problem anymore.

Ruhr looks over to the side at Zacarias, who is sitting in a chair next to hers, the two of them holding hands.

"Hey, Zac," says Ruhr, the older but familiar face looking her way. His hair has turned into tones of a strong, salted gray. "Remember that time we were in the Demon King's castle and you cried?"

"As far as I recall," replies the old man, who is used to her teasing and games after all of this time, "your face was just as wrinkly as it is now because of all the salt on it," he remarks, the two of them bickering and squabbling, but not in a bad way, as both of them argue with a smile on their faces about who cried the most back when they were young.

As one does.

And as for any spirits who left the world, be they from the chests of men or women or demons, one never really knows what happens after the exchange from life to death.

But none of these come back to plague them during their time, not during their lives nor in their dreams below a night sky that never quite becomes as bright as it once was before everything that happened.

THE END

~ [Later] ~

Now come the end of the end of days. The world is lost in a state of confused calm and quietness. The peace that covers everything is so foreign and strange that most everyone simply doesn't know what to do with it. Like a graceful being of heaven with fake wings, like a bird that has only ever fallen from the nest, they do not know how to proceed now in this new day and age, which is, in a sense, much the same but also very different from the times that were before the crisis.

The ability for men and women to look one another in the eyes is all but diminished, as everyone knows the sins they committed in order to pass through the gates of hell, and everyone assumes that everyone else knows of their transgressions. People were left behind, kicked out, abandoned to claws and teeth, frantic, desperate. Animal survival was all that mattered for so many for so long that now that the crisis is over, it seems almost impossible to go back to what was once before.

The world almost feels like it is fake, like it is an illusion.

How can it ever go back to what it was?

It can't.

And that is the truth that will take many years to relearn, as one after the other, the survivors of the Demon King's crisis slowly realize that they can never go back. There is only the forward direction remaining to them, the path onward, and nothing more than that. The shine of the bright morning light of the spring that is coming illuminates nothing more than a single road, nothing more than a single, simple path through a metaphorical valley that passes through the seas of darkness.

Forward.

The only direction is forward, and so, after some time, this is the way people move, although many at slower paces than others.

The young who grow and form into adults—those who never knew the horrors of what came during their adolescence—are the ones who change the world, who forcefully push it toward that brighter future as they live the lives people who are blessed to be free sometimes live—simple and clean, troubled by nothing more than the demons of simplicity and mundaneness.

Every day is the same, and every night is the same. Every spring is calm and gentle; every summer is lively and abuzz. Every autumn is pacifying, and every winter is hardening. And every night, they listen to the howls of those who might never recover, the people who never heal from the horrific wounds imprinted onto them by the rupturing of the soul that they experienced during the demon era.

But the young do not understand the howling men.

How could they?

For in this generation and time to come, there is no hurt, pain, or terror that comes even close to what those broken souls feel as they stare up even now toward the night sky, knowing that it has many fewer stars than it once had. The bottles in their hands and the shaking of their fingers do little to convince those fresh, new minds of the validity of their claims. Their desperate, frantic whispers and warnings of a world that could come again are all but ignored by ears that simply aren't able to contextualize their claims. And those who do remember, those who were there during the reign of the Demon King, those who know that these peddlers of madness speak the truth—they hold their silence and live on their lives until the very end in peace, not daring once to utter the name of the beast, to acknowledge the truth of what really happened during that time that felt like years on end, lest the memories spring from their own heads with claws and fangs.

Perhaps it is better to forget. Perhaps it is better to let die out the corrupted generation who knew nothing but horror.

And so they do.

Years go by one after the other, and then decades. People fall into age and illness, and they slowly begin to fade away. The world begins to heal again, the destroyed nation pushing out again from its ruptured capital. Like a seed bursting from its shell, the tendrils of life press out in all directions. They force themselves into ruins and outposts; they force themselves into the temples of forgotten orders and into the domains of witchery and forbidden mysticism. They force themselves out into forests that have regrown out of ash—greener and brighter than any in the world because of the richness of the nutrient-laden soil.

War manages to be kept at bay, despite the obviousness of it, as all nations are healing in their own way. But slowly, as the memory of the Demon King fades from the minds of the counselors and kings in power, as those days become but a story in a history book, fires begin to ignite again—passions of many fruits.

And as these fresh disruptions to peace ignite, so do they also inflame a new spark.

Artistry comes together, hand in hand not with peace and gentleness, but with times of angst. Great painters emerge from the population to capture such moments in history, and the tales of old are retold by scribes, dancers, and actors of the theater. Songs are sung, and festivities are held with traditional dishes of those days—the recipes of which are perhaps more freely invented than actually recalled, as so much documentation and knowledge of so many places were lost.

But, nonetheless, a culture of art emerges like a fresh flower breaking the melting winter ice. It takes these decades to happen, but it does eventually.

And yes, people die and kill each other; they maim, steal, and pillage from their brother nations, but this is all only in the usual metric. It is only ever enough to shift a border here or a border there by a day's march; only ever enough to serve as a spark that kindles innovation, so that the other might be better beaten.

And so it goes on.

And soon, a hundred years have passed since the crisis of the Demon King.

A new crisis emerges, and the population is once again unprepared for the raw horror to come, as those who are alive simply do not know of what came before—only the warnings of their grandparents and elders, often largely dismissed as dramatic stories of old. However, this new crisis is beaten and destroyed as well—much more readily and easily than the Demon King had been.

Propelled by this, the world changes, shifts, and grows in ways never seen before. Nations merge with one another, setting aside many differences to become global powers rather than regional ones. An empire forms and holds the world captive in awe of its stability and wealth, as people of so many creeds and origins fall under a single banner.

It feels like humanity and its ilk of all races—elves and orcs, fairies and goblins and dwarves, and everything else that falls under the mark of life—have finally found their way into a pace that cannot be broken by such powers as monsters or war.

It feels like a great peace has finally come to the world, like the shine of a day that never ends.

And it is good.

Of the past, nothing remains.

Nothing of note, nothing of significance—not a whisper. Time has flowed on like a raging river, never able to stop.

~ [A Young Girl, Many Generations Later] ~

She hums quietly to herself as she stands there, looking around in confusion at the nearly empty glade.

Where is he?

Her older brother said they would see their father today. He's been gone for a while, and she was so excited to see him again.

The young girl stands there in the rain, her hands shaking with nervousness as she clutches something firmly against her chest. The crumpled paper crinkles in her grip as her fingers press down on it while she stares down at the mark in the forest—a mark of stone that bears her father's name but not his presence.

"Where is he?" asks the child, breaking the tapping silence of the rain all around them. The thousands of droplets, striking against the verdant leaves of the forests, sound perhaps like rain to someone who is simply standing there and listening to the collage of noises all around them. The sound of the storm sounds like nothing more than what it is—a force of nature with no deeper purpose or meaning behind it than the simplicity of its existence. But for someone with a stronger imagination, someone who is viewing the world through a strange filter of confused artistry, they might hear something else . . .

She lifts a small hand, pulling on her brother's robe as she stares up at him and away from the stone marker they stand before. "Hey, where?" she asks as the rattling, tapping, and almost frightening noise of the rain strikes out all around them.

The young man's body stiffens as she touches him and her voice reaches him. His arm and fist both tighten as she pulls on his robe. "Hey!" she asks again as the young man next to her pulls his arm away, lifting his fist into the air.

"SHUT UP!" shouts her brother at her, his hand held back. She flinches, covering her face and head with her hands and the papers held within them.

It's quiet, apart from the rain, for a while.

And then a hiss comes as the man releases the air from his lungs. Her brother drops his arm, not striking her with it. But he turns away and walks. "He's dead. Idiot," he explains, looking back over his shoulder with a cold, almost judgmental gaze—as if she had done something wrong. But she doesn't really know what?

Frightened, she looks at her brother from behind the soggy paper as he walks off into the forest, leaving her alone there by the grave that she doesn't understand. She's too young. Such concepts are very fresh and unfamiliar to her, let alone the context behind them. But she does know that she's scared and confused by her brother's reaction.

Sniffling and emotional, she watches him walk away, not sure if she should run after him or not. Is she allowed to be here alone? She's never been alone anywhere like this before.

No, wait.

"Papa . . ." mutters the scared girl, turning back to the grave and looking at it, half-expecting the man's firm voice to come to her from it at any moment, as if he were simply behind a door that she's too small and weak to open. She rubs her face dry, as best as is possible, before looking at the grave again and holding out her work. The soggy papers have a scrawling on them from top to bottom in what might look like the confused scratchings of a child learning to write if one did not know better.

But as is the case with life, there are so many things that can only be seen if one has the eyes for it. Special eyes, the kind that see things that others don't.

"I wrote you another song!" she says excitedly, holding out the paper full of lyrics to the gravestone. The fresh ink runs down the wet paper, perhaps a little like blood, if one were so imaginative.

The young girl sits down by the grave and clears her throat, closing her eyes. If her father is here somewhere, but not close enough to see, then she's going to have to lift her voice so that he can hear her.

And so, she sings her song exactly as it is on the paper that almost melts in her hands as it becomes soggy and soft. But that's okay. She knows the words by heart, as she's been humming the tune all the way here to herself. She doesn't understand what makes a song good or bad, what makes a person like one or not like one—but these things don't even matter to her. What matters to her childlike mind is that the song is for her father, that she wrote it, and that she is now singing it to him. All criteria for something good have been met already.

All criteria of something that belongs to a word she doesn't really understand, but has heard before, have been met.

Beauty.

She sings a song that is perhaps not professional in the ears of the great musicians of the world, but that is beyond compare for the powers who are listening in to her lamentation in the rain that becomes stronger and more furious.

Perhaps a paranoid, confused, esoteric mind would say that the rain is trying to overpower the sound of her voice, to drown her words out and muffle them so that they might never come to the ears of those unseen forces listening to her.

Or perhaps what is more likely is that the sound of the falling rain, as before imagined by that overly creative mind, sounds like the ten thousand legs of a dancing creature, followed by ten thousand more—tapping and spinning, and dancing to the words of her song that fill the glade.

The paper turns to mush in her hands, the rough fibers of the cheap material falling apart as she is drenched, but she is too young to really care about such a concept as getting wet because of the rain, and she sings and sings, and the unseen thing with countless legs, eyes, and souls dances as it winds its way once more between the physical and the spirit worlds, creating a bridge between both that every man and woman in this era has long forgotten.

The stars in the night sky tremble in fear, knowing what is to come once again. The soil of the grave sinks in somewhat as it is saturated by water.

And perhaps a young man screams in the darkening forest behind her as something takes him into the night that promises to be very, very, very long for everyone who is now alive to see it.

But perhaps he doesn't. Perhaps there is nothing at all. Perhaps a very old, green slime that has been waiting for a long, long, long times drops down onto her head from the trees above and eats her.

Who can really say for sure at the end of the day?

After all, art is a very subjective thing.

D. M. Rhodes is a rising star author in the fantasy and LitRPG space, crushing the top rankings with popular series such as Demon Core, Dungeon Item Shop, Sunflower: The LitRPG, and Reborn as the Black Knight. Find out more at www.DMRhodes.com!

CHAPTER 71

CALL IT TREASON

I DON'T THINK we can trust that man, and I say so.

"You're probably right," my mom answers.

"It's fitting, I think, that they came from Fort Lee, and now they're headed back there."

"Why is that?" I ask.

"Fort Lee was named for Charles Lee, a general during the revolutionary war," Ms. Marrillion explains. "First of all, he was court-martialed for bungling an attack and then screwing up the retreat when it failed. On top of which, he failed to tell George Washington, who was expecting Lee's men to be somewhere else, during the Battle of Monmouth."

"That's not great," I say. "I hope I'm a better Lee than that guy."

"You are! And it gets worse. Many years later, a historian found a secret plan Lee had written during captivity which explained to the British how they could defeat the colonist's rebellion. A lot of people believe it was an act of treason."

"And they named a city after him?"

"Well, they named a fort after him, and then neglected to change it, so the town ended up with the same name. A military official, doing things he wasn't authorized to do, taking actions that could have brought down the fledgling country. I think our secret agent friend has a bit in common with Charles Lee."

"He claimed that he was trying to stop all the bad guys," I say, "but I'm not sure I believe him."

"I agree with your assessment. We're probably still in as much danger as we have been the whole time."

We stop to pick up the tactical bulletproof vests. My mom insists I put one on, even though it's so hot outside.

"The British conquered Fort Lee in late 1776," Ms. Marrillion says. "That's when Thomas Paine wrote *The American Crisis*. It says, 'These are the times that try men's souls.' And I feel like we're living in those times again. Except that I would say these are the times that try *women's* souls, too."

Once we're all wearing the protective body shields, we continue our walk back towards Manhattan. These things are hot and uncomfortable, but much better than taping a bunch of catalogs and magazines to your arms and chest. Trust me on that.

"So we'll stick with our original plan?" I ask.

"I don't believe we have any other choice," Ms. Marrillion says.

It's time to get working on our endgame.

Back in Manhattan, we duck into the George Washington Bridge Bus Terminal to lose any tail we might have. The place is packed with people, since the traffic jam we caused has delayed a large number of bus departures. People trying to get back to New Jersey are overflowing the waiting areas and little shops tucked into the sprawling complex.

Inside the Gap Outlet, mom buys a few cheap items of clothing we can use as a disguise, and then we split up since we figure they'll be looking for three of us together, or at least two.

"Try to walk close to someone else, a big man if possible, like you're friends with them," my mom says. "That should make us harder to spot."

The big sale shirt she bought for me covers the bulletproof vest, and then she also buys me an iced coffee so that I can look more casual. People fleeing danger don't usually stop for beverages, she argues.

I take all the stuff out of the bag D'Argyle gave me and transfer it into my pockets. Whatever I can't carry, I give to my mom.

"See you at the rendezvous," Ms. Marrillion says cheerfully. She must be happy this is all going to end soon, one way or another.

CHAPTER 72

THIS MUST BE THE PLACE

THE CITY IS full of places. That seems obvious, I guess. *Everywhere* is full of places. But they're closer together here than anywhere else, and there are more different kinds.

Still, it wasn't easy to choose a place for us all to meet up. That's because we had such specific requirements:

We need to be able to use the internet without it being traced back to us.

We need privacy, so that our neighbors and random strangers aren't watching or listening to us.

We need multiple escape routes, just in case somebody dangerous finds us.

We need someplace new, where we haven't been yet today, so that our movements aren't traceable and nobody is waiting for us to return so they can attack.

All that narrows things down a bit. High on the Hog is out of the running. Coffee shops are off the list. That new food hall with the bouncer who's not a bouncer would be great, but we don't know if the thug who kept getting knocked unconscious might be keeping an eye on it. The seedy hotel isn't an option, and I'm kind of glad, because it was gross.

Luckily, there's a place that's welcoming, and hopefully will lead to the happy ending Ms. Marrillion deserves after all these years.

It's a big place, and there's a sign outside that says:

COME ON IN, OR SMILE AS YOU PASS

Or, at least, there was, before mom's dreaded gentrification changed the neighborhood and developers took over the space from the church that ran it for many years.

It's the United Palace, the movie theater where I saw *The Sound of Music* and where John Wick teamed up with the Russians in *John Wick 3*. The doors are usually locked, but D'Argyle knows a back way in, through the loading area, and we can access the Wi-Fi because someone gave him the password when he was there for his cousin's graduation.

On top of all that, it's only a few blocks from the bus station, so it's a short walk for Ms. Marrillion.

No one pays any attention to me as I walk down Broadway, looking ridiculous in my disguise draped over my protective-vest. If anyone stopped to stare, they'd notice all kinds of weird angles and shapes beneath the giant Gap t-shirt.

It's noisy, as the traffic delays have spread out from the bridge entrance to the connecting streets here on Upper Broadway. Drivers are angry, shaking their heads, looking at their phones, and honking every so often, as if they think this whole citywide jam was caused by somebody who didn't notice the light had changed, and a horn is going to gently remind them to put their foot on the gas.

As loud and hectic as it is, as hard as it makes it to concentrate, I think it actually helps us blend in. The chaos means one or two suspects won't stand out against the end-of-day madness on the streets and sidewalks.

I make it to the United Palace without any trouble, and find D'Argyle by the back door, which swings open a few inches.

"It's me," I say.

"Come on in," he says.

I slip inside, and he pulls the door almost shut, with just a crack for him to see through to the street.

"Am I the first one here?"

"Yeah, but don't get too cocky. That just means you're faster than a hundred-year-old woman and your mom."

"I wasn't bragging," I say. "Just curious."

I take everything out of my pockets and put them on the floor near the door. I want to take off the vest, but I don't know if that's safe.

"My mom's bringing a vest for you," I tell D'Argyle.

His eyes bug out.

"Is someone going to shoot at me?"

"Let's hope not."

I push him aside and say, "I'll watch the door. You get to work on the next part of the plan."

"Aye aye, captain," he says.

I think he's making fun of me.

D'Argyle sets up shop in what looks like a small music studio while I keep my eyes peeled for my mom, Ms. Marrillion, and trouble.

If the man on the bridge was telling the truth, then nobody is out looking for us, scheming to grab us. But if he was lying, like we think he was, we're still in danger. Maybe it's a less chaotic danger, not random gangsters and hitmen running around anymore, but government agents and coordinated groups. Those kinds of people would be even harder to spot, although they might stand out clearly as not being from the neighborhood.

That's the thing about a community like ours. People who live here mostly get along with each other and know how to behave. People in suits from downtown are the ones who look lost, the same way I'd be sus walking around the offices near Wall Street.

Nobody seems out of place, although it's hard to get a really good view through the crack in the door. You kind of need to see the big picture to notice something unusual. I move my body back and forth to change the angle I can see out through the vertical line of light where the door meets the wall of the United Palace.

And I see a normal day, for the most part:

Restaurants with people waiting outside for carryout because it's too hot inside near the kitchen. Any place that isn't a sit-down-and-eat sort of joint doesn't turn on the AC if they can help it.

Then there are the sidewalk vendors, selling electronic junk and stolen goods, candles and sunglasses.

All the commuters headed to and from the bus station walk right past the little mall of carpets filled with goods. Locals sometimes stop and talk to them, the ones they know, or the ones they see every day.

Delivery guys with big heavy insulated food carriers like I was pretending to be earlier, except they're mostly on bikes and electronic scooters.

Guys standing on the corner checking out women passing by, sometimes yelling a crude comment, and sometimes just staring.

Pigeons fluttering around searching for crumbs or even whole sandwiches people dropped.

Delivery men, even this late in the day, loading crates full of drinks from small trucks into bodegas.

Older folks with giant bags of dirty aluminum cans, collecting them for the 5-cent deposit.

For everyone else out there, it's just another day.

There's more car traffic than usual, of course, and people seem a little angrier, more on edge. Horns are honking, but it's not like people are running around screaming. Up here in Washington Heights, we're used to problems and take them as they come.

———

Eventually I see them.

It's not that hard, as they're moving kind of slowly.

I wish they'd move faster, but then again, Ms. Marrillion is pretty old, and it would be a big problem if she fell and broke her hip like old people always seem to do. Then we'd have to go to the hospital, where we'd be sitting ducks, and we wouldn't have a chance to finish this thing.

It's painful to watch and wait, hoping they make it here without being attacked.

Part of me wants to run out there and see if I can speed things along, but that would just be risking our whole set up. In fact, even if a big van pulled up and someone reached out and grabbed them like I got grabbed earlier, I'd probably let them get taken. It'd be too dangerous to go out onto the streets, where I probably couldn't do much, and then they might see where I'd come from, which could put D'Argyle and our evidence at risk.

But maybe my instincts would win out over logic and I'd sprint out to try to help?

It's a question I don't have to answer.

They finally make it to the door, slowly, and I open it up wide to let them in.

And so here we are, together in the dark, reunited at the United Palace.

CHAPTER 73
PLAYBACK

WE HUG EACH OTHER, even though it hasn't been that long since we were together at the bridge.

My mom pats me on the head.

"All set?"

"I think so," I say. "D'Argyle's working on it in the studio."

I point to the room he was working in.

His head pops out; maybe he heard me say his name.

"I've got it all set up. It's a bit rough, you know. If I had more time, I could clean it up nice and tight."

"I'm sure you could," Ms. Marrillion says. "But I think it's probably best to get it over with as soon as we can."

I make sure the door is closed, and turn the bolt so that nobody can get in the same way we did. We all go into the smaller room, where D'Argyle has his laptop on the desk, with Audacity set up as if he's making a podcast.

I guess, in a way, he is, except one that will only have one listener.

He clicks on the spacebar, and we hear the voice of the man from the bridge.

At the CIA, though, we've been increasing our power over time. Especially after 9/11. We're the big dogs now.

We couldn't record him on our phones, but D'Argyle's podcast recorder in the bag picked up everything the CIA agents said. There were a few stray honking horns in the background, but generally their voices were clear.

Then we hear Ms. Marrillion's voice: *You're from the CIA, then?*

Yes, he replies.

There's more of it, stuff from later in the conversation stitched together to make a pretty damning recording. On its own, the audio might not be the most convincing evidence in the world, but when it's combined with video of us meeting on the bridge that D'Argyle downloaded from various local news channel websites? It's persuasive enough.

I tear open another prepaid phone that mom bought with cash on the way here and hand it to Ms. Marrillion.

She squints at the business card and dials the number the man from the CIA gave us, dialing the number slowly. Then she presses connect and we hear it ringing softly.

"I can't find the speakerphone button," she says.

"I got you," D'Argyle replies, and takes the phone, then switches it so we can all hear.

It rings a few more times, and then the man picks up.

"Let's keep this brief," Ms. Marrillion says. "I assume you're trying to track us. Is anyone else listening in?"

"No, but—"

"Don't interrupt me. Let me say what I have to say. I don't trust you. I don't trust anyone who's involved, and I just want my life back. I want you to leave me alone and make sure everyone else leaves me alone. I'm not giving you anything, because I need to hold on to it for my own safety. Now listen."

She nods at D'Argyle, who plays the audio file, and she holds the phone close enough to the laptop speakers that the man can hear his own words coming back at him.

He must be surprised because he doesn't try to interrupt while the recording plays.

"It matches nicely with the video footage from the news helicopters," Ms. Marrillion says when it's over. "It seems pretty bad for you, and for the Agency as a whole. I think you can agree, it's something we'd all want kept under wraps."

He is silent for a while.

"How do I know I can trust you?"

"You don't. You have to take it on faith. I assume you know I grew up in an orphanage. They taught us a lot about faith there, and how we had to believe in a better future despite all signs to the contrary. You wanted me to trust you, and I want you to trust me. We made it through the Cold War alive because neither side used their weapons, even though they were both armed to the teeth."

She looks at her watch.

"I think I've been on the phone long enough. What's it going to be? Do you agree to my terms?"

"I need more time. I can't authorize—"

"You're out of time. This is it. Do we have a deal? Or do we go to war?"

He sighs.

"I'm going to hang up," she says.

"Fine. Deal. You don't know what you're asking me to—"

"I'm hanging up now. If you keep your side of the bargain, I'll never see or hear from you again. I can't say it will be much of a loss. If you do your part, I'll keep all my secrets and take them to the grave with me."

"What about the mom and her kid?"

"Same deal with them. As long as they stay safe, your secrets will be too."

Ms. Marrillion nods at D'Argyle, who disconnects the phone.

"Just to be safe, let me get rid of this thing," he says. "I'll throw it in the back of a truck or some other moving vehicle."

He opens the burner up and pulls out the SIM card from inside, then slips out the back door of the United Palace.

It's just me, my mom, and Ms. Marrillion again.

"I hope that worked," Ms. Marrillion says.

CHAPTER 74

THE FUTURE I'LL NEVER SEE

I GUESS there's no real way to know for sure.

They could follow us and keep tabs on us, and we might not know it. They might come after us and try to kill us, but hopefully they're smart enough not to try. I don't think there's any reason for them to know about D'Argyle, so even if they came for me and my mom and Ms. Marrillion, he could always release the evidence.

We will have to follow through on what we promised, too, by setting up some sort of safe deposit box and method for releasing everything we know in the event that something happens to us. Ms. Marrillion even suggests that we call the number she has periodically, to remind that man we're still alive and alert, that we haven't let our guard down.

If this were a movie, I think we'd disappear from New York and start new lives in new towns. Mom would buy a fishing boat or something corny like that, renting it out to tourists in Central America. Ms. Marrillion would open a bed-and-breakfast in Europe. I'd go to college somewhere far away, traveling by train like Mekhi Phifer at the end of Spike Lee's *Clockers*, which D'Argyle made me watch one time.

Except we don't want to leave NYC. I'm no Mekhi Phifer. This is not a movie, it's our lives. The whole point of staying and fighting and keeping Ms. Marrillion alive was that this city is our home, and we shouldn't have to leave just because some idiots in the government and the mob and other institutions made a mistake 60 years ago.

While we wait for D'Argyle to get back, we talk about what we're going to do next. Not long-term planning, but the rest of today.

"I want to go home and take a shower, then go get something to eat," I say.

"We could all use a bath," Ms. Marrillion agrees. "And I'd be honored if you let me take you out to dinner, anywhere you want."

I look at my mom and she laughs.

"She means somewhere fancy, but if you want to waste your free dinner on Olive Garden, that's your prerogative."

"I can take your mother somewhere else another night," Ms. Marrillion says. "So tonight we can just go somewhere you and D'Argyle would enjoy."

"I hope our building isn't too messed up from that guy with the gun," I say.

"I'm sure the super has it repaired by now—he's always on top of that sort of thing," Ms. Marrillion says. "Although my apartment may need a good cleaning."

"You can stay with us as long as you need," my mom tells her.

"That's very nice of you. I'd hate to have to go to the hotel from last night." She scratches her head. "But maybe I'll splurge and treat myself to a night at the Waldorf. I've always wanted to stay there, but never had a good reason, since I already live in Manhattan."

I open up the laptop and start looking up the hotel online to see if I can get her a reservation for tonight. Then D'Argyle comes back.

"I got in a cab, and pretended I changed my mind about needing a ride, but stuck the phone under the seat while I was in there. Wherever his next fare takes him, the government will be looking there, if they manage to track the phone."

"Thank you, D'Argyle," Ms. Marrillion says.

"My pleasure to help, Miss Lemon-Meringue."

He *has* to know that's not really her name. I think at this point he's just messing with her.

D'Argyle packs up our stuff and we sneak back out the back door of the United Palace, ready to begin the short walk uptown on Broadway, finally headed home.

Then…

I kind of hear the yelling, but it's all a haze.

I see a flash of light and the sideburns on the face of the man from the elevator yesterday. Only this time, he's got a gun pointed at me. I hear it pop, and at the same moment I feel like somebody's hit me in the chest with a sledge hammer and I fall backward.

Everything goes black.

CHAPTER 75
GOING HOME

I COULD HAVE GONE my whole life without getting shot.

Most people do.

And I'll be happy if I never get shot again.

Because even with the bullet-proof vest I'm wearing, it *hurts*.

They rarely show that on TV shows, where it always seems like people wearing vests get knocked out for a commercial break, long enough for you to think they're dead, and then they open their eyes and act like nothing happened.

But I can already tell I'm going to have a huge bruise and it's going to keep on hurting for days.

My mom is never going to let me forget that she saved my life by making me put on the bulletproof vest we got at the bridge. I guess sometimes she knows what she's doing.

Which is more than I can say for the guy who shot me.

He picked the wrong neighborhood, and I'm surprised he didn't learn his lesson yesterday.

Right after he shot me, as he was standing in the middle of the street, somebody intentionally steered their car into him. Then a bunch of locals mobbed him and started beating on him. They might have killed him if the feds hadn't shown up and taken him away. Everyone on the block was mad about that because it seemed like they were protecting him. After everything that's happened since yesterday, though, I think he may be in for a worse fate in the hands of the government.

I watch all this from the ground while my mom is hovering over me, making sure I'm alright.

When she pulls the vest up and makes sure the guy's bullet didn't get through it, she sighs with relief.

"Probably got a broke-ass gun," D'Argyle says, and I can tell he's also relieved that I'm not dead.

"Still hurt like a—"

"Watch your mouth, Lee," my mom says. "Just because you got shot doesn't mean you can start swearing."

"Aw, mom. If not now, when?"

Ms. Marrillion laughs. "I hate to think what kind of language *I* would use if I got shot and lived to talk about it," she says.

A couple of the guys in suits make their way over from the chaos around the shooter and check to make sure I didn't get killed.

"Is the kid alright?"

"I'm fine," I say, although I don't sound fine. I'm still wheezing a bit from having the wind knocked out of me.

"We could take you to the hospital." He gets a call and listens for a second. "My boss said to tell you we didn't do that, and his offer of protection is still on the table."

"Nah, we're good," I say. "That guy was holding a grudge from yesterday. He got his butt handed to him a few times. Now that he's out of the game, we're ready to go about our lives."

The man doesn't react. He's stone faced.

But he says, into his phone, "No deal." Then he listens again for a bit. "OK, my boss says you're on your own, if that's how you want it. You keep quiet and keep your end of the bargain, and he'll let you go."

I nod, and my mom and Ms. Marrillion back me up.

After a few moments, the guy says, "Between you and me, I've never heard him this scared before. You must have really pulled a number on him." Then he motions to his partner to leave and they walk back towards the shouting and shoving near the shooter.

"Well," my mom says. "That was very scary. But the fact that the guy with the gun got so close to us tells me that the government *did* back off, like we told them to."

"Possibly the first time in history that they've kept their word," Ms. Marrillion says.

I know what she means. It goes all the way back, the lying and deceit.

"Think very hard, Lee," my mom says. "Is there anyone else like that guy who might be out to get us and so mad that they'd ignore what the government ordered them to do and just keep coming?"

I think back through the day since yesterday.

We had a lot of people chasing after us, but I think the ones who are still alive all worked *for* the government. So if they respect the truce Ms. Marrillion arranged, then we should be good.

There's a huge mess for someone to clean up, but I'm not going to worry about that. Let the CIA or the FBI figure out how to cover up the dead guy on the road from yesterday and the man who shot up our apartment. They made their bed, now they can lie in it.

"I think we're good," my mom says. "Do you feel like you can stand up?"

I'm tired and sore, but the road I'm lying in is dirty, so I sit up. My chest hurts when I do that, but I try not to wince too much. D'Argyle gives me a hand and pulls me up onto my feet.

We walk up Broadway, making our way through Washington Heights, finally heading home. We don't need to hide anymore, or run away. We've got restaurants and shops and neighbors who watch out for us, the friendly eyes on the street. Everything we need is within reach.

LATER

THE KID WITH A FUTURE

I'm away at college now, up in New England, and no longer looking over my shoulder all the time. I left the city because Ms. Marrillion offered to pay my tuition and mom agreed it would be good for me to see more of the world. Washington Heights will always be my home, but I think surviving that one summer day was like living several lifetimes on those blocks. It's good to get a new perspective on things. I know the old neighborhood's always there waiting for me during the summer and on holiday breaks.

Mom and D'Argyle are helping look after Ms. Marrillion, not that she needs much help. She's a tough old lady.

D'Argyle is enrolled at Fordham but still living at home to save money. He bikes or takes the bus to get to his classes.

None of us have heard or seen anyone coming after us since that last guy outside the United Palace. Maybe the Feds are watching from a distance. Maybe they're still hoping to get their hands on the evidence Ms. Marrillion kept from her childhood. It's somewhere safe, but I doubt they'll ever find it.

When people at my school find out I'm from Washington Heights, they're always impressed, like I must have survived something intense to make it out of there in one piece. And I did, but it wasn't the city's fault. It was mostly out-of-towners who tried to kill my neighbor and me. People in the city protected us. If someone ever comes after me again, there's no place I'd rather be when it happens than at my home, in Washington Heights.

Sometimes I go on weekend hikes arranged by the college, along mountain ridges or the Appalachian Trail. When I'm by myself, I'll head off the beaten path and bury some more of the evidence cache Ms. Marrillion gave me. Then I give her and Argyle specific GPS coordinates where they can locate the documents if they ever need to.

I guess, in a way, that's the story of America. We're constantly burying the past and hoping it can stay buried. The future seems so much more hopeful when it's not chained to the sins of yesterday, but the ground beneath our feet holds memories of the rights and wrongs of history. What happened before is the ground beneath our feet, the foundation of our country. It will always be there, if we dig deep enough.

This novel was written between 2021 and 2023, when I was living in Washington Heights, at a time when the city and the world were undergoing significant disruptions and change. For that reason, it takes place in a chronologically impossible setting. Some establishments, geography, and people date back to pre-pandemic NYC, and sadly no longer exist. Other features only came into being recently, such as the walkway alongside the George Washington Bridge, which was closed for renovations when I wrote the original draft (I have edited the manuscript to reflect the current state of the GWB). I let most of the bygone city continue to exist in print as a memorial to what once was, while I look forward to the future of my neighborhood. I hope Lee's mother won't be too unhappy with how it all turns out.

PS: There was a real Ms. Marrillion in my building, although she lived downstairs from me, rather than on the fourth floor, had no enemies that I know of, and did not have the same name as her fictional counterpart. But I helped her get groceries at the height of COVID, and those shopping trips inspired the first chapter of the book. Unfortunately, she is no longer with us—her memory lives on in this story.

R.P.

New York, 2023

9 780099 706785 9